OCEAN COVE

KEMAR DOUGHTY

ccp

June 2014.

Caribbean Chapters Publishing
PO Box 8050, Oistins, Christ Church

ISBN (paperback): 978-976-95522-7-2

To my Aunt Lisa, who ignited

within me a love for literature...

To Natalie Boyce, for

inspiring my imagination...

To Carol Pitt, who has taken

me from amateur writer to author.

CHAPTER 1

New Beginning

T*he house must be on fire*, I thought as I woke up on the first Monday of the summer vacation (July 05). I glanced at the small outdated digital clock on the table next to the bed. It said 7:16. I groaned and wiped sweat from my forehead. I was pretty sure I was having a great dream until this heat woke me up. *Isn't it against the laws of nature for it to be this hot so early in the morning*? I threw the covers off and jumped out of bed.

The sheet and cover were also damp with sweat. For the past few days it was getting hotter every day, but the heat seemed to have skyrocketed today. I walked over to the bedroom window and pushed it open hoping to let some cool air in, but this was no help. Instead of the cool air I craved, I was hit with a blast of hot, flaming air that rushed into the room like I was right outside an open oven. I slammed the window shut in frustration and decided that the only way to really cool off was to drench myself in some cold water, so I took a shower.

I was in Dallas, Texas, where the heat had reached a horrifying ninety-three degrees. I didn't live in Texas, and

I just didn't have the tolerance for that kind of fire; sorry, I mean heat. I'm more of a cold and chilly kind of guy. I was only here staying with my grandparents for a couple of days. Up until two weeks ago, I used to live in New York with my parents. My mom's a vet and dad's a marine biologist. I guess you could say we had a great life—I had friends, I was fairly popular at school, my grades were good. Well… okay. I know I liked our life there. But unfortunately things weren't so good for my parents.

My mom's veterinary practice wasn't doing so well anymore. It wasn't because she was losing her patients, it was because they couldn't pay her anymore, so now she was doing a lot of, you could say, pro-bono work. And dad's situation was worse, because he hadn't had a job in six months, and that was the longest he'd ever gone without work. They had saved some money, so it wasn't like we were broke or anything, but with bills and car payments (we had two cars) and other stuff, they were afraid we would eventually run out of money.

My parents never hid the fact that we were running out of money from me. I would often see them balancing their check books and hear them on the phone with the bank, and from the sound of their voices, things weren't going their way. But if they could, they would make sure I didn't see or hear much of that stuff. Even when I asked they put on fake smiles and said everything was fine. It was getting annoying, them treating me like I was some kid. At seventeen years old I thought I was old enough to deal with whatever they were trying to keep from me. I just wanted them to share what was going on with me.

Well, I should have been careful of what I wished for,

because two weeks ago they did just that. When I got home from school, I found them seated around the dining room table, waiting for me.

"Sit down Chase, we need to talk to you," Mom said when I got to the table. I remember feeling that they were about to give me some really bad news. Dad had pulled his chair next to Mom so they were sitting close together. At that time I wondered if it was for support. Of course it was. Strength in numbers... right.

My mom was Black. She had chocolate brown skin and neck-long black hair and she had dark brown eyes. Dad was white with emerald green eyes and he had short, dirty blond hair. As a result I had dark brown hair and light brown eyes and my skin was light, a few shades darker than my dad's.

"What's going on?" I asked nervously, looking at them both. Dad was holding Mom's hand on the table and I could tell that something would change after this meeting. Then a thought occurred to me.

"Oh, my god. Mom are you pregnant?"

She actually laughed a bit, but in a weird way, as though whatever they were getting ready to tell me would be way worse.

"No I'm not pregnant." She looked at Dad, lost for words. Dad leaned forward on the table.

"Son, you know we've been having some trouble with our jobs and money. We know it's no secret with you. Well, all that is about to change."

"You got a job, Dad?"

"Yes Chase. I got a job. So did your mother. She'll actually be working with me." They smiled at each other, but something was starting to feel odd. Why did they have such grave looks on their faces if they not only got jobs but would be working together? Isn't that what they wanted all along?

"Is there something else?" I asked cautiously.

"Well, yes. There is," Mom said. "Chase you know if there was any other way, we would choose it in a heartbeat for you, but we just couldn't find anything here, and this job is something that we've always wanted to do if we had the chance."

I started to get worried.

"What are you talking about?" I asked, still more nervously.

Dad sighed heavily before he spoke. "Chase, we're moving."

"Where? Downtown?" I asked, trying to keep down rage starting to creep out of the flame of hope I had. If it was in the city that wouldn't be so bad.

"No. East Island… in the Caribbean." Dad said.

I stared at both my parents incredulously. That had probably been their worst idea. No… it most definitely was their worst idea.

"Have you lost your mind? We can't move to the Caribbean. We have lives here. What about school and your practice? Mom, please don't do this..." I pleaded hopelessly. Dad held up his hand.

"Chase, listen to me. I know it will be hard for you, this will be hard for all of us, but we have to do this. We are doing this, whether you want to or not. We've already sold the cars and your mom sold her practice. We accepted the jobs, and they're waiting for us. We have to go."

My chest felt tight and the back of my neck pained as it always did when I was angry. Anyone could see that my parents were being irrational, and they needed to be brought to their senses before they did anymore irreversible damage.

"Mom, Dad, please don't do this. I really can't move. I'm not trying to be selfish or anything, but I can't just leave now. I'm starting my senior year in the fall, I'm going to college next year. I can't attend college here if I'm in the Caribbean," I argued as best as I could.

"We got it all sorted out. You'll be attending school in East Island. Your school has already given us all the paperwork we need and you've been accepted into a very good secondary school in East Island. And as for college, you can decide if you want to attend college here or over there." Dad said.

I wasn't ready to give up the fight just yet. I quickly rose from the chair and glared at my parents.

"You can't make me do this." I said softly, but forcefully, and turned to walk up to my room. Before I got out of the dining room Mom said:

"We've sold the house Chase. We're leaving next week. We knew you would have a hard time with this, so my parents said you could come and stay with them until we get settled in the house in East Island. We told them you'll be on a plane to Texas the day after tomorrow."

I took my bag up from the floor and ran up to my room.

Later Mom came up to my room. I was lying on my bed reading a book by Stephen King. She sat on the edge of the bed.

"I'm really sorry you have to go through this. I know

how much you love it here, I mean you grew up here, first rode a bike outside this house, you came home to this house after your first day of school, you ran home to this house with your first black eye."

Despite my anger, I snickered.

"You got your first kiss in this house; don't think I didn't know about that." Mom joked. "But we just can't stay here anymore. There's nothing left for us here and if it makes you feel any better, we don't want to leave this place either, but we really don't have a choice. Anyway, you'll love East Island. I used to live there but regretted that we had to leave…" Mom trailed off, lost in thought, probably reliving some long-ago memory. I folded the top of my page, threw the book on the bed, and sat next to her.

"That's why I don't want to leave. Because I will feel the same way. But I know we have to go." I sighed heavily. Mom took my hand and looked at me.

"We're going to be just fine. You wait and see."

She kissed me, then ran her hand through my wild, dark brown hair, trying to make it straight. I pushed her hand away and looked at her. She smiled.

"Sorry. I don't know why you keep it like that," she got up and headed for the door. Before leaving, she said: "I love you."

"Mmm…" was all I said. However, after she left I said to myself: "I love you too."

So the next day was spent saying a very sad goodbye to my friends, promising that I'd call, text, and email. The day after that I was on a plane to Texas, a place I liked to visit as little as possible because of the heat.

Now, once again, I was preparing to head off to the

airport. Today was the day. This time I was going to East Island, which I still refused to see as my new home. After my shower, I dressed in a single white shirt and a pair of jeans, then went downstairs.

Breakfast with my grandparents was always a quiet affair and I knew that today would be no different. I found them in the dining room around the table already eating. Gran-gran (that's what I called my grandmother) was sitting at one end of the small rectangular table and Granddad at the other, behind the morning paper as usual, even though Gran-gran was always telling him not to read at the table.

This morning Gran-gran had cooked sausages, eggs, bacon and toast. Since I arrived here, every morning I woke up I would always find breakfast on the table. If there was one thing I could honestly say I would miss when I left, it would be that. My parents thought I was too old for them to be making me breakfast, though Mom still did sometimes. I pulled a plate towards me and started eating.

"Chase, your parents called while you were in the shower. They said they'll be at the airport tonight to pick you up. Now once you've finished eating, you go upstairs and make sure you have everything packed, okay?"

"Yes, Gran-gran."

To get to East Island from here I would have to catch a plane to from here to Boston, then from Boston to East Island and it was about four hours on both planes, so I would arrive in East Island some time that night.

I hadn't even finished eating half my breakfast, but my stomach seemed to have decided against absorbing any more food. Whenever I had anywhere to go later in the day, I was never able to eat a big breakfast. It always made me sick and today was no exception. The fact that I wasn't going back to New York also contributed to the sudden wave of nausea.

I pushed my plate away, pulled a can of Sprite towards me and opened it. I always had tea with my breakfast, but when I got here the thought of drinking tea in this heat was just too absurd to bear, so Gran-gran consented to my drinking Sprite.

"Why aren't you finishing your breakfast honey, are you sick?" She looked closely at me. Gran-gran was a black woman with neck-long gray hair. She was fifty-five and had very few wrinkles on her face.

"No Gran-gran, I'm not sick, I'm fine." I took a swig of Sprite. She kept looking at me as though she knew why I'd suddenly lost my appetite.

"Is there something you want to say?" She asked before she took a bite of toast and drank some bay leaf tea. I opened my mouth to speak, then changed my mind. If I told the truth, that I still didn't feel any better about this move, they'd defiantly tell my parents about it and the last thing I wanted, even though I was still angry with them, was to make my parents feel guilty about something they were doing to help me. Unfortunately, once my mouth was open, it commanded itself to speak.

"I still don't feel good about this move. I know this is great job Mom and Dad got, and they can't afford to pass up positions like these, though I still know nothing about what they will actually be doing. I also know that they're doing it for me and this move is hard on them too. But what I don't know is why they couldn't get a job like that back in New York. Why did they have to leave so soon? Why did they have to sell the house? What if something goes wrong and they lose this job? Where are we going to go? Why didn't they think about this before they went out and bought a house and accepted a job in the Caribbean? That island's probably the most boring place there is..."

I was breathing hard and deep, even though I was speaking in my normal voice. I had no idea what Gran-gran was going to say because I knew she supported Mom and Dad's decision to move. I expected her to get angry with me for being childish and selfish. I expected her to tell me that I had no say whatsoever in the decision of the move and not to say anything else about it while I was here. But what I didn't expect her to do was look over at Granddad and say:

"See? I told you he still felt that way. You owe me five dollars."

Then she looked back at me. "Chase. Your parents know you're scared about this move. You'll never admit it, and that's okay. You've lived in New York for all your life. Your friends are there, your old school is there and your old house is there. But there is always some kind of change in life. Some changes we don't have to make, some changes we do have to make, and the others we have no control over. This is one of those changes you'll have to learn to live with. It's going to be hard at first, but you'll be fine. You're a handsome, smart, fun person and you'll get along on East Island just fine. Now are you sure you don't want anything more to eat?" Gran-gran asked as she got up and began taking the plates from the table.

"Nah. I'm okay."

She took my plate, but instead of dumping the uneaten food, she placed it in the microwave, then moved on to Granddad's empty plate and took it to the kitchen. As soon as Gran-gran was out of the room, Granddad folded up his newspaper, placed it on the table, and looked me straight in the eye.

"So I guess I need to talk with you," he simply said.

Granddad was tall and slim. He was black, but his skin was darker than Gran-gran's or Mom's, and for his age he was fast and healthy. But the weirdest thing about him were his eyes. They were pitch black like bottomless pits, and what really made them odd was the way he looked at you. Whenever Granddad decided to have a little chat with me, he would always lock onto me with that strange, piercing gaze of his. It always made me feel like he could see right into my soul, so instead of looking at him, I focused my gaze on the can of Sprite in front of me.

"What do you want to talk about Granddad?" I asked as I swirled my finger around the condensing water droplets on the can.

"You've got to give your parents a break, boy," he began immediately, though in a soft voice. "They're trying too hard to be putting up with your behaviour. Everyone knows how hard it is for you to move, but the truth is it's hard for most people. It was hard for your mother when we left East Island, and believe me son, she hated that we were leaving everything she loved and knew behind, but she knew the move was for the best. She never once said a negative thing about it while she was with us, although we knew she didn't like it. Chase, you need to support your parents in this. You keep talking about what you left in

New York, but what about what your parents left? They are trying to make the best out of the move, you should too."

At that time Gran-gran came back into the room and stood by Granddad.

"You know Chase, East Island is a wonderful place you'll get to love. It's beautiful and rich in history, and you just wait till you see the house your parents bought. I'm not going to tell you about it, but when you see it, it's going to blow you away."

I stifled a snicker at my grandmother's use of the phrase 'blow you away'.

"Don't forget the Island is full of legend and folklore." Granddad said mysteriously, obviously trying to get me excited. I always did enjoy legends and folklore when I was younger, but I kinda grew out of them. Still, it wouldn't hurt to find out a little about the place before I got there.

"What are you talking about?" I was sincerely curious.

"Oh, there's a lot of things like magic, and duppies and real scary stuff, like a son haunting his parents for doing something good, good Lord, it can get horrible over there," Granddad said. I gulped the rest of the Sprite and gave my grandparents an exasperated look.

"Very nice Grandad. Really funny," I said as he sat there laughing. I made to get up and throw away the Sprite can, but Gran-gran took it from me and said, "I'll put it in the *recycling bin*, like I always ask you to. You go upstairs and make sure you've got everything. Go on."

My grandparents headed for the kitchen. Before I got to the stairs, I turned back to Granddad, suddenly curious about something I've never thought about.

"Hey Grandad, why did you guys move from East Island if it was so good and all?"

When he looked at me, it was with cold, unfriendly eyes that actually made me take a step back in surprise, though I knew the look came from something painful he was remembering.

"Let's just say your grandmother and I ran into some problems we had to get away from, for your mother's sake." He replied softly, although I sensed a dark edge in his voice which left me worried. "Go on upstairs and make sure you're all packed." He said this in his normal voice, then went into the kitchen.

This time I went upstairs without interruption, both wanting to get away from whatever mood Granddad was in and to prepare for the change that was to come.

Around a quarter to ten Gran-gran came up to my room and told me it was time to go. My plane to Boston was leaving at eleven o'clock, and according to Gran-gran we should already have been at the airport. I had only one suitcase, which I carried down the stairs until Grandad insisted he would carry it, and surprisingly he took it out to the car as though it weighed nothing.

My grandparents drove an old, brown station wagon and it was a very old series, which got me to thinking that Gran-gran was right, we should have already left, because it would probably take about twice the time to get to the airport in that thing. However, according to Grandad, it drove just as nicely as another other car.

Just as soon as we were ready to go, Gran-gran said she

forgot something in the house and went to collect, leaving me and Grandad alone in the car. My grandfather was the kind of man who always told you what was on his mind, even if it was something he knew would upset you. If there was something he needed to tell you, he'd tell you and worry about your feelings later. So it didn't surprise me when he shifted his position in the front seat so he could see me.

"Look at me," he said softly. I was gazing out the window. I reluctantly turned my head towards him and met his piercing dark eyes, relieved to see they were soft and inviting.

"Chase, you're going to have to learn that change is something that happens in life. Like your grandmother said, sometimes it's something small, or it can be life-changing. I want you to promise me that when you get to East Island you'll give the island and your parents a chance to prove that everything will be alright. They need to know that you are going to at least try to appreciate the effort they're making."

"And what if say in a couple of months I'm still miserable? Then what?" I asked.

Grandad chuckled and said, "Then you can come and live with us. For once kid, just have faith in them, that's all I'm asking,"

"You know I was expecting this speech from Gran-gran, not from you." I said simply, looking at my grandfather, who was still waiting for my word. "I promise. But I hope you know I'm going to hold you to your promise as well Grandad." He laughed and turned around.

"Alright. I'm ready. Let's go." My grandmother said

now, getting in the car. I got the feeling that she only left so Grandad could talk to me, because I noticed the only new she had on her since she got back to the car was the sly smile now forming at the corners of her lips.

When I finally arrived at the airport in East Island after eight long hours of flying, it was 7:30, according to the woman who had just announced over a PA system that a flight for London would be leaving in five minutes.

Through the sea of people exiting through the arrival gate, I saw Mom tiptoeing (along with a few others), anxiously trying to find me in the crowd. As soon as she saw me, she fought her way towards me and pulled me into a tight hug in the middle of the airport. For as long as I could remember, whenever I spent long periods of time away from her, she always seemed to think it prudent to trap me in a tight hug, probably to make sure I was still alive. I decided that maybe it was because I was her only child.

"I'm so glad to have you here. I missed you so much." Mom said as she began kissing every part of my face.

"Mom please, not in public." I said softly. She chuckled as we left the airport and walked through the parking lot to our car. When we finally got to the car, I was very surprised to see it was a blue Ford Explorer truck.

"Wow. Where'd you get this? I mean it must have cost you guys a lot to rent." I said, amazed as I checked out the truck.

"We didn't rent it Chase. We bought it, as it's kind of a necessity for the work we're doing. It's big enough for both your father and my equipment and let's just say the public transportation system around here isn't very good for the convenience of a marine biologist and a vet. And hey, we like it."

I put my suitcase in the back, but kept my backpack with me. When I turned around in the light from the streetlights I could see she was smiling at me. She walked up to me and gave me another hug, but this one was light and short.

"I really am glad you're back, Chase. I know it's silly but, I was starting to feel that you would rather live in Texas with your grandparents than here with us."

"Mom, you know how I feel about that kind of heat, it's just not natural," I joked, then I remembered my promise to Granddad and decided now was as good a time as any to start making good on that promise, even though I didn't want to.

"I'm really glad to be here Mom," I said as convincingly as possible. Mom eyed me in the car park where cars were coming and going and she sighed sadly.

"You're not. I can see it in your face. You're still upset about having to come here. You know, I thought that you would decide to at least give this place a chance, give us a chance, knowing we didn't really have a choice," Mom got in the truck. I got in the front seat as irrational anger began to flare up inside me.

"I am, Mom. I really am trying so hard to give this place a chance. But it's not easy. It's not like I can just snap my fingers and say, 'hey all of a sudden I like this place.' You and Dad may have decided that this is home now, but I will not let you keep me here like some kind of prisoner, I promise the first chance I get, I am getting out of here." My voice was raised a little. I looked out through my window and saw that a man and woman were gazing at us from their car. Whether they were admiring the truck or were attracted by our raised voices I didn't know, and honestly, I didn't really care.

Mom started the truck and rolled down the windows. As soon and the couple saw me looking at them, they quickly shifted positions so they were backing us.

"Hey," Mom called. I reluctantly turned towards her. She gave me a little smile and patted my shoulder. "I'm sorry. It's just that I really want you to be happy here. Let's not fight because it's about an hour to the house and I don't want to ride with any kind of angry silence between us." After I said nothing, she seemed to give up on the patching up thing, because she sighed heavily, pulled out of the car park, and drove onto a highway.

I took the iPod from my backpack, securely positioned the headphones and started playing a selection of songs by Switchfoot. I closed my eyes, and sat back in my seat.

After a while I heard Mom calling my name, telling me we were almost there. Apparently I had fallen asleep. The only light that was available to us beside the truck's was the moonlight which shone brightly over everything I could see, which, on both sides of the road, were trees—lots and lots of trees. From what I had read on the internet at my grandparents', East Island was an advanced Caribbean island, but just about half of the island was still covered in forest. The island itself was about the size of its closest neighbour, Barbados, and had an estimated population of two hundred and ten thousand. The weirdest thing about the island to me so far was that you had to drive on the right lane.

A few minutes after she woke me up, Mom turned onto a small road lit by street lights, with a sign on one of the power line poles that read 'Sam Cove Gap'. After driving on this road for a couple of seconds, she made a right turn onto an unpaved road, but as she turned I looked back and saw that if she had kept going straight ahead we would have been driving down a small road.

"Here we are." Mom finally got past the trees and came up to a lighted house where a white pickup truck was parked. As I looked through the window I could clearly see that it was a small, white, two-storey house.

I also noticed that for some reason there was just darkness beyond it. No trees or anything, as if there was nothing there, which struck me as odd. I quickly pushed that out of my mind. I took out my earphones and threw the iPod in my backpack, opened the car door to get out, and immediately a strange sound met my ears, as though a wave of water was constantly hitting a brick wall and there was a scent in the air that smelled just like…

"Salt water. The house is by the sea?" I asked, amazed as Mom got out of the car.

"Yeah. As a matter of fact, we're on a cliff that ends just beyond the house."

"Oh man. That is soooo cool," I let slip. I had to admit that a house by the sea wasn't so bad, especially since I had been imagining that I would be somewhere far and remote, where our nearest neighbours might be a mile away.

Just then the front door opened and Dad came out dressed in a normal shirt and jeans. He came over to me and pulled me into a hug.

"Ha ha ha. Ah, it's good to have you here, son," he said as he released me and went to get my suitcase from the truck.

I was just about to head off to check out the edge of the cliff when I heard Mom shout: "I'm glad that you like it but don't you even think about going near that cliff edge in this darkness, and I mean it Chase. Stay away from there at night."

Mom said this in a menacing voice as she and Dad went inside. A little disappointed, and making a mental note to go back in the morning, I followed them in.

The front door led into a small but cosy living room. The inside walls of the house were painted white, just like the outside. There was a beige coloured, three-seater couch at the back of the room, a two seater at the left by a window and the one seater was against the right wall. There was a small glass table in the middle of the room with a vase of flowers in it. In the front corner of the room was a TV stand that doubled as a book shelf. On the shelves under the TV was the DVD player and under that was my Playstation 3. There was a very nice feeling in the living room. Left of the room, at the back, were stairs leading to the second floor, and the back right had a passage way that went further into the house. My parents proceeded up the stairs, so I followed.

My bedroom was the second room on the right side of the second floor. It wasn't a very big room, I noticed, like the rest of the house. There was my bed, a small built-in closet, a chest of drawers next to it, and a computer table with my desktop on it... Like I said, a small room, but it was just big enough for me.

Dad dropped my suitcase near the bed.

"I know how you start to feel awkward if we linger too long. The computer's up and the internet's on. If it's too hot in here you can open up the window." He motioned towards the closed window on the left wall.

"There're two bathrooms, the one right there," Dad pointed to the door opposite my room, "And there's one downstairs, through the washroom. Well, I've got some calls to make. We're going out on the boat tomorrow, so I've got to make sure everything's good." He then turned to Mom. "Don't stay here too long. The boy will be fine."

Mom gave him a glowering look as he patted me on the shoulder and left. I sat down on the bed and looked out the window, where I could see there was a tree just outside.

"What kind of tree is that?"

"Mango," she replied, "I want you to get your clothes put away tonight. You only had to travel with one suitcase so it shouldn't take you ten minutes. I've already put the rest of your clothes away so you don't have to worry about doing those. Not like you would have worried about them anyway."

"True." I muttered and she chuckled.

"There's some Lasagna in the kitchen that I cooked earlier today so you can go down and have something to eat when you're ready."

"Okay. The food on the plane was pretty crappy, so I'll be down soon."

Mom came over to me and sat next to me. "It's weird having to sleep in a new house, in a new country. Trust me I know, it wasn't easy for me the first night here either, but it isn't so bad here. You'll never have trouble sleeping—

the sound of the waves crashing on the cliff seems to have the power to just lure you to sleep." She ran her fingers through my hair, but quickly pulled away before I could say a word.

"Sorry. Old habit. It just feels so soft." She got of the bed and headed for the door, "It's really good to have you here. Whether you want to be here or not." She chuckled and left, closing the door behind her.

The clock by the computer said 8:15. I was feeling a little warm, close to hot. So I got off the bed and pushed up the window to let some air in, and just like it should be, a rush of cold night air came right into the room. It felt so good to have the cold air on my skin that I pulled off my shirt, threw it over the chair and dropped onto the bed in my jeans. As I lay there with the sound of the waves finding its way in from outside, and the cool air circulating in the room, I found it hard to focus on hating this place, because I could finally admit to myself that before long I would be calling it home. I closed my eyes for a couple of seconds, intending to get up and head downstairs, but it seemed that Mom was right about the power of those waves, because before long I was asleep with the sound of the sea in my ears.

CHAPTER 2

The Accident

When I woke up the next morning it was to a burning pain in the pit of my stomach, which I quickly came to realize was hunger. Sunlight and a soft sea breeze were pouring through my bedroom window. Weak and groggy, I stumbled out of bed. The small clock by the computer was saying five minutes to eight. Still wearing just the pair of jeans from last night, I went downstairs and through the hallway and walked into the dining room. I was so hungry I didn't even pay any attention to the room until I saw a plate of breakfast on the table under a cover. There was a note there which I picked up and read:

> *Chase, your father and I are down at the beach for an early morning swim. After you've finished breakfast please don't leave the empty plate in the sink. If you want any tea, I've left some in a mug in the microwave for you. We should be back soon.   Mom.*

I removed the cover and saw that Mom had done scrambled eggs with two hot dogs and three slices of toast. I quickly gobbled everything down. When I was done I still felt hungry so I went to the kitchen and took the lasagne from the fridge. I cut away a large piece and placed it on a plate, which I threw into the microwave after taking out the mug of tea. I set the microwave to three minutes and waited impatiently for it to finish. By the time it was done, I had already finished the tea. I got a bottle of Sprite from the fridge, and ate the lasagna right there. I washed the plate and the mug like my mom had not so subtly requested and, feeling rather full, headed back up to my room.

After a shower and a fresh change of clothes (a simple blue shirt and a pair of shorts) I decided to call my grandparents. I didn't know how much an overseas call would cost my parents, but I had a feeling they wouldn't complain. The conversation with my grandparents was brief. I apologized for not calling the night before, but they said that Mom had already spoken with them. Granddad asked if I was keeping my promise and I replied that I was trying. After speaking with my grandparents I turned on the computer. I hadn't contacted any of my friends for a couple of days. It didn't take long for the computer to boot up, and I was grateful for the high-speed internet.

As I suspected, there were lots of emails from my friends asking about how I was doing and when I would visit. I responded to a few of them, then closed the browser.

I had just decided to take a look outside when I heard Mom call out my name from downstairs. I responded, telling her I was in my room. That's when I heard the cars pull up in the driveway. As my bedroom was on the opposite side of the house, I could not see the driveway. I had to go downstairs to see exactly what was going on.

I found Dad conversing with three men sitting in the

living room. All three were dressed in shirts and shorts.

"Good morning." I said as I got downstairs.

"Good morning." They replied in unison, their voices coated with an accent.

"Chase. These three gentlemen will be working with your mother and I. This is Gibbons," he pointed to a man who was about his height and had dark brown skin, striking black eyes and a very bushy black beard. "Hamilton, but we call him Hoggie." Hamilton was few inches shorter than Dad, bald with a moustache and he wore a small loop earring in his left ear. "And this is Christopher, Christopher Faynes." Christopher was a young, slightly muscular man with light skin (though not like mine) who looked to be around his late twenties. He wore a sleeveless shirt, which allowed me to see the tattoo he had on his arm. All I could see of it was a circle and some odd star-like symbols inside it.

"It's very nice to meet you all," I said after shaking hands.

After their little morning chat they proceeded out, and of course I followed. They went into the backyard which was enclosed by a four foot high fence. There was a kind of storage shed back there that Dad had to open because it was locked, and they began moving equipment for the boat into the Explorer and the other two cars.

As Dad and the others moved the stuff to the truck, I wandered off near the edge of the cliff and peered over. The sea was calm this morning, so the waves were brushing lightly against the cliff. The cliff top itself was about seventy-five feet up from the ocean below, where just beyond the cliff huge jagged rocks that could have looked like displaced teeth jutted out of the water.

"Hey Dad!" I shouted as I walked back. "How do you get down to the beach?"

"Well you just walk up the gap, and instead of turning left to go onto the main road, you just turn right and go down the road. Oh and if you were to go straight, you'd end up at our neighbours, the Morgans." Dad was loading the last of the equipment onto the truck. Just as he did, Mom came out of the house dressed in a simple jeans and plaid colored shirt. The man named Gibbons approached them.

"Mo'ning Mrs. Rowland." His voice was heavy with what I assumed was the native accent. "Mr. Rowland, everything on de cars."

"Great." Dad replied. "I have to go change. I'll be back soon."

Dad and Mom went back into the house. Mr. Gibbons looked oddly at me as I walked over and stood by the truck. After a while he made his way over to me. I only then realised that he was several inches wider than me although we were the same height.

"So, how ya like de country so far, young boy?" He asked. His strange accent seemed so comical to me that I had to bite my tongue to stop myself from laughing.

"Well it's not like I've been here long, but so far it doesn't look so interesting, unless you like trees, because that's all there seems to be around here." I said as I motioned to the trees around the area.

Gibbons give a deep but soft laugh. "Oh I don't think dat... I bet I can change da idea fa ya. Tell me boy, ya believe in magic?" I didn't even have to think about my response.

Although I always liked legends and myths ever since I was a kid, I never believed them to be real.

"Of course not," I answered politely.

"Do ya know wha an Aquamun is?" Gibbons asked, lowering his voice and leaning closer, probably for dramatic effect, I thought at the time.

"No."

"You see lad, Aquamuns are what you kids might call mermaids and mermen. What you probably know about them is that they live in de sea and they half-human half fish, right?"

I nodded. Truthfully that was all I knew about mermaids.

"Ya see Chase, de Caribbean is a place full' o folklore an' on East Island, de most known o' all folklore creatures are de Aquamuns. First of all, Aquamuns int' half of nothin', they's one whole creature. They look like normal people, just like you an' me. The sea's like home, but they can come on land. Sometimes, mostly at night when nobody can see dem, they like ta go down by the beach to do who knows wha. An' ya know wha their goal in life is? To become mortal... like us humans. But de only way ta do da is to get a human to fall in love wid dem and then kiss de poor soul and that transfers de curse from them to the person making dem human and the other gets the curse of being a Aquamun fah de rest o' dem life."

"How do they get people to fall in love with them?" I asked curiously. I didn't believe any of this of course, but I was still mildly interested.

"Well, it's natural fa dem to get people to fall in love wid dem. It's like something in dem blood—if they got any—which meks people fall in love wid dem. And de sad

25

thing is Aquamuns can never fall in love wid a human."

"And you believe this, that they exsist?" I asked Gibbons skeptically. There was no way that even he, who must have grown up on this island, could believe in such a silly thing. But his response surprised me and I could tell he was pleased with that outcome.

"I got proof. Well, I gaw a story anyway an' in my books, dat's as good as proof. Ya see, it happened about twenty years ago wen I was in my thirties." Gibbons began with a strange look on his face as if he was talking about something he was hoping to have again.

"Me and my friend ol' Henry used to fish down in Bermintown, you know, de capital of East Island. Anyway we'd go every other Sunday mornin' and no matta wha time of year it was we always went home with a load, which was good cuz back den I used to sell fish; our spot was a good one. We used to fish on the docks just behind de old police station. Then one day when we were hulling in a mother load of fish, ol' Henry looks at me an' says '*Gibbons, ya hear da*?' Of course I ain't hear squat. So I tells him so. But he swears on his mother's grave he hear something. Anyway we soon drop that an' went on wid we work. A few days after that he started acting weird, humming tunes I never hear in me life. He'd be laughing but when I ask him about what , he'd say '*Oh, it's just a joke a friend told me*.' But ya see the thing is, he was a little weird, so I was his only friend, and he ent had no family, so I started to get worried. One night after he thought I went home I follow him to de docks. I thought he was goin' to tek de boat out, but he just sit by de edge of the dock and I saw him talking into the water. Of course I thought he was goin' crazy, but then would you believe I saw a woman's head in the water. Oh I'll never forget that face as long as I live. Long black hair and a perfectly round, smooth face that reflected de moonlight. An' then I saw her hand reach out o' de water an touch his face an' then she kiss he. Full on de lips. Then she disappeared into de water. After that I ran home so fast I could've won a medal. When I got home I tell myself first thing in de morning I gine go and talk to Henry. But then next day I couldn't find him anywhere. Everyone help search, but we didn't find he. Anyways a few days after Henry disappeared, a woman name Celia appears in town that looks jus' like de woman in de water that night. But when I asked her about Henry, she said she was a tourist and never see Henry in she life. Now on some nights people does see Henry by de docks but when they walk up to he, they say he does swim away."

Gibbons ended his story by shaking his head sadly. I looked at him, unsure of what to say. I couldn't tell if he meant it just as a story to entertain me or as what he believed was a personal experience. Then all of a sudden he started to laugh.

"Gotcha!" he said, laughing himself into hysteria. "You new people always fall fa da one."

"You mean you made that up?"

"How could you think I made that up? Look at me, do I look like the kind of person that makes up things?" He paused a few seconds, then said, "That's a story we fisherman from Bermintown tell to tourists."

Gibbons started to laugh again, and a few chuckles escaped from me. It was kind of getting to me—only a little. At that moment, Mom and Dad came out (Dad was dressed in three quarter jeans and a lime green shirt) and walked over to the truck as the other two guys hopped into their cars. Dad took one look at Gibbons then turned to me.

"He tried to get you with the mermaid story didn't he?" Dad asked. I nodded. "He tried to catch your mother and me with it a few days after we got here. Anyway we've got to go and get these things set up on our boat, then we'll be heading into town for a while, actually we might be out for the day, you think you'll be fine here?"

I looked at him incredulously. Did he think I was twelve?

"Dad. I'm seventeen, not seven. I can and already have been home alone."

"I was merely considering the fact that you've only been here for a couple of hours. But I guess you will be fine. I'll see you later son. Gibbons if you're ready hop in." Gibbons got in the back. As I was making my way to the house, Mom stopped me.

"Chase, I know you can take care of you self pretty well, but while we're gone I don't want you to go down to the beach alone."

"What?!" I exclaimed. "Mom I was really looking forward to going down there today. Plus I don't have anyone to go with as I don't know anyone here."

To my surprise she smiled, as if this was exactly where she wanted me to steer this conversation.

"Well don't you think today would be a good day to start? I would just feel so much better if I knew you were at the beach with someone else. I'm not telling you not to leave the house, don't get me wrong. I'm just advising you to try and make some friends."

I gave a heavy sigh before my response. "Okay, I'll try to meet some people today."

"Good to hear. Now, when you get hungry later, you can have some of the lasagna, actually you can finish it if you want, as your father and I will probably eat out. There's some snacks in the fridge and in the cupboards, but don't eat them off at once, and get the rest of your stuff put away please. We'll see you later."

She went back towards the truck and got in. From the front door of the house I stood and watched as the three vehicles drove away, and wondered what to do next.

After everyone left I had nothing to do, so I wandered around the house.There seemed to be an extra room built onto the house that was accessed from a door in the kitchen wall which turned out to be the wash room. There wasn't much in there, only a washing machine, a dryer and some cupboards which kept washing powder and fabric softer. The bathroom Dad spoke of was on the right side of the house, and was smaller than the one upstairs.

I went upstairs and finished unpacking, but that didn't take long enough to keep me occupied. With my bedroom window wide open I could smell the sea breeze coming in. I knew what I wanted to do, but kept reminding myself that Mom asked me not to go. I could turn on the computer or the PS-3, or go for a walk, even read a book. But none of those things held any appeal to me at the moment. Taking a deep breath to calm myself, I mentally apologized to Mom and decided to go down to the beach.

Considering that the house was only five minutes from

the cove and I didn't want Mom finding any evidence against me, I decided not to take anything with me. So with just a pair of outdoor slippers, I headed for my destination. As I was walking up the driveway flanked by trees on my left and right, I noticed that it felt good just to see the sunlight as it shone through the trees. Everything was quiet and peaceful. When I got to the crossroads, before I turned right to go down the hill, I tried to get a look at the Morgan house Dad was talking about, but my line of sight was completely obscured by trees, so I turned and continued down the road. Instead of calling it a road, it should have been called a small hill. If I had a bicycle I wouldn't have to peddle and I'd still go faster than fifty miles an hour going down there. The good news was, it wasn't too far to the bottom, so coming back up wouldn't be a problem.

Before I could take three strides down—strides because the hill was so steep that I would be close to jogging even if I didn't want to—I heard someone call out: "Hey!" I turned and saw a boy jogging to catch up with me. From the looks of him, he was about my age, the same height as me, with a kind of light brown skin, though not at all like mine. He had short black hair that looked freshly cut and dark brown eyes, just like Mom's, I noticed. He was dressed in a simple beach pants and a sleeveless shirt—dressed for the beach.

"Hey. I've never seen you around here before. Did you just move here or what?"

He had caught up with me. I noticed that his voice wasn't heavily accented like Gibbons. *Perhaps it's just with the older people,* I thought. We started walking down to the cove.

"I just moved here. My parents own the house over

there on the cliff." I pointed in the direction of our house. Realisation came over the boy's face.

"That means that you're Chase, the Evans' son right." I nodded, surprised that he knew me.

"I'm Justin. Justin Walker." We shook hands.

"How do you know me?" We were almost at the bottom.

"Well, I was down here at the beach when your parents first arrived, so I helped move their things in. They said that you were having trouble adjusting to the moving so you were in Texas with your grandparents." I just nodded as he said that. "I noticed your dad was a marine biologist, which is totally cool, do you think he'll let me go out on the boat something?"

"Probably. You could ask him."

"Cool."

We were now at the bottom of the hill and I could already hear the waves crashing on the shore. There wasn't any sand here yet, most of the road was littered with small pebbles. There were a lot of fishing boats turned upside down up here. Some were the *Blue Ocean*, the *Walter Grain*, the *Black Raven* and many more. There were a lot of trees and I could now feel the sand between my toes, although we hadn't reached the beach itself yet. There was another cliff opposite ours where I supposed the Morgan house stood. Small plants grew around us that had a small purple fruit the size of a pea on them. Justin started picking and eating them. Then he handed some to me.

"Eat them. They're sea-grapes and believe me they're good. But don't swallow the seeds."

I ate the strange fruit and they were surprisingly good. We spent a few minutes eating, then went on to the beach.

"There are fat pork trees out there," he pointed to our right. All I could say was "Huh?" I had no idea what fat porks were.

"But I suppose we could leave them for another time," Justin said.

We were now on the beach itself and the sight and sound of the waves and the smell of the sea breeze here were amazing. Justin took off his slippers and shirt, threw them on the sand and ran into the water. He dove under and disappeared from my view for a while, and then he came back and waved for me to come in. I took off my slippers and my shirt and tossed them next to his. Already I could feel the morning sun hot on my chest. Dad told me this was the hurricane season in the Caribbean. From July 1st to November 30th was when the Caribbean islands got the most rain, and hurricanes. Today was sunny, but as I looked up I saw a few grey clouds rolling in from the sea.

I took a deep breath, then ran into the water. Just as Justin did, I went under for a few seconds and then came back up. Since both my parents' jobs took them out on boats and I went with them sometimes, they thought it would be best if I learned how to swim, and I was actually grateful for that. At my school back in New York there were only a couple of kids in my year who knew how to swim. It wasn't something to brag about, but it was enough to get me attention from a couple of girls I liked.

Justin and I had a few races, then decided to see who could stay underwater the longest. After I got a little water up my nose, which stung like hell, we decided to just sit on the beach for a while. But as I was about to make my way back to the beach, I dove under for the last time and could have sworn I saw a girl who looked right at me, then swam swiftly past me and into the ocean. After I broke the skin of the surface, I dove under again, but there was no one there. When I was up for the second time I started looking around, just to be sure. I decided it was probably in my head. After Gibbons's story, I wasn't surprised.

"Hey, Chase you okay?" Justin shouted from the shore. I shouted back that I was fine and swam back to land. I sat on the sand next to Justin and looked out at the sea. Justin asked me what I thought I saw in the water. I hesitated before I replied. I didn't know Justin for very long to anticipate his reaction, but nevertheless it couldn't hurt to tell.

"One of the guys that work with my dad, Gibbons, he told me a story about," I hesitated "Aquamuns and I guess it kind of went to my head because I thought I saw someone, a girl, swim past me in the water."

"A girl?" Justin asked, without accusation in his voice.

"A girl, yeah."

"What did she look like?" He asked.

"Well, from what I could see, she had white skin and she had long, brown hair. I really didn't see her very well as she moved so fast. But like I said, I think I was just seeing things."

Justin just shrugged. I was silently glad he let it drop, as I didn't feel much like talking about a hallucination.

We then decided to pick the fat porks. They were the size of meatballs and tasted very good. I just hoped that I wouldn't get sick from eating too much. I invited Justin back to my house; I figured Mom would be glad to know that for once I took her advice. I was right about the walk up the hill not being long, but it was hard and by the time I got to the top, my legs were burning. The sun was angling to the right of the sky by the time we got to the house, which was completely empty.

"Parents must not be back yet." Then I remembered Mom said they might be gone for the day. I took a shower to wash off the sand and threw on clean clothes. I told Justin he could use the shower and I gave him a pair of jeans. We ate the last of the lasagne, then decided to have a go on my Playstation 3. We played Metal Gear Solid 4 for hours until my parents got back around five. It seemed that they went shopping because they came back with a lot of grocery bags.

"There were a lot of things we needed around here. And we had some business to take care of as well that went swiftly. Now Justin do you want to stay for dinner?" My mother asked.

"Yeah, sure. Thanks Mrs. Evans. May I go call my mother to let her know I'm here?" Justin said politely.

"Of course." My mother looked impressed. Then she looked at me. "Oh, Chase don't worry about helping me with these, my third hand is working just fine."

"Oh. That's okay, I wasn't planning on helping you anyway."

Mom gave me a very menacing look.

"Joking." I chuckled and helped her take the bags to the kitchen and began unpacking. After Justin was finished with the phone he came in and helped, then we went back on the Playstation. But before we did I gave him a quizzical stare.

"What?" he asked.

"Yeah, thanks Mrs. Evans. May I go call my mother to let her know I'm here?" I said in a fake girl voice.

"Shut up." He punched me softly on the arm. At about 6:30 we all sat down and for a dinner of mashed potatoes with fried chicken, which was a pretty normal affair. My parents asked Justin about school stuff, then he asked my Dad about his work in marine biology and questioned Mom about being a veterinarian.

All the time they were talking, my mind was free to dwell on the girl I thought I saw in the water. I barely saw her, but I could tell she was beautiful. I was quickly pulled away from this train of thought when Mom and Dad talked about work with each other, and Justin and I started talking about games. After dinner Justin offered to help with the dishes, but my mother told him it was fine and he should get home. Dad offered to take him.

"You know, that Justin is a really nice boy, very polite." Mom said to me as I helped with the dishes. "You should be more like him."

"Well, maybe you should adopt him. Or do a trade, give me to his parents and you keep him."

"That's really not a bad idea." We both laughed. The phone rang and she answered it in the kitchen.

"That was your father, he's on his way back. I am really glad to know that you've started making friends."

After all the cleaning was done my father returned. I think he planned his return to be at that exact time so he would have little or none of it to do. I watched TV with my parents, for a while and then after realising I was tired enough—I did have a long day—I said goodnight and went up to bed early.

I decided to sleep with my bedroom window open again. The sound of the waves was actually kind of soothing to me. I looked out the window and could clearly see the full moon and the starlight from dozens of stars being reflected off the ocean. At that moment was when I made a decision. I didn't usually do things like this, but I felt kind of excited by just the idea. I didn't know why I was going to do it, but I knew I was going to do it. I crept down the stairs just to get a peek at Mom and Dad. They were still watching TV comfortably, and would be for a long time. Their work schedule was hectic, so they spent as much time relaxing together as possible. I went back to my room, opened the window wider, climbed onto the tree by my window and climbed down, which wasn't that hard considering the fact that I haven't climbed many trees in New York.

I could simply have told my parents I was going out here and gone through the front door. But there would have been questions and they wouldn't relax until I stepped back into the house, and Mom definitely wouldn't want me going to the cliff's edge at night.

I should have worn a jacket, I thought as I shivered from the cold night air. I walked cautiously to the edge of the cliff and looked down. It looked like the tide was coming in slowly but surely. I could see some of the rocks just in front of the cliff jutting of the water, but the sea was beginning to cover them up again. They would become hidden hazards to any boat that passed.

As I looked down at the rocks, amazed at the wonder of the sea, I noticed something peculiar. There was a girl sitting on one of the rocks, and I knew this wasn't a hallucination. She was sitting with her knees to her chest and her arms wrapped around her legs. I noticed some odd little things around her, which I horrifyingly came to realize were pieces of wood floating in the water surrounding the rocks. She must have been in a small boat, probably a fishing boat, and lost control when the sea sent it into the rocks, which destroyed the boat. If that's what happened, she was lucky to be alive.

"Hey! Are you alright?" I shouted to the girl, but it was useless. The thundering sound of the waves on the cliff were drowning my voice.

My mind was working at the speed of light just trying to come up with a solution. If I went for help, by the time whatever help got here, she might be dead. If I went down the hill to the cove I'd have to swim against the powerful waves and through the rocks to get to her. Even if I made it, who was to say I'd make it back? I'd probably be too tired. I knew what I had to do, although knowing didn't exactly make it any easier for me to do.

I took a huge breath, then slowly lowered myself over the cliff. The wind down here was crazy cold. Now I really wished I had a jacket. I kept going down, feeling for good footholds on the cliff before I moved my hands. The further down the cliff I got, the wetter and more slippery it was getting. I could already feel sprays of water hitting me. I checked to make sure the girl was still there, and she was. In fact, even though the water level was rising quickly and she was getting wet, she didn't even move. More than once my hands and feet slipped. I never prayed so hard in my life.

My face was now getting wet, and combined with the wind, I was freezing. My hands were numb, my teeth had started chattering and my feet were tired. I started wishing I had gone for help first. I felt around for a foothold and found one. Only this one wasn't a very good one. It was wet and slippery and as soon as I put my foot on it, I slipped. I felt myself falling into space, but it wasn't like I could do anything to stop it. I heard a frightened scream and was surprised when I realised it was my own. Suddenly, as I was falling I saw the girl on the rock look up at me. Even though there was a strong chance that I would be dead in a few seconds, I still felt a tinge of triumph because it was the girl that I saw in the sea earlier. The one that was allegedly an illusion. She had the same face. I was positive it was her. The last thing I saw was the look of horror on her face, and then I hit the water—hard. I didn't expect it to hurt, but it did—and really badly. My head had collided with something hard and I felt myself fall into darkness.

I found it hard to open my eyes, but still managed to force them open. When I did I felt the worst headache I ever had in my life come over me. Everything seemed foggy, but I could hear the waves crashing on the shore and smell the sea salt on the night air.

I placed a hand on the back of my head and raised myself into a sitting position to try to at least decipher my surroundings. I realised I was on the beach, and that's when everything came back to me. The girl on the rocks, me falling off the cliff... something I wouldn't mind completely forgetting.

After a while my vision became clear again. I looked around and was surprised. There she was, sitting a foot away from me the same way as when she was on the rock, with her knees to her chest and her arms around her legs, but now her chin rested on top of her knees. She was looking straight out into the ocean as if there was something so mesmerizing out there that it was impossible to pull away from it.

Her long, black and slightly curly hair was flying in the wind and her pale skin looked like it was reflecting the moonlight in an astonishing way, just like the sea. She was wearing a short jeans and a small, plain white shirt and I noticed she was dry, as if she hadn't been in the water. I wasn't dripping wet, but my skin and clothes were damp, as if I'd been drying in the wind for a while. When I heard her voice, it surprised me. It sounded so beautiful, like music that would flow from a magical harp. It was angelic and seductive at the same time, kind of like how you would expect the goddess of love to sound. It didn't seem possible that any living being would possess such a voice.

"Are you alright?" The girl asked, her eyes still on the sea. I remained silent and just stared at her. She was stunningly beautiful, almost to the point were it could hurt your eyes just to stare at her. I tried to respond. I tried to tell her I was okay, but the words got lost somewhere in my throat because I just didn't know how to speak to someone that not only looked like an angel, but managed to sound like one too.

After she didn't get a response from me, she finally pulled her eyes away from the sea and looked at me as though she was trying to decide if I had brain damage or not. Somehow, even in the darkness of the night, I could clearly see her eyes. They stood out to me like to little stars in an otherwise black sky. I don't think I had ever seen eyes so blue before in my life; they were deep blue like the sea and as I gazed into them, they maintained a kind of hypnotic glare that could have kept me staring into them forever.

She had glared at me for about a full four seconds and seemed to come to the conclusion that I was physically fine. Then she raised an eyebrow at me and I remembered her question.

"Uh-umm, yeah I'm—I'm fine." Was what I had managed to muster in a kind of horse voice. The pain in my head was quickly reducing to nothing.

"You hit your head on one of the rocks pretty hard, you should get it checked. You could have a concussion."

I just nodded.

How did we get here? The sea's too high and rough to swim through. I thought to myself. The girl chuckled as if she realized what I was thinking.

"Don't look so puzzled, it's kind of insulting. I was able to get us to shore safely. I'm a very strong swimmer you know, if not, you'd be dead. And as we're on the subject of being dead, tell me something. What were you doing climbing down that cliff?"

I looked at her incredulously. Surely she couldn't have forgotton that she was also so close to death a few minutes ago.

"What do you think? I was trying to help you. I saw you trapped on those rocks and thought I had to do something. Didn't exactly turn out how I planned though. Getting knocked unconscious wasn't part of the plan."

To my surprise, a look of indignation crossed the girl's

face, though it didn't make her any less appealing.

"*You* were trying to save to save *me*! Well I can honestly say that's the first time I ever heard that. Did I ask for help or look like I was in trouble? No. You made a foolish assumption and almost got killed. How in the world did you come to that conclusion?"

It was my turn to give the indignant look.

"Excuse me? How was I supposed to know you're some kind of super swimmer or whatever. I thought you were in trouble and I tried to help you out, and this is what I get? Fine, since you like sitting by yourself so much, I'll leave you alone."

I got up fast—too fast, and my head felt slightly dizzy. I staggered for a moment but regained my balance and began walking away, then I heard that beautiful, compelling voice of hers.

"Wait. I don't think you should be walking yet. Look, I'm sorry, okay? I didn't mean to be so insensitive. Thank you for trying to save me, even though I didn't need saving."

I turned around and saw that she was standing, looking at me.

"Please come back, your head's injured. I would prefer you didn't move for a while."

She looked down as though she didn't want to make eye contact, then said:

"Plus I'd like your company, that's if you're willing to give me a chance."

The wind blew her hair in my direction, and the sound of the waves kept coming. I walked back over to her slowly, since my stomach was starting to feel bad and I didn't want to vomit with her around. We sat down together, though she made sure there was at least an arm's length between us.

As I sat there, a strange smell tickled my nose, and I realised it was coming from the girl. It smelled like the sea, but with something else mixed with it, like a flowery aroma. I wasn't good with flowers, so I couldn't tell if it was actually a flowery scent. It's hard to explain, but it just smelled so good that I could've sat there and inhaled it all night.

She chuckled suddenly, as if laughing at something. I then realised that my mouth was hanging open slightly. *Get yourself together*, I thought. Where were all these feeling coming from?

From the moment we sat down the girl returned to her sea-gazing, leaving me to freely glance at her, but she asked a question so quickly that the sound of her voice startled me.

"Why were you even on that cliff?" she asked, still looking out to sea.

"Well first, it's not like I wanted to kill myself or anything. I live in the house on the cliff. My parents and I just moved here, well, they were here for the past three days, I only came yesterday. Anyway, I wasn't feeling very indoorish so I decided to get some fresh air."

I don't know if I really saw it or not, but the girl actually looked a bit more relaxed after my explanation, though I couldn't imagine why.

"I didn't even want to come here in the first place and now look, I almost die on my second night, isn't that something?"

"You're not, though. Dead. You're not dead, so that should mean a lot to you. Maybe you could start trying to like it here, I mean, it's not so bad."

"How do you know I don't like it here?"

"I can hear it in your voice. You sound so sad, like you had something taken away from you."

"Thank you," I said softly after a while. She still didn't turn to me when she responded, but her voice sounded genuinely puzzled.

"For what?"

I scoffed before I answered. "For saving my life, remember? Thank you."

This time she not only looked back at me, but shifted her position so she was sitting towards me.

"You're welcome." She studied me again, though this time I couldn't tell why. "What's your name?"

"Chase."

"You're different from others, aren't you?" She asked oddly.

"What do you mean? Different from who?"

I was puzzled. She seemed to realize what she had just said and looked as though she said too much.

"I merely meant that I've never met anyone like you. You almost died tonight, you could have a concussion, yet you don't seem very scared or even rattled."

"Well, I am a little shaken, I mean I did fall like, fifty feet. But it's over and I'm alright. Plus I told my parents I was going to bed. I don't think they'd be happy to find out that I sneaked out and almost fell to my death." That's when a question occurred to me. "What were you doing out there anyway? Good swimmer or not, if something had gone wrong you could have died."

A smile slid across the girl's face and she placed a strand of her hair behind her ear.

"Like I told you, I'm a pretty strong swimmer. I like being in rough waters, you know, to test myself. Plus it helps to somehow calm me. I just like being in the sea, though I'd appreciate it if you didn't mention this to anyone. So let me ask you something, why don't you like it here?"

She now looked totally interested, as if I was about to tell the most fabulous story in world. I had to really think about how to answer, because no one had ever asked me that. My parents and grandparents seemed to think I should just accept being here.

"Well, it's not that I don't like it here. I just like my home in New York better. I have everything there—friends family, school. But here I don't have anything. It's just my parents and me."

I knew I felt this way inside, but as I said this for the first time, I actually began to feel sorry for myself.

The girl looked as though she was about to say something, but suddenly she jumped up and looked regretful.

"I'm sorry Chase. I shouldn't be here. I shouldn't be with you or even talking to you. It's not good for you to be here with me, so I have to go. I'm sorry."

She looked like she wanted to say something more, but thought better of it. I, on the other hand, jumped up in surprise. I didn't understand why she thought she shouldn't talk to me. It actually kind of hurt when she said it, but when I tried to ask her she cut me off and said:

"There is a small public hut with a bathroom to the

right at the bottom of the road, if you want to wash off. You should get home Chase, if your parents find you gone they'll start to worry."

And with that she turned and sprinted off in the direction of the hill and disappeared into the darkness. She was the most beautiful girl I had ever seen, and she was gone and I didn't even get her name.

I found the stall without difficulty. After I was free of sand I made my way up the hill and back home. I was cold and my teeth were chattering so hard that my mouth hurt. When I got home I went around to right side of the house. Climbing the tree wasn't exactly easy when my hands were so numb, but I made it. I crawled through my bedroom window and fell to the floor with a loud thud. I silently swore at the pain.

"Chase. You alright?" Dad called from downstairs.

"Yeah, I just fell of the bed." I shouted back. I got off the floor, took off my wet clothes and threw them in the corner (I'd move them in the morning and put on a dry, warm pair of shorts, and a shirt—I don't like wearing pyjamas) and climbed into bed. I wrapped the bed covers tightly around me to trap as much heat as possible, still feeling the after-chill of the wind and cold sea water.

Obviously, I couldn't get to sleep. My head was buzzing with the events of the night. It felt like my brain didn't want to slow down; I couldn't stop thinking about anything that happened tonight—about how I almost died. But mostly I couldn't get the girl on the beach out of my head. As soon as I closed my eyes, the first thoughts that entered my mind were of her. I saw her in my mind sitting on the sand with her hair blowing in the wind, gazing out to sea. The sound of the waves outside only intensified the memory in my head. But I still couldn't help wondering why she had said she shouldn't talk to me. That was the first time we met, so it's not like I did something to make her want to stay away from me. Maybe her parents didn't like mine and told her not to talk to me. It was childish, but some people would do that. But that also didn't make sense as she didn't even know me when I told her my name.

At some point after I closed my eyes I drifted off to sleep and the picture I had in my head turned into a dream. I was back on the beach and there was a girl sitting on the sand, backing me. What was weird about this dream was I could see everything around me clearly—the trees, the boats on the beach, the cliffs, even the small rocks on the sand could be easily seen, but the girl was the only thing in the dream I couldn't make out. At first she was completely covered in darkness, and even then somehow I knew it was that girl, and I was sure she wanted me to see her face, if it wasn't for that damned shadow. I walked up to the girl and stretched out my hand to touch her shoulder, but before I got too near a blinding white light emanated from her, followed by a horrible scream.

"No!" I shouted. I ran forward to grab the girl… but then I woke up. I bolted up straight in bed, breathing heavily. Sunlight came through my bedroom window and hit me right in the eyes, so I had to raise my hand to shield them from the light. I staggered out of bed and was about to go to the bathroom when I saw my clothes in the corner, right where I left them. After having to untangle myself from the tightly wrapped covers, I scooped up the still damp clothes, crept downstairs and threw them in the washing machine, since Mom already had clothes soaking in there. I went into the kitchen and saw Mom making pancakes.

"Good morning Chase," she said, turning the pancakes over.

I barely lifted my feet as I walked, still groggy with sleep. To me it felt like no more than two hours had passed since I fell asleep, though the clock in the kitchen was saying 7:30 and I was sure I fell asleep long before twelve. I went to the fridge, opened it and gazed inside.

"Chase, how many times do I have to tell you not to open the fridge and just look inside? One, you're wasting electricity and two, you could catch a cold, you just got out of bed."

I reached in, took out the bottle of pineapple juice, and drank it from the bottle. Actually the bottle didn't even touch my lips, I just tipped the bottle over my mouth and swallowed the juice, it was a skill I had acquired over time. Not exactly something to be proud of.

"Boy, how many times am I going to have to tell you to stop doing that and use a glass?"

"This way's faster. And less washing to do later. Where's Dad?" I returned the bottle to the fridge.

"He's getting some stuff together because he's going out on the boat later."

"Really? Cool. Maybe I can go out with him."

I let that linger there for a moment, as I remembered the bump on my head. I placed my hand on my head and felt the bump there. Panic rose in my chest. I wasn't sure, but I could have sworn it felt a little bigger. I had to push thoughts of tumors and blood clots out of my head before I said:

"So Mom do you think you or Dad can take me to a doctor or maybe a hospital later?"

I tried to make it sound like it was no big deal, but Mom looked questioningly at me with a hint of fear.

"Last night I tripped and fell down the stairs and hit my head. It's nothing to get upset about." But apparently it was.

"And you're now telling me this? How's your head? Does it hurt? Are you getting any kind of discomfort?"

Mom was trying to look for a bump in my head and, sadly, she found it. I heard a sharp intake of air.

"Oh, baby." She sighed.

"Mom, I'm fine. Turn those before they burn." I said, pointing to the frying pan. I heard a knock at the door and went to answer it. It was Gibbons. He was dressed in casual jeans and a striped shirt. Nothing fancy.

"You answer de door in ya underwear boy?" He asked in a kind of growl. I suddenly remembered I still wasn't dressed yet. I was still wearing the boxers and shirt from last night.

"Where ya Dad is?" Gibbons asked.

I told him he was out in the yard, then I went back up to my bedroom and got dressed. Mom had wanted us to leave for the hospital right after I got dressed, but I convinced her I needed to have breakfast, as passing out from hunger wouldn't really help things.

At about nine o'clock Mom took me to the East Island hospital, or EIH, as some people called it. Because it was the island's only public hospital it was crowded with people who were there for check-ups because of injuries and other stuff. Surprisingly, Mom knew a doctor who worked there,

Dr. Catherine Holder, and she had called ahead and the doctor kindly consented to see us. The hospital wasn't very elaborate, not like one in New York or the entire US for that matter. It was four stories tall but had a lot of other buildings, which were probably other departments, connected to it.

Dr. Holder examined me and to my relief, and Mom's of course, said I was fine.

By the time we got back home Dad, Gibbons and two other men along with Justin were waiting by the house.

"The doctor said I was fine." I spoke before Dad could even ask. He didn't make any effort to hide his relief. I really wished I hadn't told him. I couldn't even count on my own father to believe I was a little durable.

"We're going out on the sea for a few hours, you want to come?" He asked as he handed some equipment to Gibbons.

"Yeah." I responded enthusiastically. I loved going out with Dad whenever he went out on boats. It was one of the things we did together, one of the things I still loved doing with him.

As soon as everything was ready, we all bid farewell to Mom as she got back in her the car and headed off to work. Mom sometimes went along with Dad on the sea, professionally of course, but today her schedule was just too full.

Instead of a personal vehicle, parked in the driveway was a small, white pick-up truck that had a cover over the back which was where they kept the secured equipment for the boat. On the side of the truck were the words, East Island Marine Department.

As I didn't feel like going on a boat in a long pair of jeans, I changed into a red beach pants and a blue shirt.

"So how do you fit into this?" I asked Justin once I was back downstairs. He was also wearing a blue beach pants and a plain white shirt.

"Last night your Dad told me that he was going out to sea today and asked if I wanted to come. He cleared it with my parents. I only went out on a fishing boat once, but that was years ago. But now I get the chance to go on a marine biology expedition. Totally cool."

After all the stuff was loaded onto the truck we all hopped in (Justin and I in the front with Dad) and were off. I wondered which beach we were going to, but when I asked out loud it was Justin who answered.

"St. Martain's Boat Harbour, right? It's about fifteen minutes from here." Justin said, very sure of himself.

"That's right. That's where our new boat is, the *Blue Crystal*. Oh and she is a beauty." Dad often spoke of his boats with passion; he used to say if he had never became a marine biologist, he would have been a fisherman or a sailor, or giving boat rides to tourists.

"Plus, this harbour is a lot closer to us then the one in Bermintown. And it's less crowded. You'll see." Dad added.

Justin was right about the time it took to get to the harbour, because we were there in about fifteen minutes.

St. Martain's Harbour was very small and there were only about ten boats there. There was a lighthouse on a little cliff just beyond the harbour. After we arrived in the harbour, Justin and I got out of the truck while the others loaded the equipment onto the boat. The *Blue Crystal* was a white crab-fishing vessel. As soon as Justin and I were on board, Dad had us put on life jackets.

"What are you guys doing today, Dad?" I asked as he finished loading the last of the equipment, which were two long boxes I knew held the guns they used to shoot tracking darts.

"Well, there have been reports of unusual whale activity around the island lately, mainly here. And not all kinds either, people always say it's two, and always the same two. A Humpback Whale and an Orca, to be a little more specific about the species."

"Is it unusual to have whales around here?" I asked.

"Well, no." Dad responded. "See, people would probably see a whale or dolphin every once in a while, but these whales are being spotted every day and they have been getting pretty close to the island and they're not following their usual habits, so we're going to see if we can find them and tag them to see if they're the same some ones or different ones."

"And if they are, the same ones I mean." I wondered aloud.

"Then we'll have to find out why those specific two are attracted to the island so much."

"Perhaps they like the attention. Fame has gone to their heads." Justin joked. Everyone laughed.

After a while, Justin asked: "So, how are you going to tag?"

Dad opened a box and took out a small, flat object with a one-inch metal rod on it. Just like I thought: a tracking dart.

"With this. It's the latest in whale tracking technology. All we have to is shoot this onto the whale and bam, we can get sensor readings and sound recording. If something or someone out there is disturbing the whales, we'll find out what it is."

"Ya bess be hoping it ain't wha I think it is." Gibbons said while untying the boat. Everyone laughed as Gibbons went to steer the boat.

"Mermaids on the mind again." Joked Chris.

As we left the harbour and got further out to sea, we started to see flying fish, turtles and other sea creatures. It was about fifteen minutes after we left when we saw what we were looking for. A huge, brownish Humpback whale, about sixty yards away, rose out of the water and went back in with a huge splash.

Dad and the others began running around and shouting things as Justin and I hurried out of their way, but still kept good positions to keep the whale in sight.

"Get the tracker ready!!" Hoggie bellowed over the noise of the boat engine, the whale's song and the animal splashing around.

"Why isn't it already set to shoot? Gibbons get closer, don't lose it!" Dad shouted as Charlie handed him the gun, ready to shoot at the animal.

"Ya bess hold on then! Ha-ha!" Gibbson shouted, absolutely ecstatic as he spun the steering wheel to the left with all his might, causing some of us to fall to the floor. As I got up, I felt sprinkles of sea water on my face, and I saw Justin looking absolutely amazed and then when I looked straight ahead I saw the whale once again go back underwater about twenty yards away.

"Damn, he's gone!" Hoggie shouted, frustrated as he searched the ocean surface for the whale.

"No he's not. He's coming back up, we're close enough to take the shot." Charlie shouted from the sonar inside the boat. A few seconds later the whale broke the surface of the water again.

"I'm ready for him." Dad shouted, ready with the gun, but even as the whale remained visible he didn't take the shot.

"What are you waiting for? Shoot!" Charlie shouted as he joined the rest of us on deck.

"Not yet! We gotta get closer first!" Dad shouted back, still keeping aim.

"Tag it now." Hoggie prompted.

"A little closer." Dad repeated. We were now about ten yards away.

"How much closer do we have to get?" I walked over to Dad and asked.

"Not much closer."

The whale dove underwater again, and as soon as it came back up, everyone shouted "Tag it now!" I heard a small pop from the gun.

"You did it! Joe you did it!" Charlie shouted, after he ran back to the cabin and was looking at the computer screen. Everyone started cheering, but that came to an abrupt stop when Charlie said: "We got something else on sonar. It's big but not as big as the Humpback. Might be the Orca!" And sure enough a killer whale flew out of the water and dove back in.

Dad was about to shout something to the others when Hoggie shouted: "Don't worry Joe, I got the second gun armed!" He handed the gun to my Dad, who looked at me and said: "Chase come over here son."

I ran over to him as quickly as was possible on the rocking boat.

When I was younger, Dad would always tell me stories about how he'd tagged whales, and how he loved to hear their sounds. I would always ask him if I could ever tag one and he would always say, "One day soon." But I didn't expect it would be today. Dad shoved the gun into my hand.

"Dad, what are you doing? If I mess this up, you could miss tagging the Orca." I said, feeling a little scared. The gun looked like a rifle designed to shoot arrows. It already had the other tracking device in it.

"You always wanted to do this, here's your chance. I'm here and I'll help you. And if you miss it, it's your first try and that's okay. Now do you want to try this?"

I swallowed hard and stared at the rifle. "Yeah. I can do this."

"Good." Dad showed me how to stand and hold the gun and I had to admit that it did feel pretty good. By the time I was ready, the Orca was submerged again.

"Now wait till he surfaces, and we'll tell you when we're close enough for you to shoot. Make sure you've got a good shot, then pull the trigger, okay?"

I nodded. I saw the killer whale surface about fifteen feet in front of the boat. I had never been this close to a whale before and despite the fact that I was ninety-five percent sure they weren't going to attack the boat, my feet felt like they were going to give out on me. I knew that Dad was counting on me and I wasn't going to disappoint him.

"Chase, shoot now!" I heard Dad shout, but I just couldn't pull he trigger because somehow, the Orca had me mesmerized. It looked so graceful as it swam through the water and even from the distance of about eleven feet, I could have sworn the whale was looking at me.

I realised that everyone was shouting, telling me to shoot. I pulled myself out of whatever had happened to me and pulled the trigger. Along with the small pop I heard, the force of the gun shooting the tracking made me stumble back a little. I heard everyone cheering behind me. Someone slapped me on the back and I turned to see it was Justin.

"That was so cool!" he shouted.

Dad was laughing proudly. He looked at me and said: "Good work Chase. That was great. I'm proud of you."

I handed him the gun back. My hands were shaking like crazy and they were kind of tingling, and I looked over the side of the boat because all the tension had made me nauseous. That's when I saw it. The sickening feeling I was having must have been making me see things, because I thought I saw a boy swim past the boat under the water wearing nothing but a pair of shorts.

CHAPTER 3

A Strange Meeting

E veryone had run into the cabin to check on the information coming in from the devices on the whales. I heard someone ask me if I was coming, but I was so mesmerized by what I saw that their voices sounded far away, like they were on another boat. I distinctly became aware that it was Justin who was talking to me. I told him I'd be there soon and he ran in behind the others. As I scanned the water, I could see the dark outline of the boy underwater. Then quicker than I would have thought possible, he surfaced.

From his face I could tell that his skin was pale-white, but it looked good on him. It made him look handsome and it also gave him the look of a completely healthy person. He looked like he was fifteen or sixteen years old and he had jet black hair that was neck long and wild and even though he just came out the water it looked half-dry already.

He was smiling and looking around, but when he turned and realised I was looking directly at him, shock took over his face, like he'd made a dangerous mistake. Then, like he never existed in the first place, he just disappeared. I frantically searched the sea for any signs of a human in the water, but there wasn't any. The nauseous feeling I was experiencing had subsided by this time and I wondered if indeed it was that sickening feeling that made me imagine I saw someone in the water. But although I was trying to convince myself that it was in my head, I just knew that he was real.

I quickly ran into the cabin. I just had to make sure. Everyone was looking at a monitor screen with whale song recordings and video footage. At that moment I wasn't interested in that very much. I ran to the sonar monitor. There were two full red dots on the screen that I guessed were the whales, and other red dots that only appeared when the circling green line passed their location, but nothing that resembled a human.

"What you looking for?" Hoggie came over and asked me. I had to think of something convincing to say because I certainly wasn't going to tell him I saw a boy this far out in the sea.

"Just looking. Hey, um, if there was someone diving out in the sea, the sonar would pick them up, right?" I asked.

"Yeah. They would come up as a little person on the screen," Hoggie said as he pointed at the monitor. He looked back at me and said: "Chase, you did good work out there. You made your father very proud of you."

He patted me on the shoulder and rejoined the others.

"We're heading back to the harbour now." Dad came over and told me. I went back out on the main deck and looked out to sea for the rest of the ride back to land. I kept hoping the boy would come back up so I could get a proper look at him, mostly to reassure myself that I wasn't crazy, but no such thing ever happened. There wasn't even any visible sign of the whales after they'd been tagged. When I asked Charlie where they'd gone, he said they swam further out into the ocean.

Could I have really seen someone out there? I thought to myself. Then again, how could someone, even a kid, swim so for out to sea and back by himself? I didn't even see another boat in sight, plus the currents alone would have drowned him. Then again, I did meet someone who seemed to be able to swim through incredibly strong currents. Perhaps this boy could too. Even if he could, he would have been too worn out to get back to shore alive. But I had to remind myself that no one was there, as no human showed up on the sonar. Then what did I see? Was there a problem with the sonar... or, maybe me? Maybe that bump at the back of my head is something to worry about after all.

That's when the craziest thing I ever thought of occurred to me, something so silly I wouldn't ever tell anybody I even considered the existence of such a thing. Gibbons alone would have had a field day with the news. But could it be possible. Maybe the reason the boy didn't show up on the sonar or how he could swim so far was, maybe he wasn't human. Maybe he was... no. I quickly pushed this thought out of my head before it could develop into something.

"Chase. Let's go!" Justin shouted at me. I was so consumed in thought that I didn't realise we were back at the harbour and all the equipment was already loaded onto the truck. I hopped off the boat and joined the others.

On the drive back home I was silent, and Dad must have thought that was a sign of some remorse I was feeling, because when he dropped Justin and I off at our house he took me aside. His face was full of regret.

"Look Chase, I'm sorry I made you tag that Orca. I should have known you weren't ready. It's just you always said you wanted to do it and I thought you'd feel bad if you never got the chance. If it makes you feel any better, he didn't get hurt, still probably doesn't know the thing's there."

"What? Dad no, I know that. I don't feel bad about tagging the whale. In fact it was great. I'm glad you gave me the chance to do it. It's just that I've got something else on my mind, that's all." My dad looked relieved.

"You're sure?"

"Yes Dad, I'm sure."

"Okay. Well I've got to go. I'll see you boys later." He then ran back to the truck and drove away with everyone shouting "Bye" and "See ya later."

"Sorry dude, but I've got to go too. There's this big community party this evening and I promised I'd help set up. You want to come?" Justin asked me.

"What's a community party?" I asked as I imagined some big formal party.

He chuckled. "It's not as boring as it sounds. Actually it's not boring at all. It's really just an excuse for us to throw a big party for no reason. We do it every year in June."

"I don't know., I haven't really been here long enough to be going to a community party." I said, sounding uneasy.

"Come on. You are a part of the community. And even

people from other parishes come to this. You can get to meet my friends, it'll be great."

I thought about it, and after deciding I didn't want to sit around the house and dwell on whether I was going crazy or not, I said yes and Justin said he'd come back at around three, and then he left. I checked my watch, it was now eleven o' clock. "Perfect," I said to myself. Just enough time to do some quick research.

I went up to my room, turned on the computer, logged on to the internet and typed 'super swimmers' in the search bar. The results I got were a list of Olympic swimming gold medalists, people who swam the English Channel and people who seemed to enjoy swimming in extremely dangerous waters. Nothing that would really explain how a kid could swim so far out to sea or, as she came back to mind, how the girl on the beach had managed to save me and get us both out of last night's treacherous waters.

I turned off the computer and dropped onto the bed, which my body was grateful for as my bones started to relax. But even as my body rested, my mind continued buzzing. As soon as I started thinking about the girl, I couldn't get her out of my head. I remembered how her hair blew lightly in the wind, how beautiful and literally aglow she looked in the moonlight, how she smelled better than anything I ever smelled in my life. I closed my eyes and saw her more vividly in my head, looking at me with her brilliant blue eyes and a big smile on her face. I sighed and said out loud to myself: "Why do these things happen to me?" After a while I drifted off to sleep.

Bam! Someone had shot a cannon ball out of a cannon not far from me. Wait, that didn't sound right. I shot up straight in bed and saw Justin picking up a book off the floor.

"I always wanted to do that." He said, sitting in the only chair in the room.

"What time is it?" I asked incoherently, looking around as the sound of the waves slowly brought me back to reality.

"2:30." He said, sounding very much at ease.

"You're here early. How did you get in anyway?" I got out of bed.

"I got here about fifteen minutes ago and your Dad let me in. He said when he got back you were asleep."

"Well, you're going to have to wait a little longer because I've got to get ready."

"Fine with me. I'll just have a go on your PS3 while I wait." He said and dashed downstairs.

I took a shower and got dressed in black jeans and a red shirt. By the time I was done it was exactly three o'clock.

"I'm ready." I said as I walked downstairs and found Justin still playing Metal Gear Solid. He turned it off.

"Hey, Dad you don't mind that I'm going to this party, do you?" I asked as he walked into the living room and dropped himself on the couch.

"No not at all. I'm glad you're going. This'll give you a chance to make some more friends." He started flipping through channels.

As we walked up the road to get to the main road, I noticed the Morgans' house looked a little deserted. The curtains were still drawn, and all the windows were shut. That's when I remembered it was Wednesday, my second day here and I still hadn't seen anyone from that house.

"Hey Justin, have the Morgans moved out or something? I haven't seen anyone in that house yet." I asked as we turned left towards the main road.

"Nah. They always take a vacation during the summer to spend time with their kids. They'll be back soon though."

When we got to the main road we walked on the side until it took us around a corner, then we walked for five more minutes on the right side of the road, passing houses and shops until we turned onto a big field with a couple of trees here and there. There were lots of tents of many colors and tables filled with food, snacks and drinks, and there were rows and rows of colorful lights draped around the trees and hanging from poles, but they weren't on yet. When it got dark, though, it would definitely be a pretty sight. There were also piles of toys and books and household stuff available for purchase everywhere. There was a huge tent at the back of the field and under it were huge speakers and a DJ. I figured it served as a dance floor and a crowd was already under there dancing to a local song I was unfamiliar with. Even though it was evening yet, there were still a lot of people present.

Most of the people we passed seemed to know Justin very well. I guessed when you lived in a small neighborhood everyone knew you. As we walked around I noticed people were smiling and waving at me as if they knew me for years. All I could do was wave back enthusiastically, all the while trying to hide the queasy feeling I was having inside.

"Do you know everyone here?" I asked, amazed as more people still either waved or shouted "Hey!" to Justin. I probably didn't know this many people back in New

York. Justin laughed before he answered.

"Well not everyone. Some are family and others are close friends, practically part of the family." Justin said, searching frantically around, trying to see through the large crowd.

"There they are," I heard him say over the loud music. I followed him through the crowd to a group of kids our age. When we caught up with them they greeted Justin and then he introduced them to me. There were five of them.

"Chase, this is Rachael," she had long, sleek black hair, "Brandon," a muscular boy who had his hair braided, "Maranda," a tall, dark-skinned girl, "Kristian," a boy who looked slightly older than me with very tanned white skin, and blond hair. "And his younger sister, Kimberley," Justin finished. Kimberley had a small round face and small green eyes that looked like two small emeralds. Her blond hair rested lightly on her shoulders. In all Kimberley was a very good looking girl, that I had to admit, but it wasn't like I was undressing her with my eyes or anything, so I didn't understand why her brother, Kristian, was giving me such a strange look, like he wanted to convey with just looks that he hated me. It's not like I'd done him anything. That's when I noticed he had the same eyes as his sister. Feeling uneasy, I hastily looked away.

We all walked around for a while, eating and drinking everything we could. There was a wide range of food available, for free of course. There was rice and peas, chicken, fish, sheppard's pie, sweet potato pie, macaroni pie, lasagna, breadfruit and salt fish, fish cakes, and a whole lot more I didn't recognize.

After eating *a lot* of food, we just relaxed by a tree for

a while. I had to admit that Justin had really good friends. They were cool and liked making a lot of jokes, especially Brandon. I had noticed, however, that when everyone else was busy laughing, Rachael and Maranda would sneak glances at me from the corners of their eyes and would quickly turn away, blushing whenever I caught their eye. They wouldn't do it together though, as though each one didn't want the other to know what they were doing. I wondered when they would decide to try to catch me alone and when I chuckled at the thought I saw them both catch for breath. Brandon saw their expressions and then looked at me. I simply gave him a 'it—wasn't—me' look.

I had always thought of myself as okay-looking, because back in New York, although girls weren't breaking down my door, they weren't scarce either. Here on East Island however, if other girls' reaction to me was anything like Rachael and Maranda's, then my life was going to be more interesting.

I made a mental note not to say or do anything that would give Rachael or Maranda wrong signals, because truth be told, there was already a girl that caught my attention. There was just something about the girl on the beach that screamed exciting to me. At that moment, a small gust of wind came directly at me, and with it I could have sworn I could smell that same great sea-like perfumed scent she had. I kept taking huge breaths of air just so I could keep inhaling the scent.

"Dude, you okay?" Brandon asked me. The others looked around too and I was positive this time that I saw Maranda and Rachel's eyes dart to my chest. At that moment, I realised I should have worn a better shirt.

"Yeah I'm fine. The air out here is really good. Nothing like living by the cove though." I had to have a good cover story. At least that sounded better than "I thought I smelled the girl I saw on the rocks in the sea."

Maranda took her chance before Rachael could. She eased past the others and slid the tree next to me and took my hand, intertwining her fingers with mine, which took me by surprise. Rachael looked like she was about to grow horns, and I understood why. To anyone who didn't know better, it would look like we were a couple. That was probably her plan. Girls could be so devious at times.

"So I hear you live by the cove. That's amazing, I just love it down there, it's so beautiful and peaceful." She said very quickly, her face close to mine.

I blinked in surprise at our proximity to each other and said, "You heard?"

"Well yeah. You and your parents are new here. News travels fast."

I was trying in vain to find a way to unhinge my hand from hers. For the first time in my life I was desperately wishing my hands would sweat. Maranda wasn't a bad girl, but she just wasn't my type of girl.

After a while we started walking around again, and I finally got my hand free. Brandon, Justin and Kristian were trying to see who could eat the most hot dogs and Maranda, Kimberley and Rachael were talking. I walked behind the others, not because I didn't feel like part of the group, but because the girl on the beach had come back to my mind.

"Hey, are you alright?" Kimberley stopped to ask me.

"Yeah, I'm fine. Why?" I replied.

"Well, you just seem distant, that's all."

I was about to say something else when I saw Kristian giving me that warning look again. I didn't want to cause trouble with Kimberley and her brother, so I just thanked her for asking and let her rejoin the others. There was no doubt that Kristian was a bit protective when it came to his sister. I'd have to let him know I had no romantic feelings towards her before things got out of hand.

Just then I noticed a woman walking past us. She was dressed in a long, dark green dress that almost swept the ground, and had long, beautiful black dreadlocks. At first I didn't take much notice of her. What I found slightly odd about her was her eyes. They were pitch black, but that itself wasn't so odd; it was the way she used her eyes. It was like everyone she passed, she had to get a look at them. She looked at everyone she passed for half a second and went on to the next person. She did it in such a way that you wouldn't notice unless you were looking for it. When she was passing us she looked fully at the others in turn, Maranda, Brandon, Justin, Rachael, Kimberley and Kristian. It took her about ten seconds to look at them all. Then, as she was passing, she looked at me. At first it looked like she was going to move right on, then as fast as her eyes were off me they were back on. She looked at me in horror, clutching her chest as if a dark cloud of evil only she could see was around me. It actually scared me a little to see just how frightened she was.

In about two seconds she composed herself and walked on, glancing back at me every few steps. I looked around. No one seemed to have noticed what had happened. I was very grateful for that.

"Who was that woman that just passed us? The one with the dreadlocks?" I asked Rachael. She checked to see who I meant.

"That's Hilda Jones, but everyone around here calls her Miss Hilda. She's supposed to be a psychic or witch or something, at least that's what people say. She usually keeps to herself, but she'll mingle with other people every once in a while. She always comes to these sorts of events. Other than that I really don't know much about her."

She was a psychic. I really didn't believe in such things, even with TV shows like *Medium* and *Paranormal State*. It was hard for me to wrap my head around the whole supernatural thing, although because of the girl on the beach and the boy I saw in the water, it was possible that this might start to change.

The look she gave me was hard to shake off and even harder to forget, even if I was skeptical of Madame Hilda's abilities. It wasn't right for her to just come up to me and do her freaky stare and act like something was wrong. It should be against the law to do that to someone who was unprepared for it. I balled both my hands into a fist. Anger was beginning to well up inside me although I couldn't really think of a good enough reason why. Staring at people wasn't a crime. Still, it really got to me. I decided to find her and demand to know what it was all about. According to Maranda, Miss Hilda always had a tent at these events, so all I had to do was find it.

By this time Maranda was lurking near me again, but I told her I was going to take a walk alone for a while (just to make sure that she and Rachael wouldn't try to repeat their little scenario). I looked at Maranda, smiling in a friendly way, told her that we were going to be great friends (I emphasized the word 'friends') and patted her gently on the shoulder.

When I turned away from her, both she and Rachael wore dumbfounded expressions, which kind of made me feel guilty. What was I supposed to do? Behind them I could have sworn I saw Kimberley smirking.

I didn't have to walk very far or look too hard to find Miss Hilda's tent. It was green with a wooden arrow sign outside that said '*Miss Hilda, Resident Psychic*'. It wasn't exactly inconspicuous. Getting the courage to go in was a different story altogether. I must have been pacing up and down in front of her tent for five minutes (I was already seeing a path in the grass) before two kids came rushing out. One of them muttered "I told you so," before they disappeared into the crowed. Then I heard a voice inside the tent call "Well, aren't you going to come in boy, you did come to see me didn't you?"

The fact that she even knew I was out there surprised me at first, but then I convinced myself that she could probably see through the material the tent was made of. I took a few breaths to calm myself and gather my thoughts before I went in. When I entered I saw that there wasn't much inside the tent, just a long, rectangular table with a snow globe in the middle, two chairs on both sides of the table, and a life-sized mirror at the back that made the inside of the tent seem way bigger than the outside. I wondered if this was just a coincidence or if Miss Hilda was going for this effect. Either way the tent wasn't very interesting, something I thought a psychic would have wanted to avoid if they wanted any costumers. Resting on the table in front of her was a huge hardcover novel, which she was reading.

Along with the illusion of the tent looking larger on the inside, I realised the music outside was only a babble in the background. I wondered how she could do that.

Hilda was sitting in the chair facing me, but she suddenly put her hand under the table, pulled up a bowl, and started shelling peas. Well, I figured she had to do something to pass the time. She indicated with her hand that I should take a seat and hesitantly, I did, though I couldn't help seeing the way she kept glancing at me, as though she was seeing something she couldn't believe— something horrible. Hilda continued shelling the peas as she spoke.

"It's ten dollars to speak with me, and you get three questions, just so you know."

"What?" I exclaimed. "I thought this was free."

"Well not everything, plus this goes to charity. That's the way it is, take it or leave it."

For a quick second I thought about just leaving. I mean all she did to get me here was look at me. Maybe that was just a scheme to lure people here. And maybe it wasn't even me she was looking at, perhaps it was someone else. But I knew better. I knew she was looking at me, and I wanted to know why. And even if I didn't believe in her 'power', she obviously did, so she must have thought she saw something. So, silently cursing myself, I took out my wallet and handed her ten dollars. After she pocketed it, she simply went back to her shelling.

"So, what can I do for you child?" She asked. I gave her an incredulous look at her use of the word 'child', a look she didn't see.

I cleared my throat before I answered.

"Um, well I just wanted to ask you why you, um never mind I made a mistake." I had suddenly had lost my nerve. There was just something about her that made me feel weird. I just couldn't bring myself to ask her something that I knew would sound extremely stupid.

I quickly got up, but before I could get out Miss Hilda asked casually:

"Tell me boy, are you in love?"

I froze on the spot, unsure of how to answer. She had only glanced up to ask the question, then returned to her peas. This time I ignored the 'boy' jab and returned to my seat. My mind buzzed. Why on earth would she ask me that question? Maybe she saw me with Maranda and got the wrong idea or perhaps she knew about the girl on the beach and the feelings I was starting to develop for her. My heart started to race, partly from surprise at Miss Hilda's question, but mostly from thinking about the girl on the beach.

Thankfully, Miss Hilda didn't wait for my answer. I hoped it was because she guessed that I either wasn't sure about my feeling or was too shy to say anything. However, she did have an odd smile on her face. In any case she simply asked another question, one which defiantly didn't get under my 'weird' radar.

"Do you know what an aura is?"

"Umm, sure, I guess. I only know what I've heard from TV or read in books though. It's a kind of light that's around people, right? And only psychic people can see it." I never really believed in that kind of stuff.

Hilda chucked before she responded.

"An aura is defined as an invisible emotional light that surrounds a person, and is a different color depending on how you're feeling. This light can tell a lot about a person. Who they are, how they're feeling, what can become of them. I guess you can say, it's kind of a psychic journal of our souls."

I figured she said this because she had something else she wanted to say, so I decided to just stay quiet for now and let her speak.

"I can tell, just from looking at you, that you're not a person to believe in magic, you'd don't believe in the supernatural, do you?"

She was looking at me now with those bottomless black eyes of hers, no longer shelling her peas, though her hands were still in the bowl.

"No. I don't believe in the supernatural." Was my short but hopefully polite answer.

"Well then, let's just say that I'm a very gifted person, and one of my little gifts is the ability to see people's auras. All my life I've been able to see them. I've even traveled the world just to see people's auras, to see what kind of people there are in the world, and believe me, there are people out there with lives you'd never imagine."

Miss Hilda put her bowl of peas back under the table and gave me her full attention.

"The reason you came here is you want to know why I gave you that look back there in the field." It wasn't a question.

"Well, I was thinking about it," I said sheepishly. Miss Hilda looked at me oddly again, this time it was like she was trying to decide what to say.

"The reason I looked at you so oddly is because, for some reason, I couldn't see your aura. Actually I still can't see it. Everyone's aura is unique, Chase, but no matter what, I can always see it. Never in my life had I ever met someone without an aura. It just surprised me, that's all."

"Alright, let's say I believe you. Do you know why you can't see my aura?"

"No, I don't know. Maybe for some reason it's invisible to me or maybe you just don't have one anymore."

"How does it just disappear? And if I don't have one, is that a bad thing?" I asked a little nervously.

Miss Hilda fixed me with a look first, then said:

"I never heard of anyone living without an aura, though I don't think it will really mean anything if you don't have one. Now as far as how you lose it, I can't answer that."" She checked her watch. "You've been here for a full fifteen minutes. Most people only stay for ten."

After that she took out her bowl again and continued shelling her peas. I took it to mean that our little session was over. I thanked her and got up to leave, but just before I got out of the tent, I heard Hilda say: "Chase, I've met your parents. They're good people and I would hate for you to do something that would end up hurting them. Just be careful of who you make friends with."

And with that I left the tent, the music reaching its right level again, bringing me back to reality.

By the time I got back to the others it was already dark and all the lights I had seen before were now burning bright.

Justin and the others asked me where I went, but as I wasn't up for telling them about my talk with Hilda. I just told them my walk took longer than I thought it would have. They didn't question that and Kristian especially looked like he really wasn't bothered.

After Rachael suggested that we do something fun, we headed to the dance floor. Most of the people at the party were dancing and enjoying themselves. As soon as we got there, the others ran right onto the dance floor and joined in with everyone else, but as I wasn't much of a dancer, I decided to just settle in a chair for a while.

Even with all the noise and the people, I was still able to settle myself. I looked up and saw a bright, starry sky above. The moon was huge and bright and shone a kind of yellow as it hung in the sky, and that's when it happened. I caught a whiff of that perfume-like smell that had been on the girl from the beach. I got out of the chair and looked around, my heart pounding, hoping to see her again. I started to feel dizzy and my head hurt without warning. I clutched both sides of my head as if trying to block out the noise.

"Chase, are you feeling alright?" It was Rachael who asked. She had grabbed both my hands in an attempt to pull them away from my head, but strangely, when she did this, the sudden headache that had just developed disappeared along with the strong, sea-like fragrance.

I looked up and saw not only Rachael, but the others and a few strangers staring at me. I smiled before I spoke.

"I'm fine. I just had a little headache, but it's gone now."

"Are you sure? Do you need aspirin or something?" Kimberley asked.

"Yeah, I'm sure." I checked my watch. It was just after nine. I didn't even realize so much time had passed. "You know, I think I'm going to go home."

The others volunteered to walk home with me (with the exception of Kristian, who scowled at his sister for volunteering), but I declined. I didn't really feel like lying down, but with everything that had happened so far I just wanted to be alone, and the walk home would do fine.

The night had gotten cold and goosebumps erupted all over my arms, but the cold feeling barely reached my consciousness as I was deep in thought. What was really happening to me? I wasn't even in East Island for a full week and already things I didn't understand were happening.

First of all I fell off a cliff and almost died, but thankfully I was saved from deadly rough tides by a ridiculously beautiful girl who disappeared before I could even get her name. Who even does that? Then I saw some kid swimming way out in the sea without any gear or even a nearby boat. Then, a supposed psychic told me she was worried because she thought I'd lost my aura. It was a lot to take in… a lot more than most seventeen year old teenagers were equipped to deal with.

I couldn't help thinking that maybe if I could just see the girl from the beach again, everything would somehow make sense, it would all work out, like everything was somehow connected to her. She had the answers to questions I didn't even ask. It was unreasonable for me to put all this on her, but all of it started happening on the night I met her.

In a couple of minutes my house came into view, but as I was passing near the road to the cove, for a few seconds I contemplated going down there to see if the girl was there. In fact, I even turned to head down the road, until a strange sensation came over me. All of a sudden I just had this urge to get home. I didn't know why, but I felt like something was pulling me there, like my limbs were connected to invisible wires, pulling me home. With every step that brought me closer to the door, my breath got shorter and my heart began to beat faster, knowing that something was waiting for me on the other side. I finally got to the front door and opened it, and had the biggest surprise in my life.

My parents were sitting in the living room, but they weren't alone.

"Chase, these are the Morgans. They got back from their vacation a few hours ago. This is Marcus Morgan." Mom motioned to a tall man who looked to be in his late twenties. He had short, wavy black hair and surprisingly pale skin. His eyes, I noticed, were sky blue. "This is his wife, Salathia." Salathia was a very beautiful woman. She had long, blond hair and smooth-looking olive-tanned skin. She had striking dark blue eyes.

"This is their oldest son Michael." Dad indicated a boy sitting on his mother's left. He looked to be around nineteen or twenty at the most. His skin was just as pale as Marcus's, but he had his mother's honey blond hair. And then I felt like someone had knocked the air out of me, because sitting at the end of the chair next to Michael and looking extremely surprised, was someone I wasn't even sure was real in the first place. The boy I saw in the sea this morning balled his hands into fists in his lap, looked me straight in the eye and shook his head slightly as if trying to tell not to do something, which I guessed was talk about what happened this morning. If he ever thought I was going to mention that in front of all these people, he was wrong.

"That's their youngest child, Nikolai." Mom said.

Even as I stood there in front of my parents' guests though, that strange sensation was still tugging at my consciousness, pulling me to some force that I seemed to secretly desire. And as I stood there I realised that I could feel that force coming towards me, drawing nearer to me by the second.

Just as I looked towards the hallway was when she walked out. Tall and slender-looking, she was wearing a blue shirtdress and heels. Her long, slight curly black hair was bouncing off her shoulders. I couldn't tell if anyone picked up on it, but as she entered the room, it was filled with her scent, that sea-flowers aroma that always smelled so good. When she saw me, she walked past everyone and walked up to me.

"Hi. I'm Lyla. It's nice to meet you."

CHAPTER 4

Lyla

<< Good morning, East Island. The time is now 6:15. We just got word that we're in for an extremely cold morning, so to everyone out there, lock your doors, shut your windows, crawl back into bed and spend your morning with me, Krissie Anderson, right here on Flame 105.1 FM, playing the music you want to hear. >>

I rolled over and shut off the alarm radio at the same time that Krissie started to play a song by a heavy metal rock band I didn't know. It was way too early to be listening to Krissie's annoying, sleepy voice.

Unable to get back to sleep, I threw off the covers, sat on the side of the bed and just let my head fall right into my hands. I hadn't slept very well because the very vivid dreams I'd been having (though I could not remember them) were so realistic that whenever I had them I always woke up with my body aching and tired.

Stretching and yawning loudly, I got up to go downstairs, almost tripping over a pair of jeans I'd left by the bedroom door, realizing that Krissie was right about the cold from the way the floor felt like it was biting my feet.

"Well, you obviously didn't sleep well," Dad said when I got downstairs.

Mom placed a bowl of porridge in front of me when I sat down at the dining room table. Both she and Dad were already dressed and ready for work as usual. I didn't really like porridge and I started playing with it for a while, but I was so drained that after the first spoonful I started shoveling it down.

"Slow down there, or you'll get yourself sick," Dad warned with a little chuckle.

"Chase, I need you to do something for me today," Mom said, taking her things away from the table. I sighed deeply into my bowl. I was pretty sure Dad heard me, but if he did he said nothing.

Over the past two weeks Mom had been getting me to do all sorts of jobs around the house. They weren't very difficult things, but they were very time-consuming. I was hoping there wouldn't be anything more, but it seemed like I was wrong.

"I need you to take this over to the Morgans for me."

Mom placed a photo album on the table tiled: *Rural Russia*.

"I took these when I went on that veterinarian sabbatical to Russia. It's so beautiful there," Mom reminisced as she flicked through the album filled with photos of the Russian countryside and small villages. "When they were here last, Salathia saw this and loved it. She told me she grew up in Russia, but doesn't have much to remember it by, so I thought she could have this."

"Wait, the Morgans are back?" I asked as I dropped my spoon into my empty bowl in surprise.

The night after I'd met them Dad told me they'd left to visit some family in the U.S., but that was two weeks ago and even though I was always watching for their return, for some reason I didn't expect them to be back so soon, even though to me it felt like Lyla had been away for two months.

During that time I'd gotten somewhat used to the idea of living on East Island, though I still didn't like it. Dad had got me a new bike, a green BMX, something to be proud of. Mom had finally got her vet practice opened. It was a twenty-minute drive from our home, and it was pretty close to the harbor. Her reason for having it so close to home was because she felt town was too far for a lot of people in the community and other neighborhoods to have to go to see a vet. Plus she had a partner working with her, so her work with Dad wouldn't cause any problems with the vet practice.

Things were also going well for Dad. He and his team were getting lots of vital information about the marine life around the island, but they still had no idea why the Orca and Humpback kept coming so close to the island so regularly, although Dad did say over the past fortnight they almost didn't come at all.

I really didn't get to spend much time hanging out with Justin and the others because they'd decided to get summer jobs, even though there were only about six weeks of vacation left.

Mom had wanted me to get a summer job as well, but I convinced her I needed to learn more about the island first, and luckily for me she bought it, even though those were some of the crappiest lies I'd ever told. The truth was I just wasn't ready for the stress of a job. The very thought was enough to send shivers down my spine.

I was also working on getting my driver's license, but my parents refused to buy me a car so early and, to my horror, they used my own excuse on me. They thought I should learn more about road safety on the island first. One point for karma.

Something else that also developed over the last two weeks was my growing interest in Lyla Morgan. It seemed to me like I was thinking about her more and more every day. Somehow everything I saw or did found a way of reminding me of her. Even my sketch books were now filled with pictures of her.

Of course I didn't tell anyone about how I felt. Not because I was embarrassed, but because I felt it best to keep it to myself for the time being.

"So when did they get back?" I asked, concentrating a little too hard on my empty bowl. Dad gave me a suspicious look before going off to get his things together.

"Well, they got back just last night," Mom replied. "Why are you so interested?"

She added with a knowing look as though she knew something I didn't want to tell her. My mom always liked to indulge herself with the idea that she was always able to figure things about me. Most of the time, she did.

"I'm just asking," I said, taking the bowl to the kitchen. I just needed to get away from Mom so she wouldn't see my face.

"Well they just got back last night. Marcus came over

earlier because he's involved in the project, so he'll start today. I asked him to tell Salathia you'll be dropping by later, so she'll be expecting you. Oh, and I do believe Lyla will be home."

Mom turned and left the room before I could say a word.

Shortly afterwards my parents left for work, leaving me alone.

Knowing Lyla was back home, just around the corner, caused me to be jittery and impatient, yet still with enough room for me to feel extremely happy. It wasn't 7 o'clock yet and I didn't want to go over too early. The idea of seeing Lyla again had me too worked up and somehow had made time move slowly. Once I had the kitchen tidied up I decided I couldn't wait any longer. After taking a shower and getting dressed I was ready to go, but was still afraid of arriving too early, so I waited until 8:30, took up the album, and left.

Ever since I'd woken up I'd been experiencing that strange magnetic sensation I had the night I met the Morgans. Yeah, that's right, the thing that freaked me out. Once again it was like I was being inexplicably drawn towards something. But only this time the pull wasn't so strong, because even though it was there I was able to ignore it. Seeing Lyla was way more important than worrying about that.

Even though it was just minutes away, I'd never seen the Morgans' side of the cove, and for some reason I thought it was going to be just like our side of the cove.

Boy, was I wrong.

The landscape around the house was amazing. I couldn't

help but wonder how much it must have cost to have it done, because it just looked too surreal to be natural.

Not only did trees flank both sides of the road leading up to the house, but they were all a couple feet away from each other, wide enough to let the sea breeze flow freely around the area. There were also all sorts of plants around which grew a beautiful assortment of sweet-smelling flowers.

But I got the biggest shock of all when I turned the corner. In all my life I had never seen a house that looked like this. If I didn't know any better I would have assumed someone rich lived there. Then again, the Morgans probably were rich.

This side of the cliff was a lot closer to the sea than ours, about half as high as ours was. Unlike our side of the cliff, the trees on this side went right up to the cliff's edge, their leaves and branches swaying lazily in the air as I watched, giving the place a tranquil atmosphere.

As for the house, I could only describe it as an architectural wonder. It had three floors and the design made the house look like some sort of half-finished burr puzzle, but with a more exotic look. I couldn't help but wonder how the second and third floors were being safely held up.

The house was beautifully painted in red and white, and as I'd seen with some houses on TV, there was actually more glass in the walls than wall. It really did look amazing.

Gathering myself together, I walked up to the mahogany front door and rang the doorbell. I was so nervous that my body tingled, but I didn't have much time to think about this as the door was pulled open about two seconds after I pushed the bell by Salathia.

Strangely enough, the first thing I noticed about her wasn't something I saw, it was something I smelled as the scent of her perfumed wafted towards me, seductively tickling my senses the second the door was opened.

"Chase," she said with a barely noticeable Russian accent, her pale face breaking into a huge smile as if seeing me made her morning, "How wonderful it is to see you again."

"Good morning, Mrs. Morgan. I hope I didn't come too early because Mom told me you were expecting me. Anyway I just stopped by to drop off this photo album she wanted you to have."

I held the album out to her, and as her sky blue eyes slid down to it, they grew big with surprise when she saw it. She took it from me as though she was in possession of some scary book.

"Would you like to come in?"

Not wanting to be rude and glad for the opportunity at the same time, I said yes. Salathia stood aside to allow me entry and as I passed her I caught another whiff of what she was wearing. Whatever it was it was strong, not in an unbearable way, but in a make-heads-turn-in-a-crowd sort of way.

From the moment I crossed the threshold the strange metallic pull I'd been feeling suddenly became too strong to ignore. In the space of three seconds it grew so strong that I actually lost all awareness of my surroundings for a couple seconds, but was quickly pulled back when Salathia touched my shoulder.

"I asked if you wanted something to drink."

I didn't answer immediately. I just stood there, shocked and unable to explain what had just happened. The fact that it made me feel kind of happy was even stranger. I didn't know why, and that's what scared me.

"Chase, are you okay?" Salathia asked, still smiling but with concern in her voice. As I looked at her I noticed that for some reason her eyes were sweeping the air around me.

"Yeah, I'm fine," I mumbled. A strange expression crossed her face, maybe surprise, but then she realized I was staring at her and just like that, it was gone.

"Would you like something to drink?" She asked again.

I nodded. She turned and put album down on a small glass table near the door. Then I really got a good look at the interior of the house, and it made me forget what just happened for awhile.

The inside of the house was huge and very beautifully decorated. The walls and floor were painted white, while the ceiling was the same striking red as outside. This very room alone had dozens of florescent bulbs in it and I was willing to bet that every other room in the house was the same.

Beautiful, golden sunlight poured through the glass walls of the house, but I figured the windows had to be a little tinted even if they didn't appear to be, because just the right amount of light came in the house.

Salathia was taking me to their kitchen when Nikolai, the youngest Morgan, came hopping down the stairs. I had never seen anyone move so effortlessly in all my life. It was like he was levitating instead of walking towards his mother.

For some reason I couldn't fathom, she fixed him with

a look of annoyance, which he merely shrugged off and said sorry, as if he'd done something wrong. He walked up to me and extended his hand. Feeling a little awkward, I shook it.

I started to wonder about the money they spent on expensive perfumes and colognes, because when I got a smell of whatever Nikolai was wearing, it smelled just as exotic as his mother's, though there was a certain masculinity to it.

"Hi, you're Chase right? I'm Nikolai, if you remember," he said quite cheerfully.

"Of course I remember. A Morgan isn't exactly easy to forget."

Both he and his mother laughed. As I looked at him I started to wonder if this really was the boy I'd seen in the ocean before, because if it was, he wasn't acting very guilty. Maybe I was wrong, and it wasn't Nikolai. For some reason I couldn't remember it very well. That memory was now like a very thin thread that I could barely see.

"Mother, I'm going for a swim, I will be back soon and yes, I will be careful."

Salathia smiled at him and, just like my mom, ran her fingers through his messy black hair, but unlike mine, his simply fell back into place (*I so wish mine would do that*), then he said goodbye and left.

Once again I was hit by that strong magnetic pull, but this time it only lasted a second. As soon as it disappeared, she came down the stairs.

Her silky hair was moving in perfect union with her body, not one strand out of place. Lyla Morgan walked down the stairs with more grace than even her brother.

Not to be too dramatic, but I could have sworn the very air around her seemed to move differently, just for her.

Just as her brother had done, she came to a stop next to her mother and I fell into a state of nervousness again when I noticed her sea blue eyes flickering towards me for a couple seconds.

"Chase, you remember my daughter, Lyla?"

She didn't extend her hand to me, which disappointed me because I was really hoping she would, but she did smile warmly, though I took it as the smile you give people you really don't think twice about.

It was amazing how, when they smiled, they were able to show every one of their perfect teeth.

"Yes. I do remember her. It's nice to see you again." Major understatement.

"It's nice to see you again as well, Chase."

"Lyla, we were just about to have a drink, why don't you join us?"

Lyla hesitated for a while, as if she was trying to find any excuse not to, but eventually said, "Okay, why not?"

They both led me into their huge and wonderfully decorated kitchen which had an amazing view of a garden at the side of the house. Even I, who couldn't care less about décor, couldn't help but admire how the red and white walls and surfaces seemed to intensify the beauty of the room.

The most amazing thing about the room, which I didn't notice at first, was that the kitchen felt bigger than it actually was, and that's when I looked up and saw on the ceiling that there was a huge mirror that apparently was the length and width of the entire room.

"Don't worry, its secure," Salathia assured me as she handed me a bottle of coke.

After Lyla took up a bottle of water, we sat down at the kitchen counter, with me feeling extremely out of place and nervous. I was starting to wish I'd left when I had the chance.

Lyla and Salathia sat together on one side of the counter (I was sure they didn't mean to) which made me feel like I was being scrutinized as I was sitting directly opposite them, so I merely sipped my canned Coke so I'd have something to do other than look around.

There was suddenly a loud, ringing noise which surprised me and caused me to spill Coke on my shirt.

Salathia excused herself to answer the phone, leaving Lyla and I opposite each other, but when I decided it was safe to steal a glance at her, I almost fell out of my chair when I saw how intensely she was staring at me.

"What is it?" I asked, trying to discreetly mop the soda from my chest with paper towel from the counter.

"It's nothing. I'm just realizing how different you are. Like I'm now seeing you properly for the first time."

She straight-pulled the rest of her water, and after throwing the bottle in the recycling bin she turned back to me.

"Chase, there is something I need to say to you." She took a small breath and continued, "I'm sure you're a really wonderful person so I think you should know, it wouldn't be very good for us to be friends. I'm sorry. I'm sure you can find your way to the door."

And with that, she turned and walked beautifully out of the room, leaving me stunned and hurt.

A whole week had passed since I'd been over to the Morgans, and during that time I felt like I was going through some kind of emotional torture, because no matter what I was doing I just couldn't stop remembering Lyla saying we couldn't be friends, and every time I thought of it, the memory manifested itself as physical pain, which always left me feeling sick.

For some reason this strange rejection wasn't something I could just get over, but it wasn't for lack of trying. I hadn't spoken with Lyla since that day. She didn't hang out in the neighborhood much, but on those few occasions when she did I tried my absolute best to avoid her. It would have been too embarrassing for me to be close to her and remember what she said, but I had to start doing this a little more discreetly because my friends were jokingly suggesting that I was afraid of her.

The main idea was that if I didn't see her I wouldn't think about her so much. It sounded great in theory, but didn't work so well in practice because the longer I didn't see her, the more I wanted to think about her. And the more I thought about her, the stronger the urge to go over and see her got.

I should have seen this coming, but I was just too weak. I decided I had to get her to change her mind. I had no idea why she thought it would be better if we weren't talking, but I wasn't going to let that stand in my way. So that Friday night when I climbed into bed, I made the decision I was going to change her mind.

The following Saturday morning dawned with clear skies and a bright, golden sun whose light came clear and strong through my open window along with the wondrous sound of the waves against the cliff.

The moment I opened my eyes I couldn't help feeling light-hearted. The prospect of having Lyla back in my life clearly did wonders for my attitude.

After showering I headed downstairs to find that my parents had already left and didn't even leave any breakfast. Working parents. As Mom didn't leave any work for me to do (thankfully), I decided to spend my day scheming about how I would accomplish the great task and I did this over a bowl of froot loops.

There was a knock at the door. I was surprised to see that it was Kimberley.

"You answer the door in your underwear?" she asked coyly.

"Well, you never know who you might need to impress."

"Lucky for you it isn't me," she replied, though I did catch her eyeing my body. I chuckled.

"Do you want to come in?"

"Oh no," Kim responded, pulling herself together. "I'm not here to stay. See, we, Justin and the others, are riding out to the lighthouse and wanted to know if you wanted to come."

"I've never been there, so yeah, sure. Let me just grab my bike."

Kimberley started giggling when I invited her in to wait.

"You might want to think about putting some clothes on."

"I know that Kim." I stopped on my way to the kitchen and turned back to her. "Thanks for reminding me Kim."

I've never actually been out to the lighthouse. Actually,

I'd never even seen it. But I did know it was close to the harbor where my parents worked and on bicycles it was probably a forty minute ride. But once we got there, I was a little disappointed.

We rode out to the edge of a cliff and it turned out that the lighthouse was actually on the rocky beach below.

"Hmmm," I climbed off my bike as the others did. "I actually thought we were going to be a bit closer than this. Not that this isn't cool though," I added when they all looked at me.

"We can get closer, Chase," Brandon said, walking through some bushes to the side of the cliff.

When I followed, I saw that a set of old stairs and handrails had been constructed that went a couple feet down and ended just above some huge boulders on the beach, which the waves were crashing against.

After carefully hopping across, we finally landed on the shore. Even though I lived right by a beach myself, there was still something exciting about being on this completely new beach.

The second we got down, Rachael, Maranda, Brandon and Justin went running across the beach. As I didn't feel like joining them, I found one of the nicest spots on the rocky beach and sat down.

Before I even realized it, Kimberley came over and sat down.

"Are you okay, Chase?" She asked.

I looked over at her, puzzled. "Yea, I am. Why do you ask?"

"It's just, recently you've been acting, I don't know, like you're disappointed about something. And I know it's stupid because I haven't known you that long," She giggled nervously, "But I'm just wondering if everything, you know, is okay with you."

The fact that Kimberley actually saw through my attempted emotional disguise when everyone else was fooled took me by surprise, but what really stunned me was that she actually cared enough to say something.

I shifted my position so I was sure to look her in the eye, because I needed her to believe what I was about to say. I was about to lie to her, and knowing that made me feel a little guilty, but I saw no reason why she had to be dragged into my obsession with Lyla.

"You're right. I have been feeling a little depressed this past week, but it's only because I've been really missing home. I mean my old home, and my other friends. New York's been my home for as long as I can remember, sometimes I just can't help really missing it."

I saw Kimberley open her mouth, but I heard no words come out, because at that moment the strange magnetic feeling come over me again, this time with such intensity that it made me feel lightheaded for a couple seconds and I actually had to rub my temples as if I was trying to relieve a headache.

"Are you feeling okay?" I heard her ask.

"Yeah. I'm okay, really," I added when she looked like she didn't believe me, "Just a little migraine."

I was trying to sound like it didn't matter but the pull I was trying so hard to ignore was now so strong, it was starting to make me dizzy.

"Hey, you guys, we're having a game of water tag, let's go." Maranda shouted at Kimberley and I as they were about go into the water.

"Are you coming?" Kimberley asked. I got the feeling she wanted to join the others but didn't want to leave me.

"Nah, I think I'm just going to take a walk. But you go. Really Kim, I'll be fine." She looked like she was going to refuse, but after a little more urging from the others, she decided to go.

The reason I really wanted to be alone was because I was going to follow the pull and I knew exactly who it was going to take me to.

The minute everyone was in the water, I headed off towards the lighthouse, which was where the pull was leading me. The lighthouse was painted with red and white stripes and was located in a corner at the end of the beach, and stood even higher than the cliff.

As I approached the lighthouse I came to really realize something. Shouldn't it seem weird that I was following some strange feeling I'd been getting all of a sudden? Shouldn't I be concerned? Even afraid? But it didn't really matter, because I wasn't afraid of the pull or what I was being pulled to? I knew neither would hurt me.

When I walked around the lighthouse, it was just as I expected. She was sitting on top of another set of boulders in front the lighthouse. From where I stood I could see she was wearing a loose white shirt and a short pair of jeans.

She was sitting as she usually did with her knees up to her chin and her arms around her legs. She seemed lonely, like one of those women in stories who waited forever by the sea for their husbands who were away at during the war. It almost broke my heart to see her like that.

Unable to stop myself, I headed towards her. I climbed

onto the rocks and started leaping across them towards her, noticing that the closer I got, the more the pull was receding.

When I was two boulders away from her I stopped and called out to her, as I didn't want to startle her.

"Lyla!"

She spun around. When she saw that it was me, her surprise turned to annoyance. I was shocked, but this time instead of hurt, a huge flame of anger flared up inside me. After all, I'd done nothing to deserve to be treated this way and I wasn't taking it today.

"Oh, if you wanted to be alone, that's cool. All you had to do was say so." I turned to leave.

"Chase wait," she called after me. I turned around and saw that she was already standing next to me. "Is there something wrong? Did I anger you?"

I stared at her indignantly before I responded. "Are you joking? That's the second time you've treated me like I've done something to you. At first it was hurtful, yeah, but now it's just irritating."

A strong gust of wind came in with a wave from the sea, blowing Lyla's hair towards me, along with that unique aroma of hers.

"I'm really sorry Chase. The last thing I wanted to do was hurt you. Believe me, it's just…" I noticed her gaze was now focused on something behind me. When I turned around, I was surprised to see Kristian on the beach looking up at Lyla with a mixture of disgust and anger. For a couple seconds it was as though both of them suddenly forgot I was there. Finally, Lyla tore her eyes away from Kristian and he turned and left.

"That guy seriously needs to chill." Nikolai said from just behind me. I didn't even realize he was standing there. He was only wearing a beach pants, but whether he had just come out of the water or not, I couldn't tell, because he was completely dry.

"Chase," Lyla continued, as if nothing had interrupted her, "I'm sorry about just now. You didn't do anything to anger me, it just there's something different about you. Hmmm. Listen to me carefully, I, we really shouldn't be talking. Not because you did anything wrong, but because I know I would be bad for you. I'm sorry, I have to go."

She used a ruffle to put her hair in one, then walked away, leaving me alone with her brother.

"Trust me," he said. "She really believes she is doing you a favor, but for what it's worth, I think she's over-reacting. If it means anything to you, we can hang out some."

I actually laughed because he said it as if he was doing me some huge favor. At least he found the humor in it too.

CHAPTER 5

The First Attack

My hand was bleeding. It was something I only became aware of when I saw blood on the last box I was moving. The cut wasn't very deep, but it was long, cutting loose more than half of my left palm.

On my way out of the garage I saw the vase I'd moved out of my way and figured that must have been what did it. I headed straight for the first floor bathroom to patch myself up. Never in my life had I had the ambition to be a doctor, but I always enjoyed patching myself up when I got hurt. There was a certain gratification I got from it that I couldn't really explain. I blamed E.R.

After I was finished disinfecting the wound, I bandaged it and set back out to the garage. Another one of Mom's little chores was the reason I was there. There were still a lot of unpacked boxes in the garage which she wanted me to sort out so it would be easier for her and Dad when they finally got around to them.

I was actually glad to be doing it because it gave me something more to do than just sit around and think.

That's all I'd been doing lately.

I couldn't stop wondering why Lyla didn't want to be friends with me. For the entire time she was away, I couldn't help but think about the day she got back. Now it was a little hard for me to believe she wanted nothing to do with me, even after saving my life.

My job in the garage was over quickly enough, leaving me with nothing to do and I really didn't want to be hanging around because as soon as my mind had any free time, it began formulating ways and little plans to get Lyla and I to become friends, but before I could come up with anything to do I always managed to pull myself together. My parents raised me to believe that if someone didn't want to be in your life, you should leave it that way.

But Lyla was different. There was just something about her. She just needed a little push. And I was going to provide just that.

After making sure the garage would be up to my mother's standards, I set off towards the Morgans' under the pretense of seeing Nikolai. I chose not to think about the fact that we'd just become friends and I was already using that as a way to get to his sister.

When I got to the front door I rang the doorbell and didn't have to wait five seconds when the door was pulled open by Lyla. I admit that I did get annoyed when I saw her exasperated expression when she realized it was me.

"Oh, you. What're you doing here?" Before I could answer, her eyes shot down to my arm and my bandaged hand and her expression turned to concern.

"What happened to your hand?"

"Don't act like you care." I was happy at the chance to

be just as nasty as she, but I immediately regretted it when I saw her flinch in shock.

"I'm sorry," I said quickly, "I had a really stressful morning, but that's still no reason for trying to take my feelings out on you."

As she looked at me intensely I thought she was going to lash out at me, but instead, she reached out and took my bandaged hand in both of hers. This was the first time she touched me (when I was conscious) and it took me completely by surprise. Her hands were so soft, smooth and warm.

"There really is no need. I'm fine." I said softly as Lyla examined my hand, but she ignored me.

"Like I said, no need." I repeated when she saw that I was fine. At that moment she quickly let go of my hand.

"Why exactly are you here?" This time her voice was a lot softer.

"I want to talk to you. Please?" She shook her head and was about to close the door, but I held it open.

"Lyla, please. All I wanna do is talk." She looked back into her house, then stepped outside and closed the door.

"Fine, but we talk out here."

"That's fine with me." I sighed, relieved.

She led me over to a tree where she sat down on a small rock. I simply stooped down and leaned against the tree. Lyla didn't look like she was waiting for me to say something and I was glad because even though I wanted to talk to her so badly, I really didn't know what I was going to say.

"Why is it you think you will hurt me?" Was the first thing that came out of my mouth. "That's not really a good reason."

She didn't respond to that and just gazed at the flowers around us. Anything to avoid looking at me.

"Lyla, you don't know me. You know nothing about me, yet you made the decision that you and I wouldn't be good friends just by looking at me. It's like you don't even care what I think or want and I know we just met, but it still hurts."

"That's the last thing I wanted to do," she admitted hurriedly.

"But that's what you're doing. You know, believe it or not, it wouldn't exactly kill us if we were friends."

Lyla looked at me as though she wanted to say 'yeah, right'.

"Okay Chase," she said finally. "Let's try it your way."

It was Wednesday afternoon. No matter how hard I tried, I couldn't deny or even hide how happy I was. Lyla and I were finally on good terms. That itself was enough to make me feel like I was on top of the world. I couldn't imagine anything that could make me any happier and yet something did. I'd finally got my East Island's driver's license. Yes, it was true I didn't yet have a car, but just knowing I could drive if I wanted to made me feel elated; it gave me a sense of… freedom.

The only thing that dampened my feelings was Kristian's strange attitude towards the Morgans. It would have been fine if he just wasn't friendly with them, though even that I couldn't understand, but he seemed to really hate them, as though they'd done him something he couldn't ever forgive.

"What's Kristian's deal with the Morgans?" I asked unexpectedly. Everyone paused and looked over at me. It was Justin, Brandon, Rachael, Maranda and me. We had once again taken a ride out to the lighthouse beach. We found a nice spot on the sand to sit and this time we brought a bag of snacks that we were already halfway through.

"What?" I didn't like the looks the others were giving me.

"Well, it's just you seem really interested in the Morgans lately. Especially Lyla." Rachael revealed slowly. Justin piped in too.

"What's even more is she seems interested in you, which is weird because the Morgans never take an interest in anyone, but they seem to have taken a real interest in you. Now why is that?"

I stared open-mouthed at the others. All eyes were on me as though they thought I was about to let loose some insider scoop on the Morgans that everyone's been dying to hear. An assault like this was certainly something I didn't expect. I would never have thought they were watching this closely.

I was in love with Lyla Morgan. If I wasn't sure about anything else, I knew that to be true. Whenever I thought about it I started to feel great, but I knew if Lyla found out, the way she acted, she would pull further away from me. Look how hard it was for me to convince her to be friends and even now I could still tell she was fighting hard not to retreat from me. The weird thing was that at the same time I could tell she liked spending time with me. So that's why I'd decided to keep my true feelings for Lyla a secret.

I wouldn't say she was a fragile girl, just head-strange. Situations with her just needed to be handled with care.

"I don't know why Lyla and Nikolai have such an interest in me," which was actually the truth, "but we're off the point, which is Kristian. What's he got against the Morgans?"

"Well it probably has something to do with his being a Somorian," Brandon suggested. "You know how he's always bragging on about that." The others mumbled in agreement.

"Wait, um, what's a Somorian?" I was more than a little confused.

"They were kind of the first settlers on the island," Maranda simply said, but to me that wasn't much of an explanation.

"You can't just say that, you have to explain it to him," Rachael told her.

"Somorians are said to be the first settlers on the island. I think they got here over three hundred years ago. No one knows where they come from, or at least, the Somorians themselves aren't telling, but at the time it was only a couple hundred of them, according to the stories." Maranda further explained.

"And no one even has an idea of where they come from?"

"Nope," Maranda said. "And it's not like we had satellite tracking that time."

We all laughed at that.

"Their boats and pottery weren't like anything anyone had ever seen. And they were very superstitious, believed in magic and weird creatures and stuff."

"Okay, but what does that have to do with Kristian's attitude with the Morgans?"

"I have no idea. Somorians don't believe in that still, but maybe Kristian knows something we don't. Maybe the Morgans are vampires, ohhh… or witches." Maranda joked excitedly.

"How could they be vampires when no one's disappeared or witches when nothing strange ever happens on this island?" Justin asked with a raised eyebrow.

"Maybe they're the boring kind." Maranda said. That got another laugh from us.

"The Morgans aren't cool enough to be anything but human," Brandon said. Everyone agreed with him, but I simply added "Hmmm."

I wasn't saying the Morgans weren't human, but I just wanted to know if that's what Kristian *believed*, that they were something more, because he really did seem to be taking his Somorian heritage a bit seriously.

When three o'clock arrived I was still on the beach with the others, who were already in the water. Everything Maranda said played on my mind, and then something came to me.

I needed a way to get more information without actually going to the source, so to speak. So I told my friends I had something to do for my parents and left. I remembered that there was a small library in Bermintown and decided to try looking there for some answers. It might have seemed odd—the interest in Kristian's dislike for the Morgans—but I just had to know.

The architecture of the small Bermintown library made it look old. It reminded me of an old Anglican church.

When I went in, I handed my bag to the security guard, as bags weren't allowed inside.

"Excuse me, I'm wondering if you can help me," I said to a young librarian who was sitting behind the main desk. When she looked up at me, she adjusted her glasses and smiled.

"Well of course, that's what I'm here for."

"Do you have any books on Somorians? More specifically, books on their superstitions?"

"I think we have one or two," she said, walking around the desk and leading me up stairs. She took me to the back of the room to a book shelf that was labeled Caribbean History. The librarian ran her fingers along the spines of the books until she found the one she was looking for, which she took down and handed it to me.

"Caribbean Legends. They're a couple chapters in there about Somorians. If you need any more help, you know where to find me." With a last look and giggle at me, she walked off.

There were a few empty tables upstairs, so I decided to just sit and read up there. I walked over to a table in the corner by the window and sat down. After consulting the table of contents, I saw the chapters on Somorians.

As I was turning the pages someone said "What is that you're reading?" next to me. I was so anxious to get started that I hadn't even noticed Kimberley approaching, so I was startled when she spoke, which caused me to accidently drop the book.

Before I could even move to pick it up, Kimberley already had it back on the table in front of her, where she'd taken a seat.

"So you know," she said to me after she read the title. She took her long hair and placed it in one with a ruffle she had on her hand. That's when I saw the gray shirt she was wearing. I just had to comment on it.

"You know, I like the chipmunks." That actually got a chuckle out of her. "What do you mean by 'I know'?"

"That I'm a Somorian." She pushed the book back to me. Suddenly I felt like I was being very intrusive.

"Yeah, I found out today, but I'm not... it's not like..."

Kimberley chuckled. "Chase, it's okay. It's not like we have some huge big secret or dirty past or anything. I just took it as weird that you're trying to learn more about Somorians because people don't find us that interesting. And with good reason, because the truth is, Somorians really aren't that interesting. So what is it you want to know?"

It had never occurred to me that I could simply ask Kimberley about her brother. I guess there was a source after all.

"Well, it's not Somorians in general, I'm just a little curious about your brother."

"Why?" I had stifle a laugh when Kimberley said that because she made it sound as if anyone would be crazy to have any kind of interest in Kristian.

"Because I want to know why he hates the Morgans so much. I mean they've never done anything to him or your family, so why is he like that?"

Kim sighed deeply and looked through the window for a while, like she was contemplating something. She licked her lips a few times then turned back to me.

"In the old days, a lot of my people were superstitious.

They believed in everything and then some. But over time, many began to rely on science as you would expect, and leave the old ways. However, there are still Somorians today that believe in the supernatural, mainly a few of our elders. Kristian was always fascinated by that stuff. I don't know why, but he always liked it, so when he met some of those people about a year and half ago that still believe, he began thinking it may still be true that there really is some kind of magic in the world."

"Okay. So he might believe in a spiritual path. That's not so bad. But what's that have to do with the Morgans?" I asked.

Kimberley leaned closer to me as if it was important no one else hear this.

"Some people believe Somorians to be warriors of nature, agents of innocents who protect nature. Nature would be the earth and everything from it, including humans. The reason my brother doesn't like the Morgans is because some of my people believe they aren't from nature. And anything not from nature or the earth, seeks to destroy it and everything it holds."

"Wait a minute," I said as something clicked in my head. "Are you saying, that they don't think the Morgans are human?"

Kimberley nodded.

I chuckled nervously and was about to say "But that's crazy," but instead I said: "So what do they think they are?"

Kimberley looked like she didn't want to reply, but eventually she said:

"They believe they are creatures of the sea, mermaids. They are really called—"

"Aquamuns," I finished.

"Yeah," Kimberley said, shaking her head. "Just crazy. Anyway, I just came in here to pick up some books. I've got some vacation assignments I need to finish. I guess I will see you later, Chase."

"Yeah, sure," I said when I realized she was looking at me with her eyebrows raised.

She waved at me and walked away.

After leaving the library I did some exploring of Bermintown on my own. By the time I decided to head home it was just past 7:00 pm. I wasn't that familiar with Bermintown, so I did get lost a few times. Which was how it all started.

I'd made a left turn onto a street. I didn't even see the name, but it was completely deserted. All the stores were closed and only one street light was working and that was all the way on the other end.

I was used to walking alone at night and even though I was always careful, I'd never actually felt afraid. But as I walked down the unknown street, a strange feeling came over me. My spine tingled like something slimy was crawling down my back. I suddenly felt uneasy. I kept glancing around just to make sure I was alone, but visual confirmation wasn't enough, as the feeling only got worse.

And then I heard it. Something that made me feel like my heart actually stopped for a second. A deep, low, bone-chilling growl which came from in front of me just beyond the rays of the street light.

I was just about to hop onto my bike to ride off in the other direction. I wasn't going to be like those stupid teenagers you see in movies. Then whatever made that awful growl stepped into the light. Before it even did, I saw two blood-red orbs like objects moving towards me. The strange thing about them was that they seemed to hold some kind of strange power that kept me from moving, no matter how much I wanted to.

The creature finally moved into the light. I wanted to scream. Oh, I wanted to so bad, but I just couldn't remember how. It was a dog, but not like any I'd ever seen or even thought existed. It was huge. Like four or five feet tall, with fur as dark as the night sky. Even with the distance between us, I could clearly see it had huge fang-like teeth in its open mouth, where those growls were still coming from.

Without any warning, and with lightning like speed, the animal pounced at me. And with about twenty feet between us, it was actually going to make it. When the creature was about ten feet away from me in the air, something collided with it in midair and sent in crashing into a wall.

"Chase, get on your bike and go, NOW."

Lyla shouted when she landed in front of me, though she didn't take her eyes off the dog. I didn't move a muscle, because from the moment she landed in front of me I seemed to get control over my body again and I wasn't going to leave her, but she said, "Chase, please. Just go. Just trust me, I will be fine. GO."

The urgency in her voice was enough to make me comply. Without another glance at the creature I hopped on my bike and peddled off. I was in such a state, I didn't even know where I was going. When I turned what I figured was my fifth corner, I saw Lyla standing in the middle of the road. I pulled hard on my brakes and stopped just in front her.

"You and I really need to talk," she said before I could get one word out.

"Lyla, what's going on? And what the hell was that creature? And how the hell did you hit it so hard?"

We were sitting in the middle of a play park by ourselves. Lyla had led me there because she told me she was going to explain everything. She stood up and started pacing then rounded at me.

"I told you being friends with me was going to be bad, didn't I? Did you listen? No." Lyla was almost shouting.

There was suddenly a tidal wave of fury inside. I had no idea where the anger came from, because moments before I wasn't angry. Scared and confused, but not angry.

"Are you saying this is my fault?" I said, the anger beginning to show.

Lyla looked at me hard, took a deep breath, then said in her normal voice, "No, that was not your fault. I'm sorry."

"It's okay Lyla." I said, that strange anger disappearing. "Lyla, please tell me what that thing was."

"It was a Shadow Hound."

"A what?" I was perplexed. I wasn't even sure I'd heard her right.

"It's like a magical dog. But I can only think of one reason it was here."

"Lyla," I said forcefully. She stopped pacing and turned slowly towards me. "Please explain to me exactly what happened."

Lyla sighed. "I can't tell you everything. I don't even

know how we got here. To this point, I mean. I don't know what's going on." She sighed again. "Chase, I'm not exactly what you would call normal. This may sound foolish, but you have to listen. There is magic in the world, real magic and from now on, you will have to be very careful."

Despite all the things I wanted to say, I simply asked, "Why?"

"I think someone summoned that dog to kill you."

CHAPTER 6

A Maiden's Voice

"What?!" I said incredulously but softly. "Lyla, did you just tell me someone might be trying to kill me?"

She nodded slowly. The night air was just a little chilly, but even so Lyla looked perfectly fine just wearing a short shirt and a pair of black short jeans and flip flops. When a small gust of wind blew, I inhaled deeply as her wonderful aroma swirled around me.

I felt dizzy. I actually had to sit down on the park bench and place my head in my hands on my lap just to steady myself.

"And what about that other thing – that you told me?" My head was still in my heads, but I knew when Lyla came and sat down next to me.

"Chase, there are things in this world that… can't really be explained with science. I really don't know how to explain it, but the supernatural does exist. There is a lot of stuff out there people don't know about. That thing that just attacked you is proof of what I'm saying and believe me, there is a lot worse out there."

"How do you know all of this?" I asked, finally holding my head up. I didn't feel any better.

"Well, I'm not exactly what you would call a normal person." She said cautiously.

"What exactly does that mean? Because I saw how you kicked that thing and no normal person can do that, not to something that size?"

"I can't tell you everything, but I am part of that supernatural world. Me and my family, we're... different."

I got the impression she didn't want to say any more, so I didn't press that particular point. But based on what Lyla and Kimberley told me, plus what Kristian believed, could that mean that Lyla and her family are...

"Lyla, why are you telling me this? I get the feeling you don't go around telling everyone your secrets, so why tell me?"

Lyla looked at me as though I was missing something very obvious.

"Because you just got attacked by a Shadow Hound. A supernatural animal, Chase. One that has to be summoned. Which means someone sent it after you. Which means, someone with magic is trying to kill you.

"Lyla, why would someone want to kill me? I haven't even been living here that long, well not long enough to make enemies with someone who would actually try to kill me."

I was back on my feet. If sitting didn't help me to calm down, I figured some kind of walking would. So I started walking up and down just like Lyla did. That's when I realized I was shaking slightly.

"That's why I didn't want to get close to you. I was

afraid I was going to cause you trouble in some way. From the first time I met you, that night I pulled you from the water, I just knew it," she said, folding her arms.

"Why, would you say that?"

Lyla didn't answer. Instead she just stood up and looked around.

"You need to get home."

"What, isn't it safe out here?" Was my foolish attempt at a joke.

"I'm not sure, but I don't want to take any risk."

Lyla was very serious. She brought my bike over to me. From the moment she was more than an arm's stretch away from me, I started to relax. Being close to her was helping me feel at ease.

"How are you going to get home?" I asked as I sat on the seat.

"Don't worry about me, really. I'll be home shortly. I will call Michael to come pick me up and I will be perfectly safe by myself, so there is no need for you to worry about me."

"Lyla, I can't leave you here alone in the dark. Supernatural or not, it might not be safe."

She raised her eyebrows at me.

"I'm the one that saved you from the big, bad, wolf, remember?" She teased.

"You sure know how to make a guy feel good about himself."

We both laughed. It was the first time Lyla really let her guard down with me, but the second she realized how at ease we were, that same old guard was back up.

"Go on, Chase. We will talk later."

"Okay. Bye. Get home safely."

As I rode away I couldn't help looking back at her and it made me feel good to see she was looking at me too.

I was so relieved when I got home. That feeling of comfort that came over me the second I went through the door couldn't have been more welcomed. It was only a few minutes past nine, but I really was craving my bed. So I showered, said goodnight to my parents and dropped onto my soft mattress.

From the second my body started to relax, my mind wanted to replay the night's events over and over. But I had no interest in reliving the attack. If there was ever an animal that needed to be extinct, it was that dog. The one thing I didn't mind remembering, however, was my time with Lyla. She was always so careful that we never had moments when we laughed together, like tonight.

I didn't have time to dwell on it too much because I remember turning over in bed and falling asleep quickly. What I would never have known was that after I had fallen asleep Lyla came and sat in the tree outside my bedroom window to make sure I was safe.

"Sleep well, Chase. I – I love you."

I woke up to the sound of the sea just beyond the cliff, as was usual every morning. The sound of the waves bashing madly against the cliffs like soldiers trying to break down a barricaded city gate was something I'd become accustomed to, even liked hearing. Coupled with the fact that it was a sunny Friday morning and I'd slept fine the night before, I should have woken up feeling great, but I didn't and it was obvious why.

The news that Lyla gave me the day before had an odd effect on me. It made the world seem different somehow. Everything, the way the sunlight felt, the sound of the sea, even the way my own body felt to me, seemed different, like the whole world went through some kind of change overnight.

Or maybe it wasn't the world that had changed, but just the way I saw it. Things I believed to be impossible I now knew to exist all around me. So what else was going to change? What else was I going to learn that wasn't as normal as I thought?

After gathering enough will, I was finally able to push myself out of bed. I trotted downstairs, but my parents had already left which meant that today I had to make my own breakfast. So I got myself a bowl of cereal. I really wasn't in the mood to cook anything. And I was hungry.

I took my cereal with me to the couch, but just as I sat down there was a knock at the door—at 6:30 in the morning.

I took my time getting up, but the second I was up an immense feeling of apprehension washed over me. I couldn't explain why I suddenly felt like this. It wasn't like I knew who was at the door or knew where these feelings were coming from. Nonetheless, I threw that aside and answered the door.

I was shocked to see that it was Hilda.

What freaked me out the most about her was how normal she looked. She was wearing a long, green sundress and a pair of flip-flops. Her locks were kept in place at the back with a rubber band. Around her neck and wrist were a chain and bracelets that looked like they were homemade jewelry. Dangling from both ears were two flat, circular metallic pendants with strange signs on each side. I guess the way she looked when I first met her was how she always looked.

"Um, Good morning, Miss…"

"It's just Hilda to you. I came to see your mother, is she…," She dropped what she was saying and I noticed how her eyes seemed to scan the air around me. For some reason, it seemed so familiar.

"You're still seeing that girl, aren't you?" She said this kind of forcefully, actually causing me to step back a little, an opportunity Hilda used to enter. She walked past me and placed the box of herbs she was carrying on the kitchen counter. She then came back to me. It angered me how she walked around like she lived there, or was invited in.

Then, out of nowhere, something occurred to me. If what Lyla said was true, that the supernatural did exist, did that also mean Hilda's warning was valid? And did she really have magic? Was she really a witch?

"What does it matter to you if I am? It's not like anyone's getting hurt. Besides it's not any of your business."

Hilda looked like she was going to lose control of her anger, but in a flash, she changed to something I never thought I would see on her face, sympathy.

"You've got a good family. I would hate to see something bad happen to you, and so young," Hilda said softly. She headed towards the door, but turned to face me before she left.

"Let me tell you this though, if you continue to see this

girl, there will be serious consequences. Just remember that. Good morning to you."

After she closed the door, I made sure to lock it behind her. If this meeting had occurred one day before, it wouldn't have bothered me one bit, but knowing what happened, I couldn't help being curious about what bothered Hilda so much, though I just couldn't bring myself to ask her. I felt that would make her think she was right. I couldn't stop my pride from getting in the way.

I went back to the couch to finish my corned flakes, but now my mind was stuck on one issue. If Lyla wasn't human (which she admitted), what exactly was she? It wasn't like I had a list of supernatural beings I could check... or maybe there was.

Without finishing my now soggy breakfast, I left the bowl of cereal on the coffee table and ran upstairs to my computer, already knowing what I would look for. The last time I tried searching, I didn't know what to look for, but this time I typed one word in the search engine: Aquamun. Only about twenty-two results came up, spread out over two pages. This was good. There wasn't the usual crap to shift through and the junk I did come across was easy for me to dismiss with one click.

Then something caught my eye. This website didn't have the history of Aquamuns going back to some old places like ancient Greece or Egypt. It was more like a small blog, which mainly told about how Aquamuns acted and held a few more details.

From reading about the man who wrote the website, I learned he was a man whose father actually used to live on East Island in the early 1900s and believed his parents had been taken by Aquamuns. Ever since then his family had been trying to protect everyone else from them by sharing as much information as possible.

The website told that all Aquamuns had some form of blue eyes. It was proof of their connection to the sea. That really didn't sound very believable to me, but then I remembered all the Morgans really did have some form of blue eyes. But that could just be a coincidence, though it was strange that even Marcus and Salathia had the same eye color.

According to the website, Aquamuns were very hard to distinguish from humans by the naked eye, so normal people couldn't just pick one out in a crowd, but there were things that people could pick up on, like with time, coming to notice how they always seem to be comfortable in any type of weather or how they produced a scent like no other creature.

All these were things I'd noticed about Lyla and she did admit to me that the supernatural was real; that she herself wasn't normal.

Could the Morgans seriously be Aquamuns?

As I was about to close the page, I saw there was a second page and out of mere curiosity, I clicked it.

The second page was a very old drawing of a family. There were four of them. A tall, very intimidating man, a very beautiful woman with a kind, loving face, someone that looked to be their teenaged son who was very muscular, and standing next to him was a young girl who looked to be in her early teens.

The text underneath the photo said it was a drawing of a family someone believed were Aquamuns that lived on and left East Island in the 1800s. The strange thing was, they almost looked like the Morgans. The photo was drawn and it was very old and didn't have any color, but still the man and woman looked a little like Marcus and Salathia. The boy and girl, however, didn't look that similar to Lyla and Michael, but then again, if I had to guess, I would say maybe that's how they looked when they were younger. And then there was Nikolai, who was missing from the photo. But why? *Maybe he wasn't born yet*, I thought to myself.

It really could be true. Lyla's family really could be Aquamuns.

I closed the page and cleared my history.

My mind was so filled with the possibility that the Morgans might be Aquamuns that I hadn't really thought much about the fact that someone was trying to kill me; or at least that's what Lyla thought. When she first told me, I was actually a little scared. Okay, more than a little. But finding out the supernatural was real actually trumped that in my book, so unless whoever was after me had something more than pitbulls up their sleeves, I'd decided not to dwell on it too much.

The Saturday morning following the attack, my parents had a surprise for me.

"Dad," I said at the breakfast table eating a bowl of porridge. "I was wondering, since I got my license, if I could get a car."

It was something I'd been thinking about for a few days and was prepared to hear "No," but what I wasn't ready for was, "Actually, your mother and I had been thinking about that and decided that you should have a car."

"Really?" I asked, completely surprised. Where did this come from?

"Yup," Dad said, getting up from the table. "Follow me."

He took me outside where Mom's and his cars were parked. There was another one next to them.

"Dad, if this is some kind of joke, I'm going to tell you right now, I might cry. Is that my car?" I asked, pointing to the one at the end. Dad smiled broadly and took some keys out of his pocket and threw them at me.

"She's all yours. You're going to have to take really good care of this car, Chase."

It was a red 1976 Chevrolet Impala and it looked like whoever worked on it put their heart and soul into rebuilding and customizing it.

"I will Dad, I promise." I said excitedly as I climbed in and felt the interior of the car. "I'll treat Shelia like a princess."

"Shelia?" Dad asked, his eyebrows raised.

"Yeah," I said this like it was obvious. "A car's gotta have a name. How did you get this?"

"I bought it from your friend Kimberley's Dad, Jack. I had to take your Mom's car to his garage and I saw this little beauty there. When I asked him about it, he said he only restored it for the fun of it. I asked him if he was interested in selling it and he said yes."

"Wow. Seriously, thanks a lot Dad; you have no idea how much this means to me."

"Actually, I do. You're welcome. I have to take off now.

Try not to scratch it too soon."

"Is it okay if I take her out for a ride now?"

"Sure," Dad said on his way to the house, "Just remember to drive on the left."

I pushed the key into my new car and turned it excitedly. I don't even have to say how it made me feel when I first heard Shelia's engine come alive.

I was about to drive off when I suddenly got the urge to do something else. Don't get me wrong, I still wanted to take the car out for a drive badly. But for some reason I suddenly realized how important it was that I deal with this first.

I drove Shelia over to the Morgans. Once there, I felt that strange, magnetic feeling, but it was only for a second because a moment later Lyla walked from around her house.

Looking through the windshield, I noticed she was surprised to see the car. I wondered if that was because she had some kind of Aquamun ability that let her know when someone was near – like a sixth sense. The very thought surprised me, because it meant I was starting to think of the Morgans as Aquamuns.

Lyla walked over to the passenger side of the car and bent down to talk through the window.

"Hmm, nice car," she said admiringly, looking around at the inside.

"Thanks. You wanna go for a ride? I kinda want to talk to you anyway."

"Chase, I don't know."

"Lyla, come on. That night you said you would talk to me to explain things more and you never did. In fact, it kinda feels like you're avoiding me again. Look, if it makes you feel any better, I don't want to talk about you or your family, I just need some information."

Lyla looked towards her house and back then hopped into the car.

"How far are we going?" She almost sounded excited.

"No idea, but I really wanna test her out."

I started the car again, took us out of the Morgans' driveway and went onto the road, but before I had my fun with Shelia, I needed to have my talk with Lyla first.

Out of nowhere a huge feeling of nervousness rose in my stomach, which I found to be unsettling.

"So, what is it you want to talk about?" Lyla asked as trees flashed past us. I wasn't going more the forty miles per hour.

"Is Hilda a real witch?" I asked bluntly.

"Why would you ask that?" Lyla sounded completely surprised, but she quickly caught on. "You think she might be the one who sent the Shadow Hounds after you?"

"She came over to my house yesterday and knew I was still talking with you and she told me if I didn't stop… well, let's just say she said I would pay for it."

I was a little taken aback when Lyla chuckled. But it wasn't an amused chuckle.

"To be honest, that's not necessarily a lie. Chase, yes, Hilda is a real witch but I don't believe she is the one after you. She considers herself more of a protector. If she is checking up on you because of me, it's because she wants to make sure you're safe. Trust me, even though she has no reason to fear us," Lyla added softly, "I don't think Hilda is the one who attacked you. But if you're looking for suspects, I wouldn't look past the Somorians, particularly your friend Kristian."

The moment she said it she looked like she regretted it. I was going to let it go so easily.

"Why do you say that?"

She looked like she wanted me to drop the topic.

"Somorians have their own kind of magic, which Kristian might have access to. You know how he already doesn't like you because you associate with me. He might be taking it a step further."

"You think he would actually try to kill me?"

The thought that Kristian, even though we were friends, might want me dead for simply talking with Lyla was a little scary.

"Maybe, maybe not. I can't be sure of much without more proof though, so I'm not accusing anyone."

After that we stayed silent for a while. Then, when I turned onto a long stretch of road that we were the only ones on, Lyla leaned out the window as if making sure the road was clear. Then turned to me and smiled. It made me feel good to know she was finally getting more at ease with me.

"Chase, when a girl is promised a ride, she expects a ride."

I looked at Lyla for half a second and smiled coyly. I knew this day was going to be fun.

I floored it.

When I got back to the house after taking Lyla home I saw Justin, Brandon, Maranda and Rachael waiting for me inside Justin's dad's jeep.

"What're you guys doing here?" I asked when I got out of the car. They came over to look at Shelia.

"We're heading into town and wanted to know if you would like to come since you've never been," Rachael said as she checked out the outside of the car.

"What do you mean? I've been to Bermintown many times."

"Not Bermintown, dude. We're going to Ridgetown. It's the capital of our fine little island. It's bigger and better than Bermintown." Justin said.

I told them I would go, but decided to first leave a message for my parents on the answering machine in case they got home before I did so they wouldn't worry. Instead of taking separate cars, we all went in Justin's dad's jeep.

New York was pretty amazing. Even though I lived there all my life, I always loved every minute there. So I was very surprised by how amazed I was by Ridgetown after living in the big city. It was so amazing. There were a lot of modern buildings, but most of them looked like they were renovated or remodeled after old buildings which gave them a very unique and beautiful look.

Most of the buildings weren't more than three or four stories high, though they were a few that went higher. There so much to see. Night had already fallen, but the city was still alive with people, sounds and lights.

"I can't believe I haven't been here before," I said in awe. The others laughed. I'm sure I must have looked like an awestruck tourist.

We spent our time just walking around visiting stores and we bought a few things. It really was a lot of fun. Exactly what I needed at the time. The only thing that would have made it any better was if Lyla was there with me.

"Come on, Chase. Time to go," Justin said to me as we'd finished dinner in one of the fast food restaurants. It was after eight and even though I was having a great time, there were still moments I was finding thoughts miles away, but thankfully my friends were having such a good time, they didn't notice.

When we climbed back into the jeep I took a seat in the back at the left window. Maranda was in the middle and Brandon at the other end. Rachael was in the front passenger seat. Even on the trip home we were still chatting. Lyla was still on my mind, but I felt too good to get into one of my moods and to be honest, I felt things were finally getting better with Lyla. Nothing felt wrong.

Justin decided to take a short cut home, which turned out to be a long, deserted road with nothing on either side but more forest. Then all of a sudden, a strange feeling came over me. No, it was more like it passed through me. It made every part of my body tingle and made me feel like something had just tried to turn me inside out. It wasn't painful, but it was unpleasant.

Then suddenly there was a loud explosion and the jeep went out of control. We were all screaming as Justin tried to get the jeep under control, but he wasn't making any progress. We just keep swirling and spinning.

Then suddenly it all stopped. Not in a natural way, but in the same way it would if a kid was playing with a toy jeep and pressed his hand on it to stop it if it was going too fast.

Seconds after the jeep had stopped, the others were still

in a panic, but I was surprisingly alert. I hopped out of the jeep and noticed that someone had gotten out of a car on the other side of the road and was coming towards me – it was Hilda.

"Are you all alright? What happened?" She asked urgently.

"We're fine. Justin just lost control of the car for a second, but everything's cool now."

I stepped back a little from her, though I didn't think she noticed because she was busy examining the jeep. When she finally looked back at me, she seemed more at ease and said:

"You lot should get along on home. It's dangerous out here. And tell your friend he needs to be more careful on the road."

She didn't say another word. All she did was turn, get back in her car and drive off.

After calming down, Justin got out of the jeep to check for any damages and was extremely relieved when he didn't find any.

"But where did that explosion come from then?" Maranda asked when Justin got back in.

"I honestly don't know and since it didn't come from the jeep, I really don't care. I just want to get out of here."

Justin turned the key slowly, as if he was afraid if he turned it any fast, it wasn't going to start. But the engine did come on, which we were all relieved to hear.

I might not have had a clue about exactly what happened, but I was sure of one thing – that was magic. That was attempt number two on my life.

CHAPTER 7

Song of the Whales

T he rest of the ride home was a little tense. It was obvious that what had just happened was constantly replaying itself in everyone's minds; it didn't take much to tell it really shook them up. It shook me up too, but for another reason.

My friends were worried about the fact that they almost got into a car accident, while what concerned me was that whoever it was trying to kill me was willing to hurt others to do it and that made them all the more dangerous. Because of that person, my friends could have died, and they, or anyone else, wouldn't have known what really happened.

Another thing I couldn't help wondering about was the fact that Hilda appeared just after the 'accident', claiming to have been driving past and just stopped to help. *More like to find out why her spell didn't work*, I thought to myself. According to Justin, the road he took was a short cut, but it wasn't a road many used on account of how dangerous it could be, so why was she on it? Sure, a good argument would be, for the same reason we were even on it… because it's a shortcut. But I wasn't going to buy that at any price.

"Hey," Justin called, pulling me out of my reverie. I looked through my window and suddenly realized he'd just pulled up at my house. I hadn't even been paying attention.

As I was going to open the door on my side, Justin turned in the driver's seat to look at me.

"Could you not tell your parents anything about what happened? 'Cause if you do, they may call my parents to find out how I'm doing, and then my dad would find out what happened and he would have a fit."

"You're not going to tell him?" I asked, taken aback. "Are you mad?"

"Of course not," he answered, and then strangely, he looked a little embarrassed. "I'm not actually supposed to drive on that road."

"Yeah, okay. I won't say a thing."

He looked around at everyone else.

"Well?" he said expectantly. The others agreed as well.

I got out of the car and Justin drove away. As I was walking towards the front door a strange, sudden sensation of impatience and worry came over me. It was so sudden and strange that I started looking around as if I knew something was going to jump out of the tree at me. But oddly enough, these didn't feel like my own emotions. It felt to me as if someone else had just dumped them on me, though they were affecting me just the same, working their way through my body like some kind of poison, infecting my already unstable mood.

I could see through the window that the lights were

on in the living room, which meant my parents were still up. It was only a couple minutes past ten, but I was really hoping they'd be asleep by the time I got home. I didn't want to snap at them, which I knew I would do thanks to what I was feeling, I decided I'd just try to make myself calm outside for a while. Maybe the air would help me get a handle on myself.

It was low tide, but as always I could still clearly hear the ebb and flow of the sea and the strong crashing noise as it bashed against the cliff. The air coming in off the ocean was so relaxing, so soothing that it actually did a lot to calm me down, because as the soft air drifted around me, I began to feel the foreign emotions drift away as if they just floated away on a breeze, giving rise to my own calmness. For no reason at all, I looked around and I suddenly became aware of just how beautiful this place was, as if a veil had now been lifted from my senses. The seductive sound of the sea, the breeze blowing through the trees, it was all so appealing to me.

I had just started walking around the mango tree and raising my head to look up to the sky when my eyes passed over the window of my room, where, because the light in the room was on, I saw the silhouette of someone pass by. Instead of getting alarmed, I just figured it was my mom, though I had no idea what she would be doing wandering around in there. Taking one last look around, I turned and went inside.

"Chase?" I heard Dad call as I closed the front door.

"Yeah Dad. It's me," I dropped my stuff by the door, whether by choice or involuntary reflex I didn't know, because I was horrified to see Dad on the couch watching

TV, with my mom in his arms, and she was asleep. A rush of fear passed through my body.

"Hi. Goodnight, Dad. Is there anyone else here?" I said a little nervously, though luckily Dad didn't pick up on it.

"Goodnight, kid. Um, no one else is here," Dad replied, groggy. At that I sprinted off up the stairs without hearing the rest of what he said.

When I got to the top of the stairs, I crept to the closed door of my room and paused outside for a while. If I was right, and there was someone in my room, I probably should have told Dad about it, but there was always the off chance I was wrong and I didn't want to worry him about nothing. What I actually feared was that whoever was after me was behind the door, and if I was right, I didn't want my parents involved.

Taking a deep, steadying breath, I turned the doorknob and opened the door. Surprise went racing through my body as I was startled to see it was Lyla. She was sitting silently on the bed with her eyes closed, but upon my entrance, she opened them and stood up. Even though she was dressed normally in jeans and a tank top, she still looked to me like she was dressed for a fashion runway.

As soon as I saw her I felt that familiar explosion in my chest, accompanied by the nervous tingling that spread to all my limbs, making me feel I had lost the ability to stand up properly on my own. Those were just my everyday reactions to seeing her. I was about to take a step towards her, but at that moment, there was a soft knock on the door.

"Hey, kid, you okay in there?" Dad called from outside. Turning away from Lyla (which took a lot of effort) I pulled the door about a quarter ways open. "Yeah Dad, I'm good.

I'm sorry about just now."

"Yeah, what was that abo—," Dad stopped and I saw his eyes move over me and sweep the bit of the room he could see through the crack. When he spoke again, it was with a much different tone, but it wasn't anger.

"Is there a girl in there?" He asked. My heart was now pounding so hard that I was surprised he couldn't see it beating against my chest.

"What," I said in fake mild surprise, "No Dad. There's no one else in here. Why'd you ask?"

"Uh, I thought I smelled—," But he shook his head and dropped what he was going to say. I almost breathed a sigh of relief. "Never mind. Must've been inside my head. Anyway, goodnight son."

And with that, Dad turned and trotted back downstairs. I quickly closed the door, and whirled around only to find Lyla standing inches from me. I jumped back a little in surprise.

"How did you get in here and how do you do that?" I asked as I walked around her, a little wobbly, towards the bed. Being near her made me queasy and nervous.

"Well, I got in through the window, and how do I do what?" she said, following me to the bed.

I shrugged before I answered. "I don't know if it's just me, but I notice you seem to move really fast when you want to, among other things."

"I told you before, I'm gifted." Lyla said dismissively. "But that's not the issue. Are you okay? What happened to you earlier?"

"How do you even know something happened?"

"Chase please, focus. I will explain that another time,"

she said impatiently. I explained everything that happened, about the accident, about the surge of energy and finally about Hilda, how she suddenly appeared and that she was my number one suspect. Lyla seemed very interested in all this, but didn't like my views on Hilda being responsible.

"Well Chase, that's not exactly evidence that Hilda's behind these attacks. I mean, if she is the one doing this then she's hiding her tracks very well, but I just don't think it's her. For all the time I've known her, I've never gotten the feeling that she'd want to kill someone, much less a teenager. And here's the biggest question of all, why would she want to kill you? You just moved here."

Lyla dropped into the chair and looked expectantly at me. I knew she never expected me to have an answer to that, but nonetheless I did. I really didn't want to tell Lyla about the first time I met Hilda, because I was afraid the information would drive her off, but still I knew I needed to tell her.

"Well there is something she told me that I never told you. It's not even that important anyway," Lyla continued to stare at me, waiting. I sighed.

"When I first met Hilda, it was at the community party back in July, and that's where she told me she couldn't see my aura."

I made sure to say that slowly so I could search Lyla's face for any hint of surprise. But her face was unreadable. She didn't even move a muscle when I said it, which meant she was either really good at hiding things, or she really didn't know anything about it. So I continued.

"Anyway, she seemed to know that I'd met someone, a girl. Hilda told me that this girl would only bring me trouble and it would be best if I stopped seeing her, before it was out of my control. I didn't believe in any of that stuff so I didn't take her seriously, but then she came over this morning and somehow she knew I was still talking with this girl. She wasn't too happy about that."

When I was finished, Lyla nodded solemnly. Unexpectedly, she then locked her amazingly blue eyes onto mine with such a powerful stare I couldn't look away or even blink too much.

"Chase, I want you to tell me something," She leaned towards me. "Since then, have you been experiencing anything unusual? Anything at all, like losing sleep, having hallucinations or maybe… hearing things?"

I immediately thought about the strange song I'd heard, but decided not to mention it to Lyla. I didn't think it was really worth worrying her about something that only happened once, or I possibly even imagined. I wasn't prepared to worry her any further.

"No. Nothing's changed," I said.

Lyla continued to stare at me for a couple seconds more, as if determined to catch a lie, but then she nodded as if satisfied.

"I'm still not convinced that Hilda's the one after you though. She's just not that kind of person. One of the Somorians, on the other hand, could be though."

"Lyla, Kristian's a dick, but I don't think he's so bad that he'd really try to kill me."

"No. I don't mean Kristian," Lyla said, looking shocked that I came to that conclusion. "Even if he does know about the supernatural, he's way too young to have the kind of power needed to do these things. It's got to be someone older with a lot more power."

She got up and began pacing around the room exasperatedly and I watched as she silently passed me, each time producing that powerful perfume-like scent that always smelled so seductive.

As Lyla passed me again, without warning, I reached out and took her hand, intending to calm her down. Feeling sheepish, I suddenly realized this was the first time I had ever touched her. The feel of her soft, slender hands in mine sent the blood rushing through my body, quickening both my heart and my breathing. I also realized that as soon as I felt her skin, my temperature also rose a little, not enough to make me hot, but just enough to make me feel warmer, as it was a little cold in the room.

Acting on impulse, as though my subconscious mind believed I couldn't handle this, I gently pulled Lyla onto the bed to sit next to me, and I was happy when she complied without resistance.

"Lyla calm down. It's okay, relax," I said, but she shook her head.

"It's not okay, Chase. Someone wants you dead, and they're trying harder with every attempt." Our hands were still locked together and her eyes locked onto mine.

"Why are you helping me?" I blurted out before I could help myself. "Don't get me wrong, I'm glad you are, but I don't know why, because sometimes you act as though you'd rather I wasn't here. Sometimes I get the feeling you don't like me very much."

There was an explosion of emotional pain inside me, like my feelings were hurt, but once again, there was that distinctive feeling that it was an invading emotion. But I didn't have time to pay any attention. I could clearly see Lyla was distraught by what I said, even though hurting her wasn't my intention.

"Chase, that's not true. I… it's just…" she sighed and then said, "Never mind."

And with that, whatever little moment we had was gone, because Lyla very gently pulled her hand from mine (at which time my body temperature dropped back to that of the room) and stood up. I followed her.

"Lyla, I'm sorry. I didn't mean to hurt you or anything." She just put up her hand and smiled. The damage had already been done and I couldn't take it back.

"The reason I'm helping you to find out who's after you is because it's the right thing to do." She turned walked towards the window.

"Lyla, I'm sorry," I repeated, "I didn't mean to… I'm sorry," It was all I was able to say, even though I felt much more.

"I know you are, but don't be, it's not like you did something wrong. It's okay. Look, it's getting late so I'd better be going."

I didn't want her to go. In fact my mind was screaming at me, telling me don't let her go. But before I could do anything, in a move I would never expect, she turned around again and kissed me lightly on the cheek, which left me stunned and flustered, gazing at her like she was some sort of goddess.

"You are my friend, and I do like you, that's why I'm helping you."

She hopped out the window without the slightest sound. I wasn't able to see how she climbed down the tree, as I was rooted to the spot where she left me, her words running through my brain. *I do like you.*

The next day was very interesting, as for me, surprise after surprise came. First, in the morning, I'd decided to tell my parents about the near accident. I knew I'd told Justin I wouldn't, but for some reason it just didn't bode very well for me to be keeping this from them as there were other things, worse, they didn't know about. Surprisingly, they already knew. According to them, Hilda had called and wanted to know if my friends and I got home okay after what happened. Mom and Dad were concerned, but were both happy no one was hurt and as I was going to tell them, they weren't angry at me for keeping it from them.

Later that day, Justin and the others came over to the house, where they told me Justin had told his parents what happened and wasn't in any trouble. But the surprise I was least excited about came when my parents got home around five after my friends had already left. Apparently they'd gone shopping for "Your school uniform," Mom said as she unloaded the bags containing my new school clothes.

"White shirts with epaulette holders," she took out the packaged shirts, "Brown long pants…"

Mom took out five brown pants made of a soft, fine material, "…and sixth form students, that's you, and upper sixth are both required to wear a tie, though sixth formers do still have to wear epaulettes."

I took up a pack of two epaulettes. They each had four brown and green stripes, and the whole tie had the same color stripes. I was totally unprepared for this.

"You don't seriously expect me to wear this do you?" I threw the epaulettes back on the table.

"Chase, you have to wear this. It's not optional. Plus you'll look great in it. You know, I really don't understand why you're so averse to going to school here. "

"What, didn't you get the books too?" I said bitterly, dropping onto the couch. But to my horror, Dad came walking in the room with a stack of books in his hands and dropped them onto the coffee table.

"There they are. Your backpack, shoes and stationery are in the truck. So kid, you're all set for school," he said.

I merely got up and said, "I need to go for a walk. I'll be back soon." I walked past my stunned parents and out the door.

The watery orange sun was now dropping behind the trees to the west, and the air was light and cool, which was perfect for me. I didn't mean to be so unfair to my parents, but seeing that stuff just brought home the fact that I was stuck here. It reminded me that I had to go to a new school where I knew no one and which I knew nothing about, and that always kept me thinking I would be alone there. I guess anyone would just say it was the usual new school jitters.

I had no idea about where to go. As I had no intention of seeking company, I headed down to the cove. The walk down the hill seemed unusually quick to me, and I realized I didn't even hear the sound of the sea until I'd reached the beach. I guess with my mind preoccupied, I was less conscious of my surroundings.

After taking my shoes off and enjoying the feel of the

sand under my toes, I looked around and headed for one of the larger trees on the beach, sat on a low branch and just rested there for a while. It felt so good to just sit there and let my worries subside. I didn't worry about anyone being after me, about going school or anything. All I did was sit there and gaze out at the sea.

I laughed to myself. I was worried about going to school when someone was trying to use magic to kill me. I really had to get my priorities in order. That's when I heard it again. That strange, sweet, beautiful song that didn't seem to come from anything physical, as if it was in my own mind.

This time, however, I was sure the voice humming the song was Lyla's. I remembered the warnings from the book I read in the library. If Lyla really was an Aquamun, I knew hearing this song could spell trouble for me. But in that moment where it was bringing me blissful clarity, I couldn't help thinking, couldn't help feeling, this was right. Somehow I knew, for me, it was a good thing. I definitely wasn't being hurt and I was still in my right mind, not hypnotized by the song because the song didn't make me forget about my troubles, it only kind of just helped me put them aside.

Another reason I was so eager to embrace it was because I felt it brought me closer to Lyla, closer than anyone else could be. I thought that somehow her song made her a part of me, and I loved that. It just made me want her more physically and emotionally.

I knew if Lyla knew what I was doing how angry she would be and was thankful she couldn't read my mind. With that thought, I just sat back in the tree and with the wonderful song in my ears, I enjoyed the ambiance of the beach and with every passing second, thoughts of Lyla swam into my consciousness. That is, until:

"Ouch," I shouted as something which felt like a small rock hit me in the back of the head.

Rubbing my head, I looked around in time to dodge another rock which would have struck me in the face.

"What the hell did you do that for?" I shouted furiously at Kristian.

He was standing a couple feet away with another rock in his hand, and heading back up the road were two other guys who kept looking back down at Kristian, but otherwise kept on walking. They were probably friends of his.

"You're disgusting," he said contemptuously, "I warned you about that girl, I told you to stay away from her, but you didn't listen. I know you've still been seeing her, you can't deny it. You probably don't care that you'll hurt your family, not as long as you get to be like that nasty... hey!" He shouted as he ducked because I'd dropped from the tree and had thrown a rock back at him.

A fiery anger was now pulsing through my body which I wanted to take out on Kristian. Who did he think he was, accusing me of wanting to hurt my own family, but even worse, speaking of Lyla like that? And because of him, the song was gone.

I walked up to him.

"There must really be something wrong with you, if you believe that crap you're spitting at me."

I gasped in surprised as he aimed a punch towards me. I was able to move to the left to avoid it, but my foot got caught on a branch on the ground, making me fall.

Kristian, taking advantage of this, kicked me in the stomach, but at the same time, I'd grabbed and pulled his leg, which resulted in him falling hard on his back, which seemed to knock the wind out of him.

By the time he was back on his feet, I was too and before he could do anything I lunged at him, but for every blow I gave him, he sent one back.

As we were scuffling around, I suddenly felt two huge arms close around me pulling me off Kristian and holding me in the air.

"Let me go. Put me down now," I bellowed as I thrashed with all my might, but I could have been struggling against a brick wall for all the good it did.

"Dude, calm down." I recognized the voice as Michael's. Kristian had picked himself up and was looking at both of us with deep contempt, but there was also a hint of fear in his eyes. He probably thought with Michael here, we could gang up on him. It wouldn't be a bad idea.

"Michael, just put me down," I said, calming but still with every intension of knocking Kristian's teeth out. Michael on the other hand, wasn't having any of it.

"This is over, I'm serious," he said as he let me go.

Though I was still angry, the way Michael spoke kept me quiet. As I was glaring at Kristian, I saw he was bleeding from his lip, cheek and had small scrapes on his face and hands. With one last dirty look at Michael and I, he turned and walked away, and I had to stand there resisting the urge the throw something else at him.

By now the sun had already set and the first set of stars were already twinkling, but the moon wasn't out yet. I finally looked over at Michael and realized he was shirtless and wearing a pair of swimming trunks, but he didn't look as though he went swimming, as there wasn't a single drop of water on his body, yet I knew he'd just come from the sea as the smell of the ocean was strong on him. There was another strong, cologne-like fragrance coming from him I could not identify.

"I didn't need you to step in, you know. I had it handled," I said, dusting myself off.

"Sure you did," he replied with a snicker as we began to trot up the hill. When we took the turn to my house and he followed me, I realized he was making sure I didn't go running after Kristian.

"I'm not going to run after Kristian you know, I'm going home."

"All right, fine. Are you going to be okay?"

I could have sworn he looked in the direction of my house and I heard a small 'humph'. But either he did it so fast, his eyes were back on me in the same second, or I imagined it. I just couldn't be sure. All the Morgans were so strange. But then again, according to popular belief...

"I'm going to be fine," I said as I walked away, leaving Michael behind me, though when I looked back, he was already gone.

I looked over the treetops and saw the moon now beginning to peek out from behind the clouds. As I was able to see the ocean in the distance, I stood still for a while to watch the beautiful way the moonlight danced on the surface of the water, the same way it did on Lyla's skin the first time I met her.

My observations of the beauty of nature didn't last very

long, because as soon as I was still for a couple seconds, all the cuts, scrapes and bruises I'd received from the fight began aching. Pushing them aside for the moment, I continued my walk home, increasing my pace because of the anger that was once again burning inside me.

When I was hearing the song on the beach, it was acting like a kind of wall, keeping the flood of emotions away. But now that it was gone, all those feelings were coming back. But in the midst of my anger I felt something else arise—something different. It was as if my emotions were trying to calm me down, but the fire burning inside me was burning too strong and within seconds had overcome my sudden calmness.

When I finally reached home, I slammed the front door shut and headed straight for the stairs, but Mom cut me off before I got there.

"Please, tell me you– Chase, what happened to you?" She said, alarmed as she took in my appearance. I wasn't even worried about how I looked.

"Nothing happened, Mom, I fell." I tried to go around her, but Dad grabbed my arm and spun me around.

"Who did this to you, Chase?" Dad asked.

This was the point where my anger spilled out. I wasn't able to hold it in any longer and unfortunately my parents were the ones on the receiving end.

"You did this to me," I said fiercely as I pulled my arm from my father's hand. "The both of you are the reason for this, by bringing me here. How many times have I told you I didn't want to stay here, that I didn't belong here? Yet you don't listen. You tell me I'll get to love it here, that I have family here. Well, you know what? I don't care, because I don't know them. I got beat up because someone else also thinks I shouldn't be here. You have no idea what being here's been like for me. But it doesn't matter to you that my life here has been hell, not as long as your jobs are bringing in your money and I go to school like a good little boy. What else has to happen for you to realize this place will never be my home?"

And with that, I turned and shot up the stairs, not even looking back at my parents, though I was sure they were standing at the bottom of the stairs, looking stunned.

When I reached my room I slammed the door shut and fell on the bed, waiting for my parents to burst in. I didn't get up to turn on the light, and the moonlight wasn't yet spilling through my window, so I was sitting in darkness, breathing heavily and staring around at the stillness in my room.

Suddenly, out of nowhere, a strange feeling came over me, not something new, because I knew I felt it before. It was that same magnetic feeling I had a few weeks ago, when I'd first met Lyla. It was the same feeling that felt like it led me to her.

But right now, it was telling me to look back. So without hesitation, I spun around. She was standing by the wall near the window.

Strangely enough, though the room was so dark and I could barely see my own hands, I could see Lyla more clearly than anything else in the room, as though the darkness found it harder to cling to her.

Though I had no idea she was going to be here, I was no doubt glad she was.

"What're you doing here?" I asked carefully, not

wanting to snap at her too.

"I'm here for you," Lyla said simply, though looking a little uncomfortable, "I know what happened with you and Kristian, so I figured you'd want some company. If you want me to, I could leave."

"No. Please don't. I want you to stay." I responded quickly. For some reason that left a strong silence between us for a couple minutes, until Lyla finally sat at the top of the bed.

"You know even though I know what you've been going through, I don't really understand what you've been feeling. That's one of things that I find intriguing about you. Anyway, I decided I would come over here just to talk and then just now, I heard what you said to your parents," she hesitated for a moment, then said: "Do you really hate living here?"

"Yes," I replied, a little too quickly, "and no one can tell me I don't have a good reason." I turned around to face her. Wow. I had to keep telling myself to stay focused and be cool.

"Since I've been here someone's tried to kill me twice now for I don't know what and then that idiot Kristian thinks it's a good idea to attack me. It feels like the island itself is trying to reject me. I hate this place so much."

Lyla said nothing, but continued to stare at me. I turned back around, looking at the bedroom door and just realizing my parents weren't coming up. Maybe they thought it would be best if I cooled down first or maybe they were actually thinking about what I said. What they were really doing, I had no idea.

I never sat so still and silent for so long in my life.

After what I'd told Lyla, she didn't say a word, but just kept staring around. A few minutes after that I left the room to tend to the bruises on my body and take a shower, but when I returned, she was still there, and she still said nothing. Even though I wanted to say something, anything in fact, to her, something told me to be quiet for now.

Doing nothing actually turned out to be more time-consuming than I ever thought. As I sat on the bed, I watched the clock go from 8 to 9 o'clock. I'd fallen asleep before it reached ten, but woke up when the alarm sounded and saw it was 12:00 midnight.

Looking around, I saw Lyla in the exact same position she was when she arrived.

"Did you sleep well?" she asked with no sign of boredom or tiredness in her voice.

I shrugged. "It was a restless sleep, if you know what I mean. Look, I thought you said you came here to talk."

"I did," Lyla responded, "but after hearing what you said, I decided it's time to tell you the truth. And there is something I want to show you that I know will lift your spirits."

She turned around and gazed out the open window. I threw my legs over the side of the bed and sat up, but it was a little too fast, which left me dizzy for a couple seconds.

"You want to tell me the truth about what?"

"Everything. Don't worry. You'll understand soon enough."

The moon was now high enough that my room was showered with white light, which Lyla was standing in. This caused an odd effect where it made her skin look like it was glowing. I had no idea what she was going to say or do, but I decided not to question her just in case it angered her and she left. I did love her company. At around ten minutes past twelve, she finally said, "Chase, I want you to come down to the beach with me."

"What, at this time? Why?"

"Like I said, I'm going to tell you the truth about… well everything I can. Plus there is still that thing I want to show you. Anyway the beach is so beautiful at this time. If you don't want to come, I will understand, of course." There was that slight note of disappointment in her voice. It made me feel guilty even though I didn't do anything wrong.

"No, I'll go with you, but I don't think there's much you can do to change how I feel," I said defiantly. She merely responded with a "We'll see."

I watched as she climbed through the window and onto the thick branch of the mango tree outside and was amazed at her agility and how easily she climbed down the tree.

After I got down, we began our walk to the cove.

"Are you cold?" I asked, noticing the only upper body clothing Lyla was wearing was a blue tank top. She looked at me and giggled, which sent goosebumps running through my body.

"You know, for someone who used to live in New York, you sure don't handle the cold very well." I did notice that she seemed unaffected by it. "Don't worry about me, I'm fine. The cold doesn't bug me," she added.

It was a very beautiful, cloudless night. The moon was almost directly overhead and it was shining so brightly that I could clearly see everything around. There was a light breeze out, and I walked a few feet behind Lyla so I could appreciate the way her dark hair swayed in the air, as if it was crafted from the very darkness of night itself.

I wanted to say something just to hear her sweet voice, but there was something about the way she looked, as if a perpetual sadness had come over her, that left me at a loss. I began to wonder if it had anything to do with what she had to tell me.

By the time we got to the beach Lyla had already taken her shoes off, as if she wanted nothing more than to feel the sand between her toes. Without a word she simply sat down on the sand and gazed out to the sea as if deep in thought. Admittedly, there was something soothing about the way the waves came in at night. It made the sea seem more appealing somehow.

Without invitation, I sat down next to her, though not close enough to invade her personal space. Here on the beach, the air coming in from the sea was a lot colder, but she didn't seem to mind. It was the opposite for me. I guess the cold did sometimes bother me.

"I told you I'm going to tell you the truth, and that's exactly what I'm going to do."

I clearly detected a kind of nervous edge to her voice.

"The thing is though, I'm afraid of telling you because, once you know, it may be too much for you and you may become afraid of me or something. Telling you this will change your life forever. Look, from the first time I met you, since that night, things have never been the same. Everything feels so out of order."

I thought about what she was saying, and something horrible came to me.

"Lyla, are you saying, since you saved my life, I've been complicating yours?"

Lyla fixed me with that powerful stare I'd come to know.

"I'm sorry. You misunderstand me. But then how could you not when I'm blabbering. What I meant was, since I saved you, I've been complicating your life. Let me finish." She pleaded as I was about to speak.

I didn't like that she was blaming herself for all this, but I closed my mouth nonetheless.

"Chase, as you know by now, I've been keeping certain things from you. Things that if you knew would perhaps help you make the choice I'm not strong enough to make. Maybe you can make the decision I should have made after I saved you."

A kind of sad smile appeared on her face. I would have said she looked like she wanted to cry, but I didn't see a single tear.

I felt it happening again, and at a horrible time. I felt a huge emotional wave of sorrow wash over me. As usual it came so fast, it felt like it was some outside feeling. Seeing Lyla so sad was breaking my heart, but what I was feeling was worse. It felt to me like I was the one being sorry for some crime I'd committed. I wasn't able to shake it off as I was able to do with the rest of these sudden emotions. This feeling was stronger than the others I'd felt. So with a strong pain of sadness in my chest, I closed my eyes for a couple seconds and with success, managed to push the feeling away.

"Are you okay?" Lyla looked at me with concern. I simply nodded as I felt my calm emotional state returning to me. I really hated when those feelings came at me. It was like being sick, never knowing when a fresh wave was coming. At that moment, when I was taking a couple deep breaths, something incredibly ludicrous came to me. But I didn't have time to think about that now.

"I still don't understand what you're trying to say," I said, getting back to the conversation.

Lyla pulled her feet up and wrapped her hands around her knees, but didn't pull her gaze away from the sea. She sighed deeply before she spoke.

"I told you once that I was different, that I wasn't like most people. Well, the truth is it's more than that. It's a lot more than that."

I suddenly understood what Lyla was trying to say. I always knew she was different, and not because of the people that kept telling me so, or from what I managed to put together. I knew she was different from the first time I met her, though I really didn't know in what way, but I felt it. That strange magnetic feeling that kept pulling me to her was also a huge indication that something was different about her. But knowing this only seemed to make me want to be closer to her, to not push her away.

"Chase, you know what I mean when I say I'm different, don't you?"

"Lyla, do you mean that... that you're not human?" I asked in a whisper. When she nodded, it wasn't a surprise.

"You know what I am, don't you? I know you do."

It took me a while, but I nodded. Lyla still wasn't looking at me, but I got the feeling it was more because she was afraid.

"Say it," she said softly, "I want to hear you say it. Tell me what you think I am."

"Lyla, why are you doing this?"

"Say it," she repeated. I stared at her. The words were

on the tip of my tongue, but still felt unable to pass my lips. I knew once I said it, it would be true, and that would mean, up to this point everything I believed couldn't exist (even with my present situation) would suddenly be my reality. But what actually gave me the willpower to say the words was knowing, if this wasn't true, if Lyla wasn't who or what she was, she wouldn't be in my life. With that realization came the sudden wanting for all this to be true.

"You're an Aquamun," I said confidently. The absence of fear in my voice seemed to have startled Lyla, for she finally looked at me, her eyes full with questioning.

"Do you know what they say we can do to humans?"

"You mean the switching thing? Yeah, I've heard about it."

"Then why aren't you afraid," Lyla said, as if that was to be my only sensible reaction.

"Lyla, I'm not afraid of you. I know you have to want to turn me for the switch to be performed and I know that's not what you want."

I was just about to scoot over to her, but she moved over a few inches before I could. I couldn't help feeling hurt.

"You don't know that Chase," she said, turning towards me. "You see, it's true that we Aquamuns have control over our power, and all my life I've been able to control it. I have never wanted to turn anyone. But it's different with you. When I'm around you, I feel as if I have to try so much harder to keep my power in check."

"Why? Why is it different with me?"

"I don't know. And that's one of the things I'm afraid of. I could be more dangerous to you and not even know it. Chase, I couldn't live with myself if I hurt you."

She sounded so distressed it made me just want to reach out and comfort her, not because of how I felt about her, but simply because it wasn't fair for someone like her to be going through this. I could tell that this degree of uncertainty made her uneasy, to say the least.

I edged closer to her and was thankful that this time she didn't turn away.

"Lyla, you are not dangerous to me. I know that. I feel it and you should too."

"Oh yeah? How do you know that?"

"I just do." Lyla looked at me with her eyebrows together, and then as if catching the punch line of an unsaid joke, we both laughed.

"You said you hoped I could make a choice you weren't strong enough to make. What is it?"

"That you would distance yourself from me to save yourself."

"I would never do that, not to you," I looked out at the sea. It really was almost as appealing as Lyla herself.

"I figured that's what you would say, but I still had to try."

"Why can't you leave *me*? I mean, what's stopping you from avoiding me completely?"

"Well…" Lyla started, but she looked like she was afraid to say what she wanted to.

"I—I couldn't just leave you to deal with your attacker by yourself."

"Uh huh. Okay," I responded, with a coy smile.

"I'm going to admit that even though I wanted you to say we couldn't be friends after you found out about me, I'm really relieved you didn't. If you did I would've had an extremely hard time distancing myself from you, but at least you would have been safe from me."

I don't know how, but her voice sounded both relieved and disappointed at the same time.

"I know, I know," she said suddenly, the same time I opened my mouth. "You don't think I'm a danger to you?"

She then smiled at me. "You know, you're different from everyone else."

"Different good or bad?"

"Good, definitely good," she reassured me, and then silence fell between us for a couple minutes.

That's when it finally hit me: I'm sitting next to a mermaid! Lyla isn't human! I ran those two thoughts over and over in my mind, and not once did it make me feel uncomfortable.

"So, I just told you I'm an Aquamun. Don't you have any questions?"

I was intensely surprised by that. I didn't expect her willingness to be so open. Interestingly, I was actually bursting with questions. It's not like you meet an Aquamun every day. Well, I guess as it turns out, I do.

"Sure," I was trying to act as though it didn't matter. Lyla's adorable giggle told me she was on to me.

"What can you do? I mean, what kind of special abilities do you have? You never really hear what mermaids can do."

"Well, let's just say we're very strong," Lyla said with a sly smile.

"How strong exactly?" I pressed, very interested now. She stood up, looked around, then beckoned me to follow her as she walked into a grove just off the beach. After walking around for a couple seconds, we came to a sudden stop in the grove where one of the biggest trees, which had to be about thirty-five feet tall, had fallen onto a couple of other trees, leaving it at a slant. Its immense weight was clearly causing the other trees to fall.

Lyla climbed onto a huge boulder that was directly under the slanted tree, and placed her hands on the underside of the fallen tree trunk. Then she began to push. I could only watch in amazement as, with a loud rumbling noise and the rustling of branches, the tree moved off the others, and Lyla threw it onto the ground where it hit with a loud crash.

"Wow!" I shouted in awe. She smiled widely, and then in the blink of an eye she was gone. Almost a full second later I felt someone tap me on my shoulder. I spun around to find her standing behind me, her hands clasped behind her back.

"And we can move fast. Very fast."

We started walking back towards the beach.

"Having these abilities isn't always so great. Sometimes, when you have to be careful not to move too fast or to keep your strength in check, it just makes blending in all the more difficult."

We found our spot on the sand, but this time Lyla lay flat on her back, and I did the same after her.

"I think whoever's after you might be trying to kill you because of me," she said suddenly.

"Just because you saved me."

"No, it's not that," she shook her head, "You told me Hilda told you she couldn't see your aura. To be honest I don't know why that is, but we can't rule out the fact that it could be because of me. Clearly whoever is after you is probably thinking along the same lines."

She looked up at the sky, but I knew she was thinking deeply.

"If they thought I wanted to turn you, I guess they'd be attacking me, but as they're going after you, I believe they think you want me to turn you. I could be wrong though."

I watched her silently for a while as she just looked up at the stars. Then she sat up suddenly.

"What is it?" I asked, standing up.

"It's time. For the thing I have to show you, I mean," she got up and looked out toward the great, dark sea. To be honest, the night was going so interestingly, I forgot about the reason we really came out here.

"Wait, you're not going to tell me your pet's the Loch Ness monster, are you?"

"What? That's ridiculous, no."

"Oh, that's too bad," I mumbled, disappointed. "That would have been kind of cool." When Lyla laughed, it sounded as if it danced on the air.

"I said I was going to show you something to lift your spirits, but to show you, I'm going to have to take you out to sea."

"You can do that? Take me with you?"

"Well yes. The thing is, I've never done it, but I do know how. But I'm gonna to need to know if you trust me."

With her dark blue eyes locked onto me, Lyla began walking backwards into the sea until she was in the water and only stopped when it was just above her knees. As she stood in the water, it looked like the sea was dancing around her and it couldn't move her.

After finding out the girl I was madly in love with was a mermaid, instead of turning me away from her, knowing it only made me want to be all the more close to her because she had this whole different life I knew nothing about, a whole different life I could be a part of.

I pulled off my shirt and pants, threw them aside with my shoes, and stood on the beach in a pair of boxers with the cold night air blowing all around me. I began walking towards the water's edge and at the same time Lyla began walking deeper into the water, inviting me to join her by holding her hand out to me.

The way she looked, with the water playing around her body and her hair dancing in the air, simply made me want to go out to her all the more. However, as soon as I reached the edge of the water, something strange happened.

The second the water touched my feet, I suddenly couldn't move. It wasn't like some external force was holding me back. It was just the opposite actually. The moment I reached the edge of the water, one thought entered my mind causing me to pause where I was: *Can you really trust her? After she just told you what she is, do you think it's smart to trust her? She may not hurt you directly, but you do have family and friends.*

However, just like when I got those unexpected bursts of emotion, I knew the thoughts I heard weren't my own, even if I did hear them in my head. They were coming from somewhere deep in my head, like some sort of repressed memory, but it felt more like the opinion of someone else.

I tried to push these thoughts out of my head, but the harder I tried, the harder they tried to keep hold on my consciousness.

Panic was starting to course through me because the louder these foreign thoughts got, the less I felt I had control over my actions, as if, impossibly, these thoughts were taking control of me.

That's when I realized she was standing just in front me. She had me locked in that unbreakable stare of hers, and as I looked into her soulful blue eyes, I felt all my fears quickly disappear and at the same time felt like I just got pushed back into my own body, though the voice in my head was now screaming at me to get away.

"Chase you don't have to do this, but if you do, I won't let anything happen to you. I won't hurt you."

She then reached forward and took my hand in hears. From the moment Lyla's fingers interlocked with mine, the opposing voice in my head didn't just recede to some dark corner of my mind, but it disappeared altogether, and I was left fully in control of my thoughts. Then I noticed just how warm I'd become as soon as Lyla touched me, so that the water pulling at my feet and the cold air lost their chill.

"Thank you," I whispered.

She smiled contentedly, then took me a little further out until we were waist deep in the water.

"Before we go any further, I need to know you trust me completely."

"I do." I replied confidently, though breathing a little nervously.

Lyla smiled and led me deeper into the water until it was up to our necks, with our feet no longer able to touch the sandy bottom.

"Take a deep breath. Here we go."

I sucked in as much air as my lungs would hold, and

as soon as they were full, Lyla pulled me underwater. For a second we were just floating there, staring at each other, and then I felt her hold on me tighten. Before I had time to register anything else, we were off, speeding through the water faster than anything ever could.

We were moving so fast my eyes didn't have time to bring anything around us into focus, which meant all I saw was a mass of moving blackness. The only thing that was clear to me was Lyla.

Moving this fast, the water felt a lot more solid to me than it ever did, like I was trying to swim through jelly. It was like the sea itself knew I was human and didn't want me swimming so fast, but as I was with Lyla, it had no chance of slowing me down.

Before my lungs got anywhere close to burning, or before I could even get past my surprise and start to enjoy the ride, we came to a sudden stop. When we stopped the force of water hit me hard in the face. That time it really did feel like the water had won.

After we broke the surface of the water, I began rubbing my face to relieve some of the tingling.

"I'm sorry," Lyla said, looking slightly amused, "I forgot how fragile you humans can be."

Still smiling, Lyla guided me to what appeared to be a small land mass only a couple feet wide. As soon as we climbed on, I noticed that every single drop of water on Lyla seemed to drip off her, as if her body was repelling it, leaving her completely dry within seconds. Even her hair was water-free and was swaying in the breeze.

I, on the other hand, wasn't as lucky. The moment Lyla and I separated my body once more became susceptible to the temperatures of my environment, because as the night air hit my wet skin, I began shaking and shivering.

"What are we doing here?" I wrapped my arms around my body. I looked around and realized we were on one of those little patches of land just beyond the cliff the lighthouse stood on.

"We're just waiting on Nikolai. He should be here soon."

I sat down next to Lyla, all the while trying my best to keep from shaking.

"And where exactly are we going?"

"Well with Nikolai's help, we'll go to hear the song of the whales."

She started giggling at my quizzical look.

"It's not something you can really explain. You have to experience it."

As always, her eyes found their way up to the cloudy sky. The moon was barely visible through thick puffs of clouds. As was usual on the island, there were still plenty of stars out.

The same way Lyla couldn't seem to help watching the sky, I couldn't help watching her. Seeing her there, sitting so still and looking as she did made me see her more as an Aquamun. Despite having a family, no one ever seemed more alone then she did, and at that moment, it was almost too sad to think about.

Lyla looked over at me and surprisingly, held out her hand to me. This was something I'd have never expected because, apart from bringing me here, she always kept a discernible amount of space between us. I didn't question it; I simply just took her hand in mine.

The second our hands were clasped together, the chill

was thankfully gone from my body. I realized just how much I loved the feeling of Lyla's soft hand in mine.

When she began to shift her body, for a second I thought she was going to move away from me, but I was dumbfounded to see she was moving closer to me. We were now so close together, our shoulders were touching.

"How do you do that, protect me from temperature?" I only asked because I wanted to start a conversation.

"To be honest, I don't know. Strangely, that only works with you. I realized it the night I saved your life. Whenever I touched you, your body temperature matched mine and our temperature's always the same. I've never heard of anything like this before."

She paused for awhile, fiddled with her hands, then said, "May I ask you something?"

I nodded.

She shifted her gaze from the sky and looked at me with an intensity I'd never experienced before. When she spoke, there was a nervous edge to her voice.

"What does it feel like to be human?"

I was completely surprised. It was something I would never have expected to be asked in my life.

I thought carefully about what I was going to say before I spoke. "Well, I've never really thought about it before, but, I'd have to say it feels like... freedom."

Lyla's blue eyes opened wider at this. I was a little surprised by it myself, but after I said it, I understood exactly what I meant and found it strangely easy to explain.

"Being human means, you can get hurt or get sick, you get old, and you die. Sure, those can be deal breakers." Lyla giggled for a second and my heart seemed to beat faster. "But being susceptible to those things only makes us stronger. Being human means we're free to make our own choices, take risks and we shape our own destinies. I guess being human simply means we try to do the best with the life we're given."

"That's very beautiful. The life of an Aquamun is so much different. We are immortals, but it's like we never have a destiny. No purpose, no reason to live. We only have the ocean. Forever bound to the sea. It's easy to understand why some of our kind want to turn human."

"Do you ever think about turning human?"

"Of course. But I don't have any intention of becoming human. Still I always wondered what it would be like to be human, to live and experience life as you do. I think most of my kind think about that at some point, but I could never do it… change, I mean."

"Why not?"

Lyla looked at me like I missed something obvious.

"Because I could never force someone to become what I am?"

"Oh."

"Even if I could find a human who wanted to turn, I still wouldn't because that would hurt my family. We'd be torn apart. I would never be able to see them again."

Lyla and I made eye contact with such intensity that I couldn't look away if I wanted to. Our gazes seemed to be locked together by some unseen force. And then that strange feeling started running through my body again, the one that made me feel like I needed to be closer to her and before I knew it, I was leaning towards her.

"Chase, what're you doing?" Lyla whispered nervously,

but not worried as I brought my face closer to hers. I noticed that she didn't turn away.

"I don't know." I said, equally softly.

It was like my body was again moving on its own and I was just along for the ride, except I was in control and this wasn't a ride I wanted to stop.

"Please, you don't want to do this," Lyla said, but I got the feeling she was feeling the same. Before I knew it my lips brushed against Lyla's. I honestly didn't know if it lasted a couple seconds or if it stretched on for hours, but during that time I had the most exhilarating feeling of my life. I felt like all the worries and pain I had in my life never even existed. Even my troubles about moving here didn't seem to have ever been real.

This was pure bliss.

The moment her lips left mine, everything changed. I felt like a huge weight had dropped onto my shoulders and I even had to fall on my hands and knees for support. I suddenly felt stressed, like all the problems and worries in the world were now all mine.

Lyla helped me to my feet.

"Don't ever do that again," she said angrily.

"What was that?" I asked, trying to catch my breath.

"Whenever we have intimate contact with humans, somehow they seem to experience complete bliss the whole time. In a way, making them more open to us. But when you pull away... withdrawing from it can be rough on you."

"So you've never kissed anyone before?"

"Not another human."

A smile actually came across my face at the thought

that I was the first human she'd ever kissed. Before we could say anything, a figure flew out of the water with the speed of a bullet and Nikolai landed right in front of us, only wearing a pair of swimming pants. He was already completely dry. He looked curiously at me, then turned, looking both angry and scared, to Lyla.

"You told him! How could you do that?"

"Nick, it's okay," Lyla said, but Nikolai shook his head.

"No, it's not okay. You can't be sure we can trust him, and believe when I tell you, father won't like this."

I was actually very surprised to hear Nikolai's reaction. I knew he was just concerned, but I would've thought at least he, of all the Morgans, would have been cool with me knowing.

"Nick I didn't have a choice," Lyla said, then sighed, "someone's been trying to kill Chase using magic."

Nikolai looked at Lyla and me with surprise, but Lyla just raised her hand.

"I'll explain everything later. As for father, I'll be the one to tell him. Why are you so late anyway? You were supposed to be here before me."

Nikolai merely shrugged off Lyla's question.

"I got side-tracked. It happens."

Lyla shook her head, then turned to me and held out her hand. I didn't know what exactly we were going to be doing, but I took hold of her hand for the second time in an hour. Just as we reached the edge of the little patch of land, both Lyla and Nikolai spun their heads towards the cliff, fear etched in both of their faces.

"What is it?" I spun my head around a little too fast to see what they were looking at, which left my neck hurting.

Lyla glanced at Nikolai. "Don't worry, whoever it is can't see us."

"What's going on?" I asked again, massaging the back of my neck with my free hand.

"We thought someone might have been watching us from the cliffs. I swore I heard footsteps up there."

"But if someone is there," Nikolai said, "They won't be able to see us."

"He's using his power to make us invisible to everyone else," Lyla explained.

"But what if someone was there before Nikolai got here, then they would've seen you." A strange concern gripped me.

"No," Lyla said, "If there was anyone up there when we got here, I would've heard them." The concern I was experiencing just kept growing. "Let's get going. I'm pretty sure no one was there. Must've been a cat or something, you know, nothing to be concerned about."

Nikolai turned back towards the water. Lyla and I did too.

"Are you ready?" Lyla asked, holding my hand tighter.

I was still a little nervous, but my trust in Lyla removed any doubts I was feeling. I gently squeezed her hand, which looked slightly aglow, just like Nikolai, thanks to the light of the moon.

"I'm ready," I said.

"Deep breath," Lyla reminded me.

"On three," Nikolai said next to me, poised to jump into the water.

"One, two, three." Lyla, Nikolai and I leapt into the water at the same time. However, instead of splashing into the water, it was like we just slipped in, or the sea just took us in. There wasn't the slightest splash or sound. It was amazing.

As soon as we were underwater, the two Aquamuns didn't waste any time. We were off. Just like before, we were moving so fast everything just looked like a streak of black moving mass, at least to me. This time, other than Lyla, Nikolai, who was swimming next to us, was the only one I could clearly see.

We were moving so fast we were leaving three tunnel-like trails behind us, though Lyla's and mine were connected, as we softly but swiftly cut through the water. I felt Lyla's fingers close around mine more tightly. I looked around and saw that she was smiling broadly and so was Nikolai, who was flipping and turning with a speed and agility no other being could achieve.

Then suddenly, out of nowhere, it hit me.

A strange burning sensation erupted in the pit of my stomach. At first, it only felt like the burning pains you get when you wake up on mornings with excruciating hunger, but it quickly surpassed that and grew into something like a small fire raging in my stomach.

I saw the smile slip from Lyla's face the same time I felt an immense amount of worry rise inside me. The fire in my stomach began to rise up to my chest and down to my legs. Pain was now starting to spread through my whole body as if it were moving through my veins.

My hold on Lyla was weakening and she had to grip me tighter to compensate as we came to a sudden stop. The flames in my body were now licking the walls of my throat and continued to spread further. My eyes started to burn so badly I had to squeeze them shut. By now it had already reached my hands and feet and to make matters worse, it reached the insides of my lungs and felt like it used all the oxygen I had stored to burn hotter. But the worst thing of all was, in my pain, I couldn't even scream. I had to keep my mouth tightly shut.

However, through all my pain I got the weird sensation that I was going up. I felt an arm go around my waist and my head was resting on what felt like a shoulder with a hand supporting the back of my head.

The second we broke the surface of the water, I opened my mouth and sucked in as much air as possible in one breath. As soon as the fresh salty air filled my body, it seemed to extinguish the fire that was consuming my body from the inside out. All the pain was instantly gone and I felt my strength return.

"Chase, what's wrong?" Lyla asked the second we broke the surface. She sounded panic-stricken and the fear in her voice actually hurt me as much as what just happened. Someone with the voice of an angel shouldn't ever have to sound like that.

"I'm– I'm okay," I said hoarsely. The insides of my throat felt raw and sore.

"What's wrong?" Nikolai asked the moment he got up. "Why did you stop?"

"It's Chase. He's been hurt. I think someone just tried to hurt him," Lyla said angrily, then looked at Nikolai who flinched a little when she spoke. "You see now? This is why I had to tell him. I won't let him face this alone. We need to go back."

"No," I said hastily, "I'm fine now. We can go on."

Lyla shook her head in protest.

"We should get you home, in case this person attacks you again."

I spat out some sea water that got into my mouth. "Lyla, I don't think they'll try it again. And even if they do," I spoke a little louder as I knew she wanted to interject. "You can just get me to the surface again and I won't object to you taking me home. I know this song of the whales thing is something you've been waiting for, plus you did promise me."

"Lyla, he's fine," Nikolai pressed on, "He's well enough to stay and if we leave now, I don't know when next we'll be able to see it."

Lyla looked like she wanted to swear.

"Fine," she finally conceded, "but we're leaving at the first sign of danger. How much further do we have to go anyway?"

Nikolai looked around the dark water for a couple seconds, and then he said, "Actually we're close enough. I can do it from here."

He first stared off into the distance, as if seeing something Lyla and I weren't privileged to see, then dove out of sight without a word. After a while, I felt something brush against my leg.

I tried frantically to see under the surface of the dark, churning sea.

"Did you just kick me?" I asked, but Lyla just smiled at me. "They're here. Are you ready?"

"Um, yeah, I am."

The second I inhaled enough air, Lyla said, "Remember, don't be afraid." Her grip on me tightened once more, then she pulled me underwater.

Just because Lyla told me not to be afraid didn't exactly stop me from almost opening my mouth in surprise. At first I couldn't even begin to understand what I was seeing. Swimming around us were far more whales then I cared to count. And it wasn't just one species of whale. I was shocked to see all kinds of whales from five unbelievably huge blue whales, right down to dozens of killer whales.

Every single one of the whales was swimming past Lyla and I and not even bothering us, as though we weren't even there.

We found Nikolai swimming while holding onto one of the fins of a particularly large humpback, so we followed him.

I knew that these waters should have been extremely dark, but there was a beautiful white glow that illuminated the water and seemed to follow us wherever we went. After a while, when I became confident one of the larger whales wasn't going to swallow me, I began to relax a little and was actually captivated by these wonderful creatures. And from the looks on both Lyla and Nikolai's faces, they were clearly enjoying the experience as much as I was.

Then I heard it.

Something that sounded almost too beautiful and too surreal to even exist. It was similar to the harmonic sound of the Aquamun's voice, yet different, and it was coming from one of the whales. I couldn't tell which one, but I knew it was. Before long, all the other whales joined in the song. No, not just a song. This was more like a holy symphony, and every whale around us was just a piece of the whole, parts of the sum.

Obviously I had never heard anything like it. I'd never imagined that whales could make such beautiful songs. This was just the kind of thing my parents would love to hear.

As we were swimming, I looked directly under us and saw light reflecting onto something. Or maybe it was giving off its own; I just wasn't sure. Before I could get a good look at it, the creature turned and swam off on its own, but I could have sworn it was a pure white whale. Not albino, because I've seen pictures of those, but a pure, snow white whale.

Before I knew it, all the whales were dispersing in their own directions so that before long, it was only me and the two Aquamuns left. I had no idea where we were going now, but I didn't really care. What I'd just experienced was one of the most amazing things ever.

Within a short time we were crashing onto the shores of East Island.

"That was amazing," I breathed the second we dropped onto the sand, "I've never dreamed of anything like it."

"Yeah, it was even better than the first time," Nikolai shouted. He then turned and, whooping and shouting loudly, ran back into the sea.

"What's he doing?" I asked Lyla, who sat next to me. She giggled.

"He's just going for a swim. I think he likes the sea more than the rest of us."

She then turned to me. "I think we should get you home before..." I raised a hand to cut her off.

"Yes Lyla. I know you're concerned about me and I am feeling a little tired, so I won't object to going home, but before I do, I need to tell you something."

"What?"

I felt a tight knot form in my stomach, but I couldn't let that deter me from what I had to say. Somehow, hearing the whale song had given me the courage to do this and I wasn't going to let it pass.

I took a couple breaths first to steady myself as my hands were shaking and my heart was pounding against my ribs, which I was sure Lyla could clearly hear.

"I love you."

I was a little surprised at how calmly and confidently I said it, but that was nothing compared to Lyla, whose eyes opened wide in shock.

"It's true, I do. And before you say anything, it has nothing to do with you being an Aquamun. You are the most beautiful person I've ever seen. For no reason, you are willing to put your life on the line for me. I love you and I want to be with you."

Lyla stared at me for a while, directly in the eyes. For a second I thought she wanted to do something with her hands, but she simply kept them where they were, on her lap.

Happiness, fear, hope, were the emotions I was feeling, yet there was that strange sensation that there were some peripheral feelings. But I couldn't understand how, as those were what I really was feeling, unless my theory was right.

A huge wage crashed onto the beach.

"Oh Chase, I didn't want this to happen to you. I didn't want you to feel like that. I don't want to hurt you, but I can't be with you. You want to know what's even worse?...

I'm in love with you too."

I could have sworn every cell in my body was pulsing with excitement.

"Then why don't you want to be with me?" That might have sounded a little desperate, but I didn't care.

Lyla sighed heavily. "I do want to be with you and that's the truth." She placed a soft hand on my cheek. "But I can't because I don't want to hurt you, please understand that."

It was my turn to sigh heavily. "You've never been with a human so you don't know you will hurt me."

"I don't want to take that risk."

"I love you. I don't care how long it takes, we should be together and you're going to see that."

Despite this, Lyla smiled pleasantly at me. After hearing her fears about us being together, I decided that not telling her I was hearing her song was the right choice for now.

CHAPTER 8

An Eclipse of Emotions

Lyla had promised me that after I saw the whales I'd feel a lot better about living in East Island and truth was, since then I did. But it wasn't because of the whale song. What had me feeling better than I could ever remember was Lyla saying that she loved me. That single memory kept my mood lifted for the week that followed.

Every time my mind was free to wander, it drifted to that time, which usually resulted in me breaking out with a big smile for no reason, making my friends and parents ask if I was okay.

Lyla's admission of her true feelings for me made our friendship a little more tense, as now whenever we were close together, she always avoided eye contact with me, or even being too near me. But I knew she only did that because she was afraid of being closer to me, even though I knew she wanted to be.

Nine days after our excursion with the whales, on the first Monday in August, Mr. Taylor, Kristian's father, came over to finish his repairs on the shed, and I was extremely surprised when I saw that Kristian had come with him, though I figured from the brooding look on his face that he didn't have much choice.

As Mr. Taylor was making his way out back, Kristian made to follow him.

"Not so fast," I said, managing to block him in time. It showed all over his face that he didn't like the idea of me on the offensive, but as he was at my house, there wasn't much he could do.

"Why'd you come here? You don't like me and you had to know I was going to be here, maybe even with Lyla." I loved seeing his growing agitation and knowing he couldn't do anything about it. "Which means you didn't come to chat with your new buddy, so why did you come over here?"

"You think I came here to see if she was over here?"

"Well, that's hitting the nail on the head."

Kristian folded his arms in what I took to be a defensive posture.

"Kim told my dad I haven't been getting along with you, so it was his idea for me to come here to smooth things out. Well, that's how he puts it."

"But you don't think that's going to happen," I said with a slight sneer. I couldn't help enjoying having the upper hand.

Kristian scolded in response. "Well, I did warn you that being friends with the Morgans would be bad for you, but you just wouldn't listen, so don't blame me 'cause we're not going to be best buddies. You don't understand what you're getting into."

He turned to walk away, but I said, "I know exactly

what I'm getting into."

It was my pride that made me say it, but it wasn't until after the words were out of my mouth I realized maybe I shouldn't have said it. Kristian paused, then turned back around, surprised. I walked up to him.

"I know exactly what you're trying to warn me about." I took a dramatic pause, in which time Kristian seemed to be holding his breath. Then I said, "I know about the Morgans. I know what they are, and I also know about the Somorians, which also means you."

Kristian looked unsettled. "She told you. She actually told. I can't believe it. But why would she... unless I was right and she does plan to turn you."

I was dumbfounded for a couple seconds. I should have known he would find a way to get back to that. He probably only said it to piss me off.

"I think it's you who doesn't know what he's talking about. After she told me what she was, she admitted she loves me but refuses to be with me because she doesn't want to hurt me."

It was Kristian's turn to wear the patronizing sneer, which infuriated me more.

"Listen to me, they can't love humans. That's impossible. She probably only told you that to make you feel closer to her. Listen, you don't really know anything about this world and the way you're trying to force yourself into it, you're only going to end up in trouble and that's when you are going to be in deep water."

Kristian walked past me towards the yard, but before he got out of the room, he said: "Say hi to Lyla for me."

It goes without saying that Kristian's comment left me with a burning anger that didn't let up until the next morning. I was lucky that it did, because I was going out with Dad on the boat and Nikolai and Marcus were coming along and I didn't want them picking up on the fact that I was upset, because they'd tell Lyla. Then she would somehow find out about Kristian coming over and she'd just use that as an excuse for us to not be together. At least that's how it played out in my head.

"So what are we going to be doing today?" I was spreading some marmalade on a stack of toast in front of me. It was just Dad and I this morning, as Mom had already left for work at the clinic today.

"We're going back out to see if we can pick up any more unusual whale activity. We thought it was just the Humpback and Orca, but almost two weeks ago, we picked up an unusually high number of whales in the area."

"I don't think it's so unusual for a couple whales to be in the area," I said, trying to sound casual as I picked a cup of coffee.

"It is when it's over ten species together in a few hours," Dad explained, taking the coffee from me and handing me a cup of cocoa.

"Dad, I'm seventeen. I think I can handle one cup of coffee."

"You know how your mother feels about you drinking this stuff. If she ever found out, she'd have me by the gonads," he added into his cup, probably unaware that I heard him.

I really don't know how we ever thought no one would

notice so many whales in one place. In fact, two days after there was a news report about a couple of fishermen who said they spotted some whales never even seen in this part of the world, so of course they'd want to get my dad involved.

Dad chuckled and said, "Son, it's obvious there's something going on if so many different species of whales are attracted here. Of course there is the off chance that it was some kind of freak one-time thing."

"Hmmm." I was trying to sound vague, but Dad had actually just given me an idea.

"But if something new were to be discovered about whales," Dad continued, "that could explain such close cross-species interaction on such a high level, and if we were to discover it, that would be amazing."

I was starting to feel a bit bad for Dad, because although he wouldn't admit it, I knew he really wanted that theory to be true, and if he started chasing it, it wouldn't be good for his job and I just couldn't mess up my parents' lives like that, which made the success of my plan all the more important.

I had to find a way to let Nikolai know he had a very vital part in this plan, without letting Marcus know, because I had a feeling if he knew what was going on, Lyla and Nikolai were going to be in trouble.

After breakfast, the rest of Dad's team got there within a couple of minutes along with Marcus and Nikolai.

"I wanna show you something," I said to Nick. "Come up to my room with me."

"Hmmm, I don't really need to see that," he joked, following me anyway.

"Shut up." I retorted.

When we got up and the door was closed I opened my mouth to speak, but he held up his hand to stop me. His light blue eyes suddenly became unfocused as if he was daydreaming.

"Good. It's okay," he revealed, snapping back to his surroundings. "I had to make sure father was engaged so he wouldn't be listening to us!"

"Why would he care about what we're talking about?"

"Probably to make sure we're not planning any more 'reckless activities' as he calls it. He knows about the whales, and isn't very happy about it, especially as Lyla and I called them so close to the island."

"Wait a minute, he still doesn't know that I know about you?" I asked surprised.

"Are you mad? He was furious about this; he would probably explode if he knew you knew our secret. Anyway, that's why he wanted to come on this expedition. He wants to make sure your Dad and the team believe that won't happen again."

"That's great," I whispered, "Because that's what I wanted to talk to you about. I have an idea of how we can do that, but it would mean you'd have to tell your dad you came up with it if he asks. All you have to do is, get a couple of whales in the area, let them see them and then have the whales swim off back to their own places. Trust me, if Dad doesn't see them go, he'll always believe they may always be around, like the Humpback and Orca, which they're still looking out for by the way."

"Okay, you don't have to rub it in, I get it. And don't worry, I'll make sure this plan goes out perfectly."

Nick turned to leave, but I grabbed his arm to stop him.

"Are you and Lyla afraid to tell Marcus about me because he doesn't like me?"

That was something I had been thinking about all the time, but this was the first time I ever voiced it.

Nikolai sighed deeply—there was something sad about the way he did it—and turned back to me.

"It's not that he doesn't like you. He actually doesn't have anything against you. It's just that so many humans dislike us. Father just wants to protect us. He's afraid if any human finds out about us, they will expose our secret and that would cause a lot of trouble for us. It's happened before. He just doesn't want it to happen again, so he doesn't want any human to get too close to us."

"What do you mean it's happened before? What happened?"

Nikolai realized he probably said something he shouldn't have, and that kind of hurt a little, because I wanted to think he trusted me enough to know I wasn't going to tell anyone what he said.

"Don't mention that to anyone. In fact, just forget I even said it."

"Nick, I'm not going to tell anyone. You can trust me." He nodded, then we headed downstairs.

Whatever happened to the Morgan family must have really shaken them up to do that to Nikolai, but I didn't think it was such a good idea to press the issue, so I let it go.

When we got downstairs I saw that Justin was waiting for us as well. When Nikolai walked off towards his house, he and Justin merely nodded at each other.

"I still can't believe you're friends with the Morgans. They have a few friends at school, but no one from around here and they usually keep to themselves. So are you going to tell me?" Justin asked as we got in the back seat of Dad's truck.

"Tell you what?" I asked, genuinely puzzled.

"If there's anything going on between you and Lyla Morgan."

"Nah, nothing like that. We're just friends. For now," I added in an undertone. Justin chuckled. I suddenly remembered about the Aquamuns' hearing abilities and hoped Marcus wasn't listening when I said that.

I'd always envisioned Marcus to be one of those fathers who meticulously protected their daughters from everything, even harmless teenage boys.

When we arrived at the harbor the boat was already loaded, so as soon as everyone was onboard, we took off.

"How far out do we have to go?" I asked Dad while we were in the cabin with Gibbons, who was staring.

"We're going to have to go a couple miles out. It's going to take just a little time getting there and back," Dad replied. "I tell you this is one of the strangest things I've ever investigated. Actually, anyone in fact. Nothing like this has ever been documented before."

A dreamy look came over Dad's face again and my guilt returned. I knew he was thinking about the accreditation they'd receive if they did find something, but it was best to take that dream away. They'd have him chasing nothing but lies.

"Dad, maybe you shouldn't get too excited about this, because like you said, it could be a one-time thing."

He froze and looked at me with a puzzled expression.

"If I didn't know any better, and I do, I would say you don't want me to find out what's going on here."

"Weird things happen all the time. I just don't want you to set yourself up for disappointment."

That was what I replied with, but somehow I thought of saying: "Well Dad, of course I don't want you to know what's going on."

Dad merely smiled kindly at me and returned to his work. But just as I was about to leave the cabin, one of the monitors started beeping madly.

"It's one of our boys. One of the whales we tagged." Hoggie said after he ran into the cabin to check the screen. I didn't fail to notice how his eyes popped open with glee.

"And it looks like he's got company. I don't believe it. I looks like a baleen and a sperm whale!" Hoggie shouted. Chris was already on deck, holding a video camera and tracking the whales' movements.

"We could really do with some underwater shots," he said over his com while trying to get angles.

"Already on it!" Dad shouted, coming out of a small changing room inside the cabin with Marcus. Both of them were wearing wet suits.

I began thinking this was really getting out of hand fast, but then I saw Marcus look at Nikolai and he, in turn, nodded to his father.

"What was that about?" I asked Nick.

"Just letting my dad know I did have a plan."

"Come on," Justin called to us from the deck, "Get up here or you guys will miss everything."

With everything that was going on, the others paid no

attention to Justin, Nick and me, who were gazing intently out to sea, trying to spot the whales, though Nick obviously knew where they were.

Suddenly the three whales rose to the surface again, but began thrashing about madly, not like they were being aggressive, but more like they were putting on a show, like they wanted all attention on them. Nikolai was putting the plan into action.

Dad and the others were completely mystified, but very intrigued. But before they could ready a little more of their equipment, the three animals split up to swim in different directions and departed, much to the dismay of everyone on board, excepting Marcus, Nick and myself.

"What should we do?" Chris asked hurriedly. Everyone was looking towards my dad, who took one look at me and chuckled sadly.

"Look," he said, indicating the directions of the whales, "they're returning to their own territories. We can try to find out what got them here in the first place, but for some reason I just don't think we're going to find anything. We'll just document what happened, but this can just be passed off as a one-time thing."

Dad turned to walked back into the cabin, but stopped by me first.

"This is a very strange place, but I still like it here," he said, then continued on his way and, one by one, the others followed him with Marcus bringing up the rear. When he passed Nikolai, he gave him a pat on shoulder.

"Can you believe it?" Justin said, leaning on the rail and looking out towards the ocean, as if hoping to spot one last whale. "It's like they were waiting on us, just to do that."

Nick and I looked at each other and laughed quietly.

"I'm just glad it's all sorted," I said. Nikolai and Justin soon followed everyone else into the cabin, but I decided to stay out on the deck. I rested on the rail and just enjoyed the breeze on my skin.

We hadn't moved yet, but we were about to set out for home when all of a sudden the boat shook violently as if one of the whales had rammed into us. The boat shook so intensely that I was caught off guard and, to my great surprise, I fell overboard.

Unbelievably, after I fell into the water, the first thing that entered my mind wasn't fear, surprise or even anger. It was embarrassment. Of everyone on the boat, it had to be me that fell overboard.

Feeling slightly stupid, I swam towards the surface, readying myself for ridicule from Justin and Nikolai, when I realized something strange. I couldn't get through the surface of the water. At first I thought maybe I was just a little disoriented from the fall, but after two more tries and not being able to penetrate the surface, I started to panic.

Every time I made for the surface it was as if I was touching some kind of soft solid I couldn't get through, no matter how hard I pushed against the water. When I fell it was such a surprise to me that I didn't have time to take in much air, so my lungs were already starting to burn and my brain was screaming at me to open my mouth.

Through the crystal clear water I noticed everyone on the boat was frantically scanning the water, as if they weren't seeing what they were looking for. Then, even though my thoughts were starting to move to slowly, it came to me. They were looking for me.

Suddenly, through the fog that was starting to cloud my mind, I heard something familiar. Something wonderful that made the pain in my lungs and my head seem to disappear, or at least made me put them out of my mind.

All sound around me had somehow disappeared and the only one I could hear, the only one I was concerned with was the sound in my head. Lyla's song. Hearing it put me at ease. I wasn't even concerned with getting out of the water anymore. I just wanted to let the sound consume me.

Somewhere in the back of my mind I noticed a strange darkness rising from the sea floor. Whether it was because of my lack of oxygen or something more sinister, I didn't know or care, just as long as I could hear that angelic sound in my head. Then I realized the song wasn't just in my head, it was also coming from within the darkness. Somehow, that darkness held something I wanted… peace.

The fact that I was so close to drowning no longer mattered to me, all I cared about was reaching the source of Lyla's sweet voice and that was in the heart of the cold darkness.

By now my limbs were starting to get weak and vision was starting to blur, but nothing was going to be enough to stop me from getting to that voice which was beating so loudly in my ears. But as soon as I started to swim down, a pair of strong arms enclosed around my chest and began pulling me to the surface. I didn't fight like mad to get away from this person because as soon as they touched me my senses returned to me, completely pushing the Aquamun song away, and making me feel like my chest was about to explode.

Before I knew it we broke through the surface of the

water and I gulped in as much air as I could.

"Marcus. Is he all right?" Dad shouted in a panicked voice.

"I believe he is fine!" Marcus shouted, but then he lowered his head to my ear and whispered, "We will talk later." And he didn't sound too happy.

As soon as we were back on the boat I was thrown onto a bed in the cabin and Dad wrapped me tightly in a very thick blanket.

"Son, are you alright? Don't worry, we're heading back to the harbor now. I'm going to get you to a hospital."

"Dad, I'm fine," I said, trying to ignore the fact that everyone onboard was watching. "I'm not even cold so I really don't need this."

I tried to take off the blanket, but he wouldn't let me, and I quickly stopped when I saw his face. He looked as though he was at a complete loss for words and I got the feeling he was close to tears.

"I'm okay Dad, really. Nothing to worry about."

He nodded slowly, turned and thanked Marcus again for saving me, then everyone left the cabin so I could get some rest, which I really didn't need.

Sitting there alone, of all the things I could be thinking about after what just happened, the first thing that came to mind was Marcus. I couldn't stop trying to guess what he wanted to talk about. From the tone of his voice I knew it wasn't anything good. I sensed it had something to do with what happened underwater, but I would have to wait to find that out.

We soon reached the harbor. The trip back didn't feel nearly as long as the one out.

From the moment we docked, Dad insisted on my seeing a doctor, despite the number of times I told him I felt fine. To add to the horror, Mom appeared out of nowhere looking panicked, and ran to me, almost crying when she caught sight of me.

According to Justin, when everyone left me in the cabin, Dad had called my mother to tell her what happened and, just like Dad, she was demanding that I see a doctor.

After I convinced them that all I needed was rest, they agreed that I wouldn't have to see a doctor if I promised to go straight home and get to bed, which I promised. Well... with my fingers crossed. I did have more pressing matters, anyway.

Needless to say, the trip home was a silent one. On the entire drive home my accident kept replaying itself in my mind, increasing my feelings of embarrassment. Sure, I was fine, but it wasn't anything to laugh about, and for it to be me who fell over...

I kept shaking my head every time I thought of it.

Another thing I really couldn't stop thinking about was how I wasn't able to get through the surface of the water. I would never forget how it felt to be pushing against the water but still not be able to break through with air leaving my lungs by the second. And then there was the boat itself in the first place. How it rocked so hard so suddenly when there wasn't anything in the area and the sea was flat.

I looked through the front seat window as Dad was driving me home, looking at the trees blur past but not really seeing them. My mind was too busy coping with what happened to be concerned with the scenery.

That wasn't any accident. It was another attack. I had

to admit that I was amazed at how they were able to manipulate the sea like that. I guess I really wasn't safe on land or at sea.

I risked a glance over at Dad. It was just me and him in the truck as he was going to join the others after dropping me home. I got the feeling he was concentrating so hard on the road because he didn't want to look me, and I knew it was because he was afraid to look at the son he almost lost. He didn't know how to confront that.

Trying to kill me was one thing, but to do it in front of my father? The very thought of it sent powerful ripples of anger through my body. Whoever it was obviously didn't care what it would have done to my Dad to see me die like that.

Knowing that someone was using magic to kill me, and that I was unable to defend myself should have left me scared, up the wall with fear even. But I wasn't. I mean, sure, when the attacks are occurring I'm terrified, but I didn't walk around looking over my shoulder panicking about when the next attack would come. And I really hoped it pissed this guy off if he knew that. But right now, I wasn't calm. All I could think about was getting back at this person, letting them know I was still alive and fine after all their efforts.

I'd just started to relax a little when I felt a surge of white hot anger course through my body, and considering my own anger was nowhere as strong, there was only one explanation about where it came from, one I'd been turning over in my mind for a while. At first I thought it was ridiculous, but after everything that had happened... well it seemed a lot more possible to me now.

Somehow, at times I was able to pick up on Lyla's emotions. I didn't know how, or even exactly when it started, but I knew I was right. That's what it was. All those alien feelings I'd been having, the ones that sometimes contradicted what I felt, they were coming from Lyla.

What's happening to my life? I thought to myself. *For the two months I've been here, I've almost died, found out about magic and mermaids, become the intended victim of a possible murderer and now I learn I can pick up on people's feelings, or at least Lyla's anyway.*

It was enough to make anyone's head spin, but after a few seconds of introspection I found I was able to cope with it. Maybe I was suited to this life. I didn't know if that was a good thing or not.

Before long, Dad dropped me off at home.

"Dad, wait," I said before I got out, and finally he looked at me. "Dad, I'm fine. Yeah I almost drowned today, and I get that that isn't something you can just shake off, but I'm not in a coma or anything. I don't even have to see a doctor. I'm fine. So knowing that should make you happy."

My dad merely looked at me for a couple seconds then ruffled my hair and gave a hug. "Thanks Chase. You really are a good kid, you know that?"

He told me Mom would be leaving work early to spend the evening with me, then he left. I wasn't happy to hear that. I wasn't too happy about where I had to go next, come to think about it.

Marcus and Nikolai had driven up behind us, so as Mom was going to be home soon, I figured now would be a good time to go see Marcus.

I walked over to the Morgans as quickly as I could

because I was afraid if I took my time, I would be able to talk myself out of going and that wouldn't be good. I have to admit I was a little frightened of Marcus and preferred not to have him come looking for me.

When I got to their front door, I knocked with my hand shaking slightly and when Marcus answered, I had to force myself to stand my ground.

"Come in," he said softly. It was almost a whisper, but there was no mistaking the anger in his voice.

I followed him into the living room where the rest of the family was seated, each of their expressions unreadable. Now would have been a good time to get some kind of emotional reading or whatever from Lyla, but predictably, nothing came.

"Sit," Marcus said, pointing to the empty arm chair across from the others.

"What do you know about us?" He asked. Well, that was getting to the point.

It took me by surprise. And I wasn't alone. Everyone else looked towards Marcus, shocked, though Lyla and Nikolai betrayed a little hint of guilt on their faces. I wasn't sure if anyone else noticed this.

From the moment Marcus said he wanted to see me, I started coming up with responses to that very question, but none of them would pass because I was certain he didn't know for sure what I knew. He probably felt something when he saved me.

Everyone had now turned expectantly towards me for my reply, but I focused on Lyla. Because even though her face was once again unreadable, I found that looking at her calmed me. I opened my mouth to finally respond, but

Lyla suddenly blurted out:

"I told him everything."

Marcus, Salathia and Michael looked more shocked still.

"Lyla, how could you?" Salathia said.

Marcus stood up. There was a mixture of worry and anger on his face.

"Lyla, how could you do that without even consulting me first?"

"Father, if I'd asked you, you would have said no."

"Of course I would have. Do you know the kind of danger we're in now?"

"I'm not stupid you know, father," Lyla retorted with a slight note of anger in her voice. "His life was in danger and I saved him. I didn't have a choice. What was I to tell him, that I was pumped up on drugs?"

"If you had to, yes," Marcus replied, "at least we can deal with that."

"Marcus, calm down," Salathia said. "Lyla, why haven't you told us this?"

"Because I knew you both would respond this way. Chase–"

"Wait a minute," Salathia said, cutting across Lyla. She then turned her sky blue eyes to her youngest son, who seemed to shrink down into his chair under her gaze. I could see on her face that she was putting the pieces together, like she was solving some long forgotten puzzle.

"Chase is the boy that saw you, wasn't he? That's why you were so friendly with him at first, you wanted to see how much he knew." She was good.

Nikolai looked like he wanted to sink into his chair as

far as possible.

"I explained about that already and that one isolated incident has nothing to do with Chase finding out about us."

Considering that the Morgans were acting like I was some kind of liability, I did have the right to be indignant. I stood up, and even though I knew they would have heard me even at a whisper, I still spoke loud enough for humans to hear if they were in the room.

"Stop, all of you. Lyla and Nikolai didn't do anything wrong. And no one is in any danger. Look, Lyla has saved my life more than once now, and if she hadn't told me your secret, I would've probably found out on my own." Which wasn't true at all. "Now I know how important secrecy is for you guys, so when I promised Lyla I wasn't going to tell anyone and I meant it. That's a promise I intend to keep."

"How do we know you will?" Michael asked, speaking for the first time.

I glanced over at Lyla for a second before I replied.

"Because I've gotten to know Lyla and Nikolai, and I can tell this is a nice family and I wouldn't do anything to hurt you. Besides, I owe Lyla anyway, for saving me."

I knew I didn't need to convince Lyla and Nikolai of my sincerity… it was the rest of the family that didn't seem too sure.

Marcus suddenly announced: "Thia, Michael, Nikolai, may we have a moment alone?" He indicated me, Lyla and himself.

Michael and Nick got up without a word and instead of going into another room, they left the house as though they sensed oncoming tensions that they wanted to escape.

"I haven't known you very long, but for some reason I trust you. I do believe you when you say you will keep our secret. But just keep in mind, for your own safety, knowing about us may put you in danger."

Salathia got up and touched my shoulder as she left. Marcus then went back to his seat and I did the same.

"I asked the others to leave because what I am going to ask you may upset Salathia. I don't want to worry her unnecessarily."

Marcus leaned forward in his chair and said, "Tell me... are you hearing Lyla's song?"

The question was meant for me, but Lyla was the one who answered. She gasped loudly as if she'd been stung by something.

"Of course not father, there's no way. I would know such a thing. Even if it did happen, Chase would've told me straight away, wouldn't you?"

Lyla looked placatingly at me. As I gazed into those ocean blue, crystal like eyes, I realized she wasn't asking if it happened. Somehow she already knew it did, but it was as though she was holding out on the off chance that it didn't. Unfortunately, my prolonged silence was enough of a confirmation.

My chest started burning with disbelief. I didn't know you could even count that as an emotion, but it was so strong it clouded everything else I felt, even my own feelings. That's when I realized this was what Lyla was feeling. Oh yeah, now it had to kick in.

Marcus stood up again, this time not with anger, but there was a look of great concern on his young face. He looked like a twenty-eight year old man with all the trouble in the world.

"We have to stop this before it gets any further."

Lyla pulled her gaze away from mine and slowly stood up, as though she already had a plan fully formulated. Something told me I wasn't going to like it.

"You're right father. This has to be stopped now, but I will be the one to do it. I won't let the whole family pay for my mistake. We all shouldn't have to move."

"Whoa, whoa whoa," I said, getting up and shaking my head and hands like I was trying to rid myself of something. "Why are you talking about moving? So I heard the song a couple times. It's not like I'm losing my mind or anything."

Lyla opened her mouth to speak, but Marcus spoke first.

"Tell me this, are you infatuated with my daughter?"

"I won't deny that I'm in love with her. But that has nothing to do with her being an Aquamun."

"Look, Chase," Lyla said, "I'm sorry but we can't be friends anymore. This is one of the things I wanted to avoid in the first place. From the moment I met you, I just got this feeling that I was going to put you in danger. For a while I really did believe we could have made this work, but it's just too dangerous for the both of us. You won't see me again after today. I'm so sorry."

When she was finished, she walked past me without a word, but touched the back of my hand. She wanted to hold it, but changed her mind and went out the door. All this time my body felt so out of my control that I wasn't able to walk, or even talk. The second I heard the door close I snapped back to my senses. It was too late. When I ran outside, ignoring Marcus, Lyla was already gone from sight.

All through the week that followed I found myself suffering from more heartbreak than I ever had in my entire life. Every other kind of pain I'd experienced in my life was nothing compared to this. It was the absolute worst.

As depressed as I was feeling, however, I was able to hide it very well from my parents and friends, as they didn't suspect a thing. I just didn't want everyone thinking I deserved their pity because the most desirable girl on the island had rejected me.

The only person who had any idea of how I really felt was Nikolai. It was funny, but for some reason I didn't mind him being around me as I did everyone else, though that was probably because I saw him as my link to Lyla.

From the day Lyla stopped speaking to me altogether nothing strange happened to me—whoever was attacking me just suddenly decided to stop, as though Lyla was the reason they were after me in the first place. If that was true, I just hoped she wouldn't find out, because if there was any chance of us being any kind of friends again, Lyla confirming that suspicion would certainly crush that.

Even though she told me we were never going to be friends again, I didn't entirely believe that, because the connection between us that allowed us to feel each other's feelings was still working pretty well and with it I felt a huge amount of agony coming from her. It was so strong that I found it very difficult to block, and sometimes when it got mixed up with my emotions, I felt as if even breathing was causing me pain. This feeling, however, still lifted my spirits a little, because the only thing that could have Lyla feeling so horrible was the fact that she couldn't see me anymore.

It was as bad for her as it was for me. That made me feel good because I figured she wouldn't be able to stay away very long. But then again, Lyla had a lot more willpower than I did, which meant she would not come knocking on my front door any time soon.

I still couldn't ignore what I felt, from either of us. So I decided to take the situation into my own hands.

"I don't know if this is such a good idea," Nikolai said one day as he sat at our living room table, "because for one it's not like you can surprise Lyla, she will know you're coming and two, when she finds out I helped you out, it really won't end good for me."

He took an apple from the bowl of fruits on the table and bit into it.

"What?" Nikolai asked unapologetically as I stared at him.

"You look like you're really enjoying that," I simply said.

"So?" He said, raising his eyebrows. He took another huge bite.

"Well, it's just that Lyla told me you don't need to eat or can't even taste food for that matter. So, I'm wondering, why is it that you like to eat?"

Nikolai stopped chewing and looked at the apple as if it contained some kind of important news, then suddenly he just shrugged and continued eating it.

"Just 'cause I don't need to eat doesn't mean I don't like to."

"But... but you can't even taste anything," I argued. Nick just shrugged again.

"That's a small issue."

I simply shook my head and dropped it. "Anyway, you don't have anything to worry about it because I won't tell her you told me she will be home alone today."

"You're going over there now?" Nikolai asked, surprised when I got out my seat.

"Yeah. No time like the present. You can hang out here if you want."

"No thanks. I'm going for a swim. I don't want to be anywhere around here if your little talk doesn't work, because that will just put Lyla in a worse mood. If she wants to find me, she'll have to catch me first. Good luck to you though."

Nick left the house with me, but went down to the beach as I crossed over to the Morgan side of the cliff.

As the Morgans' house came into view, I started to get more nervous about seeing Lyla, because as Nikolai said, if she rejected me again—well, I didn't want to think about it. Their house seemed to be getting immensely bigger the closer I got, I had to take huge breath to calm down and stop myself from turning and running back home.

I was sure that by now Lyla knew I was coming. I rang the door bell and knocked as loudly as I could and waited for five minutes, but no answer came. I slid down the door and sat on the front steps for a couple minutes. Leaning against the door and knowing she could hear me, I said:

"Lyla, please, let me in. I just want to explain to you. At least allow me that much, the chance to give you an explanation."

Even though I knew she could hear me, I wasn't expecting anything to happen, so I was very surprised when she pulled open the front door. I stood up quickly, happy to see her for the first time in over a week. I couldn't help smiling at her.

"Hi."

"Hi," she replied in a mostly indifferent voice, but deep down I detected a note of guilty pleasure. As usual she was dressed casually in jeans and a shirt, but she somehow made it seem like she was rocking designer clothes.

"Lyla, may I come in, please? We need to talk."

Lyla's eyes gazed past me and swept the area behind me as though she was looking for something, then after about two seconds, she looked back at me.

"How did you know I was home today?"

"I just guessed. I figured you would want some time alone to yourself."

She folded her hands, cocked her head in disbelief, and looked me straight in the eyes as if she was trying to see my thoughts. I was pretty sure Aquamuns couldn't do that, but still I got that feeling again, as if Lyla's eyes could see the truth anywhere. But even thinking this, I couldn't look away. I'd missed seeing those beautiful eyes so much.

"Hmm, he'll pay for this," she whispered, then stepped back and motioned for me to come in. I followed her into the living room where we sat opposite each other.

I took a deep, steadying breath before I started.

"Lyla–" Before I could say any more, she said:

"Why, Chase? Why didn't you tell me you were hearing the song? You know how dangerous it was and you didn't say a thing to me."

"Because I didn't want to worry you." I said quickly.

"That's not true." I was taken aback at that response.

"What do you mean?"

"I'm sure you really didn't want to worry me, but be honest. The real reason you didn't tell me you were hearing the song was because you were afraid I would stop seeing you, isn't that true?"

I wanted so badly to contradict her. In fact, I'd even opened my mouth to do so, but not a word came out. I knew that lying wasn't the best option right now, and the fact that she brought it up meant that if I had any shot at making this right, I would have to start there.

"Yeah, it's true," I admitted, "I knew if I told you, you would have run in the opposite direction before I would even have a chance to say anything."

"You don't know that." She said forcefully.

"Yes I do," I replied just as forcefully, "and why are you even arguing it when that's exactly what you did?"

"Honestly I don't know why I am, I guess I just want any excuse to shout at you," she said reproachfully.

I looked at her for a couple seconds, then chuckled. But she didn't seem to find any humour in it. She stood up quickly, looking half-stern, half-hurt.

"It's not funny Chase. You know how afraid I am of hurting anyone like that, especially you, and you didn't tell me it was happening. You didn't even stop to think what it would do to my family if we were switched. We would be split apart because I wouldn't be able to live with them, and you, you would have to leave your family. Did you even think of how much it would hurt your parents if you just left home and didn't come back? And I know you didn't have my best interest in mind, because if you did, you would have thought about how it would have destroyed me if you were to be cursed like that because of me."

Lyla covered her eyes as if she wanted to hide tears she was fighting to hold back.

"You know what? It doesn't even matter now. You can just go."

She turned and made to head up the stairs, but before she moved off the spot, I grabbed her wrist to stop her. As my hand slid down into hers, she turned back around to face me. Her hand still in mine, I closed the space between us.

I felt so warm from the moment my hand touched her, and now her scent seemed to be casting some kind of spell on me, but I didn't fight it. I'd missed it too much.

"That's not true, so please don't say that," I took hold of her other hand, which seemed to surprise her from the sharp intake of breath she just took. "Look, you're right. I didn't tell you I was hearing your song because I didn't want to give you a reason to leave. It was wrong of me, and had this gone wrong, it could have caused a lot of trouble. But I was so scared that you were going to leave if you found out, I just didn't want that to happen."

"But, Chase, you should still have told me."

She sighed and looked down for a couple seconds, then looked back at me. "We can't be close to each other now, not when the risk of me hurting you is so much greater."

"Does it feel like you're gonna hurt me right now?" I asked softly, staring her right in the eyes. It was the first time I ever noticed that I was a few inches taller than Lyla.

"I – I – I don't really trust my feelings right now," she whispered back. "Chase, don't."

She said this because I was now leaning towards her, but she made no movement to stop me. In fact, it was as if she couldn't resist some charm I was casting on her, so she closed the space between us and kissed me.

It was even better than the first kiss. I still felt like I was the luckiest, most carefree person in the world. Every one of my troubles and fears were gone, but that's not what made it good. The kiss itself, having Lyla so close to me, was what made it feel so amazing.

After a few seconds, Lyla pulled away forcefully from me.

"Why did you do that? And why are you looking at me like that?" She said angrily, though she made no attempt to pull out of my hands.

"Well, that was amazing," I said, feeling just a little shy. I was still trying to catch my breath as the after-effects of the kiss were still upon me.

"That's why I'm so angry. You are always ready to take risk without even thinking of the consequences."

"Lyla, if you'd just take a minute, you'd realize that I just kissed you after being able to hear your song and nothing happened," I said triumphantly. Shock took over her look of rage.

"But... I don't understand. How is this possible? What's happening? What is it that's so different about us?"

She pondered all at once. I was sure she wasn't asking me these questions so much as thinking out loud, but I still responded.

"I have no idea. But don't you know what it means?"

When she continued to stare at me questioningly, I went on.

"It means… I'm somehow immune to your power. You can't turn me, even if you wanted to."

"Immune? Chase, that's impossible," she said defiantly.

"We just proved it, Lyla," I argued, "and that means there is no reason for us not to be together. Lyla, I love you and I know you love me, I can literally feel it. There is nothing stopping us from being together now and I hope you forgive me for saying this, but now that you can't use that as an excuse for us to not be together, you refusing to be with me just makes you stubborn."

Lyla pulled herself from my hands and turned around. For a second I was afraid she was going to reject me again, that she was going to say she could never be with me. But after adjusting her hair, she just told me:

"My father isn't going to like this."

"Isn't going to like what, Lyla?" My heart was starting to beat faster.

"It's not that he doesn't like you," she continued, ignoring my question, "it's just he doesn't want me to get hurt if someone were to find out our secret. He just wants to keep us safe."

I gently took hold of Lyla's shoulders and pulled her closer to me.

"Lyla, believe me, I won't hurt in any way. And yeah, I know your father won't like us being together. Neither will Kristian or Hilda for that matter, but I'm not going to let other people's feelings get in our way. If you just give me a chance, I can't promise you it will be perfect, but I can promise you I will try my best to be all you will ever need."

I was feeling so nervous that I was sure Lyla could hear it in my voice, even using normal human hearing. She turned back to face me and for the first time she leaned in to kiss me.

"The truth is Chase," she said, when we broke apart, "I'm tired of fighting it. I love you and I want to be with you."

CHAPTER 9

Dreams

Lyla *Morgan is my girlfriend*. That's what I kept repeating in my head day after day since Lyla and I got together and no matter how many times I said it, it always made me feel like I was on cloud nine.

We were right in saying some people wouldn't like us together. And those were the people we'd already called: Marcus, Hilda and Kristian. When we told Lyla's father the following day, I got the strangest feeling a couple hundred miles between us would've been in my best interest, as I could have sworn his light blue eyes were turning red.

"Lyla, you know the dangers and the risks such a relationship with this boy could hold for us... for you. You know how badly this could turn out. Are you sure this is what you want?"

He asked her when we were sitting in their living room that day. Michael might have been furious, though trying to keep it contained, but I could tell Salathia was leaping for joy inside, though she hadn't said a word yet.

"Yes, father," Lyla replied. "I am sure this is what I

want. And yes, I do know the dangers and risks that come with a relationship with me and Chase, but I also know of the rewards. Father, I am fine by myself, you know that, but I don't want to be alone when there is someone I love but more importantly, knows my secret and still loves me."

Marcus was about to speak, but Salathia gave him a look and he looked away and sat back in his chair.

"You two will have to be careful, but as long as you're happy, that's all that really matters. I'm sure everything will be fine." Salathia said, smiling brightly. It was a huge relief that she was on our side.

Our relationship wasn't something we could hide from our friends, as we were now spending a lot of time together. But I have to admit, the look on everyone's face was so comical the first time Lyla and I kissed in public. It was like on TV—everyone's mouths were literally hanging open. They really couldn't believe that I was now Lyla Morgan's boyfriend.

"That's like saying Brandon has a chance of dating Rihanna," Maranda joked.

"Wait a minute. Are you saying I couldn't have a chance with Rihanna?" Brandon shot at Kimberley. Everyone looked at him for a second and then laughed, even Brandon.

With no more attacks and with Lyla as my girlfriend, the last few remaining weeks of August were nothing less than amazing. We spent most of our days together and almost every night. When I went to bed, Lyla would come through my bedroom window and stay with me. Simply just having my arms around her as I slept made me feel contented, blessed. And I made sure that every night I gave thanks that my parents forced me to come to this place.

(Yeah, yeah… I know. Don't rub it in.)

One night when I was about to go to bed, Lyla was looking out through my bedroom window when she suddenly said:

"I'm going down to the beach. Get dressed and come with me."

"What? Now?"

Lyla turned around, giggled and came over to kiss me.

"Yes now. I just have this strong urge to go down there with you. Get dressed and I'll meet you down there."

Laughing, she jumped through the window. I knew she ran off to the beach the second she touched the ground. I was left standing surprised in my room. After a few seconds the same feelings, the desire to be on the beach with Lyla, came over me. I pulled a pair of short pants over my boxers, got a shirt and went through the window and down the tree after her.

When I got down to the beach I spotted her and walked over. She lay comfortably on her back on the sand with her eyes closed, and I lay down next to her. Even though her eyes were closed and I made no sound as I walked on the sand, she still knew I was there, because as soon as my head was against the sand, she took my hand in hers and laughed lightly as she enjoyed the feel of my fingers. When she finally turned her head towards me, she opened her eyes and I was immediately stunned by their beauty.

"What?" I asked, feeling a little shy when she started smiling at me. Even though I was more than glad we were finally together, I couldn't imagine what had kept her so interested in me.

"You just feel so good. So warm." She trailed a finger

along a vein on my arm.

"Really? I feel warm to you?" I said disbelievingly, "because right now, I'm actually feeling kind of cold."

Lyla propped herself up on her elbows, with her hands cupping her face and her hair casually resting on her shoulders. She laughed at my statement.

"I meant to me. Aquamuns don't have body heat, or we can't feel it," she hesitated for a moment, then continued. "Actually, we don't feel anything at all."

I stared wide-eyed at her.

"What do you mean, you don't feel anything?"

"Well, we don't have a sense of touch. Not like humans do, anyway."

"Seriously?"

"Yeah. We can detect when we touch something. We know it's there, we can tell if it's a solid or liquid, soft or hard, hot or cold. We *detect* those things, but we don't *feel* them. Like, for instance, even though it's cold outside right now, I can't feel it, but my body can detect the temperature around me. So if someone asked, I'd at least be able to say '*It's chilly out*'. It's kind of weird though, always having to pretend to be cold or hot or when the temperature's too high for a human to be 'warm', but it's something you get used to. I wish I could have one day where I could experience everything like a human... that would be amazing."
 She had such a dreamy look on her face when she said it that I knew it was something she'd thought about before.

I remained quiet for a while, taking in everything Lyla had just said, but then realized what she just said contradicted something she said before.

"So that really means you can't feel my body heat, you

can only detect it."

Lyla placed her hand on my chest and my entire body was flooded with warmth. That brought another question to me. But I decided I was going to ask her later.

"Well, that's what's odd about you. You see, every other human feels the same to me, like everything thing else... so empty, lifeless. But not you, you're different. From the moment I touched you the night I saved you, it's like a whole new world opened up for me because now... I can feel things. Well, I can only experience some things with you, like feeling your body react to me. It doesn't happen with any other human, just you. But it's still incredibly amazing. When I touch you, I'm actually *feeling* you and that's not even the most of it. When the wind blows, I can feel it on my skin. When I go swimming, the ocean feels so alive and inviting now, like I can become one with it. Chase, I don't know how or why I'm feeling these things, but I don't want it to stop. I finally know how it feels to really be alive."

"Maybe, it's me," I said after a moment of thought. "Maybe, there's something different about me, and that's why these thing are happening to you."

Lyla absentmindedly said: "Maybe," and exhaled, her amazingly sweet breath filling my lungs and dulling my mind, making me crave her more than I already did.

"There's something else," she admitted suddenly. "It's something strange. Ever since that night," I knew she was referring to the night I met her. "I've been feeling these... emotions. The thing is, these emotions, well, they weren't mine. You know what I'm talking about, don't you?" She watched my reaction closely.

I sat up and Lyla did the same, once again putting her arms around her legs. I looked at her and couldn't help but marvel at the intensity with which she regarded me.

"I do. At first, I really didn't know what to think, because I was feeling things I knew had nothing to do with me and in the beginning it had me a bit scared. But when I realized what I was feeling was coming from you, I couldn't, no, I didn't want to fight it anymore. I didn't care if I even got hurt, as long as I got to be with you."

Lyla sighed exasperatedly and turned away from me.

Through the connection we were just talking about, I was able to deduce that the anger she was now feeling was aimed at herself, for she still felt that sooner or later she was going to hurt me in one way or another. I was very surprised at how much information I was able to get just from one emotion. I reached out and turned her face towards mine and surprisingly, she complied without any resistance.

"Lyla, I love you. No amount of danger in the world could make me want to stay away from you, not even if you think that danger is inside you, which I don't think it is.

"What makes you say that?" She sounded desperate for reassurance.

"Look at us," I searched for the perfect thing to say. "Lyla, look at what we do for each other. You said the things you experience with me, you don't feel with other humans. When an Aquamun forms a bond for the switch with a human, do they have this kind of connection?"

She shook her head. "Nothing like this."

"You see? And I've never felt this way about anyone

else in my life, even though compared to yours, seventeen years isn't that long to live."

"Trust me, being immortal just means you feel every tick of the clock. Anyway, there's something else about Aquamuns I haven't told you, maybe then you will understand my worry."

"Okay, but I can tell you now, it won't change anything," I said honestly.

She took my hands in hers, pulled me up, and we started strolling along the beach, hand in hand. That got me thinking of how funny it was that I felt so at ease with being so emotionally entangled with a mermaid. Then I started to wonder... what if Lyla was human? Would half the romance between us even exist? I became aware that she started to speak and pulled myself back to our conversation.

"Chase, when an Aquamun has compelled a human to perform the switch, a kind of emotional bond similar to what we apparently have is formed between the two. The reason for it is so we can get closer to the human we want to turn, because the switch happens on an emotional level. With the link, we're able to manipulate their emotions, make them feel not only what we do, but what we want them too. Another thing is, we can go into their dreams and make them realistically see anything we want them to. I have to admit, that's something I would actually want to experience, because we sleep, but we don't dream.

"So, all the times I've dreamt about you, that was actually you in my head."

Lyla turned her head towards the sea and I had a feeling she was blushing when she said: "Well, no. Those times, it was all you. Since the connection was formed, I haven't been able to control your dreams. I admit, I tried a couple times, but I was just curious."

I laughed. "But I have been having dreams. At first, I believe I was dreaming what you were."

"What makes you think so?"

"Because I felt I was in your mind. Besides, I've seen enough of myself not to be dreaming about me the way you do, so it had to be yours."

This time I was the one that turned away shyly, but Lyla continued as if there was no interruption. "Now, I have the most wonderful dreams. Sometimes I just see colors and shapes, but at times they're just like yours, and there are times when you are even in them."

Again, Lyla led me to a tree which we sat underneath and she giggled in the child-like voice of hers that made her seem more carefree. That's why I loved it.

"Even though we can't explain what or why this has happened to us, it obviously didn't happen for any bad reason because it's brought us to each other," I said.

She just kept smiling and fell onto her back on the sand. I remained in silence for a while, just appreciating her and the ambiance around us.

I'd been living on the island for three months now. I still hadn't gotten quite used to the Caribbean sea, but always hearing the constant swooshing of its ebb and flow was very relaxing.

The air was blowing a little, but to me if felt strangely lifeless as the sound of Lyla's voice was absent from it. I just longed to hear her beautiful voice.

"Tell me more about Aquamuns."

"What do you want to know?"

"Anything," I exclaimed eagerly. Lyla laughed out loud, a beautiful, song-like laugh that was unachievable by any human.

This time, before she could reach for my hand, I took hers in mine and through our bond I felt her pleasure at this. She opened her eyes and looked up at the sky. I followed her gaze, wondering if I could see what kept her so in awe about the night sky. There were huge clouds in the sky, blocking the moon from sight, but there were still dozens of stars out, twinkling brightly as they shone down on us.

"Okay. Well first off, I um… I don't have to eat," Lyla admitted nervously, as though this bit of information would somehow be her undoing. I couldn't keep the surprise out of my voice.

"How can you not eat?"

"I didn't say I can't. I said I don't have to. Aquamuns don't have a need for food because we don't use it for energy as we get all the energy we need from the sea."

Lyla avoided my gaze by focusing on a spot above my head, as if she was afraid of what my response would be. I got the strange feeling she would now try to pull her hand out of mine, but she wasn't because I very easily kept our hands together.

"Must be interesting to never be hungry, but I got to tell you, that would be true torture because I love to eat."

"Yes Chase, everyone knows that's true," Lyla said, laughing.

"You said you don't have to, so does that mean you do eat?"

I was happy to see that a smile found its way back to Lyla's face and I felt, through our connection, that she was happy that I wasn't freaking out.

"Of course. I eat all the time like when I'm at school or out with friends, but I only used to do it for appearances sake. See, we've come to notice no matter how careful you try to be, it's the little things humans pick up on the fastest. Someone would have noticed we don't eat if we didn't sometimes. It's just I never used to like to eat because of the taste, or lack of taste I should say, food used to have and that repulsed me. Aquamuns don't have a sense of taste either, but we can sense the difference in food."

"To keep up the charade." I offered.

She nodded, her gaze still on the stars above, though with more intensity than usual, and that's when I caught onto something she said.

"Wait, 'used to'? You said you used to never like to eat? What, you do now?"

Forcefully, Lyla pulled her gaze away from above and looked at me. But as she did, I understood what she must have been implying.

"This connection between us. It's changed that too?"

"Yeah. I don't know when it started, but I first really noticed it a couple weeks ago. Father had someone over for dinner and when we sat down and began to eat, I felt every little flavor explode inside my mouth." She chuckled and continued. "I started eating everything on the table. Mr. Corner was obviously surprised and simply thought I had a 'healthy' appetite, but my family, however, have been more concerned about me."

"Hold on, did you tell them about the connection?" I

asked, a little surprised. Lyla drew herself up and looked me straight in the eyes and it was as if her amazing blue eyes were close to seeing into my soul. "Yes, I told them. But the thing is, they kind of already knew something was different about you."

"Something different about me? What are you talking about?"

Lyla looked uncomfortable, then she said, "It's past one in the morning, maybe it's time you got home…"

"No," I interjected firmly but gently. "Tell me what you mean by that."

When I told Lyla maybe there was something different about me, I had no idea that was the general consensus among her family. It's not like I was worried, at least not yet, but it did intrigue me.

"You know how the witch Hilda has the ability to see auras; well, Aquamuns can too. You told me you got Hilda's attention because she said she couldn't see your aura, well my family became worried, not because they couldn't see your aura, it's just yours is a little… odd."

"How so?"

"Well, because your aura tends to, um, well change."

"Is that bad?" I asked slowly. Lyla thought about it for a couple seconds. "We really don't know. We've never heard of anything like this before. It's so strange, whereas everyone's aura, humans and Aquamuns alike, is one color, yours is just white."

"Let me guess, no one ever has a white aura?"

"Exactly," Lyla said, "Which might explain why Hilda and the Somorians can't see it. Aquamuns probably can because of the bond you have with me. That's my best guess. And because your aura is white, it makes you untraceable."

"What do you mean?"

"Well, everyone's aura is unique and the same way you can leave a scent, your aura leaves a trail, one we can trace to find you, but not yours. That's what my family meant when they said you are different. You should know though," Lyla added, "That the only time a human's aura disappears to supernatural humans is when the connection is formed between the human and an Aquamun for the switch, but as my father said your situation hasn't been documented, we don't know what to think. Other than everything you've told me, is there anything else I should know, any other changes that happened to you?"

There was a kind of pleading in her voice as if she was hoping, no, praying I was going to say no.

Lyla's emotions suddenly pushed themselves on me. Coming from her, through the bond, I sensed her happiness at being there with me. That was her current dominant emotion, but under that there was a kind of dormant fear. Fear that what was happening was somehow going to destroy me.

"I told you everything that's happened," I said slowly and reassuringly.

"Oh, good," she muttered.

"Do you think something's happening to me?"

"I don't know, but I'm worried." Lyla moved over to me and sat down between my legs and as soon as she did, I had my arms around her and her head was against my chest.

"I think we ought to see Hilda," Lyla suggested with a

deep sigh.

"Why?" I blurted out.

"Because as much as we may not like it, she may be able to give us some answers about what's going on with us and maybe some insight on who's attacking you."

I was on the verge of saying no, because honestly I wanted to keep as much distance between Hilda and I as possible, but the pleading in Lyla's voice when she made the suggestion plus the feelings coming through our bond made me know she just wanted closure and I couldn't deny her that. When I said okay it was more to comfort her than because I actually wanted to go. She did become a little more relaxed, so I guess it was worth it.

"Simply being with you like this makes it hard to worry about myself," I whispered as I lightly kissed Lyla on her cheek. The clouds overhead had now cleared and the bright moonlight shone down brightly on us, giving Lyla's skin a kind of white glow about it as if dozens of white fireflies were glowing underneath her skin.

"Are you okay? Why so silent all of a sudden?" She asked. When she turned around, I could have sworn her eyes were glowing the most amazing blue I'd ever seen. I shook myself out of the trance I was slipping into as I stared into them.

"You are so beautiful. I'm serious. Angels probably look like you."

Lyla turned her head and let her long, black hair cover her face to hide her blushing, but that didn't matter to me. I pushed her hair behind her ears and lowered my face to hers, towards her lips, as though they were pulling me to them.

At first we merely kissed softly, but soon we gave in to a kind of fierce passion I'd never experienced before, not even with Lyla. She was finally starting to let her guard down. I now not only felt it burning inside me but, thanks to the bond, within Lyla as well.

Even though I had promised Lyla we would visit Hilda, that didn't make the thought of it any more tolerable, so for as long as possible I did my best to put it off, but that only lasted for three days, as Lyla was dead set on going.

So on Thursday afternoon, after Lyla had cornered me, we hopped into Shelia and set out for Hilda's house. The drive there felt longer than it actually was due to the silence in the car. Through our bond I felt Lyla's discomfort about where we were going increase. I didn't know if she told her family where she was going, but I figured if they knew, they wouldn't be too happy about it.

If Hilda was able to tell us anything about our connection that wasn't good, Lyla would believe it to be her fault, which was what she was dreading at the moment. It was agony for her to even think about, and all that came barreling over to me.

Taking my left hand off the wheel, I took her hand and gently squeezed it. She returned the gesture and turned to give me a smile, then went back to gazing out the window.

It occurred to me then that as much as Lyla believed that everything I was going through was her fault, the truth was that if she'd never saved my life, she wouldn't be going through this now. It really was all on me.

When we pulled up at Hilda's house, we saw her

working in her front garden and even from inside of the car, I saw the slight smile she was wearing drop a little when she noticed Lyla in the passenger seat of the car.

"Are you sure about this?" I asked Lyla before we got out. Lyla had looked at Hilda as though she was a despised rival.

"My... uh... dislike for the witch... I mean... Hilda aside, we can't deny we need her help. She may be able to give us some answers. Though I should speak as little as possible."

"Why?"

"I don't want to give her a reason to piss me off," Lyla said, getting out of the car first. Laughing, I did the same.

We walked up to Hilda with Lyla two steps behind me, and upon reaching just in front her, I cleared my throat. She looked up at me with an intensity that told me she was trying not to see Lyla.

"Good afternoon, Chase. How can I help you today?"

"I'm ready to talk to you. We..." I made sure to stress the word and indicate Lyla, "Need your help."

Hilda looked momentarily surprised, but quickly composed herself. She regarded us for a couple seconds, then stood up, dusted herself off and said:

"Very well, come inside." She walked off into the house, leaving the door open for us.

I followed her, but just as I passed the threshold I turned and saw Lyla standing just outside the door.

"What's wrong?" I asked. It was her idea to come here, so I couldn't understand why she wouldn't even come inside.

"I can't enter," she replied indifferently. Before I could

say anything else, Hilda came back to the door and removed what looked like a wind chime made of sea shells and sea glass. I noticed there were strange markings on them.

I wasn't sure if it was just me, but as soon as the wind chime was down, I could have sworn I felt a wave of heat pass through me and now the house, to me, felt strangely open, vulnerable.

Hilda smiled slyly at Lyla and said, "Sorry."

Lyla glared at her as she walked in and that's when I understood that coming here was a lot harder on her than it was on me. Hilda led us straight into her living room where we took seats around her circular table.

"What can I do for you?" she asked.

Taking a deep breath, I finally explained everything about Lyla and I to her. When I was finished Hilda was still looking at us seriously, but she couldn't keep the surprise off her face.

"It seems obvious to me what's happening to you Chase."

"No, it isn't," Lyla said, softly but forcefully. "Because I'm not trying to turn him, as that's what you're insinuating."

Hilda leaned forward in her chair, her nostrils flaring.

"I'm not insinuating anything, as it's happening right before us," Hilda retorted, waving her hand towards me. "I knew you Morgans were just the same, despite the harmless act you put on."

Now it was Lyla's turn to lean forward and through our connection, I felt a strong anger rise up inside her.

"Don't bring my family into this. None of us have ever tried to turn a human, ever. I do not know why Chase and I share this bond, nor how it allows me to experience the things I can now, or even how I am able to be in love with Chase. I don't know when it happened, but I'm glad it did. Now, Hilda, the reason Chase and I are here is to discover whether this connection can hurt Chase or if I… will change him, without intending to do so. Can you give us that information?"

After that Lyla just sat silently and looked at Hilda. The tension between them was strong. Then Hilda's black eyes came to rest on me.

"I've never heard of anything you described happening except with the switch and even with that, she shouldn't be having these kinds of experiences if it is the switch. Add to that the fact that she says it's not intentional and we've got a real mystery. I'm sorry Chase, you know I'd like to help you, but I've never heard of anything like this before. But I will do all I can to find something out."

I nodded slowly. Lyla made to stand up, but before she did, I said: "There's something else."

Both Lyla and Hilda turned to stare at me.

I'd decided to tell Hilda about the attacks because, even though coming here wasn't my idea, I was sure she could help with this. But to do this, I had to ignore the looks and emotional waves of curiosity from Lyla.

"I – I mean, we – think someone might be trying to kill me."

"That's a pretty serious thing to say. What makes you say so?"

I recounted to her all the strange attacks that had occurred since I had met Lyla. Even though Lyla told me she didn't believe Hilda to be the one after me, I still searched her face for any trace of guilt or secrets, but I saw none. But I was shocked when she admitted she knew what I was talking about.

"I knew it," she said under her breath when I was finished.

"You knew someone was trying to kill him?" Lyla said surprised, "And you didn't..."

I shot her a 'Lyla-don't-argue-now' look and she kept quiet, though she continued glaring at Hilda.

"How do you already know that?" I asked.

"Because I've been sensing it," she said simply. She seemed to be recalling something to herself before she continued. "It started a few weeks after I met you. You see, usually when someone uses magic, you wouldn't sense it unless you were looking for it. But for a while now someone on the island has been using powerful magic, very powerful dark magic. It's so strong that once it's even woken me from a deep sleep. It's had me very disturbed. I figured whoever's doing it has to be up to something very shady. Then that night I found you and your friends stranded on the side of the road, minutes after I'd just defused one of the spells..."

"What, what do you mean you defused it?" I asked.

"Well, when I sensed it, I used a spell to counter it. The counter was supposed to cancel it out, but that person's spell was so powerful it had a backlash, which was what you felt. Anyway, when I found you, imagine my surprise when I found the spell had been aimed at you, Chase, but out of all of you, you were the only, um, different one, but I had no way of knowing if that was the first time or if all the others were attempts on your life."

"So you've known about this all along. Why didn't you

tell Chase?" Lyla asked, without the attitude.

"For a couple reasons. One, I had no idea he already knew about magic or was sure he was the one being attacked. Two, if he wasn't the one, I was afraid of scaring him or putting him in danger by telling him. And besides, I'd already decided I would try to find this person by myself. They have to be stopped anyway. And three, I was afraid if I told Chase the attacker would find out and get more desperate, pushing them to more extreme measures."

"Well, do you have any idea of who it is?" I asked, but Hilda shook her head.

"Not a clue. See, since the magic this person's using is so very powerful, I was hoping it would leave some kind of trail, leading back to the attacker. But whoever it is seems to be pretty smart, because they're covering the trail and hide their location."

This was very disappointing news. However, Hilda was looking at me as though I was a long awaited gift. I had no idea why she looked so pleased, but what surprised me was when I felt the same feelings coming from Lyla.

"Can you do it without hurting him?" Lyla questioned.

Hilda nodded. "He won't feel a thing," she said as she rose from her seat.

"What are you guys talking about?" I asked.

"Hilda's going to see if she can use you to form a kind trail to find the person that's behind all of this."

"That's correct," Hilda said as she came back into the room with six candles cradled in her arms, along with six candle-stick holders.

After they were placed around the table and the candles lit, Hilda made sure all the curtains in the room were drawn.

The room was filled with a low, yellow-orange glow.

"How is this, um, link supposed to work? I mean, how can you make it if you don't even know who is behind it in the first place?"

"Well because it's already there, as this person has been directing their attacks at you from a distance. Let me explain," she said when she saw that I still looked puzzled. "This person would've had to have contact with you sometime, because when you want to inflict damage on a person using those kinds of spells, you need something belonging to the person, kind of like getting a bloodhound to find someone. With the object they have belonging to you, they can use it like a kind of beacon, allowing the spell to find you and hurt only you. Now, because some of these spells have already affected you, what I'm hoping for is for there to be a kind of residual magical link trace from you leading right back to the attacker."

"Can he use this link to hurt me?"

"No," Hilda responded at once. "If it is there, they won't be able to use it to hurt you. It's not like the one you two share. All it will be able to do is provide us with the location and identity of who is behind this."

Lyla squeezed my hand. "It's going to be okay."

"I know," I responded, not altogether truthfully.

"Give me your hand." I placed my left hand in Hilda's palm, which was surprisingly rough.

"Now, I just want you to close your eyes. And just remember, you have no reason to be nervous. You won't be hurt."

She looked over at Lyla and the look on her face was a little comical. It seemed she'd just realized she was no longer being rude to her.

"I'd like you to complete the circle, please. You're a supernatural being, so your presence will help us greatly," she told Lyla who, in turn, responded by offering her hands to us both.

From the moment Hilda and Lyla's fingers touched, still a little reluctantly, a ripple of warmth seemed to fill our little circle, but I had no idea if it was Hilda's magic or if it was Lyla.

By this time Hilda had closed her eyes and had gone incredibly still. Lyla had also done the same, so I thought for good measure I would do the same too. For a while all I felt was a rising sense of silliness almost to the point where I was getting restless, but then something strange started to happen.

The table began to shake just a little, and then the rocking grew violent and Hilda's hands began to grow mysteriously hot as if she had two burning rocks of coal in her hands. Hilda and Lyla were still not moving.

I tried to pry my hand free from hers, but she had an incredibly strong grip on me. I was starting to get worried when I looked over at Lyla and saw that her eyes were now open and she too was looking worriedly at Hilda. Before either of us could do anything, Hilda's eyes flew open and she pulled her hands from ours. I was shocked to see that even though her hands were physically fine, they were smoking as though they'd been badly burnt. But Hilda, was looking at them as though they were merely smudged with dirt.

"Are you okay?" Lyla asked, not sure what to do.

"Oh yes, I'm fine, but I'm very sorry," Hilda said,

looking at me. "Whoever's doing this seems to really know what they're doing. I tried to trace the link back to the person, but the protection spells they have in place are pretty powerful. I could not even get a general location, much less a mental print of who they are."

Both Lyla and Hilda were visibly disappointed, but strangely I didn't feel that let down. I knew Hilda could help, but for it to be this fast would have just been too easy.

"Hilda, it's okay," I said to her. "You tried your best and to be honest, I'm just glad you're not the one after me, but that just brings us back to square one, anyone could be after me."

Lyla looked over at me with a kind of fierce determination burning on her face and burning through our bond. As her gaze locked onto mine the feeling that I was being hypnotized crept upon me once again, but as usual I didn't want to fight it. Instead, I wanted to fall as far as possible into it; maybe it would bring us closer.

Suddenly Lyla gripped my wrist and it was like a bucket of cold water to the face, I was instantly back to normal and saw Lyla was now looking at me differently, half-concerned, half-exasperated. She leaned towards me and whispered: "I thought you said that stuff was over. Did…" But she broke off when Hilda came back into the room. In fact, I hadn't even noticed she'd left in the first place.

"Did something just happen? Between you two I mean," Hilda said, looking from me to Lyla, then her eyes strayed to Lyla's hand, which was still around my wrist. Lyla quickly released it, then stood up in a defensive way.

"Nothing we can't handle," she said.

Hilda merely stared at her and before she could say

anything, Lyla said:

"You can check for yourself," while holding her palm out to Hilda. She, in turn, looked taken aback by Lyla's directness, but quickly composed herself.

"I've already told you that I'm not going to hurt Chase. I don't need you to keep reminding me that I shouldn't be with him, I promised I'd do my best not to put him in any danger, whether from myself or anything else. But as my word isn't enough for you, and as we also do need your help, I give you permission to check for any lies you think I'm telling."

"You obviously know about magic, you might know a way to conceal something from me," Hilda said, raising an eyebrow.

Lyla smiled in response and said, "You're a skilled witch, I'm pretty sure you would know a way to get around any tricks I would have."

Hilda fixed Lyla with a stare as she just ran her tongue over her lips for a couple seconds.

"You do know the connection works both ways, how do I know you won't try to use it to your advantage?"

"Hilda, despite what you think, my family and I have no quarrel with you. You'll see if I'm lying."

All the while I just sat there listening, looking open-mouthed at the two of them. I wanted to get up and find out what they were talking about, but I didn't do anything partly because I felt that was something between them and maybe it would sort out their differences and anyway, whatever they were talking about, I was hoping I would be able to feel it through our bond.

I had no idea what Lyla meant when she asked Hilda to

check her, but Hilda obviously did, because she walked up to Lyla and placed her palm to hers. It seemed I was right. Whatever was happening between Lyla and Hilda was passing to me through the bond, and it wasn't anything pleasant. It felt like something slimy was passing through me, searching my soul. Only it wasn't my soul Hilda was searching, it was Lyla's emotions.

Through our connection I felt Hilda go through all of Lyla's feelings, but in a different way than I did. It was as though she was able to read her feelings like an open book. Somehow Hilda was able to sift through all the emotions Lyla ever had in her life, though she only focused on the recent ones, specifically the ones she had since she met me.

I tried my hardest to push those feelings away because I remembered the emotional turmoil Lyla went through at that time and I knew I couldn't handle all that at once. But as I tried to keep them away, somehow my own confused feelings got mixed up in whatever they were doing. Finally, they pulled apart, and I felt the huge mountain of emotions between me and Lyla subside.

From the looks their faces, I knew it was something they weren't keen on doing again.

"Do you see now that I'm not lying?" Lyla said, but Hilda was once again looking at me and rubbing her hands together as though they were sore.

"What is it?" I asked. She simply continued to stare and say nothing. She seemed then to shake herself out of her deep thought.

"Oh, it's nothing. The connection you two share allowed me to see a little into your own emotions. Not that I went looking," she added defensively, "it's just your connection is so strong, it intertwines your emotions and it was a little hard to tell them apart at first. When I was feeling through your emotions, Chase, I felt something that surprised me, that's all."

"Okay…" I said slowly. "So anyway, what do we do now?"

"Just be careful…" she sighed as she looked at Lyla, "and stay close to her. She should be able to keep you safe should she need to."

Lyla merely said: "Hmmm," and turned and walked out to the car.

"She really does love you, you know. I know she does, well I do now anyway, but believe me, that doesn't mean she still can't hurt you."

"But you're not so sure she will anymore, are you?"

"What makes you say so?"

"Because if you were, I'm sure you would have told me to stay away from her."

"I still think you should, but it would be a waste of time trying to convince you of that. So as long as she has to be around you, she might as well be of some use."

Hilda followed me to the door, her strange amulet in her hand.

"Just because I think she may harm you doesn't mean I don't believe she will protect you." She said as we stood by the door. She hung the amulet back over the door, and I felt a strange heaviness fall over the house.

Okay, so visiting Hilda gave her more information than us, but at least we knew for sure she wasn't the one trying to kill me, and knowing she was on our side greatly reassured Lyla, and me too.

Instead of going back home, Lyla and I headed to Ridgetown and as soon as we got there, headed for the first Chicken Stack restaurant we found where we ordered chicken and fries. I'd never realized how hungry I was until I started eating.

"Don't you want any?" I said as I washed down a mouthful of fries with some pineapple juice.

Lyla smiled as she watched me. "I'm fine. But I did have a feeling you were hungry. Anyone would have heard the songs your stomach was singing."

"Well, I could have gotten something to eat at home." We'd chosen a seat on the ground floor by the glass wall and I noticed that almost every guy who passed had to take a look at Lyla.

"That's true," Lyla said, picking up a chip and slowly eating it, "But you and I've never spent any real time together doing normal stuff, other than at home, so I thought we'd just use this time for that." I didn't say anything, but I was extremely excited by the idea.

Usually when we were together, our conversations had something to do with the supernatural. So after we ate we walked around town and not once did we talk about any of our troubles. It was like we were just another teenaged couple. For a short while, we were like everyone else.

My greatest happiness didn't only come from being with Lyla. It came from knowing she was happy. I was just glad that being with me brought her that happiness.

The whole time we were out and about, Lyla smiled and

laughed and held my hand with the greatest pleasure. Not once through our bond did I feel any negative emotions coming from her. She must have needed this just as much as I did.

"What?" she asked, still smiling broadly when we got in the car.

"I'm just glad to see you happy."

"Chase, I'm always happy when I'm with you, and I did have a lot of fun tonight. Thank you so much for a wonderful evening."

"You're most welcome."

By the time we got home it was just after 10:00 p.m., but Mom and Dad were still entertaining guests. Chris, Gibbons and a young black woman with long black hair that I didn't know were in our living room. When my mother saw me looking at her, she introduced us.

"Madison, this is my son, Chase."

Madison stood up from the living room couch and shook my hand, eyeing me with interest. "Chase, this is Madison. She just started working at the clinic as my assistant."

Madison smiled and shrugged that off, as if she didn't think that was anything important.

"I'm in college and I want to be a vet someday, so I thought the experience would do me good. But I only put in a couple hours a week," she added sadly, "can't afford to fall back in my studies."

"Quite right," Dad said from his seat.

At that moment, Lyla wrapped her arm around me, which resulted in my hand being pulled from Madison's, whose eyes turned to Lyla with slight interest.

"Hi. I'm Lyla, Chase's girlfriend."

There was a definite stress on 'girlfriend', to which Madison responded with a curtly nod, which Lyla ignored. I was sure the others weren't seeing any of this.

"Well, we'll just go on upstairs. And don't worry," I added, speaking to my Mom, as we starting to climb the stairs, "I know it's getting late. Lyla will be leaving soon. We won't even have enough time to get to the good stuff," I joked.

Mom's head did a double take towards the stairs, but Lyla and I had already rushed up, giggling.

"I can't believe you didn't see that," Lyla said as she dropped down on my bed.

"See what?" I asked as I pulled off my shirt, preparing to take a shower.

"It's so nice to meet you," Lyla said, doing an accurate but cruel impression of Madison. There was no way to hold in the laugh that escaped me.

"Lyla, that's not nice."

"Don't tell me you didn't see the way she looked at me."

I merely shrugged as I pulled off my jeans.

"Go on, don't let me stop you," Lyla teased with her eyebrows raised as I stood there in my boxers. I grabbed a fresh towel and wrapped it around me.

"Easy, girl," I kissed her quickly and left the room to take my shower. When I returned to the bedroom I found Lyla reading my copy of L. G Harding's novel, *The Illusionist*.

"This book is very interesting," she said as she marked her page and then put the book down.

"That's why I like it. So anyway, tell me, what you were saying before? Did you mean Madison likes me?" I fell onto the bed next to her.

"Chase, you mean to say you really couldn't tell? She practically wanted to wish me out of existence."

I laughed because I knew Lyla's pouting was merely playful banter. She knew she had no reason to be jealous. Lyla got up and headed for the door.

"You're leaving," I said, shocked. "Lyla, I really didn't notice…"

I stopped when she placed her index finger by her mouth. "I'll be right back. No need to worry."

She blew a kiss at me and practically drifted out the room. Within a couple of minutes, there was a light tap on my window.

"I just wanted your parents to think I've gone home," she said after I'd opened the window and she climbed in, but there was something strange in her voice.

"Lyla, you have nothing to feel guilty about. It's not like we're having sex or doing anything wrong. We just like each other's company."

She seemed to ease up after that. "You know, a gentleman would've walked a girl home."

"Well, I'm very sorry about that, miss. Allow me to make it up to you."

I leaned forward and kissed her, the sweet taste of her lips filling my mouth, enticing me even further. Lyla and I fell onto the bed and then parted.

"Can I ask you something?"

She turned towards me and nodded.

"Will you stay here, tonight?" I asked.

Lyla chuckled and said: "Chase, I'm here every night, I thought you would have known by now." She snuggled up to me and said, "Of course I will."

I was very surprised when my eyelids started to feel heavy with tiredness, because up until then I didn't feel the slightest bit sleepy. With Lyla here, I really didn't want to waste time sleeping. But as I should have figured, she'd already sensed it through our bond.

"You're sleepy. I can feel it. You should get some rest. I will be here in the morning."

I was about to protest, but as my mind was becoming slow and groggy, I had to focus on what I wanted to say so I wouldn't talk gibberish. During those few seconds when I tried to gather my thoughts was all it took for me to drift off to sleep.

As with a lot of my dreams, the one I was having started incoherently, but very quickly it shifted and became very life-like to me, almost like I was reviewing a memory rather than dreaming. It was so realistic.

The scene all around me was full of chaos and strangely vivid. The dream was in some kind of medieval village. People were running scared in every direction as their homes burned and the screams of the terrified and injured raked the night air. The dream was so real that I was able to feel the heat coming from the fires, smell the smoke rising from the burning homes. But what hurt the most were the cries of the children as they stumbled about, looking for their families.

Then I saw what these people were running from: Aquamuns. And by no means did it look like they were simply trying to switch with some of the villagers. They were taking prisoners and killing anyone who fought back.

One of the Aquamuns that caught my attention was a tall one with short blond hair and he was one of the only

Aquamuns riding a horse. He did look rather impressive on his black stallion. This man looked like he was in his sixties or seventies, but I knew he had to be centuries older and his physical appearance had nothing to do with how powerful he probably was. The way he acted, and how he ordered the others around, I was sure he was their leader.

Suddenly, through all the confusion, he looked at me and inclined his head, as if ordering me somewhere and to my surprise, I actually turned towards a black-haired woman lying on the ground, weeping before me. Even though this was a dream, I still felt a strange, powerful urge to end her life. But at the same time I wanted to shout "run!" to her as she slowly crawled away from me, fear beyond imagining etched on her face. I had no control over what I did or said in this dream.

That's when I crouched down and lunged at the woman. As I flew towards her, my eyes passed over a puddle of water on the ground. It was probably because this was a dream, but the time it took me to pass over the couple inches of water felt long, and in that time my eyes glanced away from the woman and into the puddle. I was horrified to see that, in this dream, I wasn't even me. I was Marcus, Lyla's father.

I sat up in bed with a sharp intake of breath. My body was trembling slightly. I looked over at the other side of the bed and saw Lyla, too, was awake, resting against the bed head.

"I just had a crazy dream. Well... more of a nightmare, I'd say," I said as I too, sat up against the bed head and started rubbing my temples.

"That wasn't a dream," Lyla said so softly, it was almost

a whisper. I looked over at her incredulously. She climbed out of bed and said, "Get dressed. We need to talk."

CHAPTER 10

Family History

A fter I too got out of bed, Lyla told me she wanted to show me something over at her house, even though it was two in the morning. So without hesitation I pulled on a pair of jeans and a shirt, then we went through the window, down the tree and walked over to her house.

A bright moon was in the sky, which provided us with plenty of light as we walked through the chilling night air. The sound of the sea crashing on the cliff was surprisingly soft, so I took that to mean it was probably low tide. Lyla and I didn't talk on our way over to her house.

Though I wanted to stop thinking about it, images from that dream or whatever it was kept flashing through my head, striking fear in my heart. I really couldn't put it out of my head. I just couldn't get over the fact that it was Marcus who helped do those things, that it was he who attacked that woman. I didn't want to entertain the idea that he killed her.

By the time we got to the Morgan house I wasn't yawning so constantly anymore and had grown somewhat accustomed to the cold. Instead of knocking or using a key, Lyla just turned the knob and pushed the front door. But then why would you need to lock your doors when you were an Aquamun?

"Aren't your parents going to be wondering what I'm doing here at this time of night?" I asked Lyla, following her up the stairs.

"They're not home," she replied, heading for the stairs, "though we can sleep, we don't have too. At night, instead of sleeping, we usually go swimming. Much less chance of being spotted. Not like there's a chance we'd be spotted in the day."

"I saw Nikolai during the day," I said defiantly.

"Only you saw him and we know you're different."

"Oh yeah, that's true."

We had just reached the third floor. Thinking on it, I realized I'd never been up there before. Unlike the others, the top floor had a very subdued look about it—the walls were the same color as the carpet, a deep blue. There were five rooms on this floor. Two on the left, two on the right and one at the end and all of them had huge mahogany doors.

Lyla turned both knobs on the second door to the right and walked in. It looked like a very sophisticated home library and it was as huge as the master bedroom, which I'd only seen once. All along the room, there were bookcases and shelves of books, most of which I figured were first editions from the way they looked.

"Chase, I'm going to explain everything you saw while you were sleeping, but first let me start by saying, my father wasn't always the man he is today."

"What do you mean?" I asked with my arms folded.

Lyla walked over to a table by the wall and began looking inside the drawers for something.

"I mean, he wasn't always civilized. He used to live primitively like most other Aquamuns. Ah, here it is."

She'd finally found what she was looking for: a silver key. She walked to the back of the room where a huge cabinet stood. She crouched and inserted the key into the keyhole of one of the bottom cupboards, and when she stood up she was holding a very large hardcover book.

"What the heck is that?" I asked, slightly taken aback at the mere size of it. The thing looked seriously old. Lyla shot me a quick look, but otherwise ignored my comment.

"It's kind of a journal," she explained as she walked back to the table. "You see, my father's very old and believes some parts of his history are too important to our family to forget, so he records important events in here."

She placed the huge book on the table.

"How old is your dad?"

"He was born sometime in the early fifteen century, though he doesn't know the exact date or year. Aquamuns who live primitively don't really keep track of time like we do. My father was born an Aquamun, but as a lot of Aquamuns used to abandon their young, he never knew his parents. So he was forced to raise himself and I guess you could say he never developed a conscience. I told you before we don't experience emotions the way humans do and that's true, but when you add to that an Aquamun who doesn't know the difference between right and wrong, well, let's just say it's asking for trouble and trust me, an Aquamun like that can cause more trouble than you can imagine."

Lyla started flipping through the book, but only turned a few pages when she came to a chapter headed, "Viktor and the house of Aselhoff."

"Sometime near the end of the fifteenth century, my father met him."

Lyla pointed to a picture of a man on the next page, who I instantly recognized as the man from my dreams. It was uncanny how accurate the drawing of him was.

"What's the deal with him?" I wondered aloud.

"His name's Viktor. He just might be the oldest Aquamun alive and they say he is the strongest of us."

"Um... exactly how old is he?"

Lyla shrugged. "Not many know. But father thinks he might be just over one thousand years old and he has the biggest house in the world."

"His house?" I asked.

"It's what we call a group of Aquamuns that live together," Lyla explained. "Anyway, to put it simply, you don't go up against Viktor or his house. Few have tried and even fewer have lived to talk about it. Viktor is a tyrant and believes in Aquamun superiority. He believes we should subjugate as many humans to our rule as possible and sees any Aquamun who seeks to be human as a traitor worthy only of eradication."

"But your dad doesn't want to be human," I explained.

"Well, yes that's true. And in a weird sort of way, that was kind of the problem. You see, when Viktor first met my father, he saw a bit of himself in him. So he took father into his house and used his savagery as a weapon and father proved to be very useful to Viktor. Here."

Lyla turned the page and pointed to the middle paragraph.

It read: "Of all the orphans Viktor had ever taken in, he seemed to take a high liking to me and saw it fit to use me on his assaults, both on humans and Aquamuns, and was very impressed with how I helped in destroying the Raze Aquamun house, something I very much regret these days. After that, Viktor was so impressed with me that he took me into his inner circle."

"Father always said Viktor thought of him as a son, which brings us to this."

Lyla turned two more pages and indicated the one with the heading "The Great Russia Attack". Under that, was a huge picture depicting an image from my dream.

It showed the village burning, people fleeing and Aquamuns running after them. There were a couple of lines under the picture which read "The village of Ominesk. It was once a thriving place, that is until the Aselhoff house attacked. Within two hours, the once lively village was reduced to nothing, though to me, no matter what might have happened here, I will always cite it as the birth place of my new life, for that was where I met Salathia, and with her came the awakening of my consciousness."

I looked over at Lyla, puzzled. I didn't understand what I had read and Lyla felt that through our bond.

"Aquamuns aren't born with a sense of right or wrong, which is why most of us never feel remorse. For those kinds, it's only logic up here." Lyla tapped a finger to the side of her head. "However, when we start to live civilized or become emotionally attached to someone, our own consciousness awakens. As our parents are civilized, ours were awakened at a young age, though Elizabeth was a bit difficult. "

"Who's Elizabeth?" I asked. There really was a whole lot of Lyla's life I didn't know about. "She's my older sister, but younger than Michael. Father told us she was very difficult to handle, so they had to live away from humans for awhile.

"Where is she now?" I was still surprised by this news.

"A few years ago she fell in love with another Aquamun and she went off with him to start their own family. Last we heard from her, they were living in Australia."

Knowing Lyla had a sister in another part of the world made me wonder just how many Aquamuns passed as human. Something then occurred to me.

"Wait a minute, how was I able to dream about that if it was your father's memory?"

Lyla dropped into the chair opposite me before she answered.

"My father passed those memories to us a long time ago. He did it so we would always know what he did in the past and how cruel some of our kind can be."

Lyla sighed heavily and a strong wave of depression came through our bond. After getting to know her, I was usually able to comfort her when she fell into one of her depressed moods. But this time I just didn't know what to say. All the information she had just given to me was still sinking in and my mind was focused only on that.

I sometimes thought that because she was an Aquamun, Lyla believed she didn't have the right to be happy.

"Lyla, you have to remember that's all in the past," I said, sitting on the table and trying to cheer her up, "your dad's a different person now. And even if he wasn't, those were his mistakes, not yours. No one can hold you to them.

"Chase, you deserve to be with someone normal. You need to be with someone who can make you happy without all of this baggage. You don't need all of this trouble."

A surge of anger flared up inside me and before I could try to stop it from passing through our link, it was already to Lyla. She jumped out of her seat nervously.

"What's wrong?"

At first I didn't want to say anything, but then decided it wouldn't be fair to Lyla not tell her why I was angry when she always opened up to me about what she felt.

"You say that all the time," I said as I hopped of the desk and turned to her. "You always say I don't deserve someone like you. And you know, that may be true, because I don't know what great thing I could have done in a past life to be rewarded with having someone as amazing as you to love me. But sometimes when you say I... it just, it just feels like you're trying to find reasons not to be with me."

Lyla quickly reached out and grabbed my hand, and she was so strong that as hard as I tried, I couldn't pull away.

"Don't say that," she said fiercely, "because you know that's not true, so don't even try it."

Lyla breathed slowly for a while, then released my hand and went back to her seat. Probably just wanting something to do, she started flipping through the pages of the book. Once I calmed down I walked behind her and placed my hands on her shoulders.

"You're right. I'm sorry. I shouldn't have said that. It's just that I get so worried that one day I'll wake up and you'll be gone. I haven't known you very long and we've been together only a little while, that's true, but I can't be without you. I love you."

The feelings flowing through our bond calmed us.

"I love you too," she replied softly. "I don't ever want to lose you."

She was still turning the pages of the book. The lamp on the table was our only source of light. When one of the pages caught my eye, I dropped my hand on it to stop her from losing it.

The page had a picture of a very strange symbol.

"What's that?"

She looked at the description beneath the picture.

"It's a siduel. It's what you call symbols and markings like these Somorians use to perform some spells. Why do you ask?"

Lyla was looking up at me for an answer, but I couldn't take my eyes of the symbol, it just seemed so important.

"I think I've seen it somewhere before. But I can't remember where."

"Maybe you saw it in a Somorian community. They sometimes use their symbols for decorative purposes."

"But I've never been to one."

Lyla read the description more closely and then said with surprise, "Chase, it says here this siduel can be used to summon good magic as well as dark. Somorians who practice magic sometimes tattoo siduels onto themselves so they would be able to summon the power as well. Maybe you saw this on the person who attacked you."

Lyla sound excited, but I didn't want to get too optimistic.

"If it's used for both kinds of magic, that might mean a whole bunch of… probably Somorians use it. I might have just seen it somewhere else and forgotten."

"Well you certainly burst that bubble," Lyla joked as she stood up, "If only we knew a Somorian who could tell us for sure."

Lyla closed the book, put it back in its cupboard and then deposited the key back inside the table drawer.

"Lyla, before we go, there's something I want to ask you. Well, actually, it's something I want to do with you."

Lyla walked back to me cautiously as though she was afraid of what I might ask.

"Okay. What is it?" She said slowly.

Excitement flooded through my body. "Just like that, you'll do whatever I ask?" I said as she came to stand in front of me.

"Anything you ask."

I smiled coyly. "Well, supposed I asked you something naughty?"

Lyla laughed and replied, "I trust you."

"Anyway, what I want to do has to do with our connection. I want to know if you're willing to do a little experiment with me. I just want to see how far our connection can go. Sometimes, when I'm relaxed, I swear I can go so deep into your feelings I can't tell yours from mine, just like how Hilda experienced. I want to know if we can really do that."

Lyla considered me for a while. I really thought she was going to say something like it sounded too dangerous or we should wait until we knew more about the connection, but she really surprised me when she sat on the ground, folded her legs and waited for me to do the same.

Once I did, she took my hands into hers.

"There's nothing wrong with trying," she said.

"How are we going to do it?"

"Well, I suppose we just have to get relaxed enough."

"I can do that."

Lyla tried to hold back a laugh, but failed.

"What?" I asked a little embarrassed. Lyla's cheeks flushed red before she answered.

"Chase, you're never really calm around me. Your breathing's always fast, which means you're usually nervous around me."

"Well you can't blame me." I replied with a smile. "You're the most beautiful person in the world. I mean I must look plain standing next to you. But it's something I'm learning to get used too. I can do this." I added seriously.

"Okay," Lyla started, "just close your eyes, relax and allow yourself to be taken in by the bond. When that happens, just try to go as deep into it as you can."

I closed my eyes and began trying to focus. Immediately and without any effort, I felt Lyla's emotions push themselves onto me. But I wanted more than just what she felt at the moment, so I pushed harder on the link.

"Chase, just relax. You're trying too hard," Lyla whispered.

I tried to steady my breathing and instead of trying to pull the connection to me, I decided to just let it come on its own. And sure enough, before long, I found myself falling deeper into Lyla's emotions.

Somewhere, I felt as if something was moving around inside me in a place I couldn't touch and realized Lyla must have been deeper inside my feelings as well. It truly was a strange sensation. I couldn't tell the difference between my own emotions and hers. There was something else too. Each emotion I felt obviously had a reason behind it. As I touched that emotion, I was able to tell the story behind it; the reason for it.

I was most intrigued by the love I felt inside Lyla, so I decided to explore that first. And the first thing that came to me was, well, me. The love in her heart was for me. There was no way, with us so closely connected, that Lyla didn't feel the amazement flowing through me right then.

The rest of the week passed without incident. The most exciting thing that happened was that, with a little more practice, Lyla and I finally learned to control our link. It turned out it was possible for us to control what went through the link. Other than that, it was a pretty normal couple of days for us.

However boring it was, I was secretly dreading its end, because the following week was the first week of…

"School. Get up Chase. It's your first day. You've got to get ready."

Mom started lightly shaking me, but she didn't need to, as I was lying awake with my eyes closed, wishing I had at least a few more days to mentally prepare.

"Chase, it's seven o'clock. You've got to get up now," Mom said a little more loudly as she turned to leave.

I groaned into my pillow and forced myself up. When I got out of bed I had to steady myself because my legs, along with every other part of my body, felt weak with nerves.

Somehow I found my way downstairs where Mom already had prepared eggs, hot dogs and toast.

"Ah, ready for your first day of school?" Dad said as he came in from outside, with Gibbons behind him.

"Not really," I said, wrinkling my nose at the food before me. I was nervous and the smell of breakfast almost made me feel like I was going to be sick, but nonetheless, I started to nibble at it.

"Well, I feel sorry fah yuh, cause yuh startin' school on de same day we goin' diving," Gibbons said a little too gleefully for me as he sat down at the table.

"What!?" I exclaimed, looking thunderstruck at my dad. "You couldn't have done this before today? Dad you knew how much I wanted to go diving."

Dad chuckled as if this was the time for it. "Sorry kid. Maybe next time," he said as he patted me on the shoulder.

"You know, I bet I would have a much better day if I went diving with you guys today and started school tomorrow."

"Absolutely not, Chase Rowland. Don't you even think about it. Neither of you in fact," Mom said, giving Dad a stern look. I was shocked to see that he was actually considering it. Damn, I should have waited until Mom left.

"Besides, it won't be so bad and it's not like you don't already know people there," Mom added. "Lyla and the others go to school there."

"Do you need a ride or will you drive?" Dad asked.

"Actually, I'm going to take the bus with the others."

I tried to gobble down as much breakfast as possible without bringing it back up.

"Well, have a great day son. We'll get going then." Dad left with Gibbons following close behind.

I felt deflated. There was just something that made school almost seem like it would make me miss the important things in life.

"Okay. I'm ready to leave, unless you want me to stay to see you off." I couldn't believe that Mom was serious when she said that.

"Mom, I'm seventeen, not seven, I'm going to be fine."

"The last time you said that to me, I came home to find the kitchen in shambles."

"Mom, you're still going on about that. It's been over a week."

"Okay, just remember the school bus comes around 8:15." Mom gathered her things. "I've left some money on your dresser and Chase, please, use a brush today."

Mom actually stopped in her haste and watched me for a couple seconds. Then she rushed forward and hugged me.

"I know you don't like it here much, but try to have, if not a good day, a tolerable one. You like what you have with Lyla and your friends. If you try, you can do that again, you can make this work." She kissed me goodbye, then was quickly out the door.

I glanced at the clock. It was 7:20. Deciding I needed time to properly prepare, I left the rest of my uneaten breakfast and went to shower.

Even though I took my time getting dressed, I was ready before eight. My friends had told me that was when they would come by, but they arrived early.

"Awww, Chase, you look so handsome," Maranda

said when she got here with Justin, Rachael, Brandon and Kimberley.

"Really," I said, relaxing a little, "Cause I think I look like a dork."

Rachael scoffed. "I doubt you've ever looked like a dork in your life."

"Clearly you've never seen my mother's home movies," I mumbled, looking at the door.

"I thought Lyla and Nikolai would've been here too," Brandon said as we left the house and started walking to the bus stop. Just then second we saw them coming around the bend from their side of the cove.

Lyla looked amazing in everything she wore, but I never expected her to look stunning in her school uniform. Nevertheless, she did in her white blouse, peach skirt and school tie.

"Wow!" The others exclaimed at once.

"I almost forgot how they looked wearing simple school clothes," Brandon admitted in a dreamy voice, looking at Lyla.

"Hey Nikolai," Rachael said, in a little-too-high-pitched voice.

Nikolai's eyes rolled over her and he smiled broadly, "Rachael, don't you look amazing."

Lyla rolled her eyes as she came to me and kissed me on the cheek.

When we got to the bus stop, there were a couple of other students there (some from our school, some from others) and everyone started chatting, but I found it hard to talk as every time I opened my mouth, my stomach started turning uneasily.

"You know, I felt every bit of nervousness you did this morning," Lyla whispered to me as we stood a couple feet from everyone else, which wasn't unusual because every other couple out here seemed to be standing by themselves.

"Really? I'm sorry, I forgot all about the bond."

"It's okay, it gave me a little practice on how to block it out, but I think I can say I didn't enjoy the feeling. Anyway, you really don't have anything to worry about; it's all going to be fine."

I agreed with Lyla, but that didn't stop that strange tickling, nervous sensation from traveling through my body. The school bus finally arrived.

I got on before Lyla and Nikolai, but after the others. When I stepped on, everyone didn't stop talking, but they did turn down their volume and I noticed all eyes were on me, but surprisingly, it didn't bother me one bit. After all, I was the new guy.

However, after I got one of the last free seats and Lyla sat next to me and we started talking, silence fell upon the bus as if everyone was stunned speechless for a couple seconds and even when they returned to their chatting, there was a lot less noise and a lot more glances our way.

"Okay. I know people are always curious about the new guy, but this is just crazy," I said to Lyla. She giggled a bit (everyone seemed to be finding some kind of joke this morning when I was as nervous as ever).

"I think their interest in you is mostly because of me. I'm usually with a couple of my friends when I'm at school, but outside of them, I tend to keep to myself. I don't have to tell you everyone at school knows the Morgans, so they've all gotten used to seeing me either with Nick or by myself when I ride the bus. So I guess they're shocked to see us so close."

I looked casually around the bus and saw that everyone was at some time shooting glances at me as though I was the most interesting thing after TV. But whenever I happened to look at any of them the same time they'd chosen to look at me, they quickly averted their eyes.

I could have sworn even the bus driver risked a glance in the rearview mirror.

Unable to shake off my growing nerves, I spent the rest of the ride in silence, being silently comforted by Lyla. When the bus pulled into the parking lot of the school, my heart started beating like a jackhammer.

"Chase, calm down," Lyla said in my ear, "you'll be fine. Come on."

I followed Lyla and everyone else into the assembly hall, seriously resisting the urge to turn around and run.

The hall was packed with hundreds of students with teachers standing to the sides of the room. Everyone was looking towards the principle, who was addressing the school.

At least I didn't have to stumble around looking for where I belonged because as soon as I was in the hall, a teacher came up to me and after hearing my name and consulting her clipboard, directed me to stand with the class I was placed in: 5-S, which also happened to be Lyla's class. I managed a small sigh of relief.

On our way across to our class I noticed that most students' heads turned to see who I was.

After assembly we were issued our timetables and I was glad to see I was continuing all my subjects from my old school. Lyla and I shared my first two classes of the morning, Math, and Carlyle, Justin and I had Biology together. By the time lunch arrived, my nerves were gone and were replaced with excitement.

"You know, I don't even know what you were so worried about in the first place." Nikolai said as he picked at his lasagna. We were having lunch in front of the school under the shade of a tree. Justin and the others were also with us.

"I think you two are causing a commotion," Brandon joked. It seemed like everyone in the school wanted to walk by just to see this new guy that Lyla Morgan was hanging out with for themselves, who now had his hand cozily around her waist, and who obviously had to be her boyfriend.

"You know, I understand what you told me about them being surprised you let someone get so close to you, but I still can't help but feel a little insulted," I said, enjoying the gentle breeze. From the tone of my voice, my friends knew I was joking.

"Oh really? Insulted about what?" Lyla asked calmly. She was propped against my chest as I, in turn, was sitting against the tree.

"When they all see me, they have this really weird look of surprise on their faces, as if they thought you would have considered me out of your league."

At that moment, everyone dropped something and they all started babbling at once, but I did catch a few words like, "No, that's crazy," and " Why would anyone think that?" but my personal favorite was Nikolai's "Duh, of course you're out of her league."

"Har-har guys. Very funny," I said as Lyla laughed away.

I'd never told anyone, but I *did* think Lyla was out of my league. It didn't make me feel bad, because I was happy and it didn't mean anything to Lyla.

Then I heard someone clear their throat next to me as if they were trying to get my attention. I hadn't even noticed someone had come up to me. Before I could even look to see who it was, Lyla sighed.

"What is it, Dre?" She said exasperatedly without even looking at him. Dre turned out to be a guy who was about my height and age. He had light brown skin and his hair was braided down to his neck. It looked kind of cool.

"Just wanted to say 'hi' and welcome you back to school." He said it innocently enough, but there was something about it I didn't like. I noticed the others had all gone weirdly silent, but Nikolai was smiling as if he was about to get some joke.

Dre was looking at Lyla longingly, but she looked as though she was trying not to notice him. It wasn't hard to figure out what was going on, and it was kind of awkward.

Reluctantly, it seemed, Dre finally turned to me and dropped his smile. I could tell he didn't like how close I was to Lyla.

"You must be the new guy everyone's talking about," he said. There it was, undisputable proof that everyone was talking about me. Through our bond, I felt Lyla's irritation at having Dre around.

"His name is Chase, Dre. Now I don't know what everyone is saying," I bet she did. "But he is my boyfriend and it's best if you give up chasing after me. I told you before, I'm not interested in you that way."

Dre's eyes flickered back to me and a nasty sneer spread across his lips.

"I'll see you later." He strolled off with his friend behind him.

Lyla sat up and looked after Dre and said with a sigh, "he's going to do something, isn't he?"

"Bet on it." Nikolai confirmed.

It seemed that my fears about school were unfounded, because over the next few days things just seemed to be getting better. I was a little ahead in the subjects I was doing, but that didn't last for long as the teachers were going through the course work quickly but carefully. Also, unkown to me at first, I was becoming popular around the school. "Hey Chase", "Yo Chase", "Chase, what's up?"; I would hear this all over school from people I didn't even know.

"You certainly settled in fast," Maranda said to me on Friday evening after school. "Adjusted and popular in your first week, now that has to be some kind of record. Where's Lyla?" She asked, looking through the crowd as we headed towards the car park. That Friday was the first time I'd driven to school.

"Oh, she's got some after-school thing. She told me not to wait for her," I told Maranda when we got in the car. I had promised earlier to take her home.

"I think she tutors. That's good. We're supposed to be involved in some kind of extra-curricular activity. It looks good on a college application."

"Well, as long as it's not mandatory, I think I'll take my chances." I said.

After dropping Maranda home my intention was to go straight home myself, it really was, but as I turned around, the path to the Somorian development caught my eye. I knew going there might be a bad idea, as whoever was trying to harm me could be there, but as nothing had happened in a while, I thought I could risk it.

I just couldn't help it. I couldn't pass up the chance to get to know more about that symbol I saw in the Morgans' book, and as it turned out, I did know a Somorian who could help me. I had just never thought of him before.

Being careful of what feelings went through the bond in order not to worry Lyla, I drove into the Somorian community. I really didn't know what I was expecting to see. For some reason, whenever I thought of the Somorian land, images of log houses always came to mind. But driving along the main road I saw that everything was as modern and normal as the rest of the island, though admittedly it took a little of the magic (so to speak) out of the place. I only stopped briefly to ask someone for directions, which, thankfully, weren't hard to follow. Had I just kept on driving, I would have found the place on my own... well, eventually.

After a while I pulled up to a garage called 'Taylor Mechanics' near the edge of a forest and saw Kimberley and Kristian's father, Jack, working on a very outdated truck. Upon seeing my car he stopped what he was doing and walked over to greet me as I got out.

"Well, this is a surprise," he said after wiping his hands on his work clothes, then shaking my hand. "To what do I owe this pleasure? Wait, don't tell me you're finally going to let me work on your car?" His eyes moved longingly over Sheila.

"No, no," I said quickly. "I came for something else. I need some advice on... well, on magic," I said cautiously. He regarded me strangely for a while, then took the cloth over his shoulder, tucked it into his back pocket and asked me to take a walk with him.

We didn't go very far, only out to the stream in the woods. His house was still in sight through the trees. The sun was now a deep orange and was now starting to fall behind the trees, which told me it was probably close to 6:00 pm.

I sat down on one of the rocks near the stream.

"Tell me Chase," Jack started, "what do you know about the supernatural?"

He spoke in a voice that was so unlike his usual carefree tone. As I needed to know all he could tell me about the symbol, I decided that the truth was my best option, so I told him everything I knew.

"I knew there was something different about you," he said once I was finished, "but as I knew the Morgans would never want to turn human, I didn't know what to think."

"You might want to tell that to your son," I mumbled as I stared into the stream. I was surprised to hear him admit he knew the Morgans didn't want to change.

"What do you mean?" he asked. Apparently he heard me.

I told him all about Kristian's hatred for the Morgans and his attitude towards me because of my relationship with Lyla. Jack shook his head sadly, but before he said anything, I asked, "Does he really know about all this, or did he just guess right or put the pieces together or something?"

"He knows," Jack confessed recently, "but only recently.

"And Kimberley?"

"Kimmie will never know about any of this," Jack said. I swore there was a note of gratitude in his voice.

"Why?" I asked, a little surprised. "Shouldn't she know about her own abilities?"

"Kimberley doesn't have nor will she ever develop any kind of powers. You see, every Somorian doesn't know about the supernatural," Jack began, taking a seat himself. "And that's because, all of us don't have magic. Only the first-born inherit the magic. Kristian is the oldest, so he got the magic, so Kimmie will not develop any powers. And once you don't have any powers, you're not informed about the supernatural world. We see it as a way of keeping the family safe. No need to drag innocent people into this, you see. Anyway, what did you want to ask me about?"

Remembering why I was there in the first place, I rummaged in my pocket and pulled out the drawing of the symbol I made and handed it to Jack.

"Do you know…"

"Where did you see this?" Jack asked in a more serious tone.

"Well, that's just it. I can't remember. That's why I came to you. I figured you could tell me what it means."

"This siduel is used to focus certain types of uncontrollable magic."

"Dark magic," I offered, but Jack shook his head.

"Death magic," he said darkly. Strangely, outside seemed a lot darker all of a sudden. "It's the most dangerous kind of magic there is. You see, even power like dark magic abides by the rules of nature. But not death magic."

Jack started shaking his head again as if he was trying to rid himself of a bad thought.

"It's the worst kind of power anyone can use because it's so uncontrollable and it's a crime against nature to use it because you need a sacrifice to make the spell work. Equivalent exchange, see. You need to use the life energy of something alive to make the spell work, that's why it's so powerful. Using this kind of magic would destroy a person, but with this siduel, the person using it gains some sort of control over the magic. But I can't understand why you would recognize this, because it's a Somorian mark. No other culture in the world uses this and trust me, we know well enough to stay away from this kind of magic."

"Well, someone's being using it on me and I want to find out who. We... I already went to Hilda, but she couldn't find who it is. Anyway, can you help me?" I pleaded.

Jack turned his eyes to the running water for a couple seconds, then slowly said, "There is something we can try, but it will be risky." He handed me back my drawing.

"Look, Mr. Taylor, I understand you don't want to put me in any danger, but I really need to find out who is trying to kill me and why. I may not have much time left," I wasn't referring to my attacker. I said this because I felt a pang of concern through the bond, which meant Lyla knew I was up to something she wouldn't like.

"Okay," Jack agreed. "Let's get back to the house. The kids are out, so we will have some privacy."

When we got back to his house, Jack introduced me to his wife Alisa and he surprised me when he told me he didn't have any Somorian magic, but his wife did. Jack led me into their living room while Alisa went to get some things ready for whatever we were going to do.

"Mr. Taylor, tell me something," I said as I took a seat, "If you don't have any magic, how do you know so much about this stuff if you weren't to be told?"

"It was Alisa who actually brought me into all this," he said with a smile. "See, she was told about her heritage when we were in our late teens and at that time, she was very rebellious. If you didn't want her to do something, just tell her the opposite. When she was forbidden to tell any non-magic users, she came and told me everything."

"Did she get into any kind of trouble?"

"Oh, no," Jack said quickly, "What they fail to tell you is there isn't any real punishment for telling people. Besides, it was okay, Alisa telling me, because when she did, we were already engaged. As you can imagine, I was very intrigued by this. So I made sure to learn as much about it as I could, even though I knew I would never have the power. Though I have to admit I am always a little jealous, it must be amazing to be able to do some of the things they can. Now, Chase, I think it may be possible for you to find whoever is after you through the spirit world."

"Come again?" I asked, taken aback. Jack didn't look surprised and merely smiled.

"It's not as absurd as it sounds, or at least, not fully. The spirit world is simply another place of existence. It's not a place where souls go when we die, it's... well it's kind of hard to explain, but essentially, from over there, you should be able to find out who is attacking you. All magic comes from the spirit world, so there will be some trace of their magic over there and with it, their identity. I should tell you though, that most people who've been trying for years have never been able to cross over and even if you do, there may be things over there that might want to hurt you. So if you do cross over, you have to be very careful."

"If I get hurt over there, will I get hurt here?"

"Your conscious mind goes over with you as well. You will believe you have a corporeal body, even though you won't, so yes. If you get hurt over there, you will get hurt here as well."

I'd watched enough movies and TV shows to know what that meant.

Pang! Another tug on the bond, this time along with irritation and concern. She knew where I was, but not what I was about to do.

"Honestly Mr. Taylor, right now, those aren't what I'm worried about. At least not fully," I said.

"In that case," Alisa said coming back into the room with a tray in her hand laden with several items. "let's begin."

Jack and Alisa shifted the furniture a little, then instructed me to sit on the floor. Once I did, Alisa took a tea cup and pot from the tray, poured a cup of tea and offered it to me, which I refused, feeling this was hardly the time, but Alisa pushed the steaming cup towards me.

"This tea is made with a special herb which helps with the crossing over."

"Then why do some people take so long to cross over if all they've got to do it drink this?" I asked, taking the tea then sipping it. I had to stop myself from spitting it out. It tasted like brewed grass and the fact that it had no sugar was no help.

"Because the tea alone won't let you cross over. We like to think of it as something that merely speeds up the process." Jack said.

As we didn't have time to waste and the cup wasn't big, I straight-pulled the tea, but it left a taste trail from my mouth all the way down to my stomach. As much as I tried, I couldn't get it off my tongue. Alisa handed me another cup, this time it was a clear liquid. I almost groaned, but Alisa simply chuckled. "I've had that tea before so I know how it is and the bitterness can last for hours. This is water, to wash down the taste."

I thanked her and quickly downed the water and was grateful when the bitterness in my mouth subsided. They made me lie on my back, then Alisa took up a small container with plain dirt, which she used to form a circle around me with.

"The spirit world is a place where newcomers such as yourself can easily get lost. Not in the sense were you can't find one place or another, but where you may become so confused, you won't be able to get back to your body." Alisa said once she had formed the circle. "This circle of earth will act as a link, keeping you somewhat tied to this world, so I can pull you back should I need too."

I wanted to say I understood, but my head now felt so groggy and my words were slurred so I simply nodded, or at least, I believe I did. My state of mind seemed to be affecting my bond with Lyla, because I felt it going out of focus. I still felt her emotions, but they felt so distorted, I couldn't tell what I was feeling.

"Now, if it works, when you get over there, things may seem a little strange, but just remember to focus on your goals and you will be fine. All you have to do is think about your attacker and the spirit world should provide you with some answers." Jack said to me. He then told me to close my eyes, which I did, and he and Alisa started chanting.

The tea made me feel I would have quickly fallen asleep from the second my eyes were closed. But I was simply lying there with Jack and Alisa chanting in my ears for hours. Finally, feeling disappointed, I decided it wasn't going to work and was about to tell them when I opened my eyes and saw that I was wrong.

It was such a strange feeling. I knew my eyes were still closed, I could almost feel it in fact, but still they were open because I was seeing everything around me. I was standing in a forest with trees so tall they seemed to stretch all the way to the clouds. Sunlight was pouring down on me but when I looked up, I saw no trace of the sun in the sky.

Time seemed to move strangely in the spirit world, because some things were moving fast while others went along at a slow pace. It was all so fascinating to watch, but I had to remind myself that I had a purpose. This was surprisingly hard to do.

I remembered what Jack told me, so I thought about finding out who my attacker was, and as soon as the thought entered my mind the trees in front of me disappeared, leaving a clear path. But did they disappear or were they simply never there in the first place? It was so hard to tell over here.

Having no other option, I took the path before me, but before I got too far along it I heard a familiar sound, one that sent shivers through my spine. It was a sound I had been hoping I would never hear again.

It was a series of strange growls and barks that couldn't come from any earthly animal, but I couldn't tell which direction they were coming from. With fear now pumping through me I started running ahead on the path before me, but strangely enough, it was as if the further I got, the further I was from where I wanted to go, and the closer the growls and barks got.

That's when I saw them ahead of me. Huge, black dogs with glistening, blood red eyes, like shinning rubies. And the teeth! Those were what I noticed first. Long, yellow, pointed, dagger-like teeth which had ropes of saliva dripping from them.

Shadow hounds.

"Run, Chase, run!" A voice in my head that sounded just like Jack's said, though I didn't need to hear it as I was already running. I didn't risk looking back to slow myself down, but I knew they were catching up. After all, this was their world.

Then, just like that, I was out of the forest. And I wasn't even running anymore, nor was I breathing like I was just running for my life… or for my soul. When I looked back toward the forest I could still see the eyes of the hounds shining through the darkness of the forest that wasn't there. Suddenly the hounds bounded out of the forest, but as soon as they did, they just disappeared.

Unconcerned with them now, I turned my back on the forest, only to realize by what I saw before me that something was wrong. Standing just a couple feet away from me was… well, me. I was just standing there in the sunlight, watching the real me. I don't know why, but upon seeing myself there my first instinct was to run. But somehow, against all the laws of physics (not that they would apply here), when I turned around, I was shocked to see I was still standing directly in front of the fake me.

"Tell me, Chase Rowland, what are you doing in a place like this?" Fake Chase asked tensely. I didn't even want to indulge him in conversation. I just turned on the spot and made to run off, but when I did, fake Chase was already standing there, already in front of me.

"You don't understand this world do you?" He said, indicating everything around us.

"This world changes according to your thoughts. Here, it really is mind over matter. But in our case, its mind over mind because this world will respond to the strongest thoughts, the strongest mind, and that's mine. Now back to my question. But I think the answer's obvious. You're here to find me, aren't you?

"What are you?" I asked, suspense getting the better of me. Fake Chase smiled darkly. "I'm the one after you and I've got to say, you have certainly been able to get yourself out of those situations I sent your way. Not without help though." After seeing how I was looking at him, he went on. "This," he gestured towards himself, "like everything else here, our appearance, also depends on our thoughts. You look like yourself because you came here expecting to look like you do. I, on the other hand, look like you because I figured you would think anyone I appeared as was the one after you, even if I told you I was just using their appearance and I didn't want anyone being blamed for something they didn't do. True, there are other forms I could have chosen, and it would be clear to you that I was just using their appearance, but I just wanted to see the look on your face when you came here and saw yourself and I have to say, it was priceless." He started laughing.

"Why don't you show me who you really are and stop hiding?" I shouted, my anger starting to get the better of me. Fake Chase remained still and said, "Because I can't have you or anyone else getting in my way any more than you already have. Chase, the truth is, I would rather not hurt you. If I thought you could separate yourself from the Aquamun, I would leave it up to you. But I know how connected you two are. I know you will never leave her. I can't let you become what you will if you stay with her. Don't you see? I'm saving you from yourself!"

"And what is it I will become? You think I will want to become an Aquamun myself?"

"I'm sorry, but I can't let it happen."

There was a kind of deranged look on his face, but I didn't have time to ponder that as he reached out with one hand and grabbed me by the throat and lifted me into the air with ease.

As he squeezed, I felt my real body crave more air. I tried to focus my thoughts to getting me away from him, but it seemed to become a hundred times harder to think all of a sudden. The pressure was becoming too much.

Suddenly, there was a kind of presence that took hold of me. The feeling was so intense I had to shut my eyes and when I opened them again, I was glad to see I was looking up at Alisa and Jack, both of whom seemed gravely concerned.

Immediately I started coughing badly. Jack helped me into a sitting position and Alisa handed me another cup of water.

"What happened over there?" Jack asked.

I finished my water, then said, "I saw him. The person attacking me, but he looked like me, so I still don't know who he is."

After insisting I was fine, thanking them for their help and promising I would keep them updated, I left and headed for home. While on the road, many things flashed through my head. I had just entered another world; I did confront my attacker, but still didn't know who he was. The thing that kept bugging me was knowing that I'd forgotten something.

When I got home, the house was in complete darkness, which meant my parents weren't home yet. I was so tired I just went straight to my room. When I got up there, I just dropped my bag on the floor and fell into the bed. But I almost jumped back up at once when I realized someone was already there. However even in the dark, I knew it was her.

Damn it, that's what I forgot, I thought to myself, *Lyla.*

I flipped on the light switch in time to see Lyla stand up and look dangerously angry.

"You better have a really damn good excuse."

CHAPTER 11

The Lillyosa

Lyla knew how to stay mad, that much was evident. Four days had passed since my trip into the spirit world—something I could never come close to forgetting. Even though she was still spending time with me, she was still slightly hostile towards me and even more intense were the waves of anger usually coming through our bond at me.

"You know, even though I've never known Lyla to be so angry," Nikolai told me when we were in the school library, "she usually doesn't stay angry very long. I have to say this is the longest I've ever known her to go. Right now, I bet it's only the idea that you got hurt that's keeping her fueled. Just give her some time. She'll come around."

"Tell me something. Do you think I did something wrong?" I asked him. Since this whole thing had happened Nick hadn't given his opinion. He didn't bother looking up from his biology homework, but he did chuckle a bit.

"You only asked that because you know I'm going to say no. No I don't think you did anything wrong. You were just trying to protect yourself. But then again, Lyla says I'm the reckless one."

Lyla wasn't the only one angry with me for what I did. Since that day I'd only seen Hilda a few times, but each time she made sure I knew how she felt, though thankfully her anger dissipated rather quickly. Despite my previous opinions of her, I'd grown to think of Hilda as a friend.

One evening I was visiting her, helping sort her herbs.

"Chase, I'm very sorry if I made you feel bad. But we are trying to keep you safe and seeing you act so recklessly seems like a serious lack of judgment on your part. It just really angered me. I'm just glad we found you in time."

"How did you know I was in the spirit world, by the way?" I asked. This was something I'd been wondering about for a while now, well at least when I wasn't trying to think of a way to get Lyla to forgive me.

"I thought you would have guessed," Hilda said, putting parsley into a basket to be cleaned. "It was Lyla. From the moment you crossed over, she sensed it. That connection between you two must be pretty strong because she can't cross over to the spirit world, yet she was still able to go over there, find you and bring you back. You two just seem to be breaking all the rules."

"Why can't Aquamuns cross over to the spirit world?"

"There are many theories why. Some people believe Aquamuns are so immune to magic that their immunity seeps down into their souls and stops the magic from working."

Something about the way Hilda kept flaring her nostrils told me she was keeping something to herself.

"You have another reason, don't you?"

263

Hilda looked at me, yet her hands were still strangely sorting the herbs correctly.

"Well, there is another theory, one I find more plausible."

"And that is...?" I said a little roughly. I knew this was something I wasn't going like.

"Some people believe, myself included, that it is because they have no soul to cross over with. That would also explain immunity to magic and also why it's so hard for them to possess emotions."

I couldn't help scoffing at Hilda's explanation.

"That's crazy. How can someone exist without a soul?"

"You don't know that they can't," Hilda said calmly, going through more herbs than me, "and besides, we're talking about Aquamuns, immortal beings, not humans."

"You said yourself that Lyla did cross over. How could she have done that without a soul?" I said that as if it was final.

"You're forgetting about your connection. I wouldn't say it's given her a soul, but it has changed her," Hilda replied as we finished sorting the last of the herbs.

"Well, it's obvious I can't change your mind, but if you were to spend any real time with the Morgans, you'd have no doubt that they do have souls. Besides, none of that matters to me. Lyla loves me and that all that matters."

Hilda rose from the table to take the baskets of herbs to the sink.

"Before you leave, tell me what happened when you were over there. Did you find out anything about whoever is after you?"

"Not really. When we were over there, he looked just like me, so I have no idea who he could be, but he did say the reason he was trying to do me in is because he would rather see me dead then turn into what I was about to become."

Hilda seemed slightly puzzled. "Hmmm, what you're about to become," she said this to herself.

"He thinks she wants to turn you, or you want her to change you. A psycho with a mission. Chase, from now on you have to be more careful," Hilda told me as she walked me to my car.

"Of course I will be," I said to her, then drove off.

When I got home it was after 7:00 and I was exhausted, but I still made sure to call Lyla. When Michael answered, he told me she wasn't at home. It's not like I had to know where Lyla was, it's just she usually told me when she would be away, so her unexpected absence left me puzzled.

Well, I knew how she felt now.

As soon as I'd hung up the phone, I decided to see what she was feeling, but I was surprised when all I felt from her was extreme calmness. Surely she wasn't trying to avoid me.

I decided to put it out of my mind for the time being. So after a shower and dinner I thought I'd get started on my biology homework, but just as I reached my bedroom door, something I hadn't felt in a couple weeks happened.

Just as I gripped the doorknob, something like a powerful magnetic feeling cruised through my body. This time it was so strong I was afraid I might actually be pulled through the door if I didn't open it fast enough.

In my haste, I pushed open the door a little too hard. There she was, lying on my bed, reading *The Illusionist* again.

"You know if you like that book so much, you can have it."

The fact that sometimes just seeing her had this effect on me just made me swell up inside with a good feeling, one I knew Lyla could feel through our bond.

She got up, dropped the book on the bed, walked over to me and took my hands.

"I owe you an apology," she said, moving one hand to touch my face.

"For what?"

"For being so defensive and pulling away from you. I was angry at what you did, yes, but I still shouldn't have acted the way I did, knowing the danger you're in."

"Lyla, you didn't do anything wrong. I won't deny that I did suffer from not having you with me," I teased as I pulled Lyla closer to me. It was she who kissed me first. It was like she was taking a long-desired drink of water after a day in the desert.

I knew now I was truly forgiven.

From then on my time with Lyla seemed somehow more special, magical, like every second with her was more precious to me than even my next breath of air.

Within a few days October arrived and with it came the heavy downpour of rain during the day and long, chilly nights. Lyla stayed with me most nights and kept me warm. She was spending a lot more nights with me and she told me it was simply because she wanted to. Because of our bond, I knew that was partially true, but I had a feeling she just wanted to make sure I was okay, to be there to help me if anything should happen, though nothing had happened since the spirit world incident.

This didn't bother me one bit. It just meant I got to spend more time with her. I even loved the times when we were together just lying in bed, both awake but not even talking, because just having her there meant the world to me.

"The sea must really be cold these days," I said one night from my bedroom window, listening to the sound of the sea hitting the cliffs while getting a full blast of the cold night wind in the face.

"Well actually, it's really not that cold yet," Lyla suddenly appeared in the tree by my window. "You knew I was down there, didn't you?" She said after a second, a little disappointed.

Recently I had discovered how to control the magnetic feeling that always led me to Lyla, so now I always knew when she was near.

"Well, who do you think I was talking to?"

"Humph, I liked being able to surprise you." She pouted mockingly. Through our bond I detected a huge surge of excitement, though I had no idea what it was for.

"What's got you in such good spirits?" I asked as she took up *The illusionist*. She'd just opened the book and threw her slick black hair behind her shoulders, smiling broadly.

"It's something amazing, one of the most amazing things in the world. It's... better if I just show you. Be outside tomorrow at 11:00 pm. This is something you won't want to miss."

I climbed into bed and Lyla snuggled up to me and continued reading, leaving me wondering what more surprises she could possibly have in store.

I didn't really see much of Lyla the next day. When I woke up in the morning I was surprised to find she'd already left. She usually waited until I was up to leave, but through our connection I knew she was with her family, so I just resolved to see her later as she'd promised. I was eager for 11:00 pm to come, because if the whale song was that good, what else could there be?

At 9:00 in the morning, 11:00 pm seemed forever away and after finishing my homework and chores it was only midday, so I headed outside and spent the day with the others.

Very slowly, it seemed, the day ended and soon it was time. When I climbed down the tree, Lyla was already there waiting.

"Are you ready to go?" Her hair was held with a ribbon.

"Yeah, I've been waiting all day. Let's go."

The two of us set off along the road, where, after we turned onto the main road, we found a jeep waiting.

"Let's go, you two," Michael called impatiently from the driver's seat. As soon as Lyla and I were in, he sped off.

"Mother and father have gone on foot. I still don't know why they're making us go, I mean if you've seen it once, you've seen it enough for two lifetimes," Nikolai complained from the front.

"Lyla, what exactly are we going to see?"

Lyla tapped Nick on the head, then said to me, "Don't mind him. If something isn't a little dangerous or reckless, he doesn't like it much. Trust me when I say, you're going to love this. On East Island, October has more than rain and cold nights because it's the only month the Lillyosa blooms."

"What?" I asked, but Nikolai was the one who answered.

"It's a rare flower that only grows on this island and it only blooms for a couple hours once a year."

"It's really beautiful," Lyla said happily, "You'll see."

I was glad Aquamuns couldn't read minds, because I had to agree with Nick on this one. About ten minutes later, Michael brought the jeep to a stop by the side of the road.

"We have to go in there?" I asked when we all go out, pointing to the dense bush that went far inland.

"Yeah, we do," Michael said, starting ahead. "It leads to a small hill we have to climb." Michael stopped and turned to Lyla. "Do you mind if we –" he indicated himself and Nikolai and before he even finished his sentence Lyla nodded her head and said, "We'll be there soon," then Nick and Michael super-sped off into the thick forest.

"How far do we have to go?" I asked Lyla as we started our walk through the bush.

"Well, it might be a while. I think it's a forty minute walk at normal speed." Lyla then looked at me, looking a little apologetic, "That's not a problem is it?"

"No, of course not," I quickly said to make it clear nothing was wrong. Though, even if it was a problem for me, I would have said the same thing for Lyla's benefit.

Just because I was a little reluctant to walk into a thick overgrowth of bush didn't mean I was afraid, because I wasn't. But I did have to keep close to Lyla as the moon was nowhere in sight, which meant I had no light to see and the fact that every tree, bush and rock looked the same only meant it was easy for me to get lost, but not for Lyla because she could see in the dark.

If it wasn't for our bond, I would have thought she was angry with me for some reason, because she didn't say a word to me on the entire trek up. But after carefully shifting through her emotions, I found she was perfectly fine and just wanted to get to the top of the hill.

The journey up wasn't as easy as I would have liked. As we got further up, the bush got more dense and the terrain got rougher. Eventually (it felt a lot longer than forty minutes) we reached the top of the hill and thankfully, because of the breeze, I wasn't hot or exhausted.

The view alone from the top of everything below made it all worth it. We appeared to be so high, I could even see the ocean from where I stood.

Lyla walked over to me.

"It's beautiful up here, isn't it?"

"Hmmm." Was all I replied. From this altitude, it was easier to understand how Aquamuns found such fascination at staring at an object.

"What we're going to see is even more amazing. Come on," Lyla said as she took my hand and guided me through the trees.

As we walked deeper into the forest up here, I became aware of a slight light spreading fast over the forest floor. I looked up through the trees to see the huge full moon emerge from behind two thick black clouds.

"Wow," I whispered, amazed. It was amazing how beautiful the forest looked in the moonlight.

"We're here," Lyla said, stopping just before a small circular clearing.

Here, the moonlight was brightest, but I quickly saw

that was because of what was reflecting the moonlight. The clearing was filled with the most beautiful multicolored flowers I'd ever seen. The leaves of these flowers were of a heavy purple, the petals were flaming red and the bud in the middle, which was now open, was a pure white. And somehow, these flowers were able to reflect light.

The flowers alone would have been enough to make this something to never forget, but it didn't end there. Every color and kind of butterfly was out in the clearing, drawn to the flowers. It was like nothing I'd ever seen before.

"Lyla, how comes no one else knows about this place?" I whispered in awe. Lyla shrugged.

"Maybe no one's ever been here when the flowers have bloomed before. I think that's a good thing. The fact that only we know about it makes it a lot more special when it does happen."

Lyla's hand was still in mine when I walked forward towards the clearing. I pulled her with me, but was extremely surprised when she quickly pulled her hand from mine.

"I'm sorry," she apologized, "but I can't go in there."

"Why not?" Lyla looked around at the flowers, sighed deeply, then walked up to the exact edge of the clearing, kneeled down and touched one of the flowers. When I saw what happened, I wanted to pull her as far away from the flowers as possible, but I didn't need to as she up and back by the tree line in a second.

"Lyla, what –" I started at her palm. It was raw and red and was slightly smoking as if she was burned, but as I was looking at her hand I saw it start to heal to the perfect way it was seconds before, right before my eyes. I grabbed her hand, turned it over and felt the flesh of her palm. It was fully healed.

"I'm fine," she said with a small smile at the look on my face. "The Lillyosas are beautiful flowers, but they are dangerous to Aquamuns. They burn us on touch. Their scent can even knock us out. The flowers aren't strong enough to kill us, but they can do a lot of damage, that's why we appreciate their beauty from a distance."

Lyla dropped to the forest floor and crossed her legs. I sat down next to her, put my arm around her and drew her closer to me. Together, we watched a wonderful display of nature only a few were lucky enough to see.

"I really don't see what's so bad about the Lillyosas, I like them." I said to Nikolai on Monday morning as we were on our way to lunch. He turned to look at me skeptically.

"You wouldn't be so quick to say that if they could hurt you. Anyway, what's going on with you and Lyla?"

"What are you talking about?"

"Well, usually she's always extra chipper around this time of the year because of the Lillyosas blooming, more than her birthday, which for some reason, considering how old we are, she always loves. But this year she –"

I touched Nikolai's shoulder to bring him to a stop. "It's her birthday?" I said a little too loudly in surprise. A few people glanced around at us, but I ignored them.

"Yeah tomorrow, and you…" Nick's voice trailed off and his eyes widened in surprise. "You forgot, didn't you?"

"I didn't even know when her birthday was, she never said. But that shouldn't be an excuse."

"What the hell can we plan for her in such a short time? In fact, she has almost everything she wants, she... let's think, generally, what can you give her that wouldn't suck?"

I punched him in the shoulder as he laughed at his own joke.

When Lyla and the others came into view and she beckoned us over to their bench in the yard, a brilliant, fully formed idea came into my head.

I stopped Nick again. "I know what I can get Lyla for her birthday. It's something I know she'll love, but I will need your help."

It wasn't easy pulling off Lyla's surprise at such short notice, but I felt I needed to do something extra special to make up for not even asking when her birthday was when I was sure she knew about mine.

I had to spend most of Monday and Tuesday evening between Hilda's house and Jack's garage, so that by the time Nikolai brought Lyla over at the appointed time—10 o'clock—I was pretty exhausted, but very determined.

"Would you mind explaining why you had him take me all over the place? I swear, if I heard 'Oh, I know what we can do next' one more time, I would have snapped his neck." Lyla said, looking savagely at her brother when they just got through my bedroom window.

I was amazed to see that Nikolai didn't seem troubled by his sister's words, but she really wasn't in a good mood. I hoped it wasn't because I'd been avoiding her all day. I'd only been doing that so she wouldn't think I was up to something.

Not too long ago I'd learned that Lyla paid less attention to the link when she was furious. And I was right. Mix together Nikolai's pestering her and the fact that she believed I didn't know it was her birthday, and I bet she never even felt a twinge of my emotions all day. It all really did sound kind of cruel, but I knew she was going to love this. It would all be worth it. I just wanted to be able to do something nice for her after all the things she'd done for me.

Actually, I needed to do it.

"Nick, thanks a lot. I'll take it from here." He gave us a salute, but before leaping through the window, said, "I'm glad you really enjoyed this Sis. Oh and we *have* to do the whole thing again. I had so much fu—" But he quickly leapt through the window before he was finished because Lyla had taken up one of my track & field trophies to throw at him.

"What's he talking about?" she asked, putting the trophy back.

Ignoring her question, I walked up to her and pushed her hair out of her face and just stared at her for awhile.

"You are so beautiful," I said dreamily to her. Even though I told her that all the time, this time it really seemed to soften her up, so at once I took advantage of that.

"I want you to come with me."

"Where?" she said, a little suspicious, a little intrigued.

"Please?" I said a little softer, unfolding her arms and taking her hands. Through our bond I felt her mood shift. "It's really important to me that you come."

I only meant to give her a quick kiss, but it was as if

I was unable to pull away from her. Not like I wanted to anyway.

Even though she was becoming more open with me every day, she was still very inhibited.

Finally I felt her anger and despair melt away. When we finally broke apart. She let out a guilty sigh. "Chase, I'm sorry. I didn't –"

I placed my left index finger on her lips.

"You don't have to explain anything to me. Just come with me and you'll understand all of this. I promise."

She looked like she wanted to say something more, but simply agreed to go with me, and as we had less than two hours, we didn't waste any time.

It was another cloudy night, but a bright moon hung to the east of the night sky, which meant it was going to be out for a while. That fitted in nicely with my plan. The air drifting in from the sea had its usual salty smell and as it blew inland all the leaves on the tress rustled loudly.

I was really getting used to this.

I picked up a jacket and pulled it on tightly. Once we were outside, we hopped into Shelia and set off. When we pulled over at the side of the road, not too far away, I felt Lyla's curiosity rise through our bond, but she didn't ask me any questions.

When we got out and I indicated we were going in the woods, she raised her eyebrows, then just put her hand in her jeans pocket, pulled out a ribbon and used it to tie her hair up.

"One of these days, you have to show me how people do that," I said, genuinely amazed. I was thankful for the small giggle I got.

The spot I took Lyla to wasn't far, but because of the dense bush around it and the fact that no one lived nearby, I knew we wouldn't be seen. The space was exactly as big and free of grass as the clearing with the Lillyosas, but it wasn't so densely occupied either, which made it do just fine.

A few tall trees grew here, and there was even a small stream that ran past us and thanks to the moon and stars, we had just enough light to make this work.

I took off my jacket and spread it on the damp ground under a tree.

"Here, sit."

"Chase, I'm fine sitting on the ground without it," Lyla said, her voice soft and serene. I just loved to hear how words and sounds seemed to flow so magically from her mouth.

"Humor me," I said. She blushed, and I felt like she was calling me to her. So when she sat down, I fell to my knees and kissed her. At once, our heightened feelings started bouncing through our bond, magnifying what we felt, what we both desired.

So with all the self restraint I had, I pulled away from her. I had a job to do.

Lyla held my face in both her hands and as she gazed at me with her hypnotic blue eyes, I couldn't help but crack. "Happy birthday, love."

Her soft hands fell from my head, but a huge smile lit up her face. I could see in her eyes she wanted to ask a whole bunch of questions, but all she said was, "Thank you. So much."

I left her for a few seconds, went behind a tree and took

up an old backpack I'd stashed there earlier. When I came back, I sat down on a dry spot of grass beside her.

"Lyla, since I've known you, you've done more for me then I could have ever imagine I deserved. Certainly more then I can ever give back. But tonight, I can at least give you a little something for this very special day; the day the world was gifted with your presence. I have a few things here for you. Sure they aren't much, but I still hope you'll like them."

I opened the bag and the first thing I took out was a brass sphere with "Lyla" and "I Love You" cut in the sides and a bottom cut out. I saw how she looked at it and chuckled.

"Hold on," I said as I dug into the bag and retrieved the spinning bottom. There were seven small light bulbs attached to it and a switch.

"I know how much you loved how the Lillyosas lit up. I can't give you that, but I can at least do this." I switched on the lights and covered it with the sphere and made it spin. It was obvious by her small squeals of glee that Lyla loved how the light poured through the markings, projecting them all around us. But what she found most amazing was the different colors that flashed through the sphere.

"Chase, that's beautiful," she said in awe, clasping her hands to her mouth, watching her name spin.

"I'm glad you like it," I said as her head turned in every direction to admire the look of the lights on the trees.

While she was gazing about, I pulled out her second gift and placed it on her lap.

"Chase, this is your sketch book. I can't take this." But even as she said it, I felt her desire to peek inside. I'd never allowed anyone to look inside it, not even her.

"It's yours now. It means a lot to me, but only for one reason. Go on, look inside."

She opened the book slowly as if it was hundreds of years old and it contained important secrets she didn't want to damage. But when she'd finally taken a good look at the drawings inside, her surprise sent my heart racing. She then began flipping through the pages of various drawings I made of her.

"Chase, no one looks this flawless, not even Aquamuns," she cried, shaking her head while looking at the drawing interpretation of when I first saw her sitting on the rocks by the cliff. I shifted myself to be closer to her. If only I could have copied that wonderful scent of hers.

"Lyla, that's how you look. That's how everyone sees you. That's how I see you. But my best ones of you are when you smile."

Not able to resist waiting, I pulled out the last gift. "This was the hardest to get, but I had to, just for you."

I was about to open the small box, but stopped and decided it was better if Lyla did. So I handed it to her.

"I think you should do it."

She took the box from me and pulled open the lid. When she saw what was inside, she looked at it for such a long time, I was afraid she didn't like it and was trying to find a nice way of telling me.

But then, slowly, she took up the semi-circular shaped crystal which hung on the end of a chain. When she held it up, it flashed beautifully as the light from the sphere and the moon as stars passed through it.

"Chase, where did you get this?" Lyla asked in a whisper as if such things should be unattainable.

"It belonged to my mom. She told me it was in her family for years. It's supposed to keep you close to the one you love. That's why the crystal rests over your heart. And look," I threw my hand inside my shirt and pulled out my half of the crystal. "See? Two halves, one whole. They belong together, like me and you."

I was struck speechless when I saw a tear roll down Lyla's face. "What's wrong?" I asked, worried.

She shook her head and laughed. "Chase, nothing is wrong. Nothing could ever be wrong with this moment. I will never forget this night, no matter how long I live."

CHAPTER 12

Ghost

The buzz from Lyla's birthday surprise hung around us both for a few days after. Even with my situation, she was finally happy and I knew it was genuine as I could feel its sincerity through our bond.

I was also pleased to see she had grown very attached to the necklace I'd given her as she was sure to wear it every day. I didn't know if it was too much pride on my part, but I felt extremely happy to know it was I who'd made Lyla so happy. Ever since I'd met her, or even from the time our relationship started, I guess I could say she was happy at moments, but most of the time there seemed to be some kind of crude sadness that always followed her around, but after her birthday it was like she didn't have a care in the world. How long this would last I didn't know, but I was going to make sure she enjoyed it.

What I really wished I could give her was some rest from school. Not that she needed it though, because I was sure school life could never tire her, so I guess I the rest from school would have been more for me. After Lyla's birthday weekend, every teacher in the school seemed to think we needed to be bombarded with work.

"Sir, Mr. Trotman, why is it every teacher is now crushing us with so much work?" A tall boy named Kevin asked from the back of the class. Almost all of the students in the class started muttering in agreement. Mr. Trotman, the Integrated Science teacher, who was actually a nice but strict teacher, actually chuckled appreciatively.

"I figured most of you would forget. Some of you will be sitting CXC exams next year. The work we're giving you is to prepare you for those exams."

Everyone stopped muttering and started talking loud at this seemingly unexpected development. I'd recently learned that CXCs were exams students in fourth year and higher sat at the end of the school year as long as they were entered by their teachers, and it was my unfortunate luck that, according to my teachers, based on the marks I got so far and from the marks from my old school, I'd been entered to do the CXCs for all my subjects. *Well, if I pass them the first time, at least they would be out of the way*, I thought to myself.

"I don't even like school that much," I complained to Lyla and Nikolai that evening as we were walking through our gap to home. "I just go because I have to. I'm not ready for any huge exams."

"Chase, are you afraid of these exams?" Lyla asked, with a teasing smile.

"No! It's not that I'm afraid, it's just huge exams like these make me nervous."

"It's no big deal," Nikolai said, "They sound a lot worse than they actually are."

I scoffed. "That's easy for you to say. You have a photographic memory and your brains are super huge and give you an unfair advantage, besides you must have done that exam a couple times."

"Only once," Nick corrected, throwing his hands in his pocket and walking with a confident stride. He really did have nothing in life to worry about. "Back in 1966 while we were living in Barbados. We lived there for about three years and passed every exam."

"No one likes an over-achiever," I called after Nick as he turned to his side of the cove.

Before Lyla followed him, she kissed me then said, with amusement in her eyes and voice, "Behave yourself when you get home." Then giggling slyly, she turned and followed her brother.

Though I was puzzled about what she said, I didn't have to long to wait to find out, because as soon as I got home I saw my parents had invited both Madison and Gibbons over for dinner again. As it wasn't yet time to eat, Dad and Gibbons were talking and laughing in front the TV and Mom was constantly refusing Madison's help in the kitchen.

"You're a guest. You don't have to do anything," she kept telling her. And that's when she found my arrival convenient.

"Chase, why don't you do me a favor and keep Madison company until dinner's ready?"

Of course it wasn't so much a favor as an order, so I didn't even waste time trying to come up with an excuse. I simply sighed deeply and went upstairs to change.

It wasn't that I didn't like Madison, because she seemed

cool. It was just I was hoping Lyla would be able to come over and spend the evening with me, but it now looked like that wasn't going to happen. *At least she'll be here later*, I thought to myself.

After I showered and changed, there was a knock on my door.

"There's something I wanted to asked you," Madison said awkwardly, rubbing the underside of her arm like she was nervous, "Um... are you hiding up here because of me or something? Have I done something wrong?"

The truth was, I was hiding in my room because of her, but the look of rising hurt on her face was so real, like she knew what I was going to say. I felt guilty for treating her like I did, partly because she did nothing wrong, but mostly because I remembered how it felt when Lyla was ignoring me when all I wanted was to be friends... at first.

"No, no no. Madison, that's not so," I answered hastily, "It's just I have some things going on with me right now and they have me kind of upset. I just don't think I would be very good company for you right now, that's all."

As I said it, it even sounded to me like an average, insincere excuse, but Madison didn't seem to think so. In fact, she now looked kind of amused, though I couldn't figure why.

Finally, she moved from the spot she was on from the moment she came in and started looking around while I simply sat on the bed and watched her.

"Wow, I can't believe you read K.J. Pollard," she said as she looked over my copy of *The Illusionist* on the computer table. "I've been trying to read his work, but the guy's worse than Shakespeare, and he's only twenty five." I actually laughed.

"He's not that bad," I said with a small shrug, "Lyla's reading it now. She understands it a lot better than I do."

"So, Chase, tell me something. How old are you?" She dropped into the chair opposite me.

"Seventeen."

"Hmmm, not much younger than me," Madison admitted and flicked her hair dramatically for a laugh. "I'm nineteen." She was about to say something else, but at that moment Mom called us downstairs for dinner.

Simply put, it was a very boring meal. Everyone was engaged in conversation with each other while I merely sat there playing with my shepherd's pie most of the time and nibbling it the rest.

At our house, I was allowed to excuse myself from the table anytime except when guests were present, then I had to wait to be excused. So I was extremely happy when Lyla and Nikolai showed up not long after and Mom let me go, though I could tell she didn't like me leaving so soon. It was certainly obvious to me that Madison didn't like the interruption.

"Thanks for coming for me. I wasn't feeling very comfortable there."

"How come? Don't tell me Madison's too much for you," Lyla joked as we walked down the driveway. I merely scowled at her while Nick looked confused but unconcerned. That's when I noticed the two Aquamuns had turned and were now heading into the woods.

"Where exactly are we going?" I asked just as I ducked under a low hanging branch. Nikolai, who was just in front me, pointed to a place not too far away from us, but he didn't need to, because just ahead, beyond a small group of trees, there was a shimmering orange glow.

"Hey, you guys finally made it," Justin said, sitting on a rock as the orange glow, which turned out to be a fire burning in an old metal barrel, was crackling away.

Along with Justin, also present were Brandon, Kimberley, Maranda and two friends I'd met at school, Carlyle and Nadira.

"What're you guys doing here?" I asked as I sat down on a small log next to Carlyle.

"Nothing big," Carlyle responded just as he threw a few small twigs into the fire and it hissed slightly as if it was an animal being fed, "we just thought it'd be good to relax like this for a while, especially after the week we had. I can't believe how fast CXC year has come." Everyone agreed and started chatting and eating the snacks the others brought.

While I did enjoy the ambience of the whole thing, for some reason I felt strangely separated from everyone else. Even Lyla, who despite the fact we shared our bond, didn't really understand what I felt. She seemed oblivious to the fact that I was peacefully watching her as she talked with Maranda and Carlyle.

Soon after, Brandon turned on the radio he'd brought and everyone got up and started dancing. They tried to get me to join in, but I felt better just sitting there by myself.

It had been a while since I was attacked and strangely enough, that had me worried. While I wasn't thrilled when these attacks occurred, they did serve one good purpose. Because of them we knew what this person was up to. But during this time of peace, I was constantly wondering when the next shoe was going to drop, when the next heart-wrenching attack was going to take place and, would it be the one that succeeds?

Watching Lyla laugh heartily with the others made me feel guilty about being with her. As much as I wanted to deny it, I was the one who brought all the sorrow and complications into her life, no matter how much she denied it.

I stood up suddenly and dusted myself off. Before anyone else had noticed, Lyla pulled herself away from the others and was about to walk over to me, but I just shook my head and said, "I'm just going for a quick walk. I'll be right back."

She looked at me oddly, then a sad expression slowly slid across her face as she realized what I was feeling. I'd forgotten to block out those emotions. I didn't want Lyla feeling sympathy for me, but it was too late. I quickly turned and walked off into the woods, also happy she didn't see my expression. I was thankful she didn't follow me because this was one of those moments when I just needed time to myself.

The woods around our neighborhood weren't very dense, but they were deep and I was so lost in my own thoughts walking absentmindedly, that when I caught myself I was so far from the others, I couldn't even hear their voices or the music. But I could still see a tiny orange spark which was the fire, so I wasn't too worried.

Finally, growing tired of walking, I sat down under a huge tree. I don't know why, but I always enjoyed quiet moments by myself. Sitting alone, I took deep, steadying breaths of the chilly thin air, which did wonders in helping me feel better. I felt all the tension and worry leave my body with every breath I exhaled.

I treasured the time I spent there by myself, but I didn't want the others to start worrying. Deciding I should find my way back to the others, I pushed myself up from the ground and as soon as I was standing, I heard a rustling of leaves just a little deeper in the woods. I glanced in the general direction the sound came from, but it wasn't any good because the darkness was so thick I couldn't see a thing.

At first I wondered if it could be one of the others, but I knew it couldn't be because everyone else was back at the fire. I supposed it could have been Nikolai trying to scare me, but then if it was, he wouldn't have made a sound. That's when I started to get nervous.

"Hello, is someone there?" I called into the still darkness, but there was no response. Not like I was expecting one anyway. "Lyla, is that you?"

I really don't know why I said that because if it was Lyla, I would have felt her presence through our bond, and I could still feel she was with the others.

Then I heard it again, more dried leaves on the ground being walked on. Goosebumps started rising all over my body and as I tried to control my breathing. That's when I noticed the air had gone completely still. No leaves were blowing and outside had actually gotten a little colder.

I felt like a lump was rising in my throat because I knew what this usually meant; another attack was coming. After all this time, it really wasn't over. Then, even in the thick darkness, I knew I saw someone standing close to one of the trees.

I heard more leaves rustle, but this time from behind me. When I spun around, I breathed a sigh of relief.

"Kimberley, what're you doing out here?"

"I could ask you the same thing. Who were you talking to just now?" she asked.

The lump in my throat felt like it was growing painfully bigger. Kimberly was standing behind me, and even in the thick darkness, she was looking this way and that, trying to see who it was that I was talking too, but when I looked back, whoever it was I thought I saw was gone.

"I could've sworn I saw some someone standing over there," I said more to myself then to Kim.

"Come on," she said, sounding a little worried, "let's get back to the others."

When Kimberley turned and started walking back, I followed her, not even noticing the air was back to being warm and thin.

"So are you going to tell me what happened to you tonight?" Lyla asked as soon as I climbed into bed. I was surprised she knew about what I thought I saw in the forest.

"Kimberly actually told you." Lyla's eyes became narrow and in the darkness of the room, they looked like two small sapphires.

"What're you talking about?"

"Nothing really. Funny story for another time. What are you talking about?" I amended quickly. Lyla looked at me puzzled for a while. She sat up against the bed head, then shook her head and continued. "I meant tonight when I felt that strong depression inside you."

I sighed as I realized what she meant. "Lyla, please, I don't really wanna talk about that."

I knew it would be way too difficult to admit to Lyla what I was going through, even if she would understand. She turned in the bed to face me, but I averted her gaze by closing my eyes. It was a coward's move on my part.

"Chase, I don't know how you think this is supposed to work, but you're in a relationship now, you're not alone, you don't have to keep things bottled up inside. I'm trying to say you need to learn to talk to me."

She sighed exasperatedly when I didn't respond.

"Well, too bad if you don't wanna talk about it, because I do. Chase what you felt was no little dip. Chase, those emotions I felt from you were... I just didn't like it. They were so strong and they came onto me so suddenly. I almost didn't have time to block them out, I mean, you have no idea how hard I had to fight just to keep them at bay. And that's only for the few minutes I felt them for, I can't imagine how hard it is for you to deal with. You really aren't going to talk about this?"

I sighed regretfully, opened my eyes and turned to my girlfriend. I smiled a little at that—the thought of Lyla as my girlfriend. It was still amazing to think about.

"No, Lyla, I'm not talking about it because there is nothing to talk about. Look, I was feeling a little grumpy before, but I'm good now." Before Lyla could reply, I kissed her lightly on the lips, then turned over and pulled the covers up to my chest.

I knew she was still watching my very intently and through our very open connection I felt her concern for me rise, but I didn't dwell on that too long because I quickly fell asleep. However, a short while later an uncomfortable yet not painful sensation cruised through my body and pulled me from my sleep so violently that when I opened my eyes I had an instant headache.

I almost screamed in surprise when I turned over and saw Lyla still sitting up in bed.

"You were awake this whole time?" I asked, sitting up and trying to catch my breath.

"You felt that too, didn't you?" She said softly. Even through the dim light in the bedroom, I could clearly see the panic on Lyla's face. She hopped out of the bed and reached for her phone on the night stand next to the bed, but before she even touched it, the phone started vibrating.

"I was just about to call," Lyla said softly into the phone when she'd answered. "I know, it shocked me too. It was so strong it even woke Chase." She explained to whomever she was speaking to. "Okay, see you in a bit," she said, then hung up.

"What's going on?" I asked. The early stages of panic were starting to hit me. Lyla, on the other hand, didn't get back into bed, but went over to the window, folded her arms and gazed outside.

"I don't know," she answered, still looking outside, "but I do know what we felt wasn't anything good. My family felt it, but what has me worried is that you felt it too." Lyla voice sounded so wrong to me, kind of how you would expect a sad mermaid to sound.

"Isn't the reason I felt it because of our bond?"

"Maybe," Lyla simply answered.

Through our bond, I felt worry from her; worry for me and for her family. She was afraid they were going to get hurt.

I sighed. If they did it would be because of me. I had to use all my resolve to keep my guilt from Lyla. It certainly wouldn't help her right now. I finally got out of bed and went over to join her. Her sweet aroma helped to calm me down a little.

"It's another attack isn't it?"

"We don't know that, I mean nothing's happened to you, right?"

I shook my head, then remembered Lyla wasn't looking at me.

"No, I'm fine, but that doesn't mean it still can't happen."

Lyla didn't respond, but she really didn't need to because I felt it all through our bond, and what I felt was fear, fear that I was right. Underneath that was a strong burning sense of desire. A little intrigued, I touched on it and wasn't surprised by what I found. She wanted it to be over. She desired some sort of normalcy in her life; after all, that's all she ever really wanted.

"That doesn't mean I blame you Chase," she mumbled as I was about to turn away. She must have felt it when I was sifting through her emotions. "I don't blame you. I blame the person out there trying to kill you. I want this to be over because I don't want him having any more chances at hurting you or anyone else. And yes, I want it so I can have some kind of normal life. With you."

She'd finally turned to face me. As it was dark in the room, I couldn't see her face clearly, but just as before I didn't need to. From the sound of her voice I could tell she was close to tears. Maybe it was her emotions overtaking me as my guard was down, or perhaps they were my own.

I neither knew nor cared, but a sudden sadness had come over me and all I could do was throw my arms around Lyla and hold her. It felt good to have her embrace me.

It was starting to seem like our efforts at trying to save my life were futile, because every one of these attacks grew more dangerous and more powerful and after all we tried we were still no closer to even an idea of who was behind them.

Lyla and I just stood there, not kissing or even being passionate, but our simple embrace was intimate. We weren't looking for intimacy in that moment, but because of the situation we both needed consoling and we provided that for each other.

A couple hours later I woke up in dazed state in my bed. For a while I was under the impression I'd had a troubling dream, but as soon as I sat up, everything came back to me, including the headache I had. I was going to ask Lyla when she had to meet her family, but she was already gone.

She probably didn't want to wake me. I climbed out of bed. I was shocked to see it was 9:30—half the morning was already gone. I hated sleeping away my mornings because I always felt I could be doing something else.

After a quick shower, I bolted downstairs and was shocked to see Mom was home, carrying a basket of clothes. From my first weekend here, both my parents worked on Saturdays and it was something I'd become used to. So it was a big surprise to find Mom home in a pair of faded blue jeans and a pink shirt.

"What're you doing here?" I asked, momentarily distracted from what I was going to do.

She was her way to the backyard with her basket of

damp clothes. She stopped and turned to me. "Um, are you forgetting I live here?"

"I know," I said rolling my eyes and following her into the yard, "but you always work on Saturdays." She threw some of the clothes at me to hang.

"I know, but that was so I could get the practice off the ground quickly. But I do have a home, husband and son to look after."

She smiled at me and did her usual thing—ran her fingers through my hair, and for some reason, that single action brought on something that never happened to me before. It happened so suddenly. A moment from my past flashed before my eyes.

It was about ten years ago. Mom, Dad and I were playing in a park, back when we were in New York. It was a time when happiness seemed to me to be never-ending.

"What's wrong?" Mom asked. It must've looked like I'd just zoned out. In response to her question, I threw my arms around her. It was the first time I realized I was a few inches taller than her.

"I love you, Mom."

"I love you too, Chase," she said nervously. 'Is there something I should know?"

"Nah, everything's good," That was a lie. I turned and headed through the gate.

"Where're you going?" Mom called after me.

"There's something I have to do, Mom." I bid her farewell then headed over to the Morgans.

"Right on time," Lyla said to me when I got there. "We have a visitor."

A little curious, I followed Lyla into her family's sitting

room. Sitting among the rest of her family was Hilda, looking somewhat uncomfortable.

"Hilda, what are you doing here?" I asked, taking a seat in the last remaining armchair. Maybe it was my imagination, but now that I'd sat down, she looked a little more relaxed. The muscles in her neck didn't look so flexed anymore, at least.

"I'm here because of what happened last night."

"They told you about it, then," I said, indicating the Morgans, but Hilda shook her head, her locks swayed slightly.

"No one had to tell me. That feeling was so strong, it could have woken the dead."

Just then Nikolai cleared his throat loudly and I had to stifle a laugh because I knew what he was getting at, and apparently so did everyone else as they all looked at him but looked away quickly. As soon as they weren't looking, he smiled at me.

"So do you know what it was?" Marcus asked Hilda, with Salathia sitting next to him. Their three children were sitting on the three-seater couch and Hilda was in an armchair across from everyone.

There was a kind of ringing command tone in Marcus's voice. I knew that was how he always sounded and wasn't trying to intimidate Hilda, but I was surprised by the indifferent way she responded, as if she could care less about what Marcus wanted to know.

"I know it was a spell and a powerful one. Had to require lots of energy behind it. I tried to get a fix on the source before the wave dissipated. But whoever it was was able to keep themselves shielded from detection."

Everyone in the room looked a little disappointed at the news, but then Hilda added, "I do know this though, it was a summoning spell, so we can expect them to be sending something after you." She looked towards me.

"Isn't there any way to protect Chase, as we don't know when this attack will take place?"

I don't know if the others picked up on it, but I could tell Hilda was taken aback by Salathia's concern. When she responded, I was glad to hear it was with a nicer voice then the one she responded to Marcus with.

"No, I would need to know exactly what's coming to come up with a proper defense and no simple defense spell will do as that summoning spell felt pretty advanced. Simple protection won't do."

Everyone got up to walk Hilda to the door.

"So what do we do now?" Michael asked as we got to the door. Hilda sighed and turned to face us all, but her eyes came to rest on me. "I'm afraid all we can do right now is wait and be careful. It's playing right into this person's hands, but as long as we're careful we should be good."

Hilda turned and stepped outside without even saying goodbye, but before she even got off the steps, her eye caught something and she said, "Huh. Those are very hard to take care of," Salathia stepped outside as well and gasped. Some of the flowers she had outside the house had withered and died. I hadn't even noticed them on my way in.

"But those were fine yesterday," Salathia said sadly, checking her dead flowers.

"Maybe it's something in the soil," I said absently, thinking of the other plants and flowers I saw that had died in the woods. Strangely, Hilda seemed a bit more interested.

"You've seen dead flowers like these ones before?"

"Yeah, flowers and plants, in the woods. Sometimes there're even dead birds around them too, which makes me think it might be something in the soil or water or something."

"No, it's nothing like that," Hilda said, looking as though she just found a missing piece of a puzzle. "They're using them for power," she uttered more to herself than to everyone. After a couple of seconds thought, she said to us, "Whoever's doing this doesn't have enough power to fuel these spells on their own, or maybe their own strength is low. The point is, they're using plants and small animals for energy. When too much energy is taken," she gestured towards the withered plants, "they die."

"Is it possible to take energy from humans too?" Marcus asked.

"Yes," Hilda responded, "but taking energy from humans weakens us quickly. Whoever's doing this could kill someone without meaning to, which is probably why he hasn't, or maybe he just isn't that strong. The good news is, however, from the amount of powerful spells this person's using and for him to be taking energy from elsewhere, it probably means his own body must be weakening from all that magical strain. His own energy must be pretty low. If he's not careful he could end up dead, but then," she stooped down by the dead flowers, picked a few, and carefully placed them in her purse and stood up, "That's probably best for you, right?"

I was hoping Hilda's views on the Morgans were going

to change. Guess that wasn't going to happen anytime soon. I was surprised when none of the Morgans responded to that and apparently, so was Hilda.

"Hmmm, I'll see if I can learn anything from the flowers. I will be in touch."

"She is a very odd woman," Michael said as they all turned to head back into the house.

"Are you coming?" Lyla asked me.

"Yeah, yeah I am," I responded.

"What's on your mind?"

I turned to Lyla. "Did you notice Hilda said 'we' and not 'you'?"

"Oh yes, I noticed," Lyla said, chuckling herself as she went inside.

I took one last look at the dead flowers and wondered just how far this person was willing to go, just as the last living leaf on one of the flowers fell off.

The fact that an impending attack was on the way unsettled me. For the whole day I kept wondering if I was going to spontaneously combust or maybe shrivel and die like those flowers. Maybe I might get hit by a bolt of lightning.

"Nothing like that's going to happen," Lyla whispered to me when we were in the library later that day. "Hilda said it was a summoning spell, which means something's going to come after you, something we can fight."

"A bolt of lightning's something, we can't fight that. Unless you Aquamuns have some kind of lightning rod powers or something," I said jokingly. We both laughed, then I noticed Lyla was staring intently at me for awhile.

"What?"

"The necklace you gave me for my birthday, do you always wear your piece?" She asked.

My fingers automatically flew to it. I nodded to Lyla and she held out her hand for it.

I took it off and gave it to her. "Why do you want it?"

"I just had an idea, but it's a surprise. Trust me though, if it works, it will come in useful." She collected her stuff, said "See you later," and after a quick kiss on my cheek, she left. And with her went my desire to finish my Social Studies assignment, so I too, collected my things, left, and hopped into my car to go for a drive.

I hadn't gotten too far when I saw Dad's truck outside an auto parts store. I parked Sheila and went in to look.

"Dad, what're you doing here?" I asked when I saw him inside, and then thought it was a stupid question. He pointed to someone sitting in one of the waiting chairs at the side of the room. I gasped when I saw Chris, who I hadn't recognized at first, sitting there.

"We came in to pick up a part for his car, then I'm taking him home. He's feeling a bit sick."

Chris looked more than 'a bit sick' in my opinion. Sure I hadn't seen him in a few days, but still, I'd never known anyone to look so different in such a short space of time.

Chris's skin had always looked clear and healthy, despite the amount of time he spent in the sun, but now it had kind of a green tinge to it that made him look like he wanted to vomit and it also made him look older. There were huge, dark circles under his eyes and the way he sat told me that he could barely hold himself up.

"Couldn't you have waited in the truck?" I asked Chris

softly, as if any louder and his ears would bleed. Hey, I didn't want to risk anything.

"It's not as if I'm dying Chase. You guys don't have to worry about me. I will be fine." Even as he spoke, his voice sounded depleted of energy.

"Dad, you can take him home now," I said, looking sympathetically at Chris as he clinched the sides of his chair. "I can wait here for the part and you can take it to him tomorrow."

My father looked at Chris intently for a while, then said to me, "Are you sure?"

"Yeah, it's cool. Just get him home."

Dad smiled, handed me his numbered ticket, then took Chris out to the truck and drove off.

My dad's number was seventy-five and they were only up to sixty, so I took a seat. I couldn't stop my mind from wondering about Chris's condition. I wondered if Hilda was wrong and my attacker was taking energy from people and Chris was one of the unfortunate ones.

I sincerely hoped that wasn't true, but if it was, I was at a loss about what to do. Like everything else, all we could do was wait to see what happened.

That thought was so depressing.

After about half an hour, one of the assistants called my number, apologized for the wait and handed me a small box. When I finally left the store it was almost 6:00 pm, so I decided to have dinner in town. By the time I was finished, it was past 7:30 and night had fully fallen.

While I was driving back home, I couldn't help thinking of how my other friends were having completely normal lives. They didn't have to worry about fearing for their lives, or maybe, because they were my friends, they did, but just didn't know it. But still they only had to worry about stuff like exams and normal relationships.

If I didn't know about the supernatural, my life would be like that; things would be so much easier, not to mention safer. But then I'd be unhappy and constantly feeling like a part of my life was missing because I wouldn't be with Lyla. Life without her wasn't worth living and any life with her was worth fighting for.

I smiled to myself as I swelled up with a tingly good feeling inside. This was one feeling I wasn't going to keep from our bond. And that's when I stepped on the brakes as hard as I could, because out of nowhere on this lonely road, flanked by woods on both sides, a woman appeared so suddenly as if she slipped out of the darkness of night itself, wearing a long, sweeping white dress.

But I didn't even get a chance to see her face, because as soon as I saw her, I could have sworn the car smashed into her. But the strange thing was, she'd vanished.

As soon as Shelia came to a stop, I hopped out, leaving the door open, and screamed "Hello!" as hard as I could.

Though my heart was beating fast with panic, I was still able to notice the air was chilly, yet deadly still, just like it was last night. Goosebumps started rising up all over my arms just as something in the back of my head told me to look at my car. When I did, she looked perfectly fine. There was no indication that I'd hit anyone. Fear started bubbling up inside me. As fast as I could, I got back in the car, locked the doors and drove off with the radio turned up for company. I was so happy when I finally pulled up outside my house.

"Took your time getting here. Wait, don't you want dinner?" Mom said from the couch with Dad.

"It's okay Mom, I already ate."

When I got up to my room, Lyla wasn't there as I'd hoped, but when I came back after a quick shower, she was sitting on the bed silently and quite still. I rushed over to her and hugged her as if she'd been gone for years.

"I'm sorry," I said when I let her go. She turned away from me and I was about to ask her why when I remembered I had to get dressed.

"Don't be. What's wrong?"

"It's nothing big," I lied. "I just had a really tough evening and really needed to see you. Lots of weird stuff going on."

Without me even telling her, she knew I was finished and turned around, but before she'd even taken a step her eyes darted to the door for half a second. Without saying anything to me, she was through the window before I knew it. I was about to run to the window when there was a light knock on the door and Dad came in.

"What's wrong?" he asked.

"Nothing, Dad. I was just feeling a little tired. Oh yeah." I took up Shelia's keys and threw them to him. "The part for Chris's car is in the back seat. How is he anyway?"

"Well it's not like he's a hundred percent better, but from the moment he got to bed, he actually started to look a little better. Poor guy overworks himself, what with working with us, his studies and his second job."

"He has two jobs?" I blurted out, surprised. I couldn't tell if Dad was going to put his face in a grin or grimace, but whatever it was, he certainly did fight hard to hold it back.

"Chase, everyone doesn't have an aversion to work like you."

I shot him a condescending look which he ignored. "He's only twenty-three and lives on his own. He's just trying to keep his head above water."

"Must be hard for him," I said.

"It is," Dad agreed, "Anyway, I'll leave these for you on the table." He shook the keys at me.

"Something's wrong with Chris?" Lyla asked as soon as the door was closed. Her appearance was so sudden, I actually flinched a little. No early bond warning this time.

"Yeah, he's kinda sick. Dad thinks it's just exhaustion, so he probably needs rest."

Lyla was staring at me as though she was expecting me to say something obvious, but after I remained quiet, she said, "Chase, Hilda said your attacker would probably be weak from the amount of spells he's been using. What if his sickness is because of the attacks on you?"

If I was an insensitive jerk, I would've laughed because that sounded so far-fetched, but after thinking about it for a couple of seconds, I saw how she could reach that conclusion, but I had to derail that train of thought.

"Chris isn't the one doing this," I said, sitting at the end of the bed as Lyla went to look through the window. "He isn't a Somorian and we know it's a Somorian doing this. Plus he doesn't even believe in the supernatural."

Lyla only said, "Hmm." As she continued to gaze out the window.

"When I saw him earlier today I wondered if maybe the attacker maybe wasn't pulling energy from him which is why he's so weak all of a sudden."

"That's what I think too. Its just…" but she didn't continue, she actually didn't have to. I knew she just wanted to have at least one theory where we have an idea of who is behind all this. She wasn't alone in that.

"Lyla, I wanna ask you something weird." She looked away from the window and looked at me seriously. I really didn't know how to ask without making it sound silly, so I just said it.

"Do you believe in ghosts?"

"Yes," she said bluntly, "and you should too." I stared at her perplexed for a while, completely taken aback by that. "The spirit hounds should have been proof enough."

"What, they're like the ghosts of dogs or something?" I'm sure that sounded stupid, but Lyla didn't laugh or anything, she just shook her head.

"No. They're like spiritual pitbulls born from the anger and greed of the dead. But there are real ghosts that remain here after they die, but no one really knows how they remain here, though there are a lot of theories. Why do you ask?"

I explained what happened earlier and the night before.

"I don't know if what you saw were ghosts or not," Lyla explained, "but if they are, why would ghosts be appearing to you?"

"Maybe they're attracted to me for some reason. Maybe I'm haunted," I added in a whisper.

"I don't think you're haunted," she said, but her divine sounding voice somehow sounded small, like she wasn't sure about much anymore. We stayed silent for a while, then her jewel-like eyes sparkled as her face lit up. She removed something from around her neck and I realized it was my piece of the crystal necklace which she dropped into my opened hand.

"It still looks the same," I said, holding it up to the moonlight, watching it spin and sparkle as if I was expecting something amazing to happen.

Lyla rolled her eyes. "I went to Hilda and had her enchant it."

"I thought she said she could only perform simple protection spells as she didn't know what was coming?" I slipped the necklace back on. I didn't know if it was just me or the magic, but as soon as it was around my neck, a strange, quivering feeling passed through my body which left me feeling strangely comforted.

"That's true," Lyla admitted, "but simple protection is better than none. The crystal will burn when you're in danger and in case anything stops me from finding you, I will be able to use my half to find you. For good measure, she also did something that will allow the crystal to emit a burst of energy that should cancel out any spells around you. But she did say it only has enough power for two blasts, if you go for a third it will drain the crystal."

I kissed Lyla softly. She looked at the ground. "I just wanted to be able to do something useful for once."

"Lyla, you're always doing useful stuff for me. I mean. If it wasn't for you, I would be dead."

"You used that one too many times."

I chuckled and kissed her on the cheek, then got up to use the bathroom. When I was at the sink, I leaned over to drink some water straight from the tap (yeah, that's right, I do that) and when I got up, half a scream escaped my mouth before I got it under control. I didn't think it was loud enough for Mom or Dad to hear, but Lyla, who did, was in the bathroom in a flash.

"What's it?" She said in a panic but I didn't answer at once. I looked around the bathroom, but saw nothing. When I'd stood up from the sink, I looked in the mirror and thought I saw a man and woman standing behind me.

"I thought I saw…" But then I thought about it and said, "Nothing. Never mind."

We went back to the bedroom, where the light was still off. As soon as I reached the door, I saw four silhouetted figures standing in the middle of the room.

There was no way Lyla could doubt me because she saw them too. But I was shocked to see Lyla was looking at me as though something was off – with me. I rushed across the room and flipped on the light switch. As soon as flourescent light flooded the room the figures disappeared, but it didn't matter because from the look on Lyla's face I could tell she knew what I saw but was skeptical it was real.

"What is it?" I asked sharply.

"Chase, I'm sorry, but I just don't see what you're trying to show me. Plus father once told me ghosts also emit a strange kind of aura we can detect, which was how I found the hounds." I knew what she was implying but didn't care. I switched off the light (the figures didn't return) and went to bed.

"It's okay Lyla, they're not here anymore."

I tried to keep my frustration to myself through our bond, as Lyla really didn't deserve to feel it. It was already too late because I heard her sigh and get into the bed. I knew she was facing the other direction. I didn't like this, so I spun myself around and threw my arm over her side and with her soft, warm hand she held mine against her body. It was funny how I believed I was seeing ghosts, yet could easily climb into bed with my girlfriend.

Sunday morning brought with it cloudy skies and a heavy, thick fog that rolled in from the rough sea and dampened everything it touched. The sunlight coming through my bedroom window was a greyish yellow, as if it was losing all its light and warmth somewhere up in the clouds, maybe because the air coming in the room was cold as though it was still night.

I got out of bed quickly (Lyla was still asleep) and once I heard how noisy the waves were bashing against the cliffs, I wondered how I could have ever slept through that.

"You're up early. I thought you would have slept longer today." Mom said when I got downstairs for breakfast.

"I like this, we don't really get to have breakfast together anymore." Dad murmured when I sat down at the table and he shoveled a forkful of pancakes into his mouth.

Just as I sat down, Mom sniffed the air and Dad wrinkled his nose, but they both stared at me.

"Did you go out last night to see Lyla?" Mom said slowly, but intently. Very discreetly, I sniffed my hand the same time I raised my fork to my mouth. Lyla's sweet scent clung to me as strongly as though I'd sprayed it on. I had to bite my tongue to stop myself from smiling stupidly.

"Um no. I... had dinner in town with her last night. Some of her perfume got me on. Must not have completely washed off," I lied. I added a shrug to make it more believable.

My parents looked at me for a while, then at each other and finally went back to breakfast, but not before I noticed the strange look that passed between them. I decided to ignore it, for the moment.

When I finished my breakfast, I went back upstairs where I was surprised to find that Lyla was still there. She was no longer sleeping, but sitting on the bed awaiting my return.

"Get dressed. Hilda called and she wants to meet us. I'm going up there now. Get there as fast as you can." Lyla was already by the window.

"Okay," I said, "See you soon."

She looked at me and smiled and said, "Can't wait till then." And with that she jumped through the window and was gone.

Within forty minutes, I pulled up in Hilda's driveway.

"Come on in," Hilda said when she met me outside, "you're going to want to hear this."

I followed Hilda into her living room where all the Morgans were sitting, looking uncomfortable, all except Nikolai who looked as relaxed as he would in his own home.

"What's going on?" I said when I sat down.

"Now that you're here, Chase, I have some news to share. I know what's coming after you." Hilda let that hang for a few seconds. The suspense in the room was almost physical. "It's a ghost." Everyone except Lyla and I seemed surprised.

"The spell this person performed was used not only to summon the spirits but also to bind them to his will, meaning they'll do whatever he wants –"

"And he wants them to kill me." I interjected.

"So why haven't they attacked yet?" Michael asked from his seat.

"Because they don't have the strength to yet."

Hilda got up and walked over to a book cabinet, ran her fingers along the spines of some hard cover books, reading the titles as she went, until she found the one she was looking for, which was a reddish brown hardcover book without any writing on the front cover.

When she found the text she was looking for, she said: "Yes. This person might've raised the ghost, but they still need a fair amount of power before they can interact with our world, which they don't have yet."

"Which is why they haven't attacked Chase. Well that's good," Salathia said, but it didn't escape my notice that Hilda had said 'yet'.

"But they can get this power right?" I said. Hilda nodded as she continued skimming through the book. "And only too easily. You see, every time they come over to this world, they get stronger. And they can even feed off the energy in the air."

"That's why it gets so cold when they're near," I said, remembering how the air felt whenever they were close. Hilda placed the book on the table and pushed it to the side, out of the way, but left it open.

"Exactly. Unfortunately it won't take them long to get the power they need. The only reason they need to gather power is because the spell brought a bunch of them over at once. That probably inadvertently links their power. Usually they have their own energy when they cross over."

"Okay. Bottom line, is there anything you can do?"

"Of course," Hilda responded to Nick, "There is a spell I can use to put them back to rest but it will have to be as powerful as the spell that brought them here. I just have to find it. I'm sure she told you about the crystal," Hilda said to me, pointing at Lyla. "Only use it when you have no other choice because it may be a while before I can perform the counter-spell. Well, I will be in touch with you."

Everyone seemed taken aback by this abrupt dismissal, but they got up to leave just the same. When I did, however, she held me back until the others were outside.

"You do know anything you tell me they can still hear from outside." Hilda smiled as she sat me back down. "I have many protection spells on this house. One of them is a kind of supernatural soundproof. They can't hear anything said in this house from outside."

Hilda sat next to me and turned to look me dead in the eye and as she did, I got the feeling like she was seeing someone else. It was freaky.

"I want you to be careful. Just because you have the crystal and the protection of the Aquamuns doesn't mean you still can't get hurt. Promise me you'll be careful."

"Yes, Hilda, I promise," I said softly.

Hilda was looking at me sadly, and then, looking as though she had to steel herself to do it, she hugged me. It was emotionally uncomfortable at first, but still I had no idea she really cared. I always thought she was helping us because she felt it was duty. It did raise one new question for me though. *Why* did she care? But I wasn't going to ask. At least, not just yet.

"Go on," she said when we broke apart. I looked at her one last time, then headed for the door. Before I was even out of the house, I felt the pressure in the house increase as she put back up her protection.

Lyla was waiting for me by Sheila. The others had apparently left.

"So, where to now?" She said when I got there, tying her hair back with a rubber band. "Home, unfortunately. I've got homework to finish that I can't put off any longer, but you can come over later, if you're not busy. You can even use the front door." I joked as we got in the car. She slapped me around the head, but still laughed.

When I pulled up in our driveway after dropping Lyla home, I saw my dad standing outside with Justin and another man I recognized to be Justin's dad.

"Hey," I called as I crossed over to them. I figured they'd just come from the beach because they were all wearing they beachwear. But when I got over there all thoughts of pleasantries left me. Justin's dad was wearing a sports vest and on his upper right arm was the troublesome tattoo, the Somorian siduel I'd seen before.

CHAPTER 13

Love and Lust

W hat!" Lyla exclaimed on Tuesday afternoon when we were alone at lunch under one of the strong trees in the schoolyard. "Why didn't you tell me this before? I told you I had a feeling she had a thing for you."

Lyla was only pretending to be angry, but through the bond I knew there was still a little jealousy there, though I couldn't understand why. But knowing she was jealous did make me feel a bit smug.

"Oh come on Lyla, you don't have to be jealous, you know you're my boo," I teased and had immense pleasure in watching her blush.

"Sweet talker. Come on, we've got to get to class," she said just after the bell signaling the end of lunch had rung. As we had different classes (I had Social Studies while she was going to Spanish) I said goodbye and watched her disappear into the rush of students.

After making sure she wasn't too concerned with the bond at the moment, I was free to let myself worry about what I had been dwelling on for the past two days: Justin's dad. I still hadn't told anyone I saw that siduel on his arm, and that's mainly because I couldn't believe he could be the one trying to kill me. Maybe he was, maybe he wasn't, but I couldn't just tell Lyla or Hilda, as I had no idea how they would have dealt with it. Either way, I needed to find out more about Mr. Pollard and I decided the best way was to talk to Justin. After that I could tell the others because then I would be sure. I just needed a way to get Justin talking without him getting suspicious. To my relief, such an excuse came in Social Studies class.

"I want to issue all of you with a little challenge, something to make things interesting," Mrs. Cox said as she walked around the room. "I want you all to get into groups of twos or threes and research the History of one of the members. Go as far back as possible. Once you have done that, write about it. Not just about the family tree, as past students have done, but about the family's history. Make it exciting, but don't fictionalize it. This is to be finished in two weeks time."

I could have done back flips then and there. Mrs. Cox had no idea how much easier she'd made my task, though it would have been nice without the extra homework. I almost swore in shock when I saw Amanda Bambang, who I knew thought Justin was God's gift to women, heading towards him and I knew she wasn't going to work in threes.

I pushed my table away and went over to him. In shock, I could have sworn I saw Amanda break into a fast-paced walk to try to beat me there, but I was only two tables away and she was across the room, so I got there first.

"What's wrong with Amanda?" Justin asked when I sat down at his table. I guess he saw the strong look of contempt she shot at me.

"Not a clue," I dropped my books on his desk. "Let's get started. Hey, I have an idea. Why don't we work on your dad?" I said with my book open and pen ready.

"Really dedicated to this class, aren't you?" Justin joked. "Why do you wanna work on my dad, though? Really, my mom's family history is much more interesting. Listen, the story is, her ancestors were part of a group of villagers that just disappeared overnight. When people from the neighboring village came to visit the next morning, they found everyone gone. Never seen again."

"I'd rather... wait, what? Really?" I said with interest, momentarily distracted.

"Yeah," Justin continued excitedly, "when they searched the villages, everything was still there, clothes, pottery, everything. Only the people were gone. The story goes, there was no sign of a struggle or fight or anything, but there was a strong, thick fog that passed through the village the night they disappeared."

"Wow," I whispered as I thought about it for a while, then shook my head as I remembered the matter at hand. "Well that is pretty cool, but I'd rather research your dad, I bet it would be easier to find facts about his family."

Justin shrugged and agreed. As the class was full and now getting pretty noisy, we packed up our stuff and with Mrs. Cox, headed off to the library.

"So, what exactly do you want to know about my dad, keeping in mind I don't know everything of his family history?" Justin said, once we found secluded seats in the library.

"Everything there is to know." Justin started telling

all he knew about his father's family and for the first ten minutes it was so normal that I started to think maybe he wasn't the one, that is until something Justin thought was important caught my attention.

"Wait, did you just say your dad grew up on a Somorian reserve?"

"Yeah," Justin said, thinking on it. "My dad's parents divorced when he was pretty young, so he was back and forth between them and his father was a Somorian, so yeah."

I tried not to seem concerned. "How much does your father know about his Somorian heritage?"

"Quite a bit. Granddad wanted him to know about his Somorian family," Justin chuckled a bit. "Actually, my dad said Granddad wanted to teach him about Somorian legends, but Dad just wasn't into that sort of thing."

Well then, how did he get a siduel too? I wondered.

"Did he have many friends on the reserve?" I pressed. I had to be sure if there was a connection somewhere, but from the suspicious look on his face, Justin was catching on.

"Why would you want to know that?" He asked, eyebrows raised.

"Just merely interested," I said quickly, "can't help it." I don't know if Justin bought that or not, but he went on anyway.

"Yeah, he had a couple friends there. He even kept in touch with them after he stopped going."

"Hmm, there's one more thing, is your dad a first born?"

"Yeah, he is," Justin replied. To be honest, I really wasn't surprised by that.

"What's wrong?" Justin said, catching the strange look on my face.

"It's nothing. Something just went through my mind. Anywho, let's see how much further back we can go."

I knew I'd promised myself I would go to Hilda and Lyla with what I knew, but I just couldn't bring myself to, not yet anyway. I couldn't explain why, except I just felt it couldn't be Mr. Pollard, so I kept quiet on the information for a couple more days at the risk of, well… my life.

I can't really say what I was waiting for, except some kind of divine sign that would tell me if I was wrong or not, but as always, it wasn't that easy.

When we last spoke with Hilda, she seemed convinced the attack would happen any day soon, but by Thursday evening I hadn't seen a single ghosts and the crystal hadn't even grown warm.

I wasn't stupid enough to think the attacker had given up, but I'd started to think that maybe with time Hilda would find a way to stop the ghost before they attacked.

That evening when I got home from school I was surprised to find Chris there, deep in conversation with my dad.

"Hey, you're looking a lot better now," I commented after I got a good look at him. I was glad to see the greenish tinge to his skin was gone, giving way to its usual tan color. And from the look in his eyes, I knew his strength had returned.

"Thanks. I feel a lot better. I guess all I needed was a little rest," he said, opening his arms as if I would be able to see his renewed spirit. "So, where's Lyla? You're usually with her whenever I see you," Chris asked as he sat back down. It wasn't meant as an insult, but it certainly did sting.

"She went out with her parents, but she told me she would drop by later." Actually, Lyla went swimming with her parents.

"What's this?" I asked when I saw an envelope addressed to us in beautiful handwriting on the dining table.

"Oh that. That's a formal invitation. The Morgans are holding a dinner party and we're invited," Dad explained as he got up from the couch with Chris to go to the kitchen to help Mom. I picked it up. It was already open, so it took it out and read:

We, The Morgan Family, are very pleased
to invite you, The Rowland family,
To a formal dinner party that will be held
in the honor of our daughter,
Lyla Morgan's 17th birthday.
The formal party will take place on
October 31st at 7pm at our residence

RSVP. Salathia Morgan

The letter was hand-written by Salathia. It was so beautiful, yet it looked almost impossible. Coming from the letter was an alluring mixture of roses and sea breeze, Salathia's scent.

"Are we going?" I asked curiously. I heard Mom and Dad chuckle from the kitchen.

"Like we're gonna keep you from this after all the horrible pain we inflicted on you by bringing you here." Mom joked.

"Everyone's going," Chris said, "even I got an invitation. I wouldn't be surprised if more people than were invited show up."

As I laughed at his joke, something came to me. It was a wonder these ideas didn't come to me any sooner. I dropped my backpack by the stairs and headed back to the door.

"Mom, Dad, there's something I have to do. Don't worry, I should be back before dinner." I said this quickly before they could get a word in and was out the door.

Minutes later I pulled up outside Jack's house on the Somorian reserve (I'd used my bike as it was close) but unfortunately Kristian and two of his friends were outside. I took a deep breath, then hopped of the bike, suddenly a little tense.

"Is your dad home? I need to speak with him." Kristian's friends started sneering, like they found something amusing, but Kristian didn't look at all like he found the situation funny.

"Why would you…" he responded, repulsed, "…need to see my father?" He began advancing on me, but stopped when he noticed his father coming towards us.

"I'm sure he doesn't have to tell you why he wants to see me."

I wasn't surprised when Kristian looked away from his father's face, because the annoyance there was obviously aimed at him.

"Go lock up the garage, now." Jack said softly but

firmly. Without a word Kristian walked off towards his father's garage, his friends following behind him.

"Come on in, Chase," Jack said, turning to walk back into the house. He led me into the living room. "What can I help you with?" He asked once we were seated and I'd refused refreshments.

"Actually, this time I wanted to ask you about someone. What can you tell me about Anderson?"

"You mean Anderson Pollard?" Jack said, completely surprised. I nodded. "A few days ago he was at our house and I saw the death magic siduel on his arm. I asked Justin about him and he said Anderson's father was a Somorian. I didn't even know that. And Justin also told me Anderson used to spend a lot of time with his Somorian relatives when he was younger."

Jack was silent. I couldn't tell if he was considering what I'd said or if he was thinking of what to say, but I could tell he knew something more.

"Well Chase, I actually know Anderson very well and even though all you've said is true, I know he's not the one after you. You see, I've known him ever since he was a boy and even up to now, he still doesn't believe in Somorian legends. He thinks they're just myths. As for the tattoo," Jack shifted uneasily in his seat, "I should have explained to you before. The language of death magic is very old and became lost to common knowledge hundreds of years ago. There are a few Somorian who study it, not to use it in the hopes of reconstructing the language, not to use it at all, but simply to regain a part of our history. Anderson got that tattoo not because of magic, but because of what it means: summoning strength. At least that's how most people translate it. It actually means summoning power from darkness. But we didn't know that when we were younger and as Anderson doesn't believe in our magic, that tattoo is useless to him."

I breathed a sigh of relief when I heard that. To think of all the trouble I could have caused had I told Lyla or Hilda. Someone was still out there who wanted me dead, but at least it wasn't Justin's dad. Something else came to me.

"Justin also told me Anderson's a first born, so why doesn't he have any magic?"

"That sometimes happens. The power can skip the first born and go to another child or not be passed on at all. It happens. In Anderson's case, it wasn't passed on at all."

I thanked Jack and stood up to leave when one more question occurred to me.

"Do you have any magic?" Jack smiled as he stood up and led me to the door.

"That would make helping you so much easier, but no. I don't have any powers. I'm actually the third and last of my parents' children, which is why I have such a fascination with magic, because I never had it."

"But I thought you said siblings without magic are never told of it."

"That's correct," he admitted, "but my family didn't tell me. I met Alisa when we were in our teens and she was a lot more rebellious back then. The rules said one thing so she had to do the opposite. I think she probably only told me to get on her parents bad side," Jack scratched his beard as he remembered days long passed. "She's the one with the magic, not me."

After that we said goodbye and I hopped back on my

bike and rode away.

When I got home it was a little later than I expected. The sun had already disappeared, though outside wasn't completely dark yet. It was more of a deep purple.

There was a strong wind blowing loudly, rustling the leaves still clinging tightly to the trees and carrying the sound of the waves crashing against cliffs far inland.

After dinner I simply went up to my room to wait for Lyla and decided to get started on my homework to pass the time, but as soon as I'd settled down, that strange magnetic feeling took hold of me and I knew where I had to go. I pushed my books to one side of the table and prepared to go down to the beach.

By now complete darkness had come, but a bright moon provided all the light I needed. Taking my shoes off and keeping them in my hand, I started walking across the beach. It was low tide and I was able to cross some rocks that otherwise would have been underwater, until I was under a small space under our cliff where I sat on a damp rock and dipped my feet into one of the pools of water left behind when the tide went out. In the other pools around me were all sorts of sea creatures such as small fish, crabs, snails, star fish and even a few eels.

Just then, a familiar presence came over me and a smile slid onto my face.

"Did you enjoy your evening without me?"

"Only the thought of your return got me through the time," I teased as I placed my shoes on a dry patch. Lyla sat down on a rock next to me. She was wearing a short jeans and a plain white tank top.

"How did you find down here, anyway?"

"It's funny really, cause I probably never would have if it wasn't for our connection."

The light under here wasn't good, but as usual, I could see Lyla quite well and she looked confused, so I explained further.

"Well, sometimes I get this strange feeling that pulls me to you. I'm not sure I can explain it properly, but it like this magnetic pull that just takes hold of me and the closer I get to you, the stronger it gets."

"Amazing," Lyla whispered. "And that's what led you here?"

I nodded.

"Wait a minute, howcome that doesn't happen with me?"

I shrugged. "Maybe it's something only I can do." That made me feel a little smug, as though she could walk into my dreams as she pleased.

"You never told me about that."

"In the excitement over, well everything, it slipped my mind."

We stayed silent for a while. I felt something pinch me in the small of my back and I pulled a small crab off my shirt.

"Come on, let's go for a swim," Lyla suggested, getting up.

"You just came from the water," I reminded her, taken aback. Lyla simply gave me a look. I chuckled and said, "Oh, right. Aquamun."

I don't exactly know what it was, but whenever Lyla suggested we do something, it was like all logic and common sense left me, allowing me to do whatever it was she wanted without fear. It was something I hoped would never change.

We ducked out from under the space in the cliff and as soon as we were out, Lyla ran gracefully back into the water, disappearing under a particularly large wave, which meant high tide was on its way back.

I, on the other hand, first walked back over to the beach before I joined her. Going back across the rocky path was not as easy as the first time. The water was quickly rising and it was making it hard to stay on the rock. I kept slipping.

The sea hadn't yet reclaimed the little space under the cliff, but it had already started on the rocks and boulders beyond. The water was now bashing against my knees was some force, though I was able to put up a proper resistance.

No matter how old I was, I knew if my parents (well, Mom anyway) knew how close I was to being caught in high tide, let's just say Dad would be more understanding than Mom, but they would both be livid.

Once on the beach again I started to strip down to my boxers and immediately felt the cold air start to bite every inch of my exposed skin.

Even though I couldn't see Lyla—she could have been miles away by now if she wanted—I still went willingly into the chomping jaws of the ocean. It was the same as all those months before when I'd fallen of the cliff. The water was so cold that after a few seconds my body felt like it was going numb, but then I felt two soft lips caress the lower part of my neck which, at the same time as calming me down, warmed my whole body.

We stayed afloat for some time, just swimming around,

and after a while she didn't have to keep holding me as the water started to feel warm enough for me. Before long I found my way back to the sand and simply lay there on my back with my eyes closed.

From the moment I did, my body started to relax. I hadn't slept well in days and with all that had been going on, I wasn't surprised at how tired my brain really was.

"I haven't felt this relaxed in a while," I whispered, the words effortlessly leaving my mouth as I felt Lyla's head rest on my chest.

She remained quiet.

"I want to ask you something. You may not want to answer."

"What is it?" she replied calmly, without hesitation.

I smiled to myself before I spoke.

"What is it you love about me? I know our connection allows you to love me as Aquamuns can't fall in love with humans, but what is it you find so appealing about me?"

For reasons I couldn't even think of, Lyla laughed for a couple seconds.

"The night I first met you, when I pulled you from the water, I remember thinking when I looked at you that you were an even sadder looking person than I was. And to be honest, that's the first thing that got me interested in you, because I wondered what a human could be going through that would make my life seem a little better."

There was a tinge of guilt in her voice.

Looking up at the stars, I realized I wasn't angry that Lyla was first attracted to me because of what I felt. Actually, I was glad for her interest in me, whatever the reason.

"After that, everything about your life, about you, seemed to appeal to me."

She rose, turned over and propped on her elbows, her hands under her chin.

"You're right about the bond." She looked down at me. "It allowed me to fall in love with you, but it's not why I love you. I love you because there is something normal and non-supernatural that draws me to you."

Lyla lowered her voice, not for secrecy, but for intimacy. When she spoke, her words seemed to flow magically. It was like they danced on the soft air on their way from her lips to my ears.

"Even now I'm not fully sure of what it is, but when I look at you, I can see it in your face. Sometimes it's like I can see it right there in your eyes, but can never tell what it is. But it's not like I need to know. At least, not yet. A girl likes a little mystery sometimes."

She lowered her head and the way she kissed me made me feel like I'd been drugged. It was a welcomed feeling. This was something I wouldn't mind getting hooked on.

"Yeah," I admitted, "A little mystery is a good thing."

I knew Lyla very well. I could even say better than any human, so I knew even though my theory about Justin's dad was wrong, Lyla would still have wanted to know, and when she did find out—I was going to tell her, when I got enough courage—I knew she was going to be pissed. The longer I took, the worse it was going to be.

With that in mind, I finally decided to tell her on Friday evening after school. So the next day when she and I were eating lunch with the others, I was a little distracted. To add to the craziness was my worrying about the attack.

According to Lyla, Marcus and Salathia spoke with Hilda, but she told them the spell she was going to cast was taking a little longer to prepare than she originally thought, which meant I was still in danger in spite of the crystal.

"I think she likes you," was all I heard Justin say. As he was sitting opposite me, I realized he was looking over my shoulder at someone behind me.

"What?" I said with an embarrassed giggle.

Lyla was sitting on my left and for a couple seconds her eyes flickered to someone sitting behind me in the cafeteria, then back to me. A small smile spread across her beautiful lips.

"You're very... appealing, aren't you?" she said. At that moment I shoved two forkfuls of mashed potatoes into my mouth and washed them down with a swing of Mountain Dew, not because I was hungry, but so I wouldn't have to say anything. Lyla felt my slight amusement through bond.

She pushed her half-eaten lunch away and stood up like it was an Olympic sport.

"I've got to go. I promised I'd help tutor in the library." No doubt because she felt through the link I thought she was leaving to get away from me.

Lyla ran her hand through my hair and told me she would see me later. Lyla might not have felt anything at hearing about the girl—I had a feeling it was Kimberly— but as she walked across the room I felt an uncontrollable pang of guilt flit through me as the ogling eyes of most of the boys in the room followed her out of the cafeteria and I filled up with jealously.

I was just about to swallow another mouthful of mashed potatoes when I felt a hand clap forcefully twice in the middle of my back, which resulted in me almost coughing up everything.

"Let me guess, she couldn't stand to be around you anymore," Dre said as he sat down in Lyla's vacated seat, smirking. I wanted nothing more at that moment than to punch his teeth down his throat, but I contented myself with contemptuous look I gave him and returned to my lunch.

Everyone at the table seemed poised for trouble except Nikolai, who was watching Dre with a slightly smug expression which, surprisingly, he ignored.

"So I was right." He leaned back in the chair and folded his arms. "I know you only want one thing from her and from the look of things," he glanced at Lyla walking away, then back to me, "you're not getting what you want. Maybe she doesn't think you're man enough." He taunted with a nasty sneer. What really surprised me was how easy it was to ignore him.

I just couldn't help answering him.

"You really are an idiot. I'm not with Lyla just for sex, which is what you're implying. I've never even thought about it." To be honest, that was a lie. I really did think about it, but that was something I would keep to myself.

"Love and lust," I pushed my chair back and got up, "are two completely different things. Maybe you should learn to tell the difference before you go mouthing a bunch of crap."

"I just want you two to remember that's my sister you're

talking about. You might want to watch what you say!" Nikolai exclaimed to both of us. His tone held a strong touch of loyalty.

When I picked up my bag, the bell sounded for the end of lunch. As I was on my way to Math, I ran into Lyla on her way back to the library and right there, for reasons I couldn't explain, I took hold of her, pulled her into a corner of the corridor and explained everything about my suspicions about Justin's dad.

Like I suspected, she was upset that I had kept this from her. When I was finished with my carefully worded confession, I watched the small smile on her face quickly turn into a frown and her eyebrows contracted in anger.

"Why is it you seem to want to do such dangerous things on your own? I would have thought after the spirit world incident, you would have thought better. But maybe you don't trust even me. If you want to do this all on your own, go ahead. You should get to class, I've got to get back to the library."

She walked past me and didn't look back despite my calling out to her. I considered going after her, but decided it was best to leave her to herself for a while. So, slightly bummed out, I headed off to Math. I got there a couple minutes late and sat at the back of the class next to an old cabinet.

Mr. Basel, the math teacher, was a small and very old teacher who was probably approaching eighty. Unlike many other teachers, he never tried to get students to pay attention to him or the work we were doing because it was his belief that if we took the subject seriously we would be attentive. That was fine by me because I wasn't very interested in Math today with so much on my mind, plus it was so hard to think with the room being so hot. Near the end of the lesson my chest felt so uncomfortable with heat I had to unbutton the front of my shirt for some air, but this did no good.

"Ouch," I exclaimed when the middle of my chest burned like someone had pressed a hot coin there. At that moment, I was looking into the reflective glass of the cabinet when I realized it was the crystal that burned me, but at that same moment, looking at me in the glass was an old woman with a shrunken face and wearing clothes that would have fit in 1850. I glanced nervously around, but didn't see anyone out of place.

What did it mean? Was she a ghost? That I didn't know, but the crystal was burning like.. I could only keep it off my chest by holding it by the chain, still on my neck, so I knew danger was near.

I looked back at the glass and saw that the old woman was reaching out to me, or at least me in the mirror. She grabbed my reflection in the mirror. She took my throat with both hands and squeezed... hard. To my horror, I began choking and gasping for air as invisible fingers tightened around my neck like a vice grip on a twig. That's how fragile I felt. My hands automatically flew to my neck but felt nothing but my own flesh and skin.

By now everyone had turned to watch me, including Mr. Bassel, who just stood still, at a loss for what to do. A few students rushed toward me, but they couldn't help.

As my hand scraped and pulled at my neck, my fingers pulled the necklace. At once the heat from the crystal disappeared, but a kind of unpleasant electric shook passed through my body and through my vision which was starting to get a little blurry. It looked like everyone else felt it too. When I looked into the mirror again the old woman had relinquished her hold on me and disappeared. I started coughing badly, but thankfully.

Seeing I was no longer in distress, everyone was crowding around me and asking if I was okay and what had happened. Just then the end of lesson bell went off, and I took that chance to grab my bag and run out of class, with everyone's eyes on me.

At that moment I didn't care if Lyla was angry with me, I just needed to find her. Not because I thought she could fight ghosts, but because I needed to know she was safe. I knew if I was near her, everything would be alright.

A hand grabbed me and pulled me out of the corridor of rushing students.

"Where were you attacked?" Nikolai said as his eyes swept the corridor as though he was looking for something.

I nodded and at the same time the crystal began to burn again. About half a dozen ghosts appeared, all of them looking barely solid and even paler than Nick.

"They're here," he said to me.

"How do you know that?" I asked, surprised as we joined the students back in the corridor.

"They seem to be giving out a strange aura I can detect, but I can't determine a specific position."

We ran to the library, found Lyla there and filled her in about the attack. At once, it seemed her anger towards me disappeared. She wasn't going to let it get in the way of keeping me safe. She motioned us outside.

"We've got to get out of here. Those ghosts are strong

enough to hurt you now, but just because you're the target doesn't mean they won't hurt others. Plus we need to get..."

Lyla stopped as we were about to pass the office. At first I thought she was looking at a teacher, but when I walked forward a bit, I saw four ghosts standing right in our path. I suddenly got a strange thought to look back and when I did, I saw the same old lady from the mirror flanked by a much younger man and a little girl no older than seven.

Lyla grabbed my hand and pulled me into a run. It was the first time I ever moved at such speed on land. If it wasn't for Lyla, I'm sure I would have been hurt. When we stopped a half second later, we were next to Sheila. Lyla got in the passenger seat, so I climbed in the driver's seat.

"Where's Nick?" I said hurriedly as I started the engine and realized I hadn't seen him.

"I told him to go to Hilda, so she would know it's happening. We need her help," Lyla said.

I exclaimed in pain as the crystal burned my chest again. I was looking into the rearview mirror to back out of my parking space when I saw the ghost of a teenage boy sitting in the back seat. He was different from the others. Every inch of him was covered with water, but even though it was running off him, not a spot of the seat seemed to be wet.

With speed similar to the Aquamuns, he rushed forward and plunged his hand through my seat and into my chest. It was the most painful thing I'd ever felt in my life. I was actually afraid my heart was going to explode.

Using my peripheral vision I saw Lyla pull something from under her seat and with lightning speed, slash something sliver through the ghost. It vanished at once.

"What was that?" I said after catching my breath and driving away. Lyla held up a silver candle stick holder for me to see.

"Ghosts are weak against sliver, that's why I brought this along."

"A candle stick holder," I said incredulously, obviously still in shock. Having your heat squeezed by a ghost wasn't pleasant.

"Well, I couldn't bring a knife in case we got searched, now could I?" Lyla said calmly.

After a while there was no more activity and I began to calm down, until we were close to Hilda's house and the crystal grew white hot again. But this time, before I could even realize it, the car was filled with them and many others were blocking our path.

"We could drive through them," I suggested after we had got rid of the ones in the car.

"The car won't be fast enough." The fear in Lyla's voice found its way through the bond and into me. There was no other choice. I grasped the crystal tightly. That same unpleasant electric shock passed through me again and this time Lyla. Every one of the ghosts, as far as we could see anyway, vanished.

"That did come in handy," Lyla said, sounding relieved, "but the next one should be the last."

I looked over at Lyla with the crystal still clenched in my hand. "That was the second time. The first was by accident."

"Then we've got to get to Hilda's. Fast." Lyla's phone rang and she answered it. She didn't say anything until

331

after a few seconds. "We'll be right there." She hung up. "Hilda found the spell to put the spirits back to rest, but she needs you to be there for it to work."

The rest of the drive to Hilda's house felt long and silent. I still felt Lyla's anger at me, but despite that she reached out and squeezed my arm reassuringly. I looked over at her and smiled.

Before Hilda's house came into view, the crystal began burning again. I couldn't take it anymore. I had to take it off.

"Don't you dare lose that Chase Rowland," Lyla said angrily.

"I'm not going to lose it, Lyla. Besides it's almost out of power."

"I'm not speaking about the magic," she clarified.

"Don't worry, I won't lose it."

I was starting to get scared, but didn't want Lyla to know. And it was the degree of heat that had me panicked. I came to realize that the greater the danger, the hotter the crystal grew, and right now it was so hot even the chain on which the crystal hung was getting unbearable to hold.

When we turned into the gap to Hilda's house; that's when I saw them. More ghosts than I could ever count. I started to breathe quickly. I looked over at Lyla and saw she was worried, but she gripped the silver candle stick holder tightly.

"I'll get out of the car first and make a path for you."

"No. they'll hurt you." I pleaded, trying to hold her back, but she simply shrugged me off.

"I'll be fine," she said, looking at me meaningfully, her deep sea blue eyes were somehow burning red. She hopped out of the car and bounded toward the ghosts. As she had predicted, it didn't matter that they were supposed to be coming after me; they saw nothing wrong with attacking Lyla too.

Nonetheless, she fought her way through them with the candlestick holder. If I didn't know better, I would have said she was doing some kind of dance with them, because she looked like she was doing it with such grace. I was amazed at how well she fought. I'd never seen Lyla, or anyone in fact, move like that in real life. She was slashing through them faster than my eyes could keep up with.

At first I thought this was going to work in our favour after all, but before that thought was even complete they all came back, all of them, and they attacked Lyla again at once.

Whether they could hurt her or not I neither knew, nor waited to see. I got out of the car and as soon as I did, they surrounded me. For the last time, I squeezed the crystal in my hand. The last blast wasn't as strong as the first two, but it was just as effective. Every one of the ghosts vanished before our eyes.

"Are you okay?" I asked Lyla as I rushed over to her.

"I'm fine, but the crystal—"

"It doesn't matter. Come on!" I shouted, grabbing her hand and running towards Hilda's house.

"They're back!" Lyla shouted. Despite being mere feet from Hilda's door. I turned around, and dozens upon dozens of ghosts were advancing slowly on us, as though they knew they had won, so there was no rush.

At that moment, Hilda burst out of the house with Nikolai behind her. Clinched in her hand was a bowl which

I supposed contained whatever it was she needed.

It was as if the ghosts understood what was about to happen, because they all turned and charged at Hilda, but before they got too close, Nikolai lit a match and threw it into the bowl. There was a huge explosion of light which, when it made contact with the spirits, seemed to burn them. They all withered and screamed as bright red flames engulfed them, and after a few seconds they exploded and left behind a huge cloud of ash which drifted on the air as easily as leaves in a slight gust.

For some reason none of us could take our eyes of the drifting ash, like they possessed a hypnotic magic of their own. However, they quickly disintegrated, releasing us from their hold. This was finally over, at least for now.

I'd turned to thank Hilda, but shock had taken over my relief.

"Hilda—no!" I shouted. Nikolai and Lyla were already crouching by her.

Hilda had collapsed.

CHAPTER 14

The Waiting Game

Nikolai took Hilda up, carried her inside and placed her on the couch. Seeing her unconscious scared me greatly, even with the assurance from the other two that she would be fine.

"Do you have any idea when she will wake up?" I said nervously two hours later when Hilda made no improvement. Both Lyla and Nikolai were seated in armchairs on the opposite side of the room. They shook their heads at my question.

"We've never dealt with anything like this before." Lyla said. "At first I thought she just fainted, but I suppose it's possible she maybe slipped into a coma."

Lyla then turned to Nikolai.

"Maybe we should take her to the hospital."

I was surprised to see Nick with a worried look on his face, and then something occurred to me.

"Wait!" I exclaimed. "I know someone who might be able to help us."

And without explaining to the others, I pulled out my

cell phone and dialed a number I always had but never used. The Ashfords. Within about thirty minutes, Jack and Alisa arrived at Hilda's, both looking confused, which turned to worry when they saw Hilda.

I hadn't explained much over the phone, so I filled them in on what happened. Both Lyla and Nikolai had left the room, as Jack and Alisa looked uncomfortable with them there.

"I'll see what I can do." Alisa said when I was finished. Jack and I moved across the room, out of her way. Alisa knelt by Hilda, placed both hands at the sides of her head and closed her eyes.

"What's she doing?" With everything that just happened to Hilda because of me, I couldn't stand it if something else went wrong. I was relieved to see that Jack wasn't worried.

"Alisa's checking to see if it's magic that's keeping Hilda unconscious. Some powerful spells give off a kind of kick when they are broken that can be harmful. If that's what's happened, Alisa might be able to heal her."

"But if it's not. If it's…" I couldn't even finish. "Would she still be able to help?"

I turned to Jack. I knew he heard the question, but probably chose not to answer because he'd seen and heard the distress in my voice and didn't want to make it any worse.

I didn't press the issue.

Alisa didn't move her hand an inch. Actually, she didn't move at all. After a few more minutes, I'd finally grown frustrated enough and was about to question her myself when she opened her eyes.

"She'll be fine. She wasn't hurt. The spell just took a lot

of energy out of her. She should be on her feet in no time."

Alisa revealed this and made to stand up, but she almost toppled over. Jack caught her before she could.

"Are you okay? What's wrong?" We both asked.

"Oh, I'm okay," she said calmly. "I just transferred a bit of my energy to her to help in her recovery. I'm just a little light-headed. I'll be fine."

Just then, and to my great relief, Hilda started to groan and actually lifted herself into a sitting position. Nikolai and Lyla came back into the room looking somewhat relieved to see Hilda up. She, on the other hand, seemed surprised, as if she wasn't used to seeing so many people in her living room.

"What're you all doing here?" She sounded a little unkind, but under the current circumstances, no one took it personally.

Before anyone could answer, a look appeared on Hilda's face, not unlike a look someone would have when they realized they were just robbed.

"The ghosts. The spell – did it work? Are they gone?"

Alisa raised her hand to calm her down.

"As you can see, everyone's fine, which means you have nothing to worry about. The spell did take quite a bit out of you, and I did transfer a bit of my strength to you, but you still need to fully recover, so you should try to relax."

Hilda looked like she was told she would need to stay in bed for a few weeks. She stood up, a little shaky at first, but eventually caught her balance.

"Thank you very much for your help, I really do appreciate it. Since you're here, I'm pretty sure that means you know the situation this boy is in," Hilda said, gesturing towards me. "Which means he still needs my help. Just because I got rid of a few restless spirits doesn't mean all this is over. Whoever's doing this is still out there and he's proven to be very smart. So I've got to do everything I can to stop him."

"But you don't have to do it alone." Jack explained, following Hilda to the bookcase where she was replacing her books. "Whoever is after Chase is abusing their power by trying to kill an innocent boy. We can't just stand by and let this happen."

"Are they like, Somorian police, to deal with these sorts of things?" I asked.

Alisa and Jack looked at each other, as if not wanting to say what they were going to do.

"Well, no, they're not like police or anything," Jack answered. "But we do have a council of elders. They're the ones in charge of everything magical going on. You see, the day we learned Chase was being targeted by a Somorian, Alisa and I went straight to the elders for help. The thing is, they were willing and going to give it too, which is something they don't usually do, but then they changed their minds."

I got the feeling they knew why, but just didn't want to say. Curiosity got the best of me at that moment.

"Why?" I pressed. But it wasn't Jack or Alisa that answered. It wasn't even Hilda for that matter.

"It's because we're involved, isn't it?" Lyla said from the doorway of the room.

Nikolai was standing behind her and even though he was the taller one, he was peering around her rather than over her, which made him seem like a shy little brother hiding behind his sister.

The others turned towards them, Alisa looking a bit weary.

"Your council has decided not to help capture an attempted murderer who's one of your own, because they know we're involved in some way and don't want to get mixed up with us, isn't that right?"

Lyla was furious. It was obvious to the others by the tone of her voice, not to mention her clenched fists, and to me by the anger now coming through the bond. It was really strong. It was not like before when I merely felt her feelings. These waves of anger were being sucked into my own sea of emotions and they were overpowering everything else I felt. I tried to use my own emotions to see if I could calm Lyla down a little. I had no idea if it worked or not.

"We tried to appeal to them to change their minds. We pleaded with them, said it was the life of an innocent human boy that was important, but they still won't help." Jack explained.

"You still haven't answered her question." Nikolai pointed out, finally stepping from behind Lyla and looking just as impressive.

"Yes. They won't lend their assistance because you are involved." Alisa said finally.

The way she looked as she spoke with Lyla and Nikolai told me she was standing face to face with Aquamuns for the first time. It was obvious she was trying not to let what she'd been taught her whole life get in the way, but it looked like she was having a hard time.

"But that's their decision. We've decided we will do

whatever we can to help." Alisa assured us, indicating herself and Jack. "Even though that means working with you." She meant the Aquamuns, but Hilda was the one who folded her arms.

"Okay. First let me ask one thing, how do we know you're not the one after Chase?"

I was shocked at her question, but I seemed to be the only one. Through the bond, I felt Lyla's feelings shift in agreement and as for Nick, Jack and Alisa, they simply looked like they expected no other question.

Maybe I was the only one that sensed the sharpness in that question.

"Because I would never be foolish enough to play with death magic, because that would be putting my family at risk and there is nothing that would make me do that."

Hilda considered Alisa for a couple seconds, then nodded and said with unusual softness, "I would be very glad to accept any help you have to offer, and thank you for coming over to help me. But you do know this will be dangerous, don't you?"

"Believe me, I know as well as you do." I could have sworn Alisa looked frighteningly at Nikolai and Lyla for a half second.

After they promised to do some searching of their own, Jack and Alisa left. A few minutes after they did, Lyla suggested we do the same, but I told them to go, as I wanted to speak with Hilda alone.

It was a sign of how far we'd come that she didn't look concerned or tell me to be careful before she left. Lyla probably wouldn't consider herself friends with Hilda, but at least there was less tension between them now.

I sighed to myself as I thought about that. One step at a time.

"You don't have to stay back to make sure I don't faint again. I'm fine." Hilda told me as she walked towards her kitchen, but when I saw her stop to lean on one of the dining table chairs for support I knew she was still in some discomfort.

"I actually wanted to ask you something." I said after she got to the kitchen and was having a glass of water. "Why are you fighting so hard to keep me safe? Why do you want to help me?"

Hilda actually froze at my question. She then set the glass on the counter and walked over to me.

"Do you remember when I first met you?"

"Kind of hard to forget. You told me my soul was in danger."

"I warned you that if you kept seeing Lyla you were sure to lose your soul, but you kept seeing her anyway, because you loved her. From the first time I met you, I saw something in you that reminded me of a dark time in my life. A time I wish I could go back and change. Maybe if I had someone who... Right now you're going through something awful, if something happened to you because I didn't try my best to protect you..." Hilda placed her hands on my shoulders, whether sympathetically or from exhaustion, I didn't know. "...well I wouldn't be able to forgive myself."

Apparently realizing her guard was down, Hilda drew herself up and after withdrawing her hands from my shoulders, walked past me and said: "I need to get some rest. Helping you is like a full time job without pay."

I had to bury my head in my pillow just to stop my brain from feeling like it was going to spin out of control.

Later that evening, after Hilda put the ghosts to rest, I went home and tried to call Lyla, but her anger had returned in full force. She told me she was busy and would talk to me when she could. I knew she just wasn't in the mood to talk, so I simply sat at the edge of my bed thinking about everything that had happened so far, and it all sounded so unbelievable that my head started to hurt trying to comprehend it all. I contented myself with knowing that at present, everything was okay. Well, almost everything.

I wasn't comfortable though. I decided to take some time to myself and go for a ride. So I hopped on my bike and just started peddling with no real destination in mind. I knew it was reckless after being attacked, but I just needed the time alone. Besides, I figured if Hilda was so worn out from putting those spirits to rest, the person who raised them in the first place probably didn't have the strength to do anything quite so soon. I really hoped I was right. To my surprise and pleasure, it was amazingly refreshing. The further I rode, the clearer my mind seemed to become.

I rode far into the country for what felt like close to an hour until I came upon a stable. I'd seen live horses before, but what made me stop was who I saw riding a tawny horse. I dropped my bike by the side of a tree and walked up to the wooden fence to watch her finish her ride. It was amazing how fearlessly she jumped over every obstacle with her long, blond her flying behind her.

When she was finished, she hopped off the horse, patted him and started walking him back to the stables when she spotted me. At first, for some reason, she looked slightly embarrassed, but she quickly composed herself and came over to me, the horse following behind her as she had the reins in her hand.

"I never took you for the cow-girl type."

Kimberly laughed. "Come around the back with me."

I gave her horse a wary look.

"He's a horse, not a dragon. Alex won't bite."

"You named your house Alex?" I climbed over the fence. For a few seconds I was a little cautious around Alex, but he seemed totally indifferent to my presence.

"Alex is one of the best behaved horses in the stables." Kim patted him again and got what sounded like an appreciative grunt from the horse. "He wouldn't hurt a fly. And yes I named him Alex. It's a nice name, but he's not my horse. Well, not legally anyway. See, he belongs to the Lovewigs. They live a little while away from here and are really nice. When Alex was born three years ago, they told me I could name him." She laughed as she remembered something. "They thought Alex was a funny name for a horse too. Anyway, they let me ride him whenever I wanted and I help take care of him and the other horses when I can."

We reached the stables, which were surprisingly clean, but still had that undeniable smell of horse crap. Before Kim placed Alex in his stall, she began taking the saddle and other stuff off him.

"Oh, and Alex is a perfectly good name for a horse."

Kim thrust the saddle at me, which was surprisingly heavy. I stood by and watched as she fed, watered and groomed the horse, then shut him safely in his stall.

She seemed so at peace as she worked, so dedicated and delicate, it was hard to believe she was a Somorian. Then again, she only was by blood. When she was finished Kimberly said goodbye to Alex and then took me on a tour of the stables, which was a little bigger than I would have guessed.

Apart from the stables, there a smaller building that served as a kind of day quarters, because, according to Kim, the Lovewigs loved their horses like children and wanted them taken care of daily. So the building was where a team of three people stayed during the day to take care of the horses and the grounds around, which were also very nicely kept.

"What do your parents say about you riding? Are they cool with it?" I asked when we sat down under the tree with my bike.

Kimberly chuckled uncomfortably.

"They actually don't know. When I was younger they let me have riding lessons. It was either that or ballet and everyone knew I was *not* light on my feet. So they paid for my riding lessons and I loved them, but after the lessons were over, that was it. I got the impression they didn't trust me with a horse, so they didn't want me riding. Afraid I would get hurt probably. So I kinda figured they wouldn't take it well if I told them about this."

We were silent for a while. While Kimberly and I were friends, this was the first time we'd ever spent any time alone together. And if what the others said was true about her having feelings for me, that would explain why she looked like she was feeling awkward around me.

"You should tell them, your parents. You should tell

them about your riding. I mean, they may not like it, but it's something you love and from what I saw, you are really good at."

Kimberly blushed at the compliment.

"I've gotten to know a little about your parents, and I've got to tell you, even if they don't like it, I don't think they will stop you from doing something you love.

"Really? You think?" I could see she took my opinion very seriously.

"Yup. And take it from me, when you keep secrets from people you love… it's just best if you tell them."

I shifted my position, which made my knee rest against her leg. She didn't seem to mind, but did become a little flustered. Then, for no reason at all, she suddenly became a little depressed and slightly defensive.

"So, what did you do?"

I looked questioningly at her. She seemed to get more uneasy by the second.

"I noticed you and Lyla aren't as touchy and gropey as you two usually are which means something happened. Now, from what I know about Lyla she never seems to do anything wrong, which points to you, and from what I know about you, well I'll just say you're no son of mother of Teresa."

We both laughed at that and I decided that telling her a carefully edited version of events was okay. Too many people were now involved as it was and I wasn't going to be responsible for bringing Kimberly into this when she was safe not knowing. It would destroy me if she got hurt because of what I said.

"Well, you're right. Lyla is mad at me and she has every

right to be. Um... sometime ago I went looking for someone that wasn't exactly good. Lyla didn't like that, and to top things off, I almost got into an accident. If I'd just listened to her, that wouldn't have happened. She wasn't mad at me very long and quickly got over me being reckless, which I admit I was, 'cause it was kind of dangerous. But then after that, I kept something really important from her, and now she thinks I don't trust her and she's having trouble with it."

"Wait a minute," Kimberly said curiously. "How do you know she felt like that?"

Damn, I didn't think she'd latch onto that, I thought to myself.

"I might not have known Lyla as long as some people, but I do know her a lot better than most," I said. I couldn't tell her I actually felt it through our supernatural connection. Well, I could, but then I would have to tell her everything, including opening the can of worms about her family.

I noticed there was a look of what could only be admiration and lust in Kimberly's soft green eyes. There was no longer any doubt in my mind about her feelings towards me. It made me kind of sad to know I couldn't return those feelings, especially as she was such a nice person.

If her feelings for me were anything close to what I felt for Lyla, her unrequited love was going to cause her a lot of pain. That made me feel guilty.

"What's wrong?" She asked, probably noticing the sad look that slipped onto my face.

"Nothing." I took up a small rock and started turning it in my hand.

"Anyway," Kimberly continued, "I think you should try to talk to her. Yeah, there are times when the guy should give the girl time and wait for her to come to him, but this isn't one of those times. You need to go to her and sort things out. Tell her you do trust her and keeping something like that from her was a foolish mistake on your part. I bet she just needs to hear you tell her you're sorry and mean it. She will forgive you. And you've got the perfect opportunity tonight."

"Why, what's tonight?" I asked, following Kim's lead and getting up. I stretched myself before I moved. Kimberly looked at me and shook her head.

"You really are something else. Lyla's birthday dinner is tonight, remember?"

It was true. I had indeed forgotten all about Lyla's birthday dinner, but apparently no one else had. When I left Kimberly at the stables, she said she was going home to get ready.

"The Morgans sent my family an invitation, though I think I'm the only one that's going." She'd told me.

"There you are." My mother sighed, half-frustrated half-relieved to see me when I arrived home around five. The living room was almost unrecognizable. The table was half-covered in assortments of hair care products. Sitting in one of the chairs was Madison, who had a blow dryer working on her hair. My mom, on the other hand, already had her hair in green curlers.

"You need to get upstairs and start getting ready. The dinner's starting at seven and we are not going to be late."

Mom said, already starting to take the curlers out of her hair. "I already sent your father upstairs, but it's been awhile. He'd better not be lagging." She added with a dangerous look towards the stairs.

I was on my way up when she said to me, "And Chase, do something with your hair."

"Would you like me to braid it?" I joked.

"What was that?"

"Nothing." I said quickly.

I trotted up the stairs, not intending to start getting dressed, but just to stay out of Mom's way. As I reached the second floor landing, I saw Dad about to dash into the bathroom, but when he saw it was me he stopped and breathed a sigh of relief, though he looked slightly uncomfortable.

"Chase, um, I was just going to…" I held up my hand to stop him. Trying to hold back my snicker, I said, "It's okay Dad, I know. Mom's downstairs in one of her 'don't be late' moods. I'm doing the same as you, just keeping out of her way.

"Good man." Dad patted me on the shoulder, then stalked back to his room like a teenager hiding from a parent—well, I guess like me.

When I got to my room, I was shocked (and a little happy) to see Nikolai there, going through my CD collection. Yeah, I still kept CDs.

"Two things: you actually listen to Wicked Wish and two, you still have CDs?"

"Wicked Wish, they are amazing and who doesn't still own a few CDs? Now, what are you doing here? What if my parents saw you?" I said softly as I closed the door, which I just realized was now closed a lot of the time, and crossed over to Nick, who in turn stood up and looked genuinely insulted.

"Chase, Lyla comes over here all the time and never gets caught. I, on the other hand, am the one with the ability to make illusions and you think your human parents are going to catch me? Please."

I shook my head, not admitting he was right. "What are you doing here anyway, what's up?"

"Well everything for the party's all set up and now that's done, mother has all of us getting ready early and it's nowhere near seven yet. You think your mother's bad? Well, at least she doesn't still pick your clothes out for you for these kinds of things. She's a nightmare sometimes," he complained, dropping back into the chair.

"So, how's Lyla?" I said kind of nervously. Nikolai was spinning around in the chair, but upon hearing my question, stopped and looked sympathetic.

"Generally, she's fine. Her issues with you, I have no idea. She's not really talking about it. I'm not the one who can read her feelings, but I think she's more sad than upset. But I do know she does really miss you."

That made me feel a little better. "I'm actually kind of scared to talk to her."

"You should be, because when she's ready she's going to eat you alive," Nick said, resuming his usual smugness. He opened his mouth to speak again but stopped, looked shocked, then sulky as his shoulders dropped.

"What is it?" I asked. His eyes were unfocused, as if he was somewhere else but upon hearing my question looked directly at me. "It's my mother. She knows I'm not there and wants me home now."

"You can hear her from here?" I said incredulously as Nick walked over to the window.

"She's shouting. If I was human I would still be able to hear her from the other side of the island, voice like hers. I'm coming, I'm coming." He mumbled and then hopped through the window.

In no time at all six o clock arrived, so I decided it was time I started getting ready. By 6:30 I was dressed and ready in a white dress pants, blue long-sleeved shirt and a white vest.

After putting on a pair of white shoes, I took a comb, applied some hair gel and with a deep sigh, started working on my hair. The end result was actually very nice to see. My usually ruffled hair was now straight and slightly wavy.

"Chase, get down here, we need to go." Mom finally bellowed from downstairs at about twenty minutes to seven. I took one final look at myself in the mirror.

Lyla was never really concerned about how I looked, but that didn't mean I still couldn't make a good impression.

When I got downstairs Dad, who was dressed in a simple tux and was sitting around the dinner table waiting, gave me a simple approving nod, but Mom, wearing an elegant, gleaming purple dress, was still fidgeting with her hair, but when she saw me, she gasped dramatically and smiled.

"Why can't you keep your hair like this?" I was surprised when she made no attempt to touch it. I guess this was too important.

"Mom, it's too much work to keep it like this every day." But she wasn't listening. She'd just pulled out a digital camera and looked excited.

"We've got a little time for a few pictures," she said with a big smile. Mom liked to document almost everything in a photo album. As I rolled my eyes I noticed that Madison, dressed in long, white, strapless dress, was looking at me in a very flattering way.

"Madison, I want to get a quick one with you and Chase."

Looking pleased and reluctant at the same time, Madison came over to stand on my right side.

After Mom had as many pictures as she needed, we finally left at ten minutes to seven. It was yet another beautiful night in East Island. A bright half moon shone above a few clouds in the sky, covering everything in a silver glow. There were hundreds of stars out tonight and the air was so nice and light.

Already there were cars parked on both sides of the road leading all the way up to the Morgan house. Some people had even parked on the road at the bottom of the hill to the beach.

When we got around the bend, we actually stopped in amazement at what we were seeing. When Nikolai said they were prepared for the party, I didn't figure he meant anything like this. Colorful lights were strung up around the trees leading up to the house. Even though the trees were way higher than any ladder could reach, the lights went all the way to the top. The lights were hung on the branches, as one would expect, but were also wrapped around the tree trunk itself, making the tree look like it was a multicolored, luminous tree.

"How did they do that?" Madison wondered aloud.

"I have no idea." I lied, knowing that their abilities were a great help.

The Morgans' front door was wide open as the entire ground floor seemed to be a mingling area.

"I'm so glad you all made it," Salathia greeted us as we went in. Mom and Dad stopped to chat with her and Madison caught the attention of a guy I figured she knew. But being alone suited me just as well. No matter how jittery I felt, I still really wanted to find Lyla.

It was only a couple minutes past seven, but probably more than half the guests had already arrived, including some of my friends who came with their families, who I merely said 'hi' to or nodded at and walked on. So many people were here now that I had to turn sideways or actually step out of the way to avoid walking into people.

After about ten minutes of frantic searching I still hadn't found Lyla, which left me frustrated because I knew she was so close, yet just out of reach. Then I remembered our bond. I hadn't been with Lyla so long I stopped using it to let her have the right to keep her emotions to herself.

But at that moment I wasn't in that state of mind, so I focused on our connection and I was immediately surprised to feel something like a jolt pass through me before the bond opened. I figured it was because I hadn't used it in a while.

Pushing that aside, I reached out to Lyla, not bothering to hide my desire to see her. The magnetic pull-like feeling I was waiting for didn't come at once and that was partly because Lyla was fighting me, but the resistance I felt disappeared quickly, as if she'd changed her mind.

I never thought I'd miss that strange magnetic pull, but

right then I did. Just as it used to months ago, I felt it take hold of me, its force wanting to lead me somewhere. Up the stairs and into Lyla's room. I was sure of it. Lyla said she'd never experienced the pull, so at least she wouldn't know I was on my way up.

Slipping past a few other people, I headed straight for the stairs, but someone grabbed my arm and spun me around.

"Mother wants Lyla to come down soon, so if you go up there now that will just offset things. And trust me, you don't want my mother on your case tonight." I didn't respond at once, because I was looking at Nikolai in amazement.

He was wearing a red dress shirt under a gray dinner jacket. The pants were an exact match to the jacket and the shoes was the same color as the shirt. And to top it off, sitting stylishly lopsidedly on the top of his head was a red bowler hat.

A bit of jealousy surged inside me at how effortlessly he pulled off the look. I knew it was an Aquamun thing, but it still wasn't fair. His cologne-like scent hung around him.

"You will get your chance to talk to her when she comes down. Come on."

Disappointed, I followed Nikolai around, chatting with our friends until finally – "Look, here she comes." Nick announced, lightly elbowing me.

I looked toward the staircase. Lyla was descending the stairs slowly. I always considered her to be the most beautiful person in the world, but as she came down in a dark blue dress that matched her eyes, I was rendered speechless.

When Lyla finally got to the bottom, I was distinctly aware that Salathia began talking to the guests, but as Lyla was all I could focus on, the two of us might as well have been the only people in the room.

"Outside to dinner," Salathia finished. I got the feeling Lyla was looking at me, but when her mother turned to go out the back way, she followed without a word to me.

I followed everyone into the Morgans' backyard where two huge tents had been erected and under them dozens of plastic tables seating five each. Mom, Dad and I were seated at a table with the Morgans, with Lyla and I facing each other. Madison and Chris were also at our table eating happily and talking with my parents. Throughout the whole meal Lyla and I kept staring at each other. Not small, quick glances but long, wanting stares. I tried to feel Lyla's emotions through our bond, but she kept pushing me away, so I was left not knowing how she really felt.

The meal was fine, but I was extremely happy when everyone got up to dance. I was going to walk right up to Lyla, but she beat me to it. "Would you like to dance with me?" I'd never been happier to hear that voice before.

"I'd love too," I answered, feeling nervous as I took her hand for the first time in over two weeks. We walked into the middle of the yard and started dancing to a slow song.

I couldn't actually dance, so I simply 'stepped', which made Lyla laugh. It made my heart dance just to hear that. We danced through that and the next song. I didn't even check the link, for fear of ruining the mood. As soon as the song was over, Lyla's hands slid from around my neck, though I got the feeling she really didn't want to. I took her hand in mine. It felt so good.

"Lyla, please… I want you to come with me," I suddenly desired to be alone with her. A Bruno Mars song started to play. People began dispersing and started mingling with each other.

"Where do you want to go?"

"Do I have to tell you?"

She considered that for a while, than her hand, which was still in mine, relaxed a little. I took her outside to the front, around her house and through the trees toward the cliff. Just as we reached the tree line, Lyla took off her heels and left them by a tree. After a few seconds consideration, I took off my shoes and socks.

As soon as we passed the tree line, we were on the cliffs. The Morgan cliff was different to ours. Instead of just being a piece of land, it looked like dozens upon dozens of huge boulders had been piled there, so much so that even though it was natural, it looked man-made.

We crossed over the rocks until we were standing close to the edge. The sound of the waves on the Morgan cliff was a lot louder and we could actually feel sprays of sea water on our face.

We were still holding hands as we walked.

"Okay, I'm just going to come out and say this," I started. "Lyla, I'm sorry. I really am. Believe me when I say I had no intention of hurting you, but I know I really did."

I stopped abruptly when Lyla started giggling. The fact that I hadn't heard that sweet sound in so long took away some of the sting I felt that she actually laughed at my apology.

"Oh, Chase, no – I'm so sorry," she said quickly, clearly forcing herself to be serious. "I'm not laughing at your apology. I was just wondering how many times you were going to force 'really' into your sentences. I do know how sincere you are. The truth is I feel I need to apologize to you too, because deep down, I knew you had no intentions of hurting me, but I just felt like I wanted you to feel how you made me feel. Honestly, though, I think you might have been right not telling me about your suspicions until you had proof, because I was so desperate for answers, so desperate to keep you safe... well, I might have done something foolish."

Lyla turned and looked out toward the sea, probably because she didn't want me to see her face. It was always easier to see her as an Aquamun whenever she did this. To me, it was such a mermaid-like thing to do.

All I could do was shake my head. I was the wrong one and the one apologizing, yet she was acting as though she'd done something far worse. That made my sense of guilt rise.

"Lyla, I really am sorry," I said when she looked back at me. I started stammering. I'd planned everything I wanted to say, but now it felt like that had just vanished. It never occurred to me before that I could simply let her feel what I wanted to say, but in the end I didn't have to do anything, because Lyla just gave in and threw her arms around me.

We held each other for a long time, during which I realized I was long forgiven.

With November also came the constant arrival of cold, low drifting mist in from the sea on the mornings and huge dark clouds which kept the island heavily supplied with rain and thunderstorms, but as Lyla and I were back on speaking terms, this didn't bother me one bit. On the contrary, I found the rain kind of relaxing in a way.

A few days after Lyla and I reconciled our differences, I woke up to find my room showered in a weak grey-golden light that obviously meant the sun was covered with bulging rain clouds. But at least for a few hours, maybe, we were going to have some sunlight.

It was a nice Saturday morning and I would have preferred to spend it with my girlfriend, but she told me she was going swimming with her family, so I decided to just finally get caught up with my homework, and as Justin was behind as well, I got him to come over so we could work together. Both my parents had already left and we'd just taken out our books, had snacks and drinks ready, when there was a knock at the door.

"Hey, Chris, um, Dad's already left. I thought you would have been with him." I said when I let him in.

He sighed heavily. "I was supposed to meet him here, but I was running late. You have friends over?" Chris asked as he saw the table and Justin's empty chair.

"Just Justin. We're studying today. He's in the bathroom."

"Oh, okay. Chase, could you get me a glass of water please? I'm going to see if I can't get your dad on his cell."

"Sure." When I came back, Justin was already back and Chris had made his call. I handed him the water and he said Dad told him to catch up with him at the harbour in Bermintown.

Just as soon as Chris finished his water, Justin started coughing badly.

"Are you okay?" Chris said looking deeply concerned. I could tell Justin was trying to say he was fine, but couldn't get the words out with all the coughing. Then I noticed his eyes were becoming red. That's when I started to panic.

"Maybe we should get him to a doctor. He's not looking so good," I said to Chris. He nodded and ran to the telephone as I went over to Justin.

"My chest is killing me!" He shouted at me. Then without warning, he went limp and collapsed onto the floor, just as if he simply feel asleep instantly.

What was going on? I couldn't explain what was happening to Justin. One minute he was fine and the next, he was unconscious on the floor.

"Yeah, that's right. He's unconscious. The poison's working his way through his body really fast. We need that ambulance now."

Oh my god, he's been poisoned, I thought as I tried to see if I could get just get him to wake up. As I was franticly calling out his name, trying anything to see if I could wake him up, something occurred to me when Chris came over and knelt next to me to check Justin.

"How do you know he's been poisoned?"

Justin's breathing was turning harsh and shallow.

"Because I poisoned him by accident."

It was one of those times when a million questions hit me at once, but mere milliseconds after, two simple answers came to me that explained everything. I stood up slowly, my shock causing me to forget to put distance between me and the person before me.

"You were trying to poison me. You're the one that's been trying to kill me."

Chris was busy checking Justin and after forcing some water down his mouth, he looked at me.

"Yes. I'm the one who has been attacking you from the start."

Justin's breathing was returning to normal and I took that as a good sign. It also seemed to bring my senses back to me as the instinct to run took over my body, but ironically, that's when I realized I couldn't move.

"If the ambulance gets here in time, your friend will be alright. That poison was made specifically for you. It would still work on anyone else, but a little water slows it a lot. Since it wasn't made for him it should only have knocked him out. I didn't expect it could kill someone it wasn't made for, which is why I chose it. I didn't want anyone it wasn't meant for getting hurt. Everything will work out fine, though. I know it."

Chris took out a handkerchief out of his pocket, held it forcefully against my face, and everything went black.

CHAPTER 15

Eyes of the Enemy

At first I thought I was having the same dreams again— the ones about the Aquamuns attacking Russia back in the fifteenth century. It had begun just the same way, people running and screaming everywhere, some houses completely destroyed and others still burning.

But there was something different about this one. Unlike the others, this dream was completely dark as if it were a starless night. I was still able to see the silhouettes of the villagers running from the onslaught of approaching danger. Everywhere you looked there were mothers grabbing children, family members running with each other, the old, abandoned and unfortunate were pushed aside by anyone and trampled by everyone.

Remembering I had some control over my actions in these dreams, I began looking around for any sign of the Aquamuns that were always here. But there was no sign of them, and now I took the time to properly examine my surroundings. I came to realize a few things.

First there were bodies all over the place, but they didn't

die from any Aquamun attacks, those were the poor souls who got left behind. Second, even though the villagers were in a panic, I noticed there weren't any Aquamuns in sight, which meant whatever was happening, the Aquamuns weren't responsible. So if the Aquamuns weren't here, who were the villagers running from?

I scanned the area in this weird dream, desperate for any sign of what these people were running from, and really saw for the first time that whatever the villagers were running from was behind me.

Before I could even turn around, one of the villagers, a particularly young and beautiful woman who couldn't be older than twenty, tripped over her dress in front of me as she tried to escape.

Even though it was only a dream, I still tried to help her up even though I was sure this was a dream I couldn't interfere in, but it seemed she could see me, because upon seeing me reach out towards her, she screamed as hard as her lungs would allow. There was a look of terror on her face so strong that I actually recoiled in surprise. Why would someone (even in a dream) be afraid of me?

Standing a couple feet away was a young man who must have been with the woman. As he looked at the woman, who was too scared to move, his face was contorted with the pain of making a terrible choice, face death trying to save the woman he loved or leave her and save himself.

It became obvious to me that the creature these people were running from wasn't behind me, it was me. Somehow, in the dream, I was their rampaging monster. Suddenly he was standing among the crowd of running people. Chris was somehow in my dream. I squeezed my eyes shut in an attempt to force myself out of this nightmare and surprisingly, when I opened my eyes again I was awake. Unfortunately, staying asleep would have been better because from the second I became conscious, my body was filled with excruciating pain that seemed to run from my chest right down to my toes. Every part of my body was screaming in agony as it was attacked constantly and ruthlessly by this unknown force, just like that night when I was with Lyla and Nikolai. The pain was just the same, only somehow if felt worse now, maybe because Lyla's presence somehow numbed the pain the first time or maybe Chris was just giving it some extra juice.

By instinct I wanted to run away from the pain, just move until it was all gone, but to my horror I realized I was unable to move. I was immobilized, as if my brain no longer had control over the rest of my body. I was completely useless from my neck down. Devoid of movement, occupied with pain. I wasn't even able to use my mouth, because somehow every sound my mind wanted to produce was lost somewhere before it got there, which meant I couldn't even scream in my agony.

Just then everything started rushing back to me at once, like tons of water rushing from a broken dam, because for a while all I remembered was that Chris was the one. I remembered discovering he was a Somorian. I thought of Hilda getting hurt fighting the ghosts just because she was trying to help me. He was the one responsible for poisoning Justin, because like Lyla said, his desperation had got the better of him and made him careless. I still couldn't believe he was the one trying to kill me.

I had no idea where Chris had taken me. Lying wherever

I was, I thought about all the times I was with him, all the time he spent working with my parents and not once had I even considered that Chris might be the one trying to kill me. I never even thought he was slightly dangerous. I was only on the island for a few months now, and during that time I had never offended Chris, at least I didn't think so. Furthermore, I had just learned of Chris being a Somorian, and he'd been trying to kill me long before that, so it couldn't be because of that.

Then a thought worked its way into my head; one that didn't really make any sense but held my interest just the same, because from the beginning everyone connected to the supernatural one way or another had the same reason for being concerned about me: Lyla. She was the only reason I could come up with to explain why Chris would want to kill me. But if it really was Lyla, why try to kill me and not just warn me like Hilda, Kristian and his dad did? Maybe he heard I ignored their warnings because of my love for her and decided to take things further. But if that was true, that he only wanted me safe, then why come after me and not her? Not that I'd want him to do that. I would rather him take me than touch her. That would be the logical thing to do, but no one said I was dealing with a logical person—for all I knew he could be insane. There were just too many possible reasons for his actions for me to guess and I didn't have time to waste on speculation.

My body might've been immobilized and in pain, but my brain was working just fine and at the moment working overtime trying to find a way out of this. I found that the less control I had over my body the more my mind was able to process. The pain cruising through my body seemed to occupy most of my thoughts.

I closed my eyes and concentrated very hard. I felt around for the connection to Lyla. If I could just kind of tug on my end of our bond, it might be enough to let Lyla trace my location. I had no idea just how long I was unconscious for (it was night when Chris kidnapped me, but I knew it was daytime now because I could feel sunlight almost directly over me, coming through the cracks in the roof of wherever I was) but Lyla would already have grown worried when she couldn't feel my end when I was out.

I remembered when she told me she can still feel our connection even when I slept and that's how she got into my dreams. So hopefully, since I was out cold, she would probably check my room and find me gone. Once she picked up on Chris's aura trace mixed with mine, she'd figure out what happened. She'd know he was the one after me.

Knowing Lyla however, from the second she lost my end of the connection, she would have started investigating, so why hadn't she already found us? I doubted Chris had done something to her, because if he could, he already would have. My best guess was that he was somehow stopping the Morgans from being able to pick up our aura trails, which meant they had no way of finding me. The only option left was for me to reach out to Lyla.

It sounded simple enough in theory, but the thing was, ignoring the pain so I could focus on the bond was a lot harder than I thought, because every inch of my body felt like tiny little claws were pinching away relentlessly at my flesh from the inside. But it was either withstand the pain or let Chris kill me.

Mustering all the strength I could, I concentrated on opening the bond while my own body was punished for some crime I couldn't remember committing. With my eyes closed and searching deep within myself, I felt the power of the bond, alive, deep inside me. It was there, I could feel its power, but something was wrong. Usually when I felt it, it was two-sided, something like a water current flowing back and forth. But now I only felt the energy from one side—my side. It felt like our bond was a cord and Lyla's side was cut but my side remained up. I tried to pull on the connection but there was no response. I tried desperately to feel for Lyla's emotional state but it felt I was running into a wall, which was leaving a pain in my head like my skull was splitting from the inside out. Reluctantly, I let go of the connection.

What did this mean? That I couldn't connect with Lyla? From the day we became bound I'd always felt her emotions. Even when we were apart, she was always still with me, so what could have happened to block off her end of the link? I suppose Chris could have been doing something to block it, but there was no way to be sure, or maybe while I was unconscious Lyla did come, but... I didn't want to think about it much, but what if the reason I couldn't feel Lyla was because, she was dead? *Could he do that*? I wondered. Could Chris have already killed Lyla? The very thought sent chills running through me. It was bad enough I was here, but it was unbearable to think about living in a world without Lyla.

She did tell me magic couldn't kill Aquamuns over a hundred years old and I knew Lyla was past that age. So if he couldn't kill her maybe he had done something to her.

The fact that he'd already done all of this was proof that I didn't really know him.

Maybe Chris used a spell to stop anyone from locating or communicating with me. He had been doing something similar to himself when he was hiding his whereabouts from Hilda. If that was the case—and I was hoping it was—the fact that I couldn't feel Lyla simply meant we were being blocked and she was safe. That would mean, however, that I couldn't count on the Morgans or anyone finding me, which left me with no other choice concerning my escape: I'd have to do it myself.

I looked around, trying to discern anything from my surroundings, and it was easy to tell I was in a small bedroom in a very old house, though it wasn't very bedroom-ish. In the corner there was a very old wooden table and chair, and it seemed I was lying on an old, red sofa Chris probably brought into the room. The wood in the roof and walls was so old, it looked like it was actually starting to turn grey, and from examining the roof more closely, I saw they were a lot more cracks than I originally thought. There was only one window in the room, but its shutters were firmly closed. I could clearly tell I was on the second floor.

I listened intently for any sound of the sea or something recognizable that would give me a clue about where Chris had brought me, but all I heard was the wind blowing through the cracks in the house. Not at all helpful in telling me where I was. I knew I wasn't near the cove or not close enough to hear sea anyway.

It looked like once again Chris had everything planned out. I couldn't escape and not even the one that had an emotional connection to me could find me. I was starting to think there might not be a way out of this.

If I was going to die, is this how I was going to spend the time I had left? I questioned myself—alone, paralyzed and in pain, both physically and emotionally. I couldn't help but wonder about my parents. Would they ever know what's happened to me? Would Chris just bury me and go back working for my parents, pretending to be sympathetic as they mourned the loss of their only child, a child they probably would think ran away based on my earlier expressed feelings towards the island. On the other hand, what if he left my body to be found, would that be worse for them, to see me devoid of life? And then what about Lyla, my love, my very life? Would she feel responsible for it, even though I'd told her she isn't responsible?

No. I told myself. I pulled my mind away from those thoughts because at the moment tears would just be a pain. I knew if Lyla was here she would tell me to fight this, she would say there had to be something I could do, and I did have too much to live for to give up so quickly.

Suddenly the bedroom door opened with a horrible noise that sounded like the hinges were in pain. There he was, standing just outside the door. I realized he was wearing a fresh change of clothes (black jeans and a sleeveless green shirt) which meant I could have been here for a while. I noticed when he looked at me that he was wearing a sad expression. He mumbled a few words and to my surprise a small grunt escaped my mouth. He gave me my voice back.

"Chris, why are you doing this?" I asked softly. The constant burst of pain was now starting to take its toll on me, but I didn't want Chris to know that. Any satisfaction he was denied was a small victory for me. But the way he looked at me told me he knew I was in pain.

"Why are you doing this?" I asked again, this time a little of the fear I was holding back filled my voice "Let me go."

Chris finally walked into the room, took up an old and many times patched wooden chair and sat down by the couch.

"I thought you would've known I can't do that Chase," he said sullenly. He had the look of a man going through some kind of emotional turmoil. His youthful-looking face now seemed aged and there were a lot of lines in his forehead. If he didn't have me captive, I would have been concerned for him.

"Actually, I don't know that," I replied. "Why are you doing this to me? And why does it have to hurt so damn bad?" The pain in my body was now burning worse than if I was exercising past endurance.

Chris looked at me again with that same sullen expression, like it was permanently etched on his face. He placed his right hand in the middle of my chest, mumbled unintelligibly again and to my surprise and relief, the pain subsided immediately, though I was still paralyzed. Chris leaned back in his seat and oddly enough began massaging his right hand, which I could clearly see had started to hurt him. Was something wrong with him? What could be causing him pain, no matter how small? That's when I remembered what Hilda said when I was being attacked, about how using so much powerful magic would eventually take its toll on the user's body. This had to be the reason why Chris was hurting and looking so worn out. It also meant that if I could get him to unfreeze my body, escape would be so much easier, as I was willing to bet his physical strength wasn't at its best, which was why he made sure I couldn't move.

"I want you to know that I'm really sorry about all of this, Chase. About attacking you, hurting your friends, which was an accident, and about what I'm going to do."

"You mean you're going to kill me." I already knew what his answer would be.

"I don't have any other choice," Chris muttered. A huge burst of fear exploded inside me when he said that. I knew he was going to try to kill me, but it was a strange thing to actually hear him say it. Like death giving you a call to tell you he'd be dropping by soon. Not exactly comforting.

"Why? Why are you doing this? I've never done anything to you."

In a flash, Chris was out of the chair, and mere inches away from my face. So close to me I could clearly see how red his eyes had become and the huge dark circles that had formed under them.

"Don't act like you don't know what this is about. I might feel awful about having to do this to you, but you brought this on yourself once you started falling for the Aquamun."

I knew this was about Lyla. No one understood her, but everyone wanted to judge her. I breathed softly. Chris's expression turned to one of disgust and he actually ejected a mouthful of saliva with traces of blood in it onto the floor. The magic had really started to drain him.

"Disgusting, all of them. I know you've been seeing her,

so don't try to lie to me. I know the truth. I know she has you under her spell." Chris said as he sat back down, more carefully than he should have needed to.

"That's not true, Lyla doesn't have me under any spell, she would never do that to me or anyone else." I snapped back. It was my original intention to get Chris angry, but he talked about Lyla like she was some kind of parasite.

Chris smiled. "If she doesn't have you under her spell, explain what's happened to your aura to me."

Admittedly, that caught me off guard. "You can see auras too," I asked incredulously.

"Yes. All Somorians can."

"Hilda doesn't know that." I blurted out in my surprise.

"Well, she wouldn't know that as we don't generally tell our secrets to anyone," Chris said in an offhand way. It was obvious he cared very little for the ways of his people.

"How long have you known about my aura?"

"The first day you came on your father's boat with us." That was the day after Lyla saved me.

"Believe me when I say, Lyla isn't going to change me."

"You don't know what you're talking about. She's changed you in ways you don't even understand, and you don't even know it."

"Well of course I've changed, being in love with someone can…"

Chris angrily cut across me.

"No, that's not what I meant. Like I said, you don't understand, but that doesn't change the fact that I have to do this. Chase, don't you see? I'm doing this for you and for everyone you love. Because anyone in their right mind would rather be dead than become what she'll turn you into."

Chris got up and started frantically pacing around the room and I began wondering if he was mentally stable. How could he come to believe the only way to save me would be to kill me? I wondered if I was related to him, would he even feel the same way. Once again I forced myself to stop thinking about such things and began trying to formulate some kind of plan to get out of this.

Considering that the more magic he used the weaker he got, all I needed for him to do was use a little more magic. Perhaps I could convince him to unfreeze me. You know, kill two birds with one stone. If it weakened him, a swift blow to the head should knock him out long enough for me to get out of here, and once away from the house I would be able to use the connection to let Lyla know where I was. It seemed easy enough, all I had to do was make it work.

"What exactly did you do to me? With the pain I mean." I needed him to keep talking as it give me more time to figure out how to get him to use his power.

"Chase, I'm not stupid, I know what you're thinking about doing." Chris said without breaking his pacing. He couldn't possibly know how I was planning on getting out of here.

"I'm sure your witch told you how difficult it can be on a person's body to use so many powerful spells, as I have. How it can start to wear down our bodies." Chris stopped and propped himself on the wall, as if merely pacing around had become too much for him.

As he stood there catching his breath, yet another horrible thought occurred to me. *Even if I do get out of here, what would stop Chris from coming after me again? Sure he's weakened now, but when he gets his strength back, he'll be as good as new, free and with his powers, so there'd be nothing stopping him from trying again.* And deep down I knew I couldn't kill another human, even one who wanted to kill me.

"There's a lot more to magic than you think. You see, it took a lot more power than I had to perform most of the spells I used. Let's just say when I was young, I didn't have much enthusiasm for this." Chris said with a weak, wicked grin. "However, I do know a few tricks, such as being able to draw on my own energy to power the spells. And it did work eventually, as you know, but as you also know, I had to try again and again, and each time I tried, the spells took more of my strength and it took longer for me to recover, but I had no choice. The energy I needed was too great to take from animals and plants, and I wasn't going to harm any other humans."

"No. Only me right?" I said. He ignored that.

"Anyway, now my body's weak, and perhaps close to shutting down. I might even be close to dying now."

He settled into his chair again. He must have greatly believed he was doing me something good, if he was willing to slowly destroy his body to kill me or 'save' me, as he put it.

Knowing Chris was probably going to die just after he killed me, that he was going to get what he deserved, made me feel good. Is that how they would find us instead, both dead in the same room? I did not want to believe we were in a house no one would discover anytime soon.

"So even if I don't escape, you're going to die right along with me?" I asked, contempt strong in my voice. It was surprising how quickly I'd grown to hate Chris. He cocked an eye at me in genuine surprise.

"Do you really think I'm going to let myself die because of this? Chase, I might be doing this to save you, but I'm not going to kill myself for you."

"But I thought you said—,"

"Yes, I'm dying now, but that can easily be changed." He actually sounded like he was the only who knew how to cure the common cold.

"I've been wondering about how to kill you in a way that's painless to you, but no one would ever be able to figure out how you died, then it hit me," he exclaimed with a snap of his fingers, "I thought of how to kill two birds with one stone. You see, my own life energy is almost gone, and that puts me closer to dying than I care to be, but you are healthy, and your energy would be more than enough, so absorbing your life force would heal me and as the energy leaves you, you would slip into a coma and die peacefully. That way both of my problems are gone in one move. This, actually, should have been quite the obvious move since the beginning really."

"You really are sick, you know." I spat at him, as he once again got out of the chair.

"You can't do this!" I shouted, half frustrated, half scared. "Let me go, you—" Fresh panic rippled through my body as the words I was about to speak were unable to produce sound. Chris had once again struck me silent.

"I'll be right back," and with that, he staggered out of the room and left me alone with my thoughts and fears. More bad thoughts came into my head. I was starting to see how easy it was for negative thoughts to take hold once you were in trouble.

My connection with Lyla ran deeper than we thought. We had never actually proven that our connection was more than emotional, but then, we weren't sure about everything our bond did. It allowed us to feel each other's emotions and go into each other's dreams, that's all we knew for sure. But Lyla did say she felt my pain once, like what was happening to me was happening to her, so couldn't that mean our connection could be holding us closer together than we thought? Was it possible, that by draining my life force, Chris would be doing the same to Lyla? Could it be that my life was literally intertwined with the one I was so in love with? Living together, both of us living for the other, both of us providing life to one another. If this was true, it meant I was putting Lyla's life in danger, I would really be the cause of her death.

If either us had to die today, I would rather it was me. It just wouldn't be fair for Lyla to die just because she went against the Aquamun's nature and risked everything and opened her heart and soul to love me. If somehow, as Lyla's life force was obviously stronger than mine, I lived and she didn't, without her, there wouldn't be a point to it, there would be no reason for me to even imagine living without her. From the time I met her, everything I was living for, every beat my heart took, was just to be with her. Without Lyla, it was pointless.

I tried to take comfort in the fact that this place blocked my connection to Lyla, thanks to whatever Chris did. I still wasn't getting any response from her end, so maybe that kept her safe, and even though she'd soon sense that I was dead, she wouldn't have to die with me. She wouldn't have to feel helpless as I slipped into death. She would be angry and sad, but at least she'd be safe.

For a few minutes I began wondering about all the things I was going to miss. Obviously, the most and best of them was being with Lyla, but there were other things too. I thought about my friends, my parents who would have to carry on without me, and of all things, even school, which I'd just started getting used to. I thought about how I couldn't even taste fresh air before I died. My eyes began to sting horribly and a couple tears fell down to my cheeks and onto the couch. In the face of doom, no one could hold this against me.

I could have sworn my heart had just stopped beating from surprise when I saw Chris suddenly appear in the doorway. When he stepped in, I saw he had a metal bowl in his hands. He slowly crossed the room, deposited a silver knife and some candles on the table, and placed the bowl on the floor.

He then placed the candles in circular position around the room and lit them with a lighter he took from his pocket. After that, he took the knife and cut the tip of my finger to draw a few drops of blood, which he dropped into the bowl, after he lit whatever was inside it first. As soon as my blood was in the bowl, I could have sworn I felt something contract around my heart. This really had to be the end. I had no great plan of escape, there wasn't going to be a rescue, and Chris wasn't going to release me.

If I'd only known today was going to be my last day, I would have done so many other things, and I would spend the whole evening with Lyla, and now I'd never get to see her again. I'd never get to touch her again or drown in wonder at her lips when I kissed her. I would never hear her funny baby-like chuckles or even just get to see her again.

"I really am sorry Chase." Chris said before turning his back on me to finish his spell... and me.

There was suddenly some kind of explosion from somewhere outside that seemed to rock the house, followed by the sound of wood cracking and glass breaking and at once the candles were extinguished. At the same time, the bands around my heart seemed to disappear.

"You've got to be joking!" Chris shouted. He shot me an odd look the same time I felt it. A strange pulse traveled through my body for a few seconds, like instead of going through water, the water passed right through me. It passed as quickly as it had come, and as soon as it did I was able to feel my body again, and my voice returned.

I felt my connection with Lyla engulf me like a life-saving breath of air. I was able to feel her emotions again and I knew from the surprise, excitement and relief she was feeling, she was able to feel me too. I wanted so badly to be caught up in our connection, but we both had other things to do.

Not questioning what was happening, I scrambled off the sofa and was ready to run through the door, but Chris raised his hand at me. Out of nowhere, an immense amount of pressure suddenly dropped onto my body, pushing me to the ground against my best efforts. But Chris didn't have time to worry about me because at that very second, Michael was standing impressively in the doorway. Chris' hand dropped in surprise, automatically releasing my body from his power. Moving in a blur, Michael rushed towards Chris, but he was ready to defend. He had his hands close together as though he was holding a small beach ball, and in that split second, just before Michael reached him, he threw something at Michael. It must have been some kind of invisible energy ball because when it hit Michael, it sent him flying through the room and down to the first floor.

Before Chris could even recover from the shock of Michael's surprise arrival, he was somehow pulled out of the room and down the stairs, as if one of the very ghosts he once conjured had taken hold of him. I scrambled to my feet. There was a series of crashes and explosions coming from downstairs, some of which were actually strong enough to shake the second floor.

As quickly as I could, I ran down the stairs, some of which had just been blasted away, and when I reached the bottom floor, I was surprised to see not only Nikolai and Hilda, but my heart skipped at the sight of Lyla. The three Aquamuns were trying to use their super-speed to take down Chris, but for some reason, they couldn't touch him. It was as if they were hitting invisible barriers around Chris.

Hilda, on the other hand, was having far more luck at inflicting damage. She seemed to be throwing the same kind of invisible energy balls back at Chris, but instead of hitting the invisible shield that were keeping the Aquamuns at bay, they were going through, hitting Chris and sending him in all directions in the empty house. Hilda would simply pull back her fisted hand and Chris would be pulled back into the room.

Chris was of course putting up a fight, but it was a feeble attempt, like he didn't have the energy needed. The energy Chris was using now seemed pretty weak, and Hilda was deflecting it with a flick of her hand, blowing up parts of the house, making holes big enough to fit an arm through.

Seeing that I would have to run through the battle to get outside, I decided to stay where I was until the fight was over, because it was clear by the way Chris was fighting that either the Morgans or Hilda would finish him off soon enough. I had to drop to the ground suddenly when I saw Chris dodge one of Hilda's blasts and it flew towards me. It missed and blew a pretty big hole in the side of the house.

Chris wasn't going to give up so easily, because he let out a terrible scream and another shock wave rippled through the house, only this one pushed everything back out of its way. Loose wood fell out everywhere, and the few glasses left in the house shattered into dozens of pieces. It even felt like the air was forced back as it rushed against me and Hilda. The Morgans and I were thrown hard against the house.

Angrily, Chris threw out his hand at Hilda. My insides felt like they were being twisted around as Hilda released a horrible scream and she began to claw at her body as if she was trying to tear the pain out of her body. Both Lyla and Michael got up and were about to rush Chris, but he already had his other hand out. However, it wasn't aimed at them, it was aimed at Nikolai, who seemed unable to pick himself up off the ground.

"I might not be able to kill you," Chris said, exhausted with sweat and blood running down his body, "but your brother here isn't as old as you, ergo, I can kill him. Take one step and he's dead before you know it."

Lyla and Michael both looked like they were being held against their will. They obviously wanted to help Hilda, but they didn't want Nikolai hurt either.

Through our bond I felt Lyla's anger at Chris flare up. I never knew she could hate someone so much. She was perhaps wondering about the same thing I was, that Chris could still come after us. There weren't any supernatural prisons, so how would we stop him? The hate I felt from Lyla was strong, probably what you would feel if two people were fighting to the death. Was this a fight to the death? Chris did say he would kill Nikolai, and he would probably kill Hilda too, if he could.

Chris raised the hand he had out to Hilda. She rose up in the air, and to our horror, was slammed into the house, still screaming in pain.

It was obvious to me that the Morgans were feeling exactly as I was, helpless, so it was weird when I saw Nikolai trying to catch my eye, to get me to understand something. At that same moment, however, Chris seemed to have realized something himself.

"Where's Chase?" he asked, looking around frantically. "No, no, no. There's no way he could've escaped. He wouldn't leave without any of you." He didn't sound too sure. The odd thing was, I was still standing on the stairs, which was still in Chris's line of sight, so I couldn't think why he was unable to see me standing right there.

At that moment, my mind was spinning with anger and worry, so it didn't make sense to me until I saw Nikolai still trying to silently tell me something, and that's when it clicked. Chris couldn't see me because Nikolai was using his power to make me invisible to Chris's eyes. From there, I didn't need any more urging. This was the chance we needed.

After looking around, I took up a piece of wood from the floor and hoped that Nikolai would make that invisible as well, as it would be a giveaway if Chris saw a piece of wood floating in midair. But he didn't seem to notice, which meant Nikolai did.

Walking down the stairs, as quickly as possible, I ran over to Chris and banged the wood against his head as hard as I could. Unfortunately the piece I chose was kind of rotting, so even though there was enough strength behind the blow, the weapon itself wasn't very strong, which resulted in it shattering upon impact. But it was still a solid object and did send Chris to the ground, and I was glad to see it had caused a gash in the side of his face.

From the second he went off balance, the hold Chris had on Hilda and Nikolai disappeared. Hilda, in turn, raised her hand above her head, which pulled Chris into the air, where she blasted him towards the wall of the house with the biggest energy blast yet. But before Chris even touched the wall, Lyla had him in the air by the throat.

"You've made the worst mistake of your life going after Chase, and trying to hurt us." Suddenly she began pushing him into the walls and floor of the house with extreme speed. When she was finished, she threw him so hard against the house, the wood actually broke from the force. "You're not worth killing." Lyla said disgustedly to Chris with one last revolting look at him. She turned away from him and was walking over to me, but the second her back was turned, Chris was back on his feet. I was starting to believe he had become obsessed with killing me, but before he was even standing properly, Lyla's hand was back around his neck.

I began to feel the weirdest sensation I ever had. It felt like there was a large serpent-like creature uncoiling inside me, only it's body wasn't made of anything solid. It was made from pure hot energy, and the more it uncoiled, the hotter it got, until it felt to me that it got so hot it exploded.

"No. You can't! Don't! No!" I heard Chris shouting.

At the same time I felt the creature explode inside of me. I could have sworn, even from where I was standing, that Chris's pupils expanded so wide, both of his eyes were consumed by some powerful darkness, however after a few seconds, the darkness seemed to have retracted back to his pupils.

As soon as Lyla removed her hand from Chris, he slid to the floor, with a blank, vacant expression on his face. The creature I felt had collected itself into a single form again, and coiled back up, going back into its slumber.

Against my better judgment, I went over to Chris's limp form and looked down into his eyes. Physically, he looked okay, but when you really stared at him, you could plainly see something was wrong with him, like something vital was gone. I looked back and saw everyone was looking at Lyla, who looked remorseful, but still content. She walked over to me, and threw her arms around me, and with her head on my shoulder, she whispered in my ear.

"Forgive me."

CHAPTER 16

Broken

How could you do that? Just run off without a word! You know what? I don't even want to hear it because there's no excuse for that, no matter how angry you were. The thing is you didn't even leave a message of any kind. You just left! We didn't know what to think. Did you even stop to consider what that would have done to us? Do you have any idea how worried we were?"

Mom shouted at me as we sat in the living with the Morgans (Marcus and Salathia as well), and Hilda. We'd just arrived home, and upon seeing me my parents engulfed me with hugs and words and praise at how happy they were to have me back. Then, once they'd gotten in all they could, they started with the scolding.

It seemed I had been gone for two days, and as they would rather have my parents believe I'd run away rather than been kidnapped, Marcus and Salathia told them that I'd told Lyla I'd had enough of the island and it seemed like I ran away. They now believed Michael, Lyla, Nikolai and Hilda found out where I was and went to get me. As this was the only story we had, and somehow my parents found it easy to believe, I had no choice but to go along with it.

"Mom, I'm really sorry for what I did, believe me." I said for what must have been the tenth time so far. Going along with this was a lie I needed to tell and, sorry to say, one I told very well. Before I found out about the supernatural, I'd never lied to my parents much, at least not about important stuff, but now it seemed all I did was lie every day about my whole life. I kept telling myself it was for their safety, and after what happened with Chris, I knew it was best.

"You keep saying that. You keep saying how sorry you are, but that's not enough now. You really hurt us Chase, a lot." Mom managed to say this before her voice became muffled as she tried to hold back sobs. Dad, who so far hadn't said a word, put his arms around her and looked at me with deep disappointment in his eyes. I flinched as if his gaze somehow burned me and turned away, wishing he'd look somewhere else. I knew I had to go along with this, but it was causing so much pain. I suddenly felt a tug on the bond as Lyla tried silently to comfort me. I had to let her know just having her here was enough.

"I think you know you're grounded." Dad said softly. "Look, just go up to your room."

I was about to protest, but he said "Now" in a voice so unknown to me that I couldn't argue. I got up, intending to go straight to my room, but instead I stopped by Lyla, hugged her tightly and after a quick kiss, whispered: "Thank you." Then I trotted up the stairs to my room and just fell down on the bed.

It felt so good to be somewhere familiar and safe again, but that didn't stop the huge waves of anger inside me. *I almost get killed and what do I get: punishment, though I would take being grounded rather than being dead any day.* I couldn't stop thinking about my parents either, about how I had hurt them. I knew it would take some time and a lot of work, but I was going to fix my relationship with them. I was going to work very hard at getting them to trust me again.

Working on me, on the other hand, was going to be more difficult as I had no idea how I really felt or should feel about what happened. I always thought people who escaped being killed by someone always felt a little out of it, and thought that was how I would have felt. But lying there on my bed, I felt fine. There was no after panic, no building fear, nothing of the sort and that got me wondering if I should be worried. Wouldn't normal people be worried? Wouldn't ordinary people be going through some kind of shock? Then again, ordinary people didn't know about the supernatural and they surely didn't have strange emotional connections with Aquamuns. What I really needed was to speak with Lyla. Even if she couldn't explain this—and I was sure she could—having her reassure me would make me feel so much more at ease.

"You okay?"

I bolted upright in the bed as I heard the voice inside my room. I quickly looked around to see Lyla standing by the window. The fact that I wasn't aware she was on her way up here puzzled me, but that flew right out of my mind when I noticed she wasn't moving, as though she was afraid of getting close to me and was going to need to escape any second. I crawled over and sat down on the side of the bed.

"What is it? What's wrong?" I asked.

She very cautiously walked over and sat next to me, but left a considerable amount of space between us. Ever since we'd left the house Chris kept me at, I noticed Lyla was acting differently towards me. It was as though she couldn't put enough physical distance between us. Even on the ride home in Michael's truck, she'd let Nikolai sit between us and through our bond, I felt she was keeping her deepest emotions to herself. At the time I assumed she felt bad about whatever it was she did to Chris, and I tried to let her know I was thankful to her for saving my life, but she was unresponsive. So I just gave her some space. Now I was starting to wonder if there something more; maybe something about me.

"Lyla, please talk to me. Tell me what's wrong."

She laughed nervously before she answered. "You know, it's funny. Even though I can feel your emotions, I sometimes have a hard time understanding what you're feeling. Human emotions are so difficult."

"I don't understand what you mean."

Lyla sighed and moved closer to me. I felt a little better, but still a little more nervous at this.

"You must think differently about me now. After you saw what I did to Chris, how could you not?" She blurted out.

I detected a kind of self pity in her words that sounded out of place in her angelic voice.

"Why would you think that? You saved my life. Believe me when I say, if anything, I think better of you."

I tried to reach out to her, but she recoiled before I could touch her as though she was protecting me from some contagious disease.

"Do you even have any idea what I did to him?"

I shook my head. "But I remember how it felt."

"Do you remember when I told you I could be dangerous to you?"

"Yes. You said you could hurt me without meaning too. But you never really explained what you meant."

She began rubbing her hands in her lap nervously, which was very unsettlingly for me because she was one of the most confident people I knew. It just felt so wrong for her to be acting this way. After a couple seconds, she began.

"The energy we use to perform the switch is powerful and dangerous. It isn't power we pull from the sea or anywhere else, it's always there, inside us. It's an energy that's ever constant and because of that we have to keep it bottled up inside us. Under the right conditions, which would be when we charm a human, when we release this power, it starts the switch." A dark look settled over Lyla's face. "But if we release this power on an uncharmed human, it becomes too much for them. The raw power is so overwhelming that it… it destroys their soul."

Lyla's voice broke on the last word and she turned her head away from me, her long curtain of hair hiding her face.

Admittedly I was shocked at what Lyla said. It was just so unbelievable, knowing Aquamuns could do that. Just another fate that was worse than death. I ran that over in my mind five times before I was finally able to really accept it. I remembered looking at Chris's limp body and getting the strange feeling that there was something missing, that he'd lost something valuable. I knew he was still alive, so I just thought he'd gone crazy, or that part of his brain had shut down.

I looked over at Lyla, who was still looking away from me. My heart began to hurt for her because I knew as much as she hated Chris for what he did, she was devastated over what she did. I knew she didn't regret saving me, but I was willing to bet that she'd never done that to a person before in her life. And knowing Lyla, she would be thinking about how she had changed Chris's life, even though he wanted to kill me.

"Lyla, look at me." I reached for her hand and turned her towards me. "I still don't think of you any differently. It's not like you go running around blasting everyone who annoys you. You saved me, and that's all that matters."

She didn't recoil or fight when I pulled her into my arms, but I did feel her unease when she said: "But what about you? Aren't you afraid of the same thing happening to you? The thing is when I'm with anyone else, it's not a challenge keeping this power inside me, but when I'm with you Chase, it becomes so much harder. What if I'm with you and I lose my control? You could end up like that, and I wouldn't be able to live with myself for being responsible for that."

"How many times do I have to tell you, I want to take the chance if it means being at risk when I'm with you. Besides, I'm not so sure you can do that to me."

A new theory entered my mind. Lyla fixed me with a curious stare. "What makes you say that?"

"Well, look at the things that happened. So far I've heard your song and you've been in my dreams, but it didn't enchant me or anything. We've been kissing for weeks now, and nothing's happened. Lyla, we're even linked emotionally. So even if you lose control of your power, which I don't think you will, there's a strong chance nothing will happen to me. I don't think your power will affect me."

"Chase, that's just you being really optimistic. I'm not going to put that to the test. You're too important to me." She said incredulously, but that faded instantly as she noticed how intently I was staring at her. It was amazing how the smallest amount of light seemed to make her beautiful face glow. I ran the backs of my fingers down the side of her face in an attempt to calm her. Immediately I saw in her eyes how emollient my touch was to her. Lyla always did say how incredible it was to her to be able to feel me.

I hope you're right, I heard in my head. I actually sprang back in surprise, but quickly reassumed my position, as I didn't want her to think she'd done something wrong.

"How did you do that?" I asked, hoping I merely sounded curious and not accusing. How could she keep that one from me?

"Do what?" She asked, alarm replacing her sadness.

"That thing you just did. You just said: 'I hope you're right,' but it's like you said it in my head." I noticed that the look of alarm still on her face.

"Chase, you know I'm not telepathic. I can't put thoughts into your head."

"Lyla I know what I heard. Didn't you just think that?"

"Well, actually yes I did." She responded slowly, looking pensive. "But how could you have heard that? The bond between us is emotional, not mental. You shouldn't be hearing my thoughts."

She seemed to be getting frustrated with herself, as if some long-time belief she had was being questioned.

"Maybe our bond is still growing. Or maybe..." Another idea was beginning to expand in my head. "Maybe the closer we get, the strong our own connection gets, the deeper and more intense our supernatural one gets."

Lyla turned this over in her head for a couple of seconds, then said: "Well we can't leave it like this. We'll have to see if that's true, but we can't test it now. I've got to go. My parents want to hear everything that happened. They're not exactly happy about what I did, even though they understand why I did it." She stood up and was about to hop through the window when I grabbed her around the waist in time and pulled her into a tight hug that I hoped was at least some comfort to her.

"You know I'm always with you, right?" I said.

"Yeah, I know." Through our connection I felt both relief and sadness at that. I reluctantly let her go. She left after kissing me on the cheek and I watched her speed off towards her house.

Slightly depressed, I lay on the bed and concentrated on our bond. Earlier it felt as if Lyla was trying to keep her feelings from me. The cause I didn't know, but now with her mind on her parents, she either forgot or didn't bother keeping her true feelings from me and I was finally able to get a sense of what she was really feeling. After shifting around, I felt the happiness and relief she felt and

I was able to tell it was for me. But further down there was also confusion, pain, remorse and regret. I could tell they weren't for Chris, so I couldn't understand why she felt this way. But what really held my attention was something I'd never felt before. Not from Lyla or even myself. It wasn't really an emotion by itself, but more of a by-product of her emotions. It was something sad. I couldn't figure it out and when I got too close to it, it began to work its way into my emotions, scaring me so much, I had to instantly push it away.

It was like she dreaded it so much it came out of her fear. Just then I felt a pull in the connection. Lyla was happily acknowledging I was there. But she must have felt what I was doing, because her dark, sadder emotions suddenly disappeared as if hidden behind some cloud or fog. For a while I tried to sift around silently, hoping to pick up something real, but all I got was what she wanted me to feel: happiness, relief and love.

After a while—when she was probably still in the meeting with her family—two new, more familiar emotions appeared. Fear and anger. But almost instantly those were also pulled behind the fog. I pulled myself away from the connection, and as I lay on my bed staring up at the black roof, I finally knew she was keeping something from me.

My parents decided to keep me home for the rest of the week, but it wasn't as exciting as it sounded. Along with being grounded, I also wasn't allowed any company, I couldn't use the computer, I couldn't do anything but read. So during my time at home I had nothing to do but catch up on the assignments which my friends brought over. Maybe I should say ex-friends. The first day Brandon and the others came over to bring me my homework, I was glad to see them, but I was really hurt (though I won't be telling them that) to hear them tell me they aren't going to be friends with someone who thinks they're too good to live in East Island. That was a hard blow for me. I wondered if Justin would take the same view when he got out of hospital.

My parents believed I wasn't seeing anyone. But every night Lyla would come over and spend the night with me, and sometimes even Nikolai would and try to persuade me to sneak out, but I always declined. Every time Lyla came over I asked her if everything was alright and she always say yes with a convincingly sweet smile. But I would feel a trace of her emotions behind the fog again, and that was really beginning to disturb me.

When I returned to school everything didn't go back to normal as I'd hoped, because even then, and even though I was with her a lot of the time, she always felt so far away. She never joined in any conversations the others started. Every now and then she'd smile or nod or chuckle a little and that seemed enough for everyone else, but it wasn't for me. And it wasn't even just her. Nikolai was acting really strange all of a sudden, really out of his character. He was acting unusually... normal, as if something had tamed his spirit. And I noticed he'd always give Lyla strange looks that I couldn't understand. Too bad I wasn't connected to him too.

I knew Lyla's mind was on something else. I just couldn't figure out what, which made me think it had to be something I didn't know about. And then one day when we were at lunch, our other friends were happily discussing something and Lyla was once again staring off into space (still no one else noticed her change as long as she looked at them every now and then). I was sitting next to her, playing with my mashed potatoes and strangely enough, wishing I could read her mind.

BAM! That's when it came to me. Maybe I could read her mind. Since that time in my room it hadn't happened or wasn't mentioned again, and it wasn't like her to forget something that important, which got me thinking maybe she didn't want me to control that link. What else was a guy to do?

I looked over at her. It was amazing how still she could remain still for periods of time and just concentrate on nothing. There was a light breeze blowing; not enough to blow paper away or anything, but apparently it was strong enough to make Lyla's jet black hair dance and fill the area with both her and her brother's aroma. I realized I was staring at her longingly, so I pulled myself out of my stupor to concentrate on what I wanted to try.

She was distracted, which was rare, so this would be the perfect time, when she wouldn't fight me.

"Hey, I gotta go," I said, suddenly getting up and pushing my untouched food away. "I just remembered I've got an assignment to finish, so I need to get to the library 'cause Mrs. Best refuses to let me borrow the book 'cause the school only has two copies, as if they've never heard of the Salvation Army."

That was supposed to be a parting joke, and it fulfilled its purpose. Everyone laughed; even Lyla chuckled. I wondered if it was real or for show. Before she could get up, I bent down and kissed her quickly.

"You don't have to come. I can do this alone. Stay and finish your lunch. I'll see you later," I said to her slyly. I said goodbye to the others and left.

I knew I would obviously need to concentrate and as the classrooms were all locked at lunch, I headed straight for the library. Once there I deposited my bag and looked for a place that was both empty and secluded. Lucky enough for me, I found such a place at the very back of the room. It was almost completely surrounded by bookshelves. I took an information technology book from the shelf, just in case anyone wanted to know what I was doing. Once I was well secured in my hidden position with the book open in front of me, I leaned back in the chair and closed my eyes to focus, because I figured I'd have to apply the same practice to the mental search as the emotional one.

As soon as my eyes were closed, my ears seemed to have become sharper because the noise around the school of people playing and others laughing seemed to boom louder than ever. But surprisingly, it wasn't an annoyance. Usually whenever I'm submerging myself into our bond, I have to shut out all noise, but this was a great deal more than I was used to, and even though all the windows were open and the fans on, the library was uncomfortably warm. Concentrating extra hard, I ignored all noises and distractions and focused on Lyla. If there really was a mental link between us, I had no idea what would trigger our connection. So I focused on trying to bond with her mind instead of her emotions. It wasn't exactly an easy task. At first, our emotional bond kept pushing itself toward me, as if by now it knew when I wanted to be one with Lyla. As this wasn't what I wanted, I had to be constantly pushing it away.

After nearly twenty minutes (lunch was almost over) the only thing I achieved was drifting off to sleep for a few minutes. I got nothing even remotely close to Lyla's thoughts in my head, and I was becoming conscious of the fact that I was still alone and hidden as if I'd done something wrong. Apparently Mrs. Best also shared this opinion, because every now and then she threw suspicious looks at me from behind her desk.

I opened my eyes, got up and kicked the desk in frustration, which earned me looks from everyone in the room, including Mrs. Best, all of which I ignored. The IT book fell to the floor and I bent down to pick it up. The second my hand touched it, a horrible pain flashed through my head. It was so intense I stumbled into the book shelves behind me, but thankfully, it was gone as quickly as it had come. When I looked up, I saw Mrs. Best hurrying towards me, her small, bony face full of concern.

"Are you all right? Do you need help?" She gently took hold of my shoulder as to prevent me from falling again.

"No ma'am. I'm alright, I just stumbled," I said as I handed her the book.

She looked at me oddly, but simply took the book and walked away. As soon as she was behind her desk again and everyone had stopped staring, I fell back into the chair, mostly because I wanted to get off my feet in case something happened again. I'd never experience anything like this before.

I wondered if Lyla felt it. If she did she would be

concerned and that was the last thing I wanted to happen. I closed my eyes and rubbed my temples in an attempt to relax, but as soon as I did this, sounds and images I'd never had and couldn't control began flashing through my mind and they were all of Lyla. Some were of her childhood from decades ago. Some were of her family and past friends and then there were some of me, and these were the most frequent. What surprised me the most were the flashes of memories of Kristian's dad, which was odd, because from what Lyla told me, I figured the Somorians kept well away from the Morgans, so I couldn't think of why they would be meeting.

In these memories Mr. Taylor always looked grave, as if he was giving some kind of bad news. The memories were incoherent and out of sequence, but one phrase that struck me was: '...has caused unease in the community. There needs to be a meeting.' After this memory followed another of Nikolai telling Lyla she needed to make her mind up about me. At that moment, the bell began ringing, signaling the end of lunch, startling me and pulling me away from the memories. Along with the other students in the room, I took up my bag and headed off to my fifth lesson, giving Mrs. Best a smile on my way out as she was still peering at me.

I took my time walking to English, even as other students kept brushing me as they hurried to class. There was a lot I needed to think about and I just needed a few minutes to do it. I couldn't believe it actually worked, it was nothing like our emotional bond, yet now that I was out of her mind, I felt that same longing to go back as soon as possible. All the memories I'd pulled from Lyla's mind were still swimming around at the front of my head. I felt like they were just behind my eyes, like all I had to do was close my eyes and I'd start seeing them, like a quick video of her life. They seemed to be just banging against my skull, begging to be seen. I knew if I even glimpsed them I wouldn't be able to stop, so they'd just have to wait for later.

No matter how many ways I thought about what I saw, I couldn't make sense of it. *Why is Mr. Taylor constantly seeing Lyla? Exactly what sort of meeting has to be held? Why does he want her to meet with whoever it is he wants her to see? And what is it that Nikolai keeps telling Lyla to talk to me about?*

I sighed deeply. These were just more questions I couldn't answer by myself, so I headed off straight to class. When I finally reached the third floor I was the last student there, but Ms. Harris hadn't arrived yet. I scanned for Lyla in the class and saw her seated in the back the window. She was chatting away avidly with Charice, which was all I knew about her as we only had this class together. Lyla obviously knew I was on my way even before I arrived, but still looked surprised when I came in, probably for the sake of appearances. To my utter bewilderment, however, when she beckoned me over to the empty seat next to her, although she looked happy I felt an intense anger that was actually aimed at me, and to be honest, I was a little scared. I cautiously took the proffered seat and, once I did, she continued her conversation. Through the whole double-period, she said nothing to me. She just focused on the lesson and I decided to do the same. Not that I found MacBeth very interesting, but I knew that once the class ended she wasn't going to hold back what she had to say.

So after English was over I collected my things and tried to hurry out of the class, but she caught hold of my arm, took me outside, led me into an empty classroom and closed the door.

"You know, we're going to be in trouble if…" Lyla held up her hand and cut me off.

"Don't. Don't you dare say anything," she said in a forced soft voice, "What the hell did you do? And don't lie to me, because I know exactly what you did. I felt it, just as you did. I know you searched around in my mind." For some reason she now sounded scared as well as angry. "Tell me the truth. What did you find?"

I told her of everything I saw except the part about Nikolai. I thought it best not to let her know I knew she was keeping something important from me. I myself felt betrayed because she was keeping something from me.

"Lyla, why does Mr. Taylor want to see you? You're keeping me out of everything. I know it's your business, but not telling me what's going on just makes me feel like I'm not a part of your life anymore, and that really hurts. Please tell me what's going on," I pleaded.

Lyla ran her hands through her hair and dropped into one of the chairs. Seeing her like this tore me up inside, because I felt like I should be able to help her.

"Chase, the Somorians have their own little communities and families. They care for one another. Chris was a part of one of those families. They know everything Chris did to you, and of what we did to help you. But some of them think I used my power on Chris, not as a last resort, but out of prejudice."

"That's crazy. How can they say that? He was going to

attack us, if it wasn't for you, one of us could be hurt, or worse right now."

"Well Chase, they don't see it that way, and to be honest I understand where they're coming from. If it was the other way around, if one of them had hurt someone from my family, I'd say it was done on purpose just because they hate us. I'd want revenge too."

"Whoa. Revenge? Who's talking about revenge?"

"I guess that's too strong a word. Justice is more suited. That's why Kristian's father has been coming to see us. He's acting as the Somorians' delegate. According to him, a lot of them are really fired up about this. They think they're beginning to get restless."

"But that makes it sound as if Aquamuns are some kind of uncontrollable creatures," I said as if nothing could be more incorrect.

"Well, that's exactly what they think," she replied simply. "And to tell the truth, it's not exactly wrong. Some Aquamuns are like that, the ones that are proud to be Aquamuns. They like to live life on the edge. They go anywhere and do whatever they want, without any repercussions. That's how the Somorians know us to be. But my family is not like that, and have proved it a long time ago, but they don't care about that."

"Well maybe if I talk to them and explain…"

"NO!" Lyla shouted. "No Chase. I kept this from you because I don't want you involved. Besides, I'm sure anything you say they'll either ignore or try to spin it to make it sound bad. They're just looking for an excuse to come after us." She sighed, then said: "I was really hoping to have this settled by the time I told you this, but according to Paul, the civilians may want to attack us, but a fight's the last thing the Somorians and my parents want. So Paul's been trying to get me to meet with the elders to explain everything so they can have this resolved."

Lyla said this so matter-of-factly that I couldn't help but be amazed at her lack of fear of a potential impending attack.

"So when is this meeting supposed to happen, anyway?" I finally sat down now I was sure she wasn't too angry anymore.

"It's tonight. My family's coming along with me. Of course we don't have to go. We aren't bound by their authority, so they can't really do anything if we refuse, but father would prefer to have this over with now. "

"I wish you had told me all this before." I whispered, trying to hide the pain in my voice. It was very disconcerting to learn that what I suspected was true. Lyla wasn't just keeping one secret, it was quite a few. Truth be told, what got to me wasn't that she was keeping things from me. I was sure she could fill a library with the secrets she kept in her hand over the decade, but it was more the fact that she couldn't tell me something this important.

"Chase, don't feel like that, please." Lyla muttered. "I didn't tell you because I didn't want to add anything more to your load. Chris was trying to kill you for weeks, and whether you admit it or not, it's taken its toll on you. So I decided I'd handle this one on my own and let you rest. My intention wasn't to hurt you. I just want you to have a life without all this supernatural drama. A normal life. "

"But I don't want a normal life. Don't you know I'd take all the horrors and drama in life as long as I get to be with you?"

Lyla opened her mouth to say something, but changed her mind, seemingly upon remembering something. Then she said: "Wait a minute. I'm supposed to be angry with you. I thought we agreed we'd wait awhile to try the mental link thing."

"Actually we didn't. You just said we didn't have time that night."

Lyla ignored me. "What if doing that caused some kind of brain damage to you? And most of all, why didn't you just ask me first, before feeling like you had to go through my head to find out what you want?"

She was no longer angry. I, on the other hand, was starting to breathe harder with indignation.

"If I'd asked you, would you have told me? No, you wouldn't. The only reason you did was because I'd already seen some of it in your head. The reason I did it is because nowadays, you don't seem to tell me anything, even when I ask!"

I was beginning to shout, and Lyla looked completely taken aback.

"Ever since I got back you've been acting different towards me no matter how many times I try to make you understand—I don't think of you any differently. You're always so withdrawn from me now, and you'd think that wouldn't really happen with us as we have this connection. I'm sorry, but..." I got up and turned away and lowered my voice, now feeling a little lugubrious. "I felt like it was the only way I could find out what was going on with you. But, I did violate your privacy and I am sorry for doing that."

Lyla was just yelling at me for being nosy. You'd think I'd learn to give her some space. I knew she only minded when I found out something she didn't want me to, but I couldn't help checking our emotional bond.

"Chase, I'm concerned about you, me, I'm worried about what this meeting tonight could mean. It's a lot of this."

"Why are you still worried about me? Everything's fine now. No one is trying to kill me and there's no sign of the switch between us. Everything's good, right?"

I knew she worried about me because she was afraid of inadvertently changing me. But as we got this far without much incident, I thought she would have relaxed a little. I guess I was wrong.

Lyla got up and sat on the desk in front of me. "It's not that," she looked at me with such intensity it felt as if her emotions were rolling off her onto me. "I'm also worried about the Somorians finding out about our bond."

"Why?"

"Because I'm afraid some of them may react the same way Chris did. I don't want to put you in that position. Not again. All they need to know is Chris wanted to kill you just for knowing us. That's why I don't want to bring you into this. I just want it to be over."

I didn't need any sort of connection with Lyla to know how to comfort her. I took hold of her hand and pulled her off the desk towards me.

"I want you to remember, however long this takes, or how difficult it gets, you've always got me by your side."

"You know, even though I already know that, it's still good to hear." She paused for a couple seconds, during which I simply stared at her in awe and inhaled her amazing scent. It made me feel little light-headed.

Then Lyla muttered, "Please don't ask me if you can come tonight. Because if you do, I won't be able to say no, and I think that's a bad idea. I know you want to be there with me, but this is something I have to do without you."

She put her hand on my shoulder. Her hair felt like a kind of solid liquid. I felt like it was my duty to be there with Lyla, like I needed the Somorians to know I was going to stand by her, even if they didn't like it or me. But after hearing what she had to say I realized I underestimated her strength. I should have known better. Lyla was an incredibly strong person. It had nothing to do with her being immortal. She had a strong heart and a powerful soul.

So along with being deeply in love, we were connected like no two people were and we spent so much time together, I figured maybe it was time to give her some space. I knew she would always come back to me in the end.

"Okay. I won't ask you to go, but, you have to come see me tonight and tell we what happened. Deal?"

"Deal." Lyla kissed me. It was so free of tension and wonderful that it immediately lifted my mood, and hers. Maybe everything was going to be fine after all. *Hopefully everything would change for the better soon*, I thought to myself. At that moment I embraced the euphoria that had risen inside me.

"Excuse me." I heard from behind me. I turned around to see a skinny, fourth year boy enter the room and take a seat, dropping his heavy bag on the floor.

"Aren't you two late for class or something?" he asked as he took off his glasses to clean them. With Lyla's hand in mine, we left the room chuckling and passed the boy's classmates who were waiting outside, watching and giggling as they saw us leave.

That night, dinner with my parents wasn't the tense affair it always seemed to be recently. They actually seemed to realize how sorry I was for 'running away' and really wanted to make amends, and they'd invited Justin, who was discharged from the hospital three days earlier. Even though he was out his doctor still hadn't declared him fit for school yet, so he was now home most of the time, but went down to the harbour that day for the first time since he was discharged, which was how my parents saw him.

It was really good to have a (mortal) friend to talk to. Every one of my other friends in the neighborhood still wasn't talking with me, and I was very happy when he didn't decide to do the same after he learned what happened. He wasn't happy to hear it, though.

Having Justin over was also an excellent way to pass the time, as I would have been stuck in my room letting the hours slide by, waiting for Lyla to come. Even after dinner my parents allowed him to stay over longer, though I figured that was more for his benefit than mine. But it suited me just fine all the same. But all the distractions in the world couldn't have stopped me from checking the bond every couple of seconds, and every time I did I felt nothing but Lyla's surface emotions—mostly anxiety for the meeting to be over. That was something we both shared at the moment.

At a few minutes past ten, Dad walked Justin home, despite him saying he'd be fine alone. I was pretty worn out by that time, but very determined to hear what Lyla had to say. I'd actually become nervous because now I wasn't feeling anything through our bond for a while now, which was causing my panic to grow by the second.

I expected her to be back by now, and her prolonged absence was made me uneasy. Even worse, I knew the reason I wasn't feeling anything. She'd somehow closed off our connection, as if she didn't want me to know anything unless she told me. So I had no idea what was going on. I paced up and down in my room for about twenty full minutes until I finally got so frustrated that, without thinking, I spun around and kicked the computer table. I wasn't even phased by the fact that I'd almost destroyed it, but what did catch my attention was an object that was hidden behind all the junk on the table, which rolled to the edge and fell right into my waiting hand.

It was a snow globe. One I hadn't seen in a long time. The glass sphere was a little dusty, but once I'd cleaned it, the little inside could clearly be seen. Distracted from my frustration and caught up in the moment, I gave it a little shake and held it up to the light. As the tiny sprinkles inside fluttered back down, the light passing through the glass caused them to sparkle in different colors, enough to make it look like a broken rainbow was falling on the village.

"Do you remember how you got that?"

I spun around to see Mom propped against the door frame. I shook my head. A dreamy, reminiscent look came over her face.

"You've had that for a long time." She pointed at the globe. "Since you were five, to be precise. See at that time, you used to love swinging on the fridge door, even though your father and I kept telling you to stop. One day, it was just you and I at home, and I'd fallen asleep studying. I remember it was a crashing sound that woke me. When I got to the kitchen, you were crying and the fridge door was lying on the floor. It's actually kind of funny now, but at that time, I was mad as hell. You got such a beating, you cried yourself to sleep."

We both laughed the same way.

"After that you wouldn't talk to me for a week because you felt I didn't love you anymore. I tried everything to change your mind, and it hurt me so bad to know I made you feel that way. That's when I bought you that. When I gave it to you, I told you no matter what, I will always love you."

I looked at the snow globe again. "How strange I should find it at a time like this then, huh. Maybe I should give it back to you." I held the globe out to my mother. She sighed deeply, then came in and sat on the bed. I sat next to her.

"I gave you that so you would always remember I love you."

"Then why are you avoiding me? Ever since I got back you and Dad have barely said a civil word to me. And you know what Mom? That kinda hurts."

"I'm sorry Chase. But it seems like these days we don't know how to talk to you anymore. You used to tell us everything that was going on with you. But now you seem to be keeping so many secrets from us."

Mom shook her head and looked at me sadly. Keeping secrets from my parents? She'd voiced the very thing I felt guilty about. Almost every child kept secrets from their parents. I knew that. But the ones I was keeping weren't what the average person had to deal with.

"Mom. I'm not trying to keep you and Dad out of my life, but there are just some things I can't tell you about."

"Why?"

"Because they're my situations to deal with and not something my parents can help me with. Look Mom, I'm not doing anything wrong or illegal or anything of the sort. But it is something I won't get you involved in."

"Does it have to do with Lyla?" I figured she already knew the answer to that and didn't need me to tell her, so I said nothing. "Okay. Chase, I do trust you and love you. So does your father. He's just... no. We're just a little disappointed."

"I know." I whispered. It had started to rain. My mother fiddled with her fingers for a while, then got up to leave, but before she could I gripped her in a hug.

"I love you Mom, and I never wanted to hurt you." She looked at me with a smile on her face, then ran her fingers through my hair. I shook my head slightly and she grinned.

"Sorry." It was our old routine and I loved it.

"Hey Mom, one more thing," I said as she headed for the door. "Am I still grounded?"

She laughed, turned to leave, then said: "Of course." I had my Mom back.

We said goodnight and as she left I put the snow globe

on the top shelf of my closet. As I did that, my hand passed across something. Leaving the snow globe up there, I pulled the object down. It was a mahogany framed picture, but unlike the snow globe, I'd never seen this before. *Just how many foreign objects can this room hold*? I thought to myself. The photo was of Mom's family. She was standing in the centre, wearing a long white dress and shoes, and her hair was in braids. She must have been about ten in the photo.

Standing behind her were my grandparents. Granddad was dressed in a black suit, and Gran-gran was wearing a white dress similar to Mom's. They looked like they were going to church. But what, or who interested me the most was the young man standing in the front next to my young mother. He was black, tall, about the same height as Granddad, and looked to be around eighteen years old. He was also wearing a church suit.

He looked just like Mom, though his features were closer to Granddad's—the chin and nose, but mostly the eyes, which had a small hint of blue, making the boy look like a much younger, handsomer version of Granddad. I had no idea who he was, but I figured he'd be family, which would explain why I felt I was somehow connected to him. I felt as if I should somehow know him, like we were alike.

"Mom!" I shouted over the sound of the rain banging against the house. My mother was back in my room within a couple of seconds. "Um, could you tell me who this is?" I held the picture up to show her. For a while, it was as though this picture was the only thing in her universe. She fixed it with such a strong look of longing on her face.

"Mom." I said, slightly alarmed. She looked at me as

though she'd just woken up. She took the photo from me and touched the part with the boy, as if hoping he could reach back.

"Where did you find this?"

"In my closet. Mom, who is he?"

"My brother."

"I—I didn't know you had a brother. Where is he? And why have I never met him? Don't you guys talk anymore?"

Mom looked at me with sadness in her eyes. "Chase, Jonathan died twenty-six years ago, when he was eighteen. I was ten when it happened."

She turned back to the photo, leaving me stunned. I didn't expect anything like that. I'd never even heard her talk of having a brother.

"I don't remember him well," she said, still mesmerized by the photo, "just some small memories. Little things here and there, you know. But those are the things that keep him alive for me. This was actually taken a week before he died. It's the only picture of him I have, but I thought I'd lost it a long time ago."

"How did it happen?" I said carefully.

Mom took a few breaths before she answered. "We think he drowned."

"What do you mean 'think'?"

"Well, you see Chase, my brother loved everything to do with the sea. Every day he'd be at the beach and sometimes Dad used to have to go drag him home. Sometimes he used to go out in a sail boat he got when he was sixteen, even though my mother didn't like it when he did. One day, he was planning to go out, but the sea was rough, and my parents asked him not to go, but he went anyway. They were so worried. I will never forgot the pain it caused them when a fisherman brought back the boat and told them Jonathan wasn't in it when he found it. They were so determined to find him. They even went out with the search parties to try to find him, and even keep looking when Search and Rescue and Search and Recovery were both called off. Accepting that Jonathan died took something away from my parents, I could never tell what, but after that they were different. Not the normal way parents are after a child dies. I can't really explain it, but they were never the same again. Okay, I can see that's enough for you." Mom said after looking at me.

She probably thought I was feeling horrible about what she'd just said and I was, but what I was really thinking about was how she and Dad almost had to go through that same thing, if Chris had had his way. They would have had no idea what happened to me. They wouldn't have deserved that.

"I'm okay Mom," I simply uttered.

Mom nodded and said, "Do you mind if I take this?"

"Mom, it yours. Go ahead." She smiled at me and left the room.

And that's when it happened. At that moment, just like at school, a flood of images and sounds came rushing into my head. And even though at first I didn't understand them, after a couple of seconds my brain was able to put everything in the right place so I was able see it as one whole memory. The abrupt stop of Lyla's memories and the shock of what I'd just found out made me stumble to the floor. Mom came running back into the room, and she asked me something. I could see her lips moving, but I couldn't hear a word she was saying and that was because the blood was rushing to my head way too fast because of the pounding of my heart.

Getting myself together, I got up and ran past my mom without a word. In a couple seconds, I was out of the room, down the stairs and out of the house into the pounding rain. All that mattered was getting to Lyla before it was too late. I didn't have much time, because I knew, just like before, she felt what happened and would know I was on my way. That weird tingly feeling I got when I was nervous was now rushing through my body, which made me quicken my pace.

By the time I'd reached the bottom of the hill to the beach, I was soaked and I felt a horrible stitch in my side, but I didn't care. I just needed to get to Lyla… to stop her. But by the time I got to the edge of the water (past Nikolai and Michael, who were standing on the beach looking somber) I knew it was too late. Lyla was already shoulder deep in the water when I yelled.

"Lyla don't do this!! Come back. Please!" She only looked at me.

"Please don't go! I'm sorry if I've done anything wrong," I said as I waded into the water.

I felt someone's hands close around my arms, but I shrugged them off. I was about to dive right into the water, but I froze when I heard Lyla shout: "Chase. I'm so sorry." And then she was gone.

I shouted her name for what felt like hours. I ran up and down the beach looking for her (Michael and Nikolai refused to let me in the water). I even tried our bond, which was closed off to me. I fell to the ground, weak-kneed and dizzy, with a horrible sadness trying to force its way to me. Michael and Nikolai joined me, the three of us just staring off towards the empty black sea.

CHAPTER 17

Something Is Missing

For the next two weeks, the days seemed as though someone had hit a fast-forward button on time, but somehow left me going about at my normal pace as if they wanted to prolong my suffering as much as possible. Everyone around me was going about their lives normally, as if a great tragedy hadn't taken place, whereas I felt like I'd grown distant from the world around me because of that tragedy, and was contented with retreating into my own little place in my mind, where the outside world couldn't interfere and I could drown in my pain in peace.

I felt like everyone around me who was laughing, happy, or enjoying themselves in any way was making a rude, obscene gesture. Lyla was usually the source of happiness for me and as she was now gone, there were no good reasons for such behavior. Lyla's departure meant nothing to them. She was just another person to them. Someone they didn't have to think about.

Without Lyla to really give them purpose, the days started to lose all appeal to me and I passed them almost like a robot, only having enough time for my sadness and depression.

With December also came the sudden, constant, heavy downpour of rain that felt like crushed ice on my skin whenever I got caught in it. It was becoming a usual thing for me to wake up in the morning to find a kind of weak grey-golden sunlight in the room because of thick, dark clouds lying low in the sky. Though most people would see this as a hindrance, there was something calming about it for me. I always loved rain, and now it kept me calm when I felt like I wanted to explode. But it wasn't good enough to bring me out of my despondency.

My parents were actually getting worried, as they were sure I was falling into some kind of depression. They didn't come right out and tell me this. It would have been awkward for us. A few days after Lyla left, I noticed them watching me very closely, but whenever I tried to catch them at it, they'd conveniently be engaged in something else. It was the last thing I wanted, but my parents knew I wasn't getting much sleep and they were concerned about me.

Every time I closed my eyes I would see Lyla smiling and staring at me, and that I could handle. But it was too much to fall asleep and have to watch her leave over and over again. I'd always wake up a few hours after falling asleep with a huge, unbearable pain in my chest.

I woke up on Tuesday morning (I'd actually been awake for hours) of the second week of December to the same cloudy sky. Rain hadn't yet fallen, but the sound of thunder was loud in the sky and the air carried that scent that preceded showers. I got out of bed with the same empty feeling I was carrying around for weeks.

When I got downstairs for breakfast, I said good morning to my parents as I normally would, to give them the impression I was doing fine, but from the sympathetic looks on their faces, I knew it didn't work. I sighed deeply, sat down and tucked into my pancakes and eggs. Mom and Dad were soon engaged in their own conversation, leaving me to myself. As I ate, as I'd been doing every day since she left, I tried to connect with Lyla, both emotionally and mentally. But just like every other time there was nothing there, like our connection no longer existed. I figured I wasn't getting anything because Lyla was probably blocking our connection, but some irrational part of my brain always wondered if our connections failed because Lyla's feelings towards me were gone. I didn't entertain those thoughts very long, because I knew how Lyla felt about me, and those feelings didn't just disappear no matter how far or how long she went away.

However, knowing she was the one blocking the link hurt a lot worse than being stuck back here without any information about her. I didn't like feeling that every day took me further away from her.

As soon as I was finished eating, I pushed my plate away, got up and left—fully aware of my parents' gaze at my back—to get ready for school, and once I was done I tried to leave without saying much more than goodbye, because I knew what was coming…

"Chase, wait." Mom said as I swung my bag over my shoulder, about to head for the door. "I was wondering… if you would mind if I drove you to school today?"

"I'm riding with Nick today, Mom. Sorry. Next time,

okay?" I replied half-apologetically, half-rushed, and then ran through the door. Once I was a couple feet from the house, I sighed with relief and that actually got a smile out of me—the first in weeks. I'd just escaped a weird conversation. When I realized what got me to smile, the smile faded immediately. With all the conversations my parents were having about me, I figured one of them would have tried talking to me about what I was going through, and I honestly thought Dad would have tried first.

It was a few minutes to eight when I reached the bus stop, so there were already lots of other school kids around. I found Nikolai sitting alone, sulking and somehow still managing to look like a carving of a sad, Greek god.

Apart from me, Lyla's departure was hardest on Nick because they were so close.

"Any news?" He knew what I meant.

"No, sorry. Nothing."

The bus came into view, so he took up his backpack and stood up.

"I was actually going to ask you that, or aren't you still getting through?"

I shook my head, and I saw his face fall a little. I knew he and his family were depending on my connection with Lyla to know how she was doing.

As soon as the bus stopped, most people rushed for the door as usual. But today was the first time I noticed something strange. Even though the door was completely blocked, somehow everyone kind of absentmindedly moved out of the way to let Nick pass. All I had to do was stick close to him.

"Seriously, dude, how do you do that?" I asked as we

climbed onto the bus.

"How do I do what?" He replied innocently. I shook my head in amazement.

I took a seat in the middle of the bus, and Nikolai was about to sit next to me when Kristian zipped past him and dropped into it so fast, it left us both taken aback. I soon recovered from this sudden surprise and wondered if Kristian knew how much danger he was in. Nikolai and I, especially Nikolai, would have loved to take our pain out on him.

It seemed like he did know, because he threw up his hands and whispered to me, knowing Nick would hear, "I don't want any trouble. I just want to talk. Seriously."

Nikolai leered at Kristian for a few seconds, but when his eyes flickered to me, I nodded and he took the seat behind us on the left. Two rows ahead of us on the left, I saw Kimberly's head turn towards us a couple times. Seeing me and her brother together definitely made her nervous.

"What do you want?" I asked abruptly and acidly, not looking at Kristian. He took a deep breath, as if to force down a retort that would usually follow, before he responded.

"My dad told me about the meeting and about your – that the Morgan girl left. I'm sorry."

"No, you're not," I spat at him.

"What?" Kristian replied, stunned.

"You're not sorry Lyla's gone," I said, turning to look through the window. "You didn't exactly keep it a secret that you didn't like her. In fact you're probably glad she's gone. One less soul sucker on the island, right?"

I was deliberately not looking at Kristian because I didn't want him to see the pain on my face, so I forced myself to look unnerved before I turned around.

"What makes it worse is, you hated her just for what she was, even though she hadn't hurt anyone. And you hate me because I—I love her. If you had known the kind of person she was, you wouldn't have been so quick to judge her."

I wanted what I said to hurt him, but I knew better than to hope for that. When I looked back at him, Kristian was merely staring at me with his mouth open as if he was contemplating whether to say what was on his mind or to play nice. I seriously doubted he was actually lost for words. But then again, it really didn't matter to me.

The bus made a sharp, sudden right turn, which made Kristian slide onto me. I pushed him off, which must have seemed rude but I didn't care.

"What is it you want, Kristian?" I said bluntly.

I caught a small glimpse of annoyance on his face, but surprisingly he kept it to himself. He sighed deeply than said:

"A couple days ago some of the council members were over at our house, talking with my parents. I overheard my dad talking, and he said you... that you went on a spirit walk."

The bus stopped again and another group of students got onboard, talking loudly with friends. The last few to get on had to remain standing as there were no more seats and those who stood to the front blocked Kimberley from our view.

"So, what's it to you?" I asked.

"Well, the thing is, I've been trying for months and I know it's not an easy thing to do, but it's never worked."

"Why?" I was slightly intrigued.

"I'm not really sure, but my dad told me you have to have strong focus and the mind has to be ready. I've been trying to condition myself for months, but nothing ever happens, which is why I wanted to talk to you. Since you did it on your first try…"

"You want to know exactly what I did to make it work."

Kristian turned his head away shamefully. I knew coming to me for help took a great deal of courage from him, but in my current state, I had no sympathy for him and felt no remorse in taking pleasure from that.

"I had a need, a purpose." I admitted after a moment's silence. "I didn't just want to do it for the sake of doing it, so I guess that kind of fueled it."

"Thanks," Kristian said softly, about to get up, but before he did, I said, "I hope killing Aquamuns won't become your purpose, 'cause see then we'd have a problem."

He ignored that and walked to the back of the bus. I guess he preferred to stand with his friends than sit next to me. It was a relief to know that.

Before anyone could take the seat next to me, Nikolai took it.

"You know, I'm really sorry you didn't provoke him. I would have enjoyed kicking his ass. Plus his face would benefit from a little… readjusting."

Despite how I felt, I managed another smile, though it fell away as quickly as the one before. There was no real joy left in my world.

From that moment my day sank back into its usual

routine. I went to my classes, depressed and detached from the world around me, where I tried my best to focus on my lessons, but the voices of all my teachers were unappealing to me, which resulted in my mind constantly drifting off to the very thing or person I didn't want to think about.

By the time I'd met Nick for lunch after Social Studies, I was agitated and had grown tired of school, and unfortunately for him, Dre picked this time to pester me. Nikolai and I were at one of the good lunch tables alone, where I was sadly watching my ex-friends, when he came over with his three friends and dropped into the seat next to me. I really hoped this wasn't going to be a regular thing. His three friends stood close by.

"I always figured you weren't a very smart person," he said, "but I thought even you would've known how great Lyla was and done your best to keep her. But I underestimated you, you managed to freak her out enough to make her leave the country."

I was surprised to actually hear fury in his voice, as if he was hurt Lyla was gone. Did he actually have true feelings for her?

Nikolai leaned forward as though he was about to hit Dre, but before he could I shook my head to tell him no. Dre just needed to be put in his place, not a couple broken bones. But then he turned his eyes on Nick.

"And let's not forget about you. How could you let him do that to your sister? Just chase her away and still hang around with the guy. If it was my sister, I'd beat the crap out of him, but then maybe you can't, or maybe you don't care enough about your own sister to do anything,"

He finished with a slight sneer. He just couldn't help

taunting us, which was unfortunate for him. Even without his supernatural strength, I don't think even a dozen people would've had the strength to keep Nick in his seat. As soon as he stood up, Dre's friends walked over to him, probably believing they could take him in fight.

Not that Nick needed my help, or that I was even afraid he would hurt them, but I jumped in as well, just because I needed to blow off a lot of anger, and at the time a good fight seemed the perfect way to do just that.

Without any regrets, and before Dre had time to even stand properly, I punched him in the left side of his face, with a huge amount of gratification. But faster than I cared for, he recovered and threw a punch into my stomach. I immediately doubled over in pain as the air rushed out of me. He wasted no time in pounding every part of my back he could reach, but I quickly recovered from his first punch and tackled him to the floor, where we matched each other blow for blow. I also expected Dre's friends to try and get in as well, but remembered Nikolai must've been bored only having to deal with the three of them.

By now, most students in the school had surrounded us to watch the much loved 'entertainment'. Those who weren't in the crowd watched from the balconies on the second and third floors. A few daring boys (and one or two girls) even climbed the trees to get a good view.

As I narrowly missed a blow from Dre, I noticed all the students were running away in every direction, which meant one thing – a teacher was on the way. Dre seemed to realize this too, because he backed off, shot me a dirty look and ran off into the crowd with his friends, who I was glad to see were all pretty beaten up.

That's all I need, to be labeled a troublemaker, I thought angrily to myself. "Let's get outta here." I told Nikolai, who seemed just fine.

"Dude, trust me, they're going to find you before school's over," Nick said with a smile, handing me my backpack as he swung his over his shoulder.

"No," I said taking Nick's arm, leading him away from the scene of our fight. "I mean let's ditch this place. I can't stand it here anymore, I need to get out of here and do something, anything fun."

Nikolai forced me to stop when we reached the back fence. There wasn't a gate back here and the fence was like seven feet high, but I felt like every step I took away from school was a step in making me feel better.

As Nick looked at me, I looked back at him, straight in the eyes, and for the first time I saw the older, more experienced man he really was, but the second he blinked he was back to his normal self.

Without any warning, Nikolai took hold of my shoulders and with ease, lifted me off my feet and threw me over the fence. By the time I'd hit the ground on the other side, Nick was already there and helped me to my feet.

"Dude, let's tear this place up," he shouted with a wicked smile playing on his lips. I smiled too, and this time it stayed there.

Ditching school is never a good thing, I knew that. I also knew my parents were going to be really angry when they found out about the fight and that I had left school early. But this was one of those times when you just couldn't worry about consequences. Besides, Nikolai was such a good distraction and company I didn't even worry about that until later.

We headed straight to the beach, one not too far from our school, where we spent the rest of the afternoon playing games, eating and swimming, though a couple times, Nick did ditch me to frolic with a couple girls, but I didn't feel bad about that. It was good to see him somewhat back to normal. I used to do the same with everyone else when I was with Lyla.

Around 6:00 pm we hopped into Sheila (Nikolai went home for it), headed to town and somehow Nick got us onto a private party on the Catamaran *Cathleen*. No one seemed concerned about our age, so we saw no problem with enjoying the party.

By the time it was over, it was obvious I was hurt (that's Caribbean talk for drunk – the place was growing on me), so Nick had to drive us home. Alcohol had no effect on Aquamuns.

"Whoa, something just hit me," I mumbled, my words slurred.

"Bug in the face?"

"No." I was feeling incredibly uneasy, so I had my window fully rolled down as I rested back in my seat. "You're the first person I ever let drive Sheila. That's like really huge, dude."

"Yeah it is." I heard Nick say with humor in his voice as I concentrated on flashing scenes outside my window. "And so were all those bottles of vodka that seemed to strangely disappear around you."

At that moment, my head started to spin and I moaned.

"Don't worry, we're almost home." I could still hear that sneer in Nick's voice. "Though if I were you, I'd consider wanting to sleep somewhere else."

My head started to feel strangely light on my slumped body, and worst of all, I kept saying everything that came to mind.

"I love sleeping in my bed. It reminds me a lot of Lyla and I really miss her. I miss her so much."

"Yeah, me too," Nick mumbled the same time we passed under a streetlight. There was no trace of humor when he said that.

"You're pretty funny," I babbled to Nick suddenly. It even seemed to startle him. "I really needed this. Thanks a lot Nikolai."

"You might want to hold off on the thanks till you've seen the tattoo."

I started giggling uncontrollably. "There's that humor again. You really are a good friend, I don't think I've ever told you that so there it is. Ever since Lyla left, you've been there for me, even though you needed support yourself and I was too wrapped up in me to help, you still stood by me. Thanks a lot."

I could tell Nikolai was caught off guard by what I said (so was I, for that matter). He was actually stunned for a couple seconds. We bumped fists, then he chuckled.

"Don't expect me to hug you while I'm driving."

"You're lucky I don't make you say 'I love you'." I didn't see the concerned look on his face because I was looking through the window at the cold blackness beyond. That's when I got the urge. Even though I knew nothing was going to happen and it was only going to make me feel worse, the allure of the possibility that this was the time was too strong. I just couldn't resist, but when I tried to reach out to the bond, I could barely feel it, which I figured was the result of my intoxication.

"Lyla. I love you and I miss you so much. I want you to come back, please."

My chest tightened with pain and a tear rolled down my face. Nikolai placed a comforting hand on my shoulder, but I didn't notice any of this because I'd fallen asleep. When I woke up, before I even opened my eyes, the sunlight in my face felt like it was going to burn my eyes out, and I would have sworn my head was swollen from the way it hurt. I felt so weird at first I couldn't even get up, but when I finally did I began wishing I hadn't because I had to run to the bathroom, even though every step sent a terrible, splitting pain to my head. When I'd finally pushed the bathroom door open and dropped to my knees by the toilet, I vomited worse than I ever did in my life.

I'd never drunk so much alcohol. It wasn't something I cared to go through again. Every single sound was like a new assault on my ears.

When I was sure I was done being sick, I flushed the toilet with a shaky hand—it sounded like a waterfall— dropped onto the cold bathroom floor and let my head fall onto my knees. I wasn't going to be sick again, not physically, but I did feel horrible about how I let my emotions control my actions, though I didn't regret it. If Lyla knew how I'd been acting (for all I knew she did) she would be disappointed. *But then if she cared, she wouldn't have left*, I thought to myself.

Since Lyla left I experienced moments of irrational

bursts of anger towards her, and I would always convince myself I was being unreasonable. But this time I just wanted to let it consume me, because if anything it could help me focus more.

"Chase, get down here now." Dad bellowed from downstairs. "Don't make me come up there for you." After that, I heard him unloading loudly to Mom about my recent behavior.

Through the alcoholic buzz I was feeling, I felt a strong stinging pain at the way my father sounded talking about me. I guess I didn't prefer the shouting at all. With a heavy sigh, I forced myself onto my feet. Dizzy and staggering slightly, I headed downstairs.

My father was aggressively pacing around the living room, constantly rubbing his hands together the way he always did when he was frustrated. When I got there, he just looked at me and continued his pacing, so I went and joined Mom at the table. Although it was more passive, I could see the same frustration on her face. There wasn't any breakfast, which was a good thing owing to my queasy stomach, Mom just sat there avoiding my eye by drinking her coffee and reading one of the two newspapers on the table: The *East Island Times* newspaper. The headline on the front page of a folded edition of the *Daily Sun* lying on the table caught my eye.

Lifeless Man To Be Sent To Geriatric Institution

I took up the paper and unfolded it to see huge picture of Chris, which appeared to be taken after we'd left him in the old house. He was in the same slumped position and the camera even caught that eerie, empty expression on his face. There were only a couple lines under his picture:

> Doctors at the PHH (Prince Henry Hospital) have been left baffled as they have finally concluded they have no answers or even theories as to what could have happened to Christopher Weeks, who was admitted to the hospital more than three weeks ago. What makes this case so strange is the fact that Mr. Weeks seems to be in perfect health.
>
> Christopher Weeks was admitted here because, according to close friends and colleagues, he wasn't suffering from any mental illnesses," Reports Dr. Hansel, "which suggests whatever brought on this complete unresponsive state he is in, is medical. However we've run all manner of test on his body and brain, and have yet to find a cause for his sickness. So as he doesn't require medical attention, he will be sent to a geriatric hospital, where there will be trained professionals who can care for him. However, we will still continue over investigation into this strange case."

The rest of the article told of how he was found, so I threw it back down. At least he can't hurt anyone else now. The same time the paper hit the table, my father stopped pacing and looked at me. For a second I thought he was going to hit me. He had never punished me, that was always Mom's thing, but then they never had to deal with anything of this magnitude.

"I don't even know what to say to you right now," Dad began, looking like he was straining to keep as calm as possible, which wasn't any good as he was already close to shouting.

"Joe, calm down." Mom got up and went over to him, but he shrugged her off. "No Lilly. We shouldn't have to be dealing with this. We give him everything he wants, give him more freedom than he can handle and this is the thanks we get. Acting out, running away, fighting, skipping school and now we can add getting drunk to the list. And what's worse, you took Nikolai with you." Dad was now in a full rage. "It's a good thing he's such a good a friend. He made sure you didn't get hurt and got home okay. I would like you to tell us what prompted this behavior this time. No, wait," Dad said, putting up a hand to cut me off, though I had nothing to say. Dad let loose a short, sharp laugh that held no humor in it. "Let me guess: Lyla."

I flinched in my chair. These days Lyla's name coming off the tongue of others was like a sharp knife across my skin.

Dad glanced over at Mom, who was looking at him as though warning him to calm down.

"I know how you felt about her, but you're taking this way further than you should. You two were only together for a couple months, and it's not like she'll be your last."

I was prepared to listen to what my parents had to say (or shout) at me and prayed they didn't punish me too heavily. But hearing that Lyla was supposed to be just another girlfriend wasn't something I could just let slide.

"You don't know what you're talking about. You have no idea. I —" I was shaking slightly and on the edge of my seat. I wanted to say so much, but it felt like it all wanted to spill out at once, which left me speechless. I balled my hands and took two deep, steadying breaths before I continued.

"When I came here, we all know I hated it. I was unhappy, a mess. But then I met Lyla. She... she didn't just get me to love it here, she changed my whole life. I fell in love with her and through some miracle or act of God, she loved me back. And I'm honest with you, I never went out looking for someone to love, but I found her. These last few months with her have been unbelievable. I was closer to her than I've ever been with anyone else in my life and now she's gone and I don't know if she's ever coming back or if she even wants to and it's all because of me. Everything reminds me of her and it hurts too much to ignore or just get over."

I'd pushed my chair back and was standing up. My Dad still had the same angry expression on his face, but Mom's had changed, though I couldn't tell to what. She walked up to me and spread her arms out to me, but I stepped back, out of her reach.

"No!" I shouted. For some reason my voice was weakening and my eyes were starting to sting with the tears I'd been desperately trying to hold back. "I can't stay here anymore. It's just too hard. I need to leave."

"Leave?!" Mom repeated, obviously caught off guard. "Leave and go where? This is your home."

She almost sounded like she was pleading. She looked at Dad for help, but he just remained silent. How was it we got to this? Was I really responsible? Did I really drive us apart?

"It doesn't feel like home anymore."

I walked past my horror-struck mother and went up the

stairs, but not before I noticed the mixture of anger and disappointment on my father's face.

"I'm so happy you get to spend Christmas with us this year. For some reason the house always feels a little dull around the Christmas holidays." Gran-gran said, trying to decide which of two bags of sugar to buy. We were shopping inside Cost-Mart, the local superstore.

"But Granddad's with you," I said, pointing to the first bag of sugar. She smiled and placed it in the half-full cart. "Well yes. But it's always better with more family around. Plus your grandfather seems to think the holidays are a time to eat and sleep."

"Aren't they?" I joked. Gran-gran and I laughed heartily.

It was Friday and it was my second day here. On Wednesday morning when I'd declared I wanted to leave, I called my grandparents, who had already heard about me skipping school and were very concerned about me, so they agreed to let me stay with them.

It was strange, but from the time I landed in Texas I felt as though most of my worries had been left in East Island. Here you couldn't find anyone more normal than my grandparents. Here there was no magic (that I knew about), no one trying to kill me and no supernatural problems to worry about. But knowing I had nothing to worry about only left me with one thing to think about—Lyla. She was constantly on my mind these days, despite my best efforts to keep thoughts of her away, and that was mostly because I'd finally got something from her from our connection.

It happened when I was on the plane to Texas. I was inevitably drifting off to sleep when they were showing

Pretty Woman. My head was feeling light and dizzy and that's when it happened. It was like falling into a dream while still knowing you're awake. I was standing on the beach looking up at our house with strong feelings of longing and desire. I felt like all I wanted was to go up to the house I'd come to know so well. The only one I ever loved was in there.

"Is he okay?" Asked someone behind me in a beautiful, musical voice. Whoever it was, walked closer to me and said: "Physically, he's fine. Emotionally, well according to Nikolai, he's not doing so well, but he is getting through. Whenever I see him, it seems as though he's struggling through every day, but he's a strong young man."

I looked away from the house and turned towards the sea where Marcus was standing, looking at me. "It's not so easy for us either Lyla, we do miss you."

"Oh father, I miss you too, but I can't return as long as Chase is here, I'm too much of a danger to him. When the time comes I will come home, but now's not that time. Father please don't tell anyone I was here." Marcus sighed, moonlight dancing on his skin the way it did with Lyla's. As a wave crashed onto the shore, he came closer to me and drew me into a hug. "I won't tell them. Just remember how much we love you," Marcus said, drawing back.

"I love you too, father. Goodbye." I looked back at the house on the hill, the one that was home to my love, bid goodbye to my father, then ran back to the comforting depths of the sea.

At that moment the mental bond closed, but through

our emotional bond I felt a huge wave of affection towards me, but that was also quickly closed to me, and I woke up with a heavy heart.

From then I'd been constantly trying to connect with Lyla, hoping to catch her off-guard so I'd be able to get some kind of idea of what she was feeling. But I had no luck, and as I still had no idea of how to control our mental link, that wasn't even an option. I was willing to bet Lyla had that secured too, just in case. So I was left only to hope she was trying to contact me, though I soon came to believe maybe that was a one time thing, whether intentional or not I didn't know. After a while I convinced myself that I'd be able to get through the days better if I just tried to think of her less. As impossible as it seemed, I had to try.

As soon we finished shopping, Gran-gran and I headed home, mostly in silence, only exchanging a couple words during the entire car ride. From the moment I arrived I'd expected one or both my grandparents to sit me down to have a talk, much like the last time I was there, but up until now they hadn't so much as looked at me seriously, which led me to believe they were going to wait until after Christmas so I could enjoy the holidays. I had no problem with that. I felt so comfortable here, so strangely relaxed that the days seemed to just drift away from me as easily as a leaf on the wind.

I was home most of the time. As there was always something to occupy my time, I failed to even notice how fast the days were going until Christmas Eve had arrived.

My grandparents celebrated Christmas like most people in the Caribbean. The whole house had been cleaned, curtains changed, furniture polished and the dishes and cutlery washed. Most of the food was prepared on Christmas Eve night, so at around ten that night the house was filled with the mouthwatering smell of baking ham and both plain pudding and the classic Caribbean Rum Cake. At one point I could have sworn that, like on TV, the aroma was actually steam which turned into a ghostly hand beckoning me to the kitchen.

"Mmmm," Granddad moaned from the living room. "The thought of your puddings at Christmas are just one of the things that get me through the year." Gran-gran and I laughed.

"Does your mother still make her own puddings or does she go for the store bought ones now?" Gran-gran asked, pouring the last pudding batter into a pan.

"She still does make her own," I answered, scooping up the last of the batter in a spoon and eating it. "Two years ago she wanted to try the store ones, but we didn't like it nearly as much as hers, so we went back to tradition. Mmmm, Gran this batter is really good."

"Lilly doesn't let you have the batter at home?"

"Nah, she's always talking about salmonella or whatever," I said, licking the last of the cake batter. I stopped suddenly when I saw my Grandmother staring at me intently.

"What?" I asked.

Gran-gran placed the last cake pan into the oven and turned back to me.

"Let's sit over here," she said, indicating the table in the kitchen. I sighed when I realized what was happening. The talk I was dreading was finally here.

We sat at the table and Gran-gran wiped her hand in

the kitchen towel she had over her shoulder. She remained silent for a couple minutes, probably making sure she knew what she wanted to say.

I really didn't want to go through with this conversation because it would inevitably find its way to Lyla, and I was afraid from the moment I talked about how I truly felt when she left, that all that pain would come racing back to me all at once.

I would have run out of the house at top speed and gone somewhere, anywhere actually, but I knew that would have done no good and decided it was just best to get the talk over and done with now. If there only was the slightest chance at avoiding this...

"Gran-gran I think I know what you're going to tell me."

"Well maybe that's true, but I think it would be better for you if we still talked. It does help to say things out loud. Chase, tell me what's going on with you."

I opened my mouth to speak, but I actually had no idea what I was going to say. The last thing I thought I would have said slipped out.

"I don't think I can go on any longer without her," I whispered, looking away from my grandmother. Now that I'd started, I felt like I couldn't stop. Everything I'd kept bottled up just forced its way to my mouth. "Ever since Lyla left, I've felt like she took the best part of me with her, leaving this angry, bitter person behind. She is the best part of me."

There was a new found sadness to my voice I hadn't even noticed coming on, and there was nothing I could do about it.

"Without her I feel… empty… and lost… and I feel like I've lost my place in the world. Now I'm always angry and most things people say upset me. Every day I wake up thinking today's the day Lyla's coming back, but she never does. Somehow I know she's never coming back, no matter how many dreams I get, but that still doesn't stop me from having useless hope. It doesn't stop that voice in my head from telling me maybe she will come back. Every day I miss her. Gran-gran, every day, and it makes me feel like… my life will never get better. You know, you always hear people say 'it gets easier' but the truth is, it never does."

"Well, Chase, maybe that's true, but you do learn to live with it."

"That's the most depressing thing I've ever heard," I said, taken aback. "I don't want to learn to live with this pain. I don't want it at all."

Gran-gran sighed. Not in an exasperated way, but like her heart was breaking just by looking at me.

"Chase, you're only seventeen. You will find someone else. Lyla was only your first love. You will have another."

"I don't want another." I said softly, looking down at my hands because I could feel a few tears starting to escape. "I just want her back. I feel like Lyla's my true love. Even if I were to find someone else I liked, even if they had a year, they couldn't make me feel as happy as Lyla could in an hour. You can understand that, right?"

Gran-gran didn't respond for a while. I knew a little of what I was saying had gotten through.

Actually voicing my true feelings made me feel somewhat better, like a weight had been lifted off my chest, but I regretted it almost instantly when I saw the look my grandmother now had on her face.

"Don't look at me like that, please."

"Like what?" Gran-gran asked, looking at me calmly.

"Like you're sorry for me. Like you pity your little grandson who just got dumped. Well, I'm not little so... I..." I sighed and just stopped, but she continued to look at me as though she knew I had more to say.

"How could she just do that? She said she loved me, she said she would always be here for me. I always tried my best to treat her great. What did I do wrong? It's not fair. I don't feel like I deserve this."

Gran-gran came over to me and hugged me while I was sitting down. "Everything will work out in time, Chase, just have a little faith."

I heard my grandfather clear his throat and when I turned around I was shocked to see him standing in the doorway to the kitchen with both my parents behind him. I stood up just as they moved closer, all three of us unsure of what to do. Certainly my Dad looked like he was in standby mode.

"What're you guys doing here?" I was finally able to say. Mom dropped her bag and came over to hug me. "This was supposed to be our first Christmas together in East Island. Even though that's not going to happen this year, we weren't going to be apart as a family on Christmas when we really didn't have to be."

When Mom released me and stepped aside, I took a deep breath and walked up to my dad.

"Dad, I –" Before I could say anything else, he pulled me into a hug. "I'm sorry, Dad. Really."

"I know you are son. Me too."

It wasn't the perfect Christmas or New Year's, but I'd finally patched things up with my parents, though I still wasn't healed. But that was the first time I really felt like I wouldn't hurt this bad forever.

CHAPTER 18

The Return

I t was like something had shocked me in my sleep. It felt to me like some strange electric current seemed to pass through my body with lightning speed, zapping every part of me, ripping me from my dreamless sleep and making me sit straight up in bed.

I hopped out of bed and without even pausing to turn on the light, I ran to the window, almost tripping over the covers as I went, and threw it open in my anticipation. My heart began thumping hard as I wondered about the blissful ramifications of this feeling.

Nothing but cold night air, darkness and the sound of the sea greeted me. This didn't hinder my hopes though. I thought maybe I just couldn't see her, that maybe my eyes hadn't yet caught her silhouette, but after nearly twenty minutes of pointless hoping, I finally admitted that Lyla wasn't there.

I was so sure that the surge I felt had something to do with Lyla being close by, but perhaps this was more like some kind of withdrawal, and these false alarms were nothing more than my body adjusting to Lyla's constant absence from our link.

From the day Lyla left, I'd always hoped she'd come back. There was always something in me that hoped one day she would open her end of the connection and upon feeling my emotions again, would decide to return to East Island. The truth is, that small glimmer of hope I kept inside was all that kept me from completely losing it. It was the rope that kept my sanity intact.

But at that moment, standing by my bedroom window, I finally admitted to myself she wasn't coming back. I hadn't felt her open her end of the link in weeks, so I had no idea where she was or how she was feeling, which meant I had no way of knowing if I even had a chance at changing her mind. And as for the mental link that recently developed between us, she was doing her very best to keep her thoughts away from me.

My chest began to feel heavy as I fought to hold back the pain that came when I realized just how much I had lost, and how much I could have gained if Lyla had stayed.

I had left the window open and was walking back to bed when I felt someone's hand grip me gently below my elbow. Anyone would be surprised or even scared if a hand just touched them when they were alone in the dark, but from the second that hand touched me a rush of warmth flooded my body, accompanied but a strange yet familiar calmness. How could I not recognize those soft, slender fingers that caressed my face so many times? I turned quickly on the spot and even though it was dark, I could clearly see the silhouette of a girl standing next to me. It was Lyla.

"Chase," she uttered this with that same beautiful voice I was accustomed to but was sure I would never hear again. I couldn't whether she was happy or sad, but I was simply too happy to just have her there to care.

Without even thinking about it, I flung my arms around her and felt like I needed to stay like this or she would disappear forever. I even welcomed her unique aroma which aroused all my senses. It just seemed to smell more amazing than I remember.

When I felt Lyla's hand touch me as she hugged me back, I was sure that nothing could have been better than this, to have her in my arms again, but she relaxed her control over the bond, and I felt her desire for something more. I didn't exactly have to think about what she wanted, but before I could do anything, her lips were crushed against mine in a way she had never allowed before. The kiss was amazing. Lyla had never kissed me with such fierceness and passion before because she was always afraid of losing control and hurting me.

The emotional part of the kiss was weird, but in a good way. I felt every pleasure a kiss like this could give me. It took away all the pain and worries I had when Lyla was gone. It was like every bad thought I had was wiped away leaving nothing but pure happiness, just like the first time we kissed. I also felt every pleasure it gave Lyla. Through our bond, I felt how much she not just longed to kiss me, but to kiss me like this. I felt how much she was simply happy to be here, and I felt how powerful this one kiss was to her, how much it meant to her.

When we finally broke apart (though our heads remained together) I still felt happy, but it was no longer the only or dominant feeling I had. Looking at Lyla, I started to feel angry and hurt, and from the look on her face, I knew she felt this through our bond.

Suddenly I started to feel like I wanted to make her feel the pain she caused me, even if it was only for a few minutes. But I told myself it wouldn't be fair to her because she left to keep me safe in the first place.

Knowing this did nothing to quell my anger. I released her and walked over to the other side of the room near my bed. Without turning to look at her I said, "You left me here. You left me alone."

There was a soft whoosh in the room that meant Lyla had super-walked to me, but she didn't do anything but sit on the bed. When I looked at her she was fiddling with her hands in her lap.

"Do you know what it was like for me, always wondering if you were ever coming back, always hoping you would come back? Every night I woke up just hoping to find you here, but you weren't. Every day and night I went down to the beach, praying you'd swim back, even if it was for a little while, because I just needed to see you. What made it worse was the fact that I could still feel you through our bond, but I couldn't be with you. Then you just started to close yourself off from the link altogether. Lyla, how could you do that? How could you just leave? Do you know how much that hurt?"

I sat down next to her on the bed. I so wanted to just put my arms around her and just to lay there, but I needed to know.

She finally looked at me.

"Of course I know how much it hurt. How do you

think I felt every time I felt your emotions tugging on my consciousness? I felt your pain, and I knew I was the cause, but I couldn't do anything to help you. Chase, I wanted to come back for you so badly, but I couldn't because distancing myself from you was the only way to keep you safe."

"How do you figure that?"

"Everyone kept saying we shouldn't be together because they thought I wanted to turn you, but even though we both know I would never do that, it didn't mean I couldn't indirectly hurt you in other ways."

Lyla got off the bed and started pacing.

"For instance look at what Chris did. It's all because of me. Those things didn't happen because you love me, it's because I love you. If I hadn't been around you, none of that stuff would've happened and you would've had a normal life."

I jumped off the bed, filled with shock and indignation.

"Are you out of your mind?" Lyla recoiled a little in surprise. "Do you think I would give up all I've had with you for, what you call 'a normal life'? I would go through that ten times more if it meant I could be with you forever. Being with you has been the best thing that could've happened to me, but it's like you don't understand that."

"I do understand, really. I just want you to be safe." Lyla whispered in her angelic voice.

"So what made you finally come back?" I just realized that something must have made her change her mind.

Lyla finally stopped pacing and turned in the bedroom light. "I came back because you're in danger and I've got to get you out of here."

She walked over to the chest of drawers and was about to start pulling out my clothes before I caught her hands and turned her to me.

"Whoa. Slow down. What do you mean?"

She merely pulled away and started throwing clothes onto the bed.

Seeing Lyla acting so frantic and feeling a sudden wave of panic and fear rushing through our bond from her scared me more than if she had actually attacked me. I reached out to her again.

"Lyla, please tell me what's happened."

She sighed, dropping the remaining clothes back into an open drawer.

She took my hand and guided me over to the bed. After a few moments of silence, she finally said: "When I left, which was the hardest thing I've ever had to do, I went to England."

"Okay. I remember you told me your time there was one of the happiest in your life."

"Well, I thought if I went back I might be able to find some of that happiness again. I had hoped with time it would ease my pain over you, but once I got there, nothing I did made me feel any better."

I had to concentrate hard on blocking my end of the connection, because I actually felt some satisfaction at hearing Lyla say she couldn't get over leaving.

"I stopped going on land altogether. I just wanted to go full primal and lose myself in my instincts. It's not something I'm proud of wanting to do, but I didn't want to hurt anymore and I believed if all I brought was trouble to the person I loved, I didn't deserve any kind of happiness.

After a while I came across another Aquamun named Andréus. At first he only came around to watch me, but he soon started talking with me, and to be honest, I welcomed his company. But after a while I realized that he, well, he kind of wanted to acquire me."

"He wanted to what?" I blurted out, unable to help myself. The way Lyla said it sounded like he thought she was some kind of object he could buy. Lyla smiled at my indignation. "That's how most Aquamuns refer to it. It simply means he wanted me to be his mate."

Lyla watched me closely to see my reaction to this news. Truthfully, when I heard the word 'mate', something hot seemed to contract in my stomach.

"What happened next?" I tried to sound like I merely wanted to hear the rest of the story rather than fearing the girl I loved was about to tell me she loved someone else.

"Well I had to explain to him that I was already in love with someone, and if I couldn't be with him, I didn't want anyone else."

I turned my face away. I didn't want Lyla to see my blushing.

"Okay, believe me when I say that's good to know, but that doesn't really explain why I have to leave. What are you afraid of?"

I moved closer to her and took her hand in my palm. Suddenly she started talking as if she was giving a murder confession and tears began flowing down her cheeks.

"Chase, I'm sorry. I was so lonely and took the chance for company. I didn't realize what kind of Aquamun he really was. I told him things about me, about the island, but mostly about you. I told him your name, where you live, what you look like… I'm sorry."

At that point I finally realized what she was getting at. I remembered something Nikolai told me a couple months earlier. He said if two Aquamuns wanted the same mate they would settle it with a fight to the death. "The one who survives would claim the Aquamun as their mate. In our world, there's nothing more terrifying than an Aquamun fighting for a mate."

I didn't need Lyla to finish. I knew what was happening. It was the hunt and that meant an Aquamun was coming after me.

"He's coming after me." It was a statement of fact, but Lyla slowly nodded a confirmation and after drying her eyes, stood up.

If a rampaging Aquamun was after me, I really didn't see any way out of it. When Chris was after me, he did it indirectly with his magic, and Hilda and the Morgans were there to help me. But if an Aquamun was coming, it changed everything. I'd seen what the Morgans could do with their abilities. The fact that someone was going to use those against me was bad. Very bad. There was nowhere in the world I could hide. Anyone I was with or around was in danger.

With my mind made up, I got off the bed and grabbed a bag pack out of the closet, and threw some of the clothes Lyla had on the bed into it.

"You're right. I've got to get out of here." I went to get my passport and my ATM card.

"I won't let anything happen to you Chase, I promise. You don't have to be scared."

Lyla took hold of my hands, then kissed me. Hearing

her ready to put herself in the danger that was coming scared me more than the Aquamun himself.

"Lyla, no. I don't want you to fight him. He can actually kill you. Look, I'm not leaving because I'm scared… well, I am. But I'm more frightened for my friends, I'm scared for my parents, and I'm terrified for you. If I stay here, I'd be putting everyone in danger, and I wouldn't be able to live with myself if I knew that any of them got hurt because of me."

Lyla cupped my face in her hands and said: "Chase you don't have to go through this alone, we can help you."

"What do you mean 'we'?"

"My family. You're a part of my life, which means you're a part of our family and we protect each other. Now I have no idea when Andréus plans on coming, but we're prepared anyway. Right now Nikolai's in the sea, patrolling the island's borders and Michael's just below the cliffs in case Andréus gets past Nikolai. We already called Hilda for help. Mother's over there with her now, and father's already left for England."

"He's gone to find Andréus?"

"He's gone to the Aselhoff house. Viktor is Andréus's father,"

"He's part of the Aselhoff house?"

"Yes. Father's going to try to convince Viktor to get Andréus to call off the hunt, seeing as you're human."

At first I was lost for words. The fact that this was all happening because of me was unbelievable. I obviously wasn't happy, but after hearing what everyone was doing for me, I was no longer afraid for myself. I felt ready, like I just wanted to find Andréus and fight him, but as he was probably a billion times stronger than me, that would be suicidal.

Lyla took my hand and squeezed it in a reassuring gesture, which I returned.

"Okay. I'll do it your way. But what about my parents?" I suddenly remembered they would be caught in the middle of this if something wasn't done.

"Don't worry," Lyla replied. "I know how to get them off the island. They'll be gone by the day after tomorrow at the latest. Get that bag." She pointed to the backpack now stuffed with clothes. "We have to wait for Nikolai's signal. When we leave, we'll go out the window, meet Michael out front with the jeep and Nikolai will join us there too."

"Where are we going?" I asked.

"Hilda's. We'll figure out our next move there. Plus, you're going to be staying there, where she can protect you until this is over."

Suddenly there was a bright flash of light, accompanied by a loud boom.

"What the hell was that," I asked, startled when everything had gone back dark and silent. Lyla cursed under her breath.

"That was Nikolai's signal. I told him to make it simple. Good thing only we were meant to see it. Come on."

We were just about to go when something occurred to me.

"When my parents realize I'm gone with a bag of clothes, they're gonna freak. They'll think I'm making another break for it."

"No they won't." Lyla actually sounded kind of smug. "Because in the morning, they'll find their son sleeping in because he got a cold. Nikolai will be taking care of that with a little compulsion. Chase you don't have to worry, we're going to take care of this." Lyla said, both promise and worry strong in her voice. Then with more grace and agility than a cat, she jumped out the window, then shouted back up. "Throw down the bag, then climb down."

After throwing the bag out, I went through the window and down the tree. Then, with only the moon and stars as a source of light, we ran to the road where Michael met us with the jeep. As soon as we were in, we sped off into the night.

"Where's Nick?" Nikolai wasn't in the jeep with us.

"He's running behind us to make sure we're not being followed. Andréus might get some of his father's men to help track us. We can't be too careful."

I knew Nikolai was an Aquamun, which meant he could handle a lot. But because he looked even younger than me, it made me feel bad because he had to do so much and put himself in harm's way.

"Don't worry, he'll be fine," Lyla said, but I couldn't help but hear the concern in her voice. My worries were probably barreling across the bond towards her. We both knew because of Nikolai's illusion powers, a lot would depend on him, and even though I knew he was willing to do it, it still felt unfair to expect so much from him.

No one said anything for the rest of the trip. We just sat in silence and I knew that, like me, Lyla and Michael were both contemplating the danger we were in. After about ten minutes, Michael arrived and parked at Hilda's house. As soon as we pulled up, Salathia danced out of the house in a blur, and before I barely recognized it, she hugged me and ushered us all into the house.

"Thank God you're all okay. I was so worried."

"What's going on, Mother?" asked Nikolai, suddenly appearing with us.

"We'll explain inside."

No matter how many times I was inside Hilda's house, it still freaked me out. I mean, why couldn't she be like a normal witch and have a creepy house? At least then I'd feel like I was in the right place. We found Hilda sitting in the dining room around the circular table. After we all sat down, Salathia began with a grave face.

"Marcus called shortly before you arrived. He spoke with Viktor, but he won't help. He said Andréus has the right to start the hunt as it is the Aquamun way and they refuse to defend a human."

"Where's father now?" Michael asked.

"When he called he said he had picked up Andréus's trace but it led out of England, which meant he'd already left. So he's on his way back. He should be here soon."

"So what do we do now? We can't just sit back and let Andréus attack." Lyla said, frustrated that there was no good news so far.

"Settle, Lyla. There may be a way for us to find Andréus," Salathia said, looking at Hilda to continue.

"You've already met him Lyla," Hilda said as she switched seats with Michael so she was sitting next to Lyla. "Which means you've sensed his aura. I can use that to try to use magic to find his location."

Hilda held out her hands, and Lyla placed both hers, palms down, on them.

"Now I want you to think of Andréus, and of him alone,

understood?"

Lyla responded with a nod and closed her eyes as Hilda did the same. A couple minutes went by and I began wondering if anything was even happening. But before long, they both slowly opened their eyes.

"Where is he?" I asked.

"He's somewhere in the Atlantic ocean, but I can't give you a more precise location because it seems he's using magic to hide his location." Hilda said.

"I didn't know Aquamuns could perform magic." I said, surprised.

"We can't," Salathia said. "But the Aselhoff house is very powerful. Viktor has witches under his command as well. One of them must've performed the spell for Andréus."

"Actually, Hilda, that's very helpful. I've got his scent and his trace. We know he's coming here and now with a general idea of where he is, it will be easier for me to find him." Lyla explained.

"What do you want to do now, Lyla?" Salathia asked. Lyla studied me for a while. It was clear to me what she was feeling, but it would have been nice to know what she was thinking. Every time I tried our mental link, there was always that small buzz that told me she was blocking the connection. Why, I had no idea.

"You," Lyla indicated her mother, "Michael and I will go looking for Andréus. He's not on the island yet, he's staying away for now for whatever reason, and I'd like to keep it that way. When father picks up our trace, I'm sure he'll join us."

She turned to Nikolai. "Nick, in the morning, compell Joseph and Lilly. Make them think Chase is still there, and use your influence over the whales to get them to do something, anything interesting really so they'll have an excuse to leave the island. When you're done, trace our location, we'll need you."

Nikolai nodded in acknowledgement.

"Hopefully, we'll find him in time and between the five of us, we can convince him to give up the hunt," Lyla sighed loudly, and judging by the expressions on everyone's face, it was clear they were sure it wouldn't be that easy.

As I was going over in my head what Lyla had planned, what everyone was thinking burst from my mouth.

"Tell me something. Let's say you find Andréus, but he refuses to give up the hunt, what are you going to do then?"

Everyone in the room was looking at me as though they were all afraid, but Michael cleared his throat in a business-like manner and answered.

"When an Aquamun is on the hunt, and a third party interferes like we're going to, one of the hunters kills the person for getting in. So to answer your question, if Andréus refuses to end the hunt, which he probably will, he'll come after us too, and it won't stop until one of you is dead, so we may have no other choice but to kill him."

And there it was, out there for all of us to hear.

Everyone in the room was quiet. I knew that neither the Morgans nor Hilda had ever taken anyone's life, supernatural or human, and here now, because of me, they faced having to do just that. When it was Chris who was after me, Lyla had the chance to kill him, but instead, she took away his soul. Now they were up against another Aquamun and as Lyla told me before, the touch wouldn't destroy an Aquamun's soul. The only option would be to take him out for good.

Even though Aquamuns killed each other all the time, it wasn't the Morgans' way. Hilda claimed to hate Aquamuns, but did she have the resolve to kill one? And who was to say if they did go up against Andréus, would they all survive? With protection as strong as this, it was easy to believe I would live through this. The real question was, would everyone else here live through this? I looked around at everyone and felt a pang of guilt and emotional pain at the thought that, maybe a month from now, one or more of the people I loved could be dead.

"How?" I asked suddenly, pulling everyone from their train of thought. All eyes were on me again. "How do you kill an Aquamun?"

"Because of our healing abilities and our bones being so strong, it's not an easy thing to do." Lyla began. "And in Andréus's case, he is well over one hundred years old, so magic is out, but we do know of two ways. The first is the touch."

"I thought you said the touch doesn't work on Aquamuns," I interrupted.

"No. I said it won't destroy our souls. The energy works differently on us. Instead of destroying our souls, it would kill us. But the thing is, father said some Aquamuns are immune to the power, so it may not work on Andréus. The other way would be to break the neck. Remember I said our bones and healing are why we're so hard to kill? Well our necks are our weak point."

Lyla paused, and with everyone else looked at Hilda when she gave a "Hmmm" at Lyla's words.

"Our bones might be strong, but we are strong enough to break them. What people don't know is, if you can break an Aquamun's neck it would paralyze us for a couple minutes because it slows down the healing process. Once that's done, we can completely break the bone connecting the head to the spine, which would kill an Aquamun."

It sounded so complicated. If they tried to take out Andréus like that, there was a huge chance he could turn the tables on them.

"When are you leaving?" I wasn't too keen to see any of them go, especially knowing that any one of them, my new family, might not come back.

Lyla rose from her seat, walked over to me and lightly kissed me on the cheek. After a quick nod to her family, who had also risen gracefully from their seats, she said, "We're leaving now."

CHAPTER 19

Protection

The next couple of minutes flew by in a blur of color and that was because everyone was pacing around Hilda's living room going over what they were to be doing for the final time, which could be disastrous if it went wrong.

Lyla, Michael and Salathia were going to try to find Andréus and stop him from coming here. According to Lyla, Marcus was to meet up with them in the sea.

Nikolai was to go to my house and compel my parents to make them believe I was still home. To make sure they were safe and out of the way, he was going to use his ability to create some whale activity near the island that would require my parents to leave for a few days. That way Andréus wouldn't be able to use them against us. Once that was done, he would meet up with the others.

Finally, I was to stay with Hilda at her house, where she would put up some extra defense.

Without me realizing it, everyone else had left the room one by one so I was left sitting all by myself. The silence in the room was now so absolute I could clearly hear the ticking of the second hand on the clock, which was now saying 3:15 am. Any thoughts of sleep had long since left me.

Without any real reason, probably because I had nothing else to do, I started remembering days from months before, when around this time Lyla and I would be asleep, my arms wrapped around her, her body keeping me warm and the sound of my heart beat and my dreams keeping her comfortable. Those were cherished moments that now seemed an entire lifetime away.

"Those really are good memories," Lyla said, now walking back into the room. "And believe me, we'll be making many more, I promise you that."

I looked at her and smiled. It was the first time I really smiled since she came back. "You can read my mind now, can't you?"

Lyla chuckled. "Not all the time. And sometimes only what you're thinking in the moment. I'm still learning to control it. When this is over, we can practice it together."

"I would like that." I walked over and hugged her.

I checked the link and shifted through her feelings. Anger, fear, regret. Those were what I expected to feel from anyone who went through what Lyla did.

Over time I'd learned that she was pretty good at hiding her base feelings from our connection, but I found that if I tried hard enough, I could tap into her true emotions. But when I did I was surprised, because I felt emotions from her I didn't think she would be feeling right now: happiness, hope, content.

The only reason I could think of that she would hide these feelings from me was if she was ashamed. I knew the reason she felt so good was because she was finally back home with her family, with me. I didn't care how bad she thought that was at a time like this, I was glad she was back.

After disentangling herself from my arms, she kissed me with that same fierce passion she kissed me with before. When we broke apart, she said, "I'm so sorry I brought this on you. It seems whatever I do, I put you in harm's way. I get close to you and someone almost kills you for it. I leave to keep you out of danger and still, someone else is after you. It makes me feel so helpless."

The thing about having an emotional connection is that emotions can take you by surprise at any time. Just as soon as she said it, her despair hit me painfully in my chest.

"Lyla, this isn't your fault. Just because you love me doesn't mean when something bad happens to me it's your fault." I knew nothing I told her would make her feel better yet, but I still had to try.

A series of audible footsteps told me someone else was here, and I saw Michael standing by the threshold. Knowing that even as big as he was as an Aquamun, Michael could walk without making a sound, which obviously meant he wanted me to be aware he was coming.

"Lyla, mother said it's time to go." He told his sister, and then looked at me. "You shouldn't worry so much, this is all going to work out."

I tried to give him a reassuring smile. To be honest I had no idea what look was on my face. Looking like he was intruding on something personal, Michael eased out of the room, a lot more gracefully then he came in. Clearly everyone knew how hard saying goodbye again so soon would be for us.

Lyla, looking soulfully at me with her piercing blue eyes, took my right hand and placed it on her cheek, then placed hers on my chest, over my heart. Suddenly, a strange kind of feeling came over me. It felt more physical than emotional. It was beyond anything I'd ever felt in my life, happy and wonderful, yet so much more.

The Aquamun song, Lyla's song, was loud in my head. The loudest I'd ever heard it. Somewhere, deep in my head, I felt a presence in my mind, another consciousness: Lyla. Somehow, our mental and emotional connections had become so strong, it was as though they were one. I not only felt Lyla's feelings, but I also heard her thoughts as well and not just what she was thinking at that moment, it was like I had access to all the thoughts and memories she'd ever had, and popping up all around in her mind was me. In that moment, which felt like it could stretch on forever, I knew just how much she loved me.

I don't know how I said it, with my mouth, mind or emotions, but I said to her, "Lyla, I will always love you." I knew she heard me.

Shortly after the Morgans left (around 3:23) I sat down on Hilda's couch just to rest for a couple minutes, but what felt to me like a few minutes later, I opened my eyes to find the house bathed in sunlight and I was lying down with a blanket over me.

After throwing it over the back of the couch, completely forgetting I didn't live here, I got up. I saw on the clock that it was five minutes past nine.

"Hilda," I called a little hoarsely, but was only answered by the ringing silence of the house. Stretching my still tired body, I walked around Hilda's living room for a while, looking at the pictures depicting her life and came to realize something. All of the pictures in Hilda's house were of her when she was younger, but she didn't have any of herself after her late twenties.

I took up one of the photos which depicted a scene of a younger, much happier looking Hilda, posing for the camera with a group of other women. It was so hard for me to imagine the past Hilda and the present one as the same person. Judging from the photos, their personalities seemed entirely different. It made me think of how much I didn't know about Hilda, not that she was the sharing type.

"What is it?" Hilda's voice said quietly from behind me. I spun around in surprise. Did everyone supernatural have the ability to sneak around so quietly?

"Looks like you slept well enough, but from now on you can sleep in the room I prepared for you upstairs."

I figured she was outside when I called, as she was wearing her gardening stuff with the gloves in her hand. I saw her eyes drift down to the picture in my hand and even though she said nothing about it I got the strangest feeling me holding it was making her uncomfortable, so I carefully put it back in its place.

"Would you like some breakfast?"

She walked into the kitchen. I followed her.

"You don't have to make me breakfast, you know," I said even as I sat down to a plate of fried eggs, hot dogs and toast.

"Well of course I know that, but it's not like I get many guests here anyway. Now, if you don't mind, I would like your help with a few things around the house."

I nodded as I sipped a cup of tea.

Hilda watched me for a moment as I drank my tea, but just when she was about to speak, I asked, "Do you think they're going to be okay?"

I could tell she read the worry on my face, but I didn't care. I just needed to hear something good.

"Chase, there's five of them against one Aquamun, I'm sure they're going to be fine."

Because of her tone, her words didn't reassure me. Instead it brought more worry. I loved the Morgan family as if they were my own and the thought of losing any of them made my stomach turn.

They'd already done so much for me, but this time it seemed like there was a lot more to lose, as if this time the mission at hand was way more dangerous. Maybe it was because Chris had no direct way of killing them, but as an equal, Andréus did. It just hurt me to imagine one of them not coming back if Andréus fought them and for some reason, I knew he was going to.

"Chase, I won't lie to you. There's a chance one of the Aquamuns could get hurt. This Andréus sounds like a tough character, but you have to have faith. You need to believe they're going to be okay or you'll drive yourself mad with worry. Plus if he does manage to get here, you're going to have to be ready, so try not to worry so much."

After a quick, sympathetic smile, she stood up, pulled back on her gloves and was back in her usual mode.

"Once you're done, you can come on outside. The

garden fence needs painting and it won't paint itself."

"Can't I shower first?" I moaned through a mouthful of eggs.

This time, Hilda's smile was shrewd.

"Trust me, showering now isn't going to matter in a few hours, not when I'm done with you."

The days that followed the Morgans' departure were far from blissful. We didn't have any contact with Lyla and her family, so we had no way of knowing how they were doing or where Andréus was.

Hilda still kept trying to use magic to look for him, but somehow now even that was not picking him up. As we had no idea where he was, we decided it was best if I stayed home from school. At Hilda's house I had the best protection. I had left my cell phone home, so no one knew where I was.

Even though I knew they were off the island and safe, I still couldn't help thinking about my parents. This whole situation was messing with their lives, even though they didn't know it.

I spent my time helping Hilda as much as possible, because even though it didn't calm my mind, it did help me pass the time.

On the third day after the Morgans had left, outside seemed like it was permanently overcast. Huge dark clouds had settled over East Island, leaving the place dark and windy.

I was upstairs sitting in the room Hilda prepared for me, wondering just how the cove sounded in this weather, when Hilda walked in.

"Looks like there's a storm coming." She stood behind me as I looked through the window at the dense forest beyond. "I want you to have this."

I turned around and was surprised and a little shocked to see she was holding a sheathed hunting knife out to me.

"I, um, don't think this is going to hurt Andréus if he gets here, Hilda," I said as I took the knife from her.

"Well normally, no, it wouldn't, but this knife has been touched by magic. It's been charmed." She added at my puzzled look. "I'm betting it won't kill him, but if he does get close to you and you use it on him, it will do some damage. Enough for you to escape anyway."

At that moment I felt a strong pang of frustration in my chest.

"I don't think they're having much luck," I said, then explained to Hilda what I just felt through the bond. Even though we had no idea what Lyla was feeling so frustrated about, Hilda decided to increase the protection around the house.

I had no idea how she was going to do that, but I was really concerned about it. From the time Lyla left, I hadn't been able to connect with her through the bond and that worried me a lot because I couldn't help but remember the loneness and pain I felt the first time she left. That was the hardest part. Having to constantly reassure myself that she would come back, that she was just keeping the bond weak so I wouldn't be checking it in concern all the time. But I just had to know she was okay. Now that I did feel something from her end, however, I had just had to know that they were okay. It appeared what I felt only got through because Lyla temporarily lost control, because as soon as I was about to check the link, I felt it close off again and my own anger began to rise.

I knew Lyla only wanted me to be safe, but I couldn't roll with the fact that she was keeping me in the dark about everything. Just because I didn't have any supernatural abilities didn't mean I needed to be kept from everything. I began wishing I had some way of letting her know how I felt when, to my surprise and relief, one such way did arrive later in the afternoon that day.

Hilda called me downstairs and when I got into the dining room, I was excited to see Nikolai sitting at the table, eating an apple. It was gone within seconds of me reaching the room.

As he was only wearing a pair of shorts, Hilda came into the room holding out a T-shirt to him that I was sure was mine. Nikolai eyed it sadly, but took it and pulled it on.

"What are you doing here?" I asked, the surprise disappearing, giving way to panic. "Did something go wrong? Is Andréus here? What's wrong?"

"Nothing's wrong, well except the current problem, which is why I'm here." Nikolai pulled two more apples from the fruit bowl on the table and bit into one.

"Why is it you eat so much when your kind don't even need to eat?" Hilda wondered.

"Some organic foods actually have taste to us. Weak and quick, but it still has an appeal to me." Nikolai replied through a mouthful of chunks.

"And apples are one of those foods?"

Nick nodded as he took another huge bite.

"Why are you here?" I asked again, a little more sharply. "And maybe you can tell me why Lyla's been keeping me out of what's been going on."

"Dude, she hasn't been doing that to keep you out. She didn't want to be distracted by the connection, so she closed it to focus on Andréus. And that hasn't been going very well." Nikolai suddenly became very serious.

"What do you mean? What exactly has been going on?" Hilda asked. She pulled out a chair and sat down.

"Well, first, I don't think I need to tell you that he refused to give up the hunt."

"So what have you been doing this whole time?" I demanded as if I was accusing him of doing something wrong. He simply looked at me and started on his third apple.

"Well, we've been trying to pin him down. When we first found him, he was near Australia. Lyla actually convinced him to talk to us, but when he heard what we were asking, let's just say he wasn't too keen on the idea of giving up to a human. Sorry."

Hilda was about to protest, but as I was hungry for information, I spoke a little louder. "Wait, what was he doing near Australia. I thought he lived in England?

"I think he was trying to avoid any interference as he figured Lyla was going to try to stop him. Luckily for us, Lyla already had a pretty strong sense of his aura, so she was able to pick it up. Well, from that time on, he's been trying to get to the island, but we've been throwing him off, though it hasn't been easy. Believe it or not, he's actually smarter than he looks."

"Has he been getting close to East Island?" Hilda asked,

getting a little tensed.

"Well, not really," Nick admitted, thinking on it. "The closest he got was the British Virgin islands. Once we blocked his way, he then tried to shake us off, but with Lyla and me being so fast, he usually has a hard time shaking us off." Nikolai looked a little nervous, and then said, "He sometimes uses distractions, the worst so far was when he attacked a small fishing vessel."

Both Hilda and I gasped in horror. I'd never imagine Andréus would hurt complete strangers just to get to me. But then he probably only thought of them as mere humans.

"Did he kill any of them?" Hilda asked.

"No," Nick replied, "But a few of them were badly injured. I compelled them to forget how they sustained their injuries, but the boat's been damaged so people will probably think pirates or something."

"It seems he's getting desperate. Or frustrated," Hilda said. Nick nodded in agreement.

"That's what father said. He also thinks Andréus may be getting help somehow."

"I thought Aquamuns go on the hunt alone," Hilda said. I looked to Nick who shrugged.

"Well, we do, but this isn't a typical situation. We aren't part of the hunt and we're helping Chase, so to even things out, maybe Andréus got someone from his house to help him. But it's only a theory, and Andréus hasn't been acting like he's getting any help from anywhere and father doesn't want to split us up for an unsupported theory, so he sent me to tell you to be on your guard. And yes, we're all okay."

Nick got up to leave.

"Thanks for coming to tell us Nick. It's been horrible being without you, I gotta say, though I thought you would have sent Lyla as she's the fastest."

Hilda and I walked Nick to the door, where he turned and looked back at me. Nikolai, out of everyone I knew, knew just how much Lyla and I loved each other, even if he couldn't understand it. He knew how I felt as he had his own special connection with her. It was anything but supernatural, but it was strong. I'd never forget how much it hurt him when she left.

"As Lyla's the fastest, she's the one who's best able to keep up with Andréus. He's pretty fast himself. Lyla and I are the ones usually on his tail. Chase, Andréus wants Lyla, remember. He won't hurt her."

"But that isn't true for the rest of you."

Nick gave us a small smile. "Don't worry about us. We'll be fine. If he decides to fight us, we'll handle him. I've got to go, hopefully the next time back, this'll all be over."

He gave us a quick wave and sped through the door, disappearing from sight in under a second.

"If I'm not careful, he may actually start to grow on me." Hilda admitted as she hung back the protective medallion over the door.

"I hope you realize he took my shirt with him," I joked. The first clap of thunder rolled through the after sky, sounding like drums of war, signaling the danger to come.

Even with the existence of magic, I still didn't believe in omens. However, I didn't take it as a good sign when the overcast sky got worse over the next two days. This was supposed to be the sunny season, yet outside was cold, dark and wet as rain pummeled the island due to a passing tropical depression.

Since Nick's visit, Hilda had upped the magical protection, not just on the house, but on me as well. She'd given me a ring to wear she said would protect against an Aquamun's touch and she'd made one for herself.

I'd seen her doing other things around the house that had to be powerful because she'd begun to get exhausted really quickly. She spent more time sleeping the regain her strength, which wasn't good, as I knew that meant she was tapping into her own life energy.

"Maybe you should go easy on the magic," I suggested one evening when Hilda was resting on the couch. She eyed me disbelievingly.

"Chase, you know I can't do that. Andréus could be a lot older than the Morgans, in which case my protection wouldn't hold for very long, so I've got to put up as many spells as possible. One small spell could mean the difference between life and death."

Shaking my head in defeat, I drifted back up to my room. As I was too agitated to keep still, I took my clothes off and took a shower. By the time I was finished, rain had already began to fall, sounding like rocks falling on the house, and I actually jumped in surprise as a huge bolt of lightning showered the house in light for half a second, which was followed by an explosion of thunder that was enough to sake the windows.

I knew Andréus didn't have the power to make storms, but the worsening of the weather made me very nervous and made me think of what Lyla said, about Andréus being just like his father.

After getting dressed, I decided to ask Hilda if everything was okay, but after searching the whole house, I couldn't find her anywhere. I even tried calling out to her, but got no answer.

My heart was already racing with worry. Since I came here to stay, Hilda had never left without telling me, so I knew she didn't just go off somewhere. I supposed she could have just been in the shed outside and couldn't hear me over the pounding of the rain, but when I went out there, I still couldn't find her. I couldn't quite tell what it was, maybe it was all in my head, but something just felt wrong.

Getting myself together, one thought came to me— getting to the knife Hilda gave me, because if she really was in danger, that knife would be my only hope of helping her.

I dashed back into the house, rushed upstairs, dug into the top drawer of the chest-of-drawers and pulled out the knife.

After I took it out by its wooden handle, I couldn't help but marvel at it. Another bolt of lightning flashed across the sky followed by another explosion of thunder, illuminating the room and making the sliver blade of the knife glow in the light.

At that moment, the realization of the situation and what I was about to do came to me. If Andréus really was here, if he'd somehow found a way around the Morgans, then they wouldn't be far behind and would simply deal with him. But if he somehow managed to slip past them without leaving a trail, if he was way ahead of them and the Morgans weren't able to get here anytime soon, that would mean Hilda and I were on our own with him and I'd have to try to find Hilda by myself.

If he was willing to take Hilda, I knew he wouldn't have a problem going after my parents; it was a good thing we got them away from here. It was a relief not having to worry about them too.

Taking a deep breath and mentally pulling myself together, I gripped the knife tightly in my hand and confidentially strode out of the room only to walk into a completely soaked figure wearing a wind breaker.

"Aaaaahhhhh!!" I screamed, only to realize it was Hilda.

"Where the hell have you been? I've been looking everywhere for you. I was so worried. I was just about to go out to look for you." I said, half-relieved, half-exasperated.

"I was out strengthening the protection around the house when I thought I saw someone lurking just behind the trees so I went to look, but I didn't find anyone."

"Well that's good, right?"

Hilda gravely shook her head. "Just because I didn't find anything doesn't mean someone wasn't there. Anyway, it made me increase the power around the house. We can't afford to be sloppy with him out there."

Then Hilda's face became kind. It was something I was still getting used to.

"I'm sorry I worried you. I didn't expect to be gone so long. And it's good to see you've finally got that out." Hilda said, pointing to the knife in my hand. "It's best if you keep it with you from now on."

"Why must you be so negative? I'm sure the Morgans

will handle this."

"It's not that I'm being negative, I'm being careful. The young one…"

"Nikolai." I corrected.

"He told us Andréus was trying to shake them off by leading them all over the place but when I thought about it, it sounded more to me like he was trying to keep them occupied, away from the island, away from you."

A flash of lightning lit up the sky again and was quickly followed by its companion, thunder.

"Even if that's true, that he's trying to keep them away from the island, so what? It's not like he's here to do something. He can't be in two places at once."

"He might not be here, but like the Aquamun suggested, he could have a partner that's just waiting for the right time. Now if that's the case, the Morgans won't be here to help us, which means we'll have to fight for ourselves. I'm going to get out of these clothes and I want you to keep that knife with you at all times, okay?"

After I didn't reply, Hilda grabbed me by the shoulders and looked me in the eye. "Do you understand?"

"Yes, yes, I got you."

"Good," she said as she released me and went to her room, leaving me to ponder about the severity of her words.

The storm that had hit East Island didn't let up by the next day as I'd hoped. In fact it wasn't until midday the day after when the lightning and thunder ceased and the rain was reduced to a drizzle. However, huge, dark clouds still drifted slowly across the sky.

I was actually glad when the rain slowed because Mom and Dad were still at sea. Around two in the afternoon, Hilda told me she was going out to strengthen the protection around the house. When I watched her from inside I saw her mutter as she walked around the area of the house. I noticed strange rocks and seashells were placed around the house. As I glanced at her through the living room window, she seemed agitated as she kept glancing towards the forest, as though she expected something to jump out at her. Something or someone.

Before she'd left the house, Hilda told me to stay in the living room and keep the knife with me, which was now lying on the coffee table behind me. There was something in her voice, like panic or fear. Whatever Hilda knew, it had her scared.

Suddenly, as I was staring out the window, I could have sworn I saw a figure just beyond the tree line. A humanoid figure. But as quickly as I had seen it, the figure disappeared. For the smallest part of a second I'd actually thought maybe the Morgans had returned, but if they did, they would not hide. They would come and let us know what was going on. That only meant either Andréus was here, or like Hilda said, he had an accomplice.

My head started to spin. Every beat my heart took seemed to send vibrations through my body that made my vision blur. My whole body felt out of my control. Then I remembered, Hilda had the house protected. Even if an accomplice of Andréus was here, as long as I stayed inside until the Morgans got here, I would be safe.

Wait a minute. That's when I remembered Hilda was

still outside. I looked out the window but couldn't spot her. Panic filled my body, making my arms and legs tingle in that unpleasant way.

Without thinking about it, I grabbed the knife off the table and put it in the waist of my pants where I could feel the cold brass handle pressing against my skin. Very quickly, I ran through the door and into the drizzling rain. Although the lightning and thunder had stopped and the rain lessened, the wind remained as strong as ever. As soon as I got out, the wind had started blowing the rain in my face, lowering my visibility. I started calling out for Hilda, but my voice was carried away by the wind.

By now my clothes were completely soaked and I had to keep wiping water out of my eyes. Adding the wind to the mix, I was freezing cold. I was about to turn when I felt a hand grab my shoulder. I quickly spun around, only to be relieved to see it was Hilda.

"Chase we've got to go now. We're in danger." She shouted over the wind, her eyes wide with shock and fear. The hand she had on my shoulder was trembling violently.

"Hilda, what's wrong?"

"He's coming. Andréus is on his way. The protection I placed around the house won't hold. We've got to get away from here."

"Where can we go? If the protection you put on the house won't stop him, what will?"

I was starting to feel like the end was near, like everything everyone did for me was in vain, and in no time Andréus would be able to kill me.

Hilda grabbed my shirt and started pulling me towards the forest as she said: "There's an old abandoned chapel deep in the woods. Its walls have powerful magic that will keep Andréus out."

I pulled myself free of Hilda and stared at her.

"What about Lyla and the others? What happened to them, are they okay?"

Hilda looked at me, the urgency temporarily disappearing from her face.

"Chase, I'm not sure what happened to them, but if they're okay, I'm sure they will be here soon and when they get here, I know Lyla would like to see you alive. Everything will be fine. There are five of them against Andréus. I'm sure he only slipped past them but didn't hurt them. Lyla will be fine. I promise you."

Hilda motioned towards the trees with her head then took off at a sprint, faster than I would have thought she could run. I took one last look at Hilda's house and the feeling that I was going to lose everything I loved rushed over me. I turned and took off after Hilda.

As I was following her into the forest, I began to realize I'd never been out here before, so I had no idea where I was going.

The trees were a lot closer together and taller, and there were a lot of low-lying branches that felt like they were trying to catch me. After a couple minutes of running, I started breathing hard and had to slow down as I had a terrible stitch in my side that felt like a knife had pierced my ribs. I had stopped to take a breath when I saw Hilda was just in front of me.

"We're here. Come on." Hilda said. I looked around and saw we were now standing in a very small church yard with a very old and majestic looking chapel just ahead of us and all of this was in a small enclosure inside the forest.

As we walked up to the chapel we passed through the graves and crypts. They were about thirty in all.

"I would have never guessed this was here."

"There's a lot you'd see if you just opened your eyes," Hilda said as we got to the chapel, but then she turned to me and held out her hand. "I'm sorry to ask this, but I need your ring. I need to use a spell and require a little extra power."

Without thinking on it too much, I slipped the ring she gave me off my finger and dropped it into her open hand. She looked at it for a second then placed it in her pants pocket.

Hilda walked up the chapel steps, then opened the doors and stood aside for me to enter. The rain had finally stopped and the wind had simmered down somewhat.

I walked up the steps past Hilda and into the chapel. The inside gave away the fact that this place hadn't been used in a long time. There were leaves and dust all over the floor and benches. The benches themselves were scattered all over the room as if everyone left in a hurry and threw them out of their way.

Colorful pieces of glass from the broken windows littered the floor, glittering brightly as weak sunlight shone on them. Huge networks of spider webs were across the whole room. In all, the deserted chapel had a very sad look.

There was a loud bang which I assumed was from Hilda closing the door. I turned around and stepped back in surprise as she was already standing in front of me. I didn't even get the chance to ask her how she did that. All I saw was the back of her hand as it collided with my face and I went flying across the room.

CHAPTER 20

On the Hunt

Pain. That's the first thing my mind registered above all else after Hilda hit me. A huge burst of pain engulfed my face. Hilda had so much power behind that one blow that it sent me across the room where, after I hit the floor, I slid all the way to the opposite wall and crashed into it.

Make no mistake, it hurt like hell, but it made me remember the knife I had. Hilda didn't ask about it, so maybe she didn't know I had it on me. But then, it wasn't like I could use it on her. She was my friend.

"Hilda, what are you doing?" I asked as I stood up, my left cheek stinging. I was afraid of her answer. She stared, walking towards me at a slow pace.

"This will be easy," she said in a voice that was very much unlike hers. "You're human, weak, fragile. I don't see how Lyla could have ever fallen for you. Admittedly you are handsome and I suppose she did have to occupy her time with some form of amusement. But a human? It's just so… wrong."

I felt like I finally had control of my body again and got

up quickly, but just as I did, a huge burst of pain exploded in the lower right side of my back. I looked down at the spot where I was. I saw a piece of broken wood covered in blood. I moved my hand to the place where the pain was coming from and I felt some moisture there, which meant I was bleeding.

I didn't know if it was serious or not, but from the size of the wood that did the damage, I was willing to bet it wasn't too bad.

"Hilda, why are you doing this? Why are you helping Andréus after everything?"

A wicked smile spread across Hilda's face, making her look evil and unfamiliar to me.

"Watch and be amazed," she said.

Suddenly Hilda started to grow. Her locks started to undo and seemed to be retracting into her head. Her whole body looked like it was liquefying and changing. The arms grew bigger, more muscular and the hair was now neck long and looked untidy.

The liquid mass finally began to solidify, and now standing before me wasn't Hilda, it was Andréus. He was tall and slightly muscular, with incredibly pale white skin. Even with the distance between us, I could see his eyes were a misty blue color and he was gazing at me malevolently with them from behind his curtain of untidy hair that was slightly damp.

Seeing him in person seemed to jolt my brain into remembering I had the knife. I put my hand behind my back, grabbing the hilt. My heart began racing, which I knew he could hear. I began thinking I might have a chance if he would just come close enough to me for me to plunge the knife right into his heart.

"How did you do that? What happened to Hilda?"

"You know it's really amazing what some Aquamuns can do. You see, very few people know that I have the ability to shape-shift. All I need to do is touch the person I want to become. It was actually easy getting to Hilda. While she was outside protecting the house, she herself wasn't very well protected. She had on her some kind of protection ring, but… well let's just say I came here with a little magic of my own and that took quick care of her little decoder ring. I didn't have any more to deal with yours, though."

He slipped his hand into his pocket and pulled out my ring.

"Which is why I had to get you to give it to me." And right there he crushed it in his hand with that nasty smile on his face again. He brushed the pieces onto the floor and said, "Well that's useless now. Oh and don't worry about your witch. I didn't kill her, I just knocked her out and threw her into her storage shed. Then I shifted into her and waited for you to come out looking for her once you couldn't find her, as I knew you would. You see, Lyla told me about how caring you are."

Andréus had stopped walking and for some reason seemed to be mesmerized with one of the pictures on the windows. That's when I realized something about him. He was a bragger. He was one of the types that loved to savour the moment just before victory and achievements, that's why I wasn't dead yet. He wanted to be sure I knew how clever he was before he killed me.

Well, that was fine with me. It gave me time to come

up with some kind of plan to try to get out of here and back to the house where Hilda and I would be safe until the Morgans got here. And speaking of the Morgans, why weren't they here? If something had happened to them, he would have said something. He probably wouldn't be able to resist it. If something had happened to Lyla, Andréus would have been furious and I would be dead.

"Where are the Morgans?" I asked, sounding braver than I felt. Andréus didn't take his eyes off the pictured glass when he answered.

"I don't know where they are and that's the truth. You see, when I first left home to look for you, I wasn't alone. I knew that Lyla would've tried to protect you, so I brought along a friend. This friend of mine has the ability to copy another person's power. It was simple really, all he had to do was copy my power, shift into me, and have the Morgans follow him for a while and they would have never guessed because when I shift into someone my aura changes to match theirs, which meant they didn't know they weren't following me and all I had to do was wait for the perfect opportunity."

"Lyla will never forgive you for killing me. She will hunt you down."

"After I kill you, yes, she will be mad, but we have forever ahead of us and you're just a human, she'll forget about you in time. Or," he said, thinking on something. "I could just frame your witch. Have them believe by the time I got here she'd already killed you. It's not so hard to believe when you think about it. Lyla told me she doesn't like our kind. The Morgans will think she just snapped and thought of you as one of them."

I actually started to laugh and it scared me a little, because I sounded just like him. It was just hard to imagine that someone could believe Hilda was capable of murder.

"No one would ever believe that. Hilda would never kill anyone. Everybody knows that."

But Andréus just shrugged and finally turned to look at me.

"Maybe that's true, but it's my problem to deal with. You, on the other hand, don't have a thing to worry about."

"Because you're going to kill me."

"Well, this is a fight to the death. However as you are human," there was strong contempt in his voice when he said the word 'human', "I'll make you a deal. If you leave Lyla and have nothing to do with her ever again, I will spare your life. How does that sound?" He had a look his face as though he'd just told me I won the lottery. I ignored his question.

"How do you know your friend won't hurt the Morgans?" I asked, ignoring him. He actually chuckled, and it sounded so normal you would have thought he was laughing at a joke.

"Well, he knows not to hurt Lyla, but I can't say the same about the rest of her family. Or your witch, if she gets in his way. I will say this for her, she does know her stuff. She was able to keep me away for a while, but her trust took her down. When I approached the house looking like Lyla, she sensed something was wrong, but because I was able to tell her what she wanted to hear, she let her guard down. You humans are so gullible." He moved a strand of hair from his eyes. "What about my offer, do you accept or not?"

I gripped the knife a little tighter. I knew after I gave him my answer he would attack me.

"No." I answered strongly.

He simply smiled at me and said, "Well, you die."

He was standing right in front of me and for a split second I caught a whiff of his aroma. It was sweet, like something sticky, but deep down, that amazing sea scent was present, but before I could appreciate it Andréus gripped me tightly by the neck with one hand, and lifted me off the ground. Gasping for breath and feeling like my head was going to pop off, I pulled out the knife and plunged it into his chest.

There was a horrible scream and I felt myself hit the ground as Andréus released me. He had a mystified look on his face, as though he couldn't believe it was possible that a knife could injure him like that as his hands fumbled with the hilt, like he was afraid of pulling it out.

Not waiting around for the outcome, I pulled myself up and headed for the door, but just as I reached it I felt someone grab my upper arm. I spun around and saw that Andréus had pulled the knife out and he looked pissed.

With fury bright in his eyes, he pulled my arm so hard it came out of the socket and to add further pain, he squeezed my arm until he broke it. The scream of pain that escaped me was one to rival Andréus's.

For the second time, he threw me across the room, away from the door. I collided with the back of the chapel—again—and that wall wasn't soft.

Pain flashed through my whole body and my already dislocated shoulder seemed to want nothing more than to torture me with agony. It felt like every part of my body was attacking me from the inside.

As I pulled my head off the ground, I looked up and felt a trickle of sweat drop into my eye, stinging me. With only my right eye open, I saw Andréus walking towards me with the knife in his hand and his shirt stained with blood.

I let my head fall back to the floor, resigning myself to the fact that I wasn't getting out of this; that I was going to die here.

Now who's the negative one? I thought to myself. I knew that whatever happened, Lyla wasn't going to have that monster in her life and this calmed me somewhat.

There was suddenly a huge crash and two loud bangs as what sounded like the chapel doors crashing onto the floor. Curiosity getting the best of me, I looked up and saw Andréus being held by someone from the back. Whoever it was had his hand with the knife in the air and an arm around his throat. Then, with what looked like little effort and amazing strength, they threw him into the air, where he flew so high he collided with a very thick beam with a loud bang and left it broken in two. Andréus fell to the floor, but landed on his feet, though I was glad to see he did stumble a little, and placed a hand over his chest. It seemed the wound did more damage than I thought.

By this time, the Aquamun that stopped Andréus was now standing in front of me and that's when I realized it was Nick. He had taken a defensive position in front of me, but Andréus was blocking our way out of the chapel and going through the windows was out of the question, as the low ones were sealed with bricks. Nikolai wouldn't be able to break through before Andréus got to him.

"Let me guess, you're Lyla's little brother, Nikolai,"

Andréus taunted. I knew he said 'little' just to rattle Nikolai, but for all it was worth, it didn't do any good, because Nick remained as he was, poised for battle, perfectly still. So still, in fact, that with his pale skin you'd think he was some sort of 3D figure. For every inch Andréus moved, Nikolai adjusted himself.

For all the time I'd known him, I'd never seen Nick so serious, even when we were looking for Chris or planning to stop Andréus. It was like a whole new side of him, like a different personality.

A dark frown had replaced the sneer that was on Andréus's face.

"Get out of my way before I have to hurt you too. He's mine."

Nikolai actually did one of his funny comebacks.

"I think my sister would say he's her's, but I'm sure you two kids can share."

If someone wasn't trying to kill me or I wasn't in so much pain, I would have laughed, but it seemed Andréus didn't find it too funny as he sped towards Nikolai, who in turn ran towards Andréus. After they collided, they were moving so fast I couldn't tell what was happening during much of the fight. After a while however, I did notice that they were out of the path to the door, which meant that I could escape.

There was no way I could leave Nick here, but I was hurt. Bad. What could I do? Then I remembered… I could call Lyla. I still had no idea why she and her family still weren't here with Nikolai and that had me a little worried, but if I opened the connection wide enough for my thoughts to flow to her, she would see what was going on and would know Andréus was here. So, trying extremely hard to close out what was going on (Andréus threw Nick onto the floor but he was up before Andréus could do any damage) I closed my eyes and focused on opening the connection. However, instead of feeling Lyla's emotions, I felt nothing.

Well not exactly nothing, but instead of the bridge I usually felt, there was an almost non-existent thread-like connection, so small it wasn't enough to contact Lyla, which meant she was trying to hide her emotions from me.

"Damn it!" I shouted in frustration. No way to contact Lyla, no way to help Nick. I just felt so helpless. Suddenly Nikolai flew across the room and slammed so hard into the wall that huge, deep cracks appeared and the place where Nick hit seemed now to be dented, but Nick was unharmed.

However, Andréus had used this time to find the knife he dropped and once he had it, he looked at me with animalistic rage and ran at me. Before he got too close Nick once again grabbed him from the back.

This time, however, Andréus was ready. He turned the knife backwards and plunged it into the left side of Nikolai's stomach. I couldn't tell who was more shocked, me or Nikolai. Seconds later blood started running out of the wound and onto Andréus hand and that's when he pushed Nick onto the ground, where he stayed.

"No!" I shouted at the same time someone else said it. I saw Marcus standing in the doorway, silhouetted against the sunlight. Less than half a second later, he was standing by Andréus where he grabbed him by the shoulders and threw him against the east wall, which made a deeper impression than the one Nikolai made. Marcus then forgot about Andréus and ran towards his son. In the space of time it took him to get to Nick, Andréus was inches away from him, but before he could get his hands on Marcus, Michael, Salathia and Lyla sped in, dragged Andréus away from us and engaged him in fight.

Weak but determined, I crawled over to Nikolai in time to see Marcus pull the knife out of his stomach. He screamed for a second and was covered in sweat. I'd never seen any of them sweat before, which meant this was getting worse.

Marcus took off his shirt and I was horrified to see that not only was the wound deep, but Nikolai's skin was getting paler and what looked like veins were showing up all over his body, carrying what looked like dark blue blood which seemed to be originating from the wound.

"What's wrong with him?" I asked Marcus, though I was afraid of the answer.

When Marcus answered, his voice sounded grim.

"He's still young. His body doesn't yet have a defense for such an injury. He's dying. We have to do something now or he'll die. Lyla." She was crouching next to us. "You have to take Nikolai." Marcus told her gravely.

"Now, Lyla. You're the fastest of us, he doesn't have much time. We will take care of things here. Lyla go. Do whatever you have to to save your brother."

And with that our connection was back open and I felt everything she wanted to say. *I love you.*

Lyla took Nikolai in her arms and sprinted out of the church in a blur. As soon as she was gone, I turned towards the fight and saw that Andréus had his hands full. Marcus and Michael were both in front Andréus, taunting him with their actions, and Salathia was behind him. Taking her chance, she ran and jumped onto Andréus's back, wrapping her legs around his middle. She grabbed his head with both hands and quickly twisted it to the side with a sickening snap, then she pulled it back, which was followed by another snap and a scream, then Andréus's dead body fell to the floor with a thud.

The last thing I remember seeing were the Morgans walking towards me, then I finally gave in to my pain and exhaustion, and passed out.

CHAPTER 21

Acceptance

W hen I next opened my eyes I felt so disoriented that I had no idea where I was at first, but soon enough I realized I was in the hospital. What made me aware of this wasn't what I saw or heard, but what I smelled. There was that weird smell of medicine and it was strong in the air and it was horrible. I pushed myself into a sitting position, and felt instantly uncomfortable.

As soon as I did this, I saw someone peek into the room and upon seeing me awake, in rushed my mother, closely followed by a nurse. Mom hugged me tightly around from the left to avoid my bandaged hand which was in a sling, and forcing the disgruntled-looking nurse to go around my other side to tend to me.

"Mom, what are you doing here?" I said, just remembering she and Dad were supposed to be at sea.

Taking the opportunity to try to fix my hair now—I couldn't stop her—she said, "We got a call Wednesday night from Karen; she said you got into an accident and was hurt. I was so scared on the way here. Chase, you have got to be more careful. I keep telling you, be careful when you are on that bike."

I looked up at her, surprised, because as far as I knew my bike was at home or… well at least it was supposed to be. I decided it was best to just go along with the story as I didn't know what the Morgans had told her about my accident.

"How much did they tell you about what happened?" I said slyly, trying to sound embarrassed. My mother sighed and dropped tiredly into the chair beside the bed.

"Lyla told us you were riding down the hill to the cove. Somehow, some rocks had gotten into the road, which you couldn't avoid and crashed. You broke your arm and got a pretty bad cut on the lower right side of your back, but Karen says you'll make a full recovery though the cut may leave a scar."

A scar on my back wasn't so bad as long as I was alive. I thought about this as the nurse finished examining me and left after taking some notes.

Thinking about my own life caused me to remember that of someone else's: Nikolai.

"Mom, have you seen Nikolai since you got here? There's something I need to ask him."

I didn't want my mother to really know what I was worried about. However, she still did regard me oddly. Maybe when you just woke up after having an 'accident' like mine, petty little questions weren't really important. But I had to know if my best friend was dead.

"No, I haven't seen him since I got back. Actually, I haven't seen much of anyone for the past twenty-four hours. See, your father and I have only been to the house and back. We did see the Morgans a while ago, but I don't remember seeing Nikolai with them."

Panic began to rise inside me. Perhaps the reason Mom didn't see him there was because he was... gone. If he really was dead, I had no idea how I was going to handle it, as he got into that situation to save my life. I had to know for sure.

Then, right on cue, Lyla drifted beautifully into the room, danced over to my mom, and gifted her with a cup of black coffee. As soon as she was in the room, that powerful scent of hers filled the room and did more for me than all the flowers there.

"I thought you might like that," she said as Mom cravingly sipped the coffee. "Mr. Rowland asked me to tell you he's downstairs sorting out some things for work, so the both of you will be able to spend time home with Chase.

"No!" I shouted, stunned, surprising even myself.

Both Lyla and Mom eyed me, startled, but I saw Lyla standing behind Mom, silently giggling and I was sure she knew what had shocked me from our bond. I loved my parents very much and would do anything for them, but I just couldn't stand spending days with them trying to tend to me. They could get really annoying at times and it would drive me mad.

"No Mom, you guys don't have to do that. I'm not even hurt that badly. Plus, I've got Lyla if... You know, I don't need anything."

"You don't want your parents hanging around all the time. I understand. I'll speak with Karen and if she says you are well enough, I will talk to your father."

After one last kiss I couldn't avoid, she said goodbye and left. As soon as she was out of the room, I had to ask Lyla about Nikolai.

"Lyla how is Nikolai? Is he alright?" I was now sitting up, supported by the back of the bed. My heart was pumping fast from anxiety, but Lyla actually answered the question matter-of-factly, as though she had something more important to address.

"Oh Nikolai's fine. So fine in fact, that's he's joking, saying he wished he had a scar to show off," Lyla said, gazing out the window. I finally started to relax. He was okay, and from what Lyla said, back to normal.

"Well that's good. So where did you take him?" I remembered how he looked when he got stabbed and the memory sent shivers through my whole body. He was weak and so pale-looking (even for him).

"I thought you would have guessed," Lyla said softly. "I took him to the ocean. Remember I told you we're connected to the sea. Well it's more than just a need to return to it. You see, if an Aquamun is ever mortally wounded by something we can't heal from, if we can get to the sea in time, the connection we have with it becomes so strong, it heals us. But I have to admit. For a while I did think I was too late. Nikolai was barely breathing and he wasn't moving. But luckily we did get there in time."

"What about Andréus? What did you do with his body? Did you bury him?"

Lyla finally settled herself into the chair, and shook her head.

"No. We don't bury our dead. We return them to the sea, if we can, and their bodies dissolve and become one with the sea."

The way Lyla said that got me thinking. That sounded like something they would do for family or friends, maybe sometimes complete strangers. But were mermaids so above reproach that they would give someone like Andréus a proper sendoff? By the contempt in Lyla's voice, I highly doubted it.

"Lyla, what did you do with him?" I asked, not accusing, but just purely interested.

She turned her gaze towards the ground. Her hair fell over her face like a long, sleek curtain, hiding pure beauty behind it. When she spoke, it was it with the voice of a kid who was admitting to what bad thing she had just done.

"I burned his body. Actually, we all did."

"Is it a bad thing if you burn the body of a dead Aquamun?"

Lyla looked up. Her face was unreadable, but I still felt her emotions, which were mostly anger towards Andréus, but under that I felt two other conflicting emotions, which were fear and hope and they were both because of me. She was afraid I would be repulsed by what she did and hoped I would understand and forgive her.

"When we burn the body of an Aquamun, it is seen as a dishonorable cast away, as they can't rejoin the sea. It's something usually left for enemies. Chase I'm sorry. Please forgive me, but after all he did to us, I felt he deserved it."

"Lyla, Lyla please don't." It was hurting me to see her like this. "I don't think of you any differently. In fact, if I was in your place, I would have done the same thing, especially after everything he put you through."

Lyla flew into my arms, and I just held onto her, because

there was no need to move. Then I suddenly remembered Hilda.

"She's okay. Andréus just knocked her out and threw her into the shed. Let's just say she wasn't too upset to learn he was dead."

As she was lying next to me in the bed, I felt her mood shift. It wasn't through our bond I felt it, but from her body language. She had become tense, and she was now looking up gravely at me.

"Chase, I don't know what to do, about your safety I mean." Lyla sighed. "Whatever I do, whether I stay or remove myself from your life, someone just wants to kill you."

"Well, maybe it has nothing to do with you. Maybe they just don't like my good looks."

I smiled, but Lyla wasn't finding any humor in the situation.

"Well then, stay Lyla. If I'm going to be in danger whether you're here or not, wouldn't it make sense, wouldn't it make us both happier if we were still together?"

Lyla was about to say something, but I interjected what I had to say first.

"No. I want you to listen to me. From the first time we met, you were adamant about protecting me from your world, and that's a really sweet thing to want to do in theory, but in practice it's kind of insulting because it makes it seem as if you don't believe I can stay alive without your help. Look, even though you aren't human, that doesn't mean you're invincible. You can't protect me from everything. But I know you'll still try, and believe it or not, I'm cool with that. What I'm not okay with is you deciding on your own if your being here with me puts me in danger or not. As I'm involved in this, don't you think you should at least tell me what's going on? Lyla the truth is, I know all about your world now, and because of that, I might always be in danger, if you are here or not. So don't you think it's better for us to be together if I'm still going to get hurt if you leave?"

Lyla moved up on the bed and rested her head on my chest.

"I just don't want to lose you," she said softly.

I put my good arm around her. "Don't worry Lyla. I'm not going anywhere."

"Mom, that's enough. We're going to be late," I said, almost pouting.

It was a couple minutes after seven and Justin, Brandon and I were outside my house with my mom who'd ambushed us with her camera as we were about to leave. We were on our way to our school cruise and dressed quite sharply.

"It's not like we're going to a formal event, it's just a couple of kids having a party on a boat."

But it was like my words reached deaf ears as she lined us up for another batch of photos.

"Well, we've been here seven months so far and this is the second time I'm getting pics of you and your friends. I'm not giving this chance up. I just can't wait to see Lyla. She's going to be stunning."

Mom's words about Lyla's impending arrival excited me. She, after all, was the one who convinced me to go to this cruise because, as she put it, we were going to experience a normal teenage relationship even if it killed us. So she spent the day with her friends, getting ready, which meant I hadn't seen her for the whole day, which is the longest we've been apart since I got out of the hospital (a full three weeks now). So I was very interested to see how she would look. To tell the truth, I was just anxious to see Lyla period. Whatever she wore would just be an extra treat.

"Mom, first, it's not like this is the last time you will be getting pictures of me and two, please don't say pics again. Ever."

Mom began to laugh, but stopped abruptly and stared behind us. As we were facing the house, we had to turn around to see what she was looking at. My mouth fell open in awe.

I could have sworn I drooled a little when I saw her. As there were no street lights covering the distance between our house and the Morgans, Lyla and her brother were once again illuminated by the moonlight and I was, as always, stunned by her striking beauty. She was wearing designer black pants with a sparkling shirt and black heels. Ignoring the usual stunned looks from the others, Lyla walked up to me, kissed me lightly on the cheek and said:

"Hi everyone. Sorry we're so late, but, well, you know how Nikolai can be."

Nikolai merely shrugged and said: "Well to be as handsome as I am comes at the price of tardiness."

He was wearing a long-sleeved shirt, Levi jeans and a pair of really expensive Jordans.

"You two look amazing," Mom said, standing there

looking completely flabbergasted. And she wasn't alone as Brandon, Justin and I couldn't help but marvel at how great both of them looked—like perfectly carved ice sculptures, the way their bodies reflected the moonlight. As if on cue, as they got to us, a small gust of wind blew in our directions and Lyla and Nikolai's individual scents reached our noses, which would explain the blank looks on the others' faces.

"Well, I think it's time we get going," I said loudly, pulling Mom, Justin and Brandon back to us. Lyla, however, looked at me with fake surprise on her face.

"And deprive your mom of more pictures? You've got to be crazy."

So without another word, we were pulled into various positions and poses for Mom, although I had to admit (to myself of course) that Lyla being here made the whole exercise a lot more bearable. When Michael arrived with the jeep, I wasn't sorry to get going, though Lyla made sure to take her time going through the photos with my mother.

The boat was leaving the harbor in Ridgetown, but the way Michael drove, we got there within twenty minutes. I was actually surprised we got there without getting reported by the police. After Michael parked and we got out it was easy enough to spot our boat, as there were still a lot of people running on and off and teachers on duty stood watching, and it was the brightest lit and most lavishly decorated boat docked. As we walked up to the boat, everyone we passed stopped and stared. I knew they were really staring at Lyla and Nikolai, who sometimes walked as though they were gliding on air.

Lyla simply ignored the looks, but Nikolai, on the other

hand, basked in it.

"I'll see you guys later," was all we heard him say before he ran off towards a group of staring girls. I, on the other hand was just about to walk off with Lyla, but Justin caught hold of my arm and pulled me towards the left side of the ship.

"You're gonna spend most of the cruise with Lyla, we all know that. But for now, you're my wing man."

At the same time some of Lyla's friends took her off to another side of the boat, but not before she waved goodbye with a hearty smile. Then I felt her open our bond wider to keep us in contact with each other. I couldn't help but notice Lyla's friends taking her towards a group of drooling guys. I never really did like those girls. I felt her playful amusement at my reaction.

"What's so funny?" Brandon asked as he heard my laugh.

"Nothing," I replied hastily.

A while later, after the boat finally left dock at around 9:00 pm, the party really began. Even though it was our school cruise for students only, I saw a lot of people I was sure attended other schools.

As the first hour progressed, I spent a lot of the time walking around with Justin and Brandon, talking, laughing—they were a lot of people dressed funny—and I had a few dances with some of the other girls, but by 10:30 I was aching to be with Lyla.

I was finally able to get away from the guys. I was about to go look for her when I realised she was looking for me too. So I waited on the top deck for her.

It was the smallest of the five decks on the boat. It was

very small and semi-circular. There were only four other people up here: a guy and a girl I recognized from school, who were sitting on the staircase with two guys by the rails.

It was more than chilly up here, but I really didn't mind. I walked over to the railing and wondered if I should call Lyla, but knew instantly she'd already felt my burning desire to be with her. I leaned on the cold body of the rails and looked out to sea. It was a very starry night with no clouds in sight. It was just the impassive blackness of night and dozens of stars out shining. And then, as if to complete some romantic package, the full moon was out, shining a bright slivery white, its light reflected on the smooth, placid surface of the sea.

Just then I felt a smooth, warm hand rest over mine on the rails which startled me, because I hadn't even felt Lyla approaching.

"I like that," she murmured, standing next to me and staring up at the sky. I followed her gaze, perplexed. "The moon."

Lyla chuckled. "Yes Chase, I do like the moon, but I was referring to your surprise. With our bond, you always know when I am coming or near you. I like that I can sometimes surprise you," Lyla said as she kissed my cheek. I walked behind her and wrapped my hands around her waist, but this time no heat rushed to my body and I knew it was because I didn't need it. This was one of our perfect moments and we were fine just the way we were.

Suddenly I felt a pang of pain through our connection. The feeling behind the pain felt like loss. And as we—or at least I—still couldn't use our mental link at will, I wasn't able to see what she was thinking that could cause her to feel this way.

"What's wrong?" I asked softly, but I guess she heard the concern in my voice anyway.

"Nothing's wrong," she replied, reaching back and stroking my cheek. It was amazing how I never got used to Lyla and her capabilities, especially the way her body produced that sweet fragrance of hers. It made her smell like some scared flower of the sea, if there was such a thing.

"I was just thinking about all the times I almost lost you."

"But you didn't. I'm here. I will always be here."

We stayed quiet for awhile, just enjoying each other's company. That's when I realized the music and sounds from the rest of the boat weren't reaching us up here. I was grateful for this. It just felt like a quiet moment.

"We did have to go through a lot to get here, though, didn't we?" I whispered.

Lyla nodded.

"We sure did. But we're here and no one or nothing can change that," she said, as if daring anyone to try. She then turned around and pressed her soft lips to mine. I could honestly say, it was a kiss like no other. A kiss to get lost in, a kiss to forget everything and everyone around us. It felt to me like this very boat didn't even exist, and Lyla and I were just somehow supported on the surface of the water, under the moon and the stars. Our night sky.

When we pulled apart, there was no feeling of the world crashing down on me.

"That's getting better," Lyla said.

"I hope you mean those after-effects and not my kissing, cause you know, I've got a fragile ego."

Lyla gave a laugh so beautiful it seemed to rebound right off the sea. This really was a perfect moment. There were no supernatural problems to worry about, no tense moments or feeling from either of us, and most of all, we were both looking forward to what tomorrow had to bring.

"Lyla?" I breathed with my head on her shoulder and she was once again stroking my cheek.

"Hmm?" she answered.

"I will always love you," I said a little nervously.

I knew she was smiling from the way she sounded when she said, "Chase, you are my true love, and with you is where I want to be forever."

COMING SOON:

OCEAN TIDE

I was about to turn around and head out of the forest, as I was pretty sure the others were already out, but that's when I heard, the ominous sound of twigs snapping under the weight of someone's foot.

I spun around quickly and scanned the place where the sound came from, but couldn't see anything other than the forest and the thick darkness trying to cling to it. Even with the moonlight, I still could not see much and the dead flashlight in my hand was of no use.

"Nick, if that's you, its really not funny, man."

Before these words even left me, I knew it was not Nikolai, or any of my friends for that matter. My heart was beating harder than ever. I could see or hear nothing more beyond the trees into the darkness, but I knew there was someone... or something there. Strangely enough, that's when I realized the forest was dead silent. I couldn't even hear any crickets. Even the leaves swaying ever so gently on the trees weren't making any noise as the night breeze passed through them. It was as if nature itself was holding its breath.

Just then, the air rang sharp with an ear-splitting roar that seemed to rattle every nerve in my body and clear my mind at the same time. Out of the shadows came a creature. It was unlike anything I had ever seen. It was about six feet tall and was covered fromhead to toe or... paws, in gray fur. Its features reminded me of a dog, or moreso, a wolf.

The beast was standing on two legs and had long, powerful, arms that ended with five sharp claws on each arm. It let loose another fearsome roar which, now that it was out of the darkness, allowed me to see its many sharp teeth. Without wasting another second, I turned and ran. It wasn't hard to tell that the creature didn't come to be petted.

As I ran through the forest, willing the muscles in my legs to go faster with every second, I had to keep ducking or jumping to avoid low lying branches or some of the small trunks and branches that littered the forest floor. I knew as I ran that I needed to keep my eyes in front, that to look back could cause me to fall or slow me down. But I still couldn't help it. The first chance I got, I glanced behind me and was shocked to see that the creature was running on all fours, and was extremely fast and agile. I was surprised that I was actually keeping a distance between us.

Suddenly I saw a gap in the path before me. Without even needing to think on it, I jumped it and landed on the other side, but my feet seemed to lose all the strength they had, so I dropped to the floor and hid behind a tree.

From the way my heart was beating, I feared it would explode it my chest. The creature roared again, but it puzzled me this time, because it seemed so far away. I took a deep breath and chanced a look around the tree behind me. My mouth fell open in shock. I had to be so focused on escaping the creature that I didn't realize the size of the gap. It was impossible. I shouldn't have made it. No human should have, because the gap had to be at least forty feet wide.

FIND 'OCEAN COVE' ON FACEBOOK
Post comments/questions to:

www.facebook.com/oceancove

www.ingramcontent.com/pod-product-compliance
Lightning Source LLC
Chambersburg PA
CBHW020823030726
47496CB00001B/69